David Davenport is a very successful man by most standards. He has money, influence, and the Manse, his private gay club. Still, that's not enough to make him happy. Despite all his privilege, David is a lonely man. While at lunch with an old friend, David finds himself enchanted by the charming young waiter, Shea Whittier. Unlike David, Shea does not have wealth or influence. He does have problems, though, and David is more than willing to help. As the men grow closer, Shea's submissive nature responds to David's dominance, bringing a powerful intensity to their relationship, and leaving them vulnerable to an unexpected danger. (M/M)

"I'm not leaving you here," David said. The reply was cool, composed, and very fucking confident. He ushered Shea forward, supporting him as they began their climb upward. "I'd never forgive myself if I allowed you to stay in this situation."

"Huh," Shea said thoughtfully. "I don't even know what to say to that. You totally get bonus points for sounding so sure of yourself."

"I'm always sure of myself," David replied, seriously, and Shea smiled.

"Must be nice."

They reached the third floor and walked down to his door. The key slid into the lock, he turned the knob and diligently ignored the two people waiting behind him, because if he didn't, he might just start laughing hysterically at the whole thing. His head was unbearably hot, but his body was cold enough to give him goosebumps. Maybe David did have a point with that whole 'rest' idea.

Also recommended...

You may also enjoy these other ForbiddenFiction works:

Bound by Lies by Lynn Kelling
Brayden Clare never wanted to return to small town life. Blond, athletic, and struggling with his sexual identity, a casual relationship on the beach in Florida suits him much better. When a family emergency calls him home, he is forced to trade his personal freedom for a job as a bartender in a town where everybody thinks they know who he is, and nobody has a clue — including Brayden. Jenner Parrish is the owner and operator of Parrish Pub, the social hub of Robertsville, Pennsylvania. Jenner is charming, dominant, and popular since they were both in high school together. Brayden finds his new boss intimidating, and is daunted to find that turns him on. Jenner finds his new recruit intriguing but mustn't dare to ask an employee to submit to him. The two men find what they're seeking at a masked BDSM ball in the next town over, and are startled to discover their desires rest much, much closer to home. (M/M)
http://forbidden-fiction.com/story/LK1-1.000108

Don't... by Jack L. Pyke
"Don't... open me." Three simple words that tease Jack, taking him places from his dark past. For Jack, BDSM is a way to resist his worst impulses. Yet, the stranger calling himself The Unknown seeks to use that to seduce him. As Jack slips further down into the abyss, two men hold the power to save him. Will it be Gray, the Master who knows Jack's every secret? Or Jan, the first man to give Jack a reason to hope? With deadly ghosts coming out to play, Jack may lose everything, even his life. (M/M)
http://forbiddenfiction.com/story/JP2-1.000134

Loving the Master

Lynn Kelling

ForbiddenFiction
www.forbiddenfiction.com

an imprint of

Fantastic Fiction Publishing
www.fantasticfictionpublishing.com

LOVING THE MASTER
A Forbidden Fiction book

Fantastic Fiction Publishing
Hayward, California

© Lynn Kelling, 2016

CREDITS
Editor: Rylan Hunter and D.M. Atkins
Cover Design: Siolnatine
Cover Art: Photo by Arturkurjan at Dreamstime.com.
Mask Vector Icon by Freepik Production.
Editor: Erika L Firanc
Proofreading: Kailin Morgan

SKU: LK1-000225-02
ISBN: 978-1-62234-276-1

Published in the United States of America

DISCLAIMER

This book is a work of fiction which contains explicit erotic content; it is intended for mature readers. Do not read this if it's not legal for you.

All the characters, locations and events herein are fictional. While elements of existing locations or historical characters or events may be used fictitiously, any resemblance to actual people, places or events is coincidental.

This story depicts fictional BDSM; it is not intended to be used as an instruction manual. It contains descriptions of erotic acts that may be immoral, illegal, or unsafe. The characters are not models for the Safe, Sane and Consensual forms embraced by most current practitioners of BDSM. The author takes license with the use of BDSM for dramatic effect. Do not take the events in this story as proof of the plausibility or safety of any particular practice.

For my beloved Matthew,
who never let unfortunate circumstances or a bad turn of fate
rob him of his kindness or sense of humor.
I'll miss you always.

Contents

Chapter 1

Disconnected Decadence

"It's not enough to want someone. The motives need to mesh—theirs and yours. You know what I mean? The prettiest face in the world might mask the blackest heart."

"I know you're frustrated, David," Elet told him on a sigh.

"Frustrated?" David laughed. He bit his lip, studying the exceedingly pretty slave bound before him. "No, more like... disappointed. Maybe it just isn't possible to train someone to be kind."

Pacing around one of the few places where he was usually truly at home—a dimly lit but decadent dungeon on the lowest level of his primary residence—David Davenport felt farther than ever from where he knew he needed to be. It was amazing how, no matter how many resources he had at his disposal, there was always something out of reach. Money couldn't touch everything. Life was funny that way. Some days, he would have gladly traded his empire to switch places with one half of the older couples he'd see sitting together on park benches, holding hands with absolute understanding, respect and hard-earned love. They had found the one thing his swollen bank accounts could never acquire.

Elet was tall and elegant in his dark grey suit and tie. Posed against the bruised red wallpaper, he made quite the alluring yet imposing picture with his flawless, mahogany skin gleaming in the flickering candlelight. A series of sconces lined the lush, private, windowless room; the only source of light. Reclined in a cherry-red armchair, Elet sipped an amber drink and smiled indulgently. He was David's closest friend and most trusted confidant, which was why the patronizing flavor of that particular grin hit David hard.

1

"I can't let it go this time, El," David warned.

"I didn't ask you to. The rules are in place for a reason. You're taking this personally. Why is that?"

"Hmm." David mulled over the question. He wandered over to the boy held trapped like a monarch butterfly caught in a net, too preoccupied with his predicament to care about the Masters' musings. The boy's name was Thierry and he had the most intriguing eyes David had ever seen, though at the moment they were hidden by a blindfold. Thierry's complexion was dark, his skin a warm, rich, medium-brown, but his eyes were a startling, impossible light blue. Like the monarch, Thierry was starkly beautiful at first glance, though not nearly as delicate or innocent. "I can't stand cruelty," was David's quietly spoken answer.

Anger was an emotion he rarely displayed openly, but there was a tightening of his jaw as he looked at Thierry... and thought of others close to him who had been cruel. The whip called to him, which was why he resisted using it. It wasn't entirely because of Thierry that David was riled, and it would be wrong to make the boy pay for the sins of others.

Thierry, whose arms were held loosely above his head in comfortable, leather shackles, moaned through parted lips, his head tipping to the side as a shiver worked its way through his lithe body. He was a practically a child — twenty-one years old, but more like a teenager with his brashness and selfishness. Just a glance at him told David everything. Thierry cared too much for himself and too little for others. It was a trait David struggled to forgive, especially when it caused the pain of those in his care. Maybe it was more aggravating because of how much possibility he saw in Thierry. But, like so many other submissives that David had taken for a scene or a night, as well as business associates, acquaintances, family members and staff, Thierry's motives were highly suspect. David was used to people trying to use him, or the perks of being in his company, to their advantage. But when David's friends were mistreated while doing so, consequences needed to be paid.

Caressing over the right side of the rounded swell of Thierry's ass with a leather-gloved hand, David touched the place where the boy was breached by a long phallus impaled on a pole bolted to the floor between Thierry's feet. David could almost taste how badly Thierry wanted to writhe and twist, but he was taken so deeply, movement was impossible. Sweat trickled down the planes of his body, over lean, defined muscles. Thierry's cock was flushed dark, jutting up stiffly between his thighs, wet with pre-come and begging for attention.

Physically, Thierry was irresistible. But he was arrogant. He was always the first to be caught standing back, laughing, whenever someone less fortunate nearby was hurt. Of course, that was only when he thought David, Elet, or one of the other Masters weren't looking. When he was with his Masters, Thierry was more likely to fall to his knees at their feet with soft, suspicious, tempered pleas to serve and submit.

A few hours earlier, David had personally seen Thierry snickering at some of the newer patrons of Manse, the private gay club David owned and ran out of his home. That was why the boy was currently strung up so, his hearing muffled with noise-canceling headphones and a blindfold masking his sight. When Thierry had been bound there, a number of the youngest attendees had been present to watch the spectacle. They'd since left, but Thierry was none the wiser. Let him wonder, David thought, if he was the one being laughed at now. The young ones were busy with better sources of amusement, but David remained, and Elet along with him. David didn't intend to leave until the job was thoroughly done.

Humiliation was a key tool within David's BDSM arsenal, especially with slaves like Thierry who were burdened with an overinflated ego. David had been deeply grateful when his own Masters had thoroughly humbled him during his training. It was healthy, now and then, to be made to see your own modest place in the grand scheme of things. That training, more than anything else, had taught David that no one person was more valuable than any other. It didn't matter what class you were born into, or how many possessions you had, or the subjective quality of your appearance. Once David's eyes had been opened, and he gained more experience in the worlds of business and privilege, the more he saw that, for some, being counted among the most fortunate minority from birth sped the process of rot within the soul.

Greed, pride and ignorance were stubborn human conditions he consistently strove to fight in his own, small ways. They had, after all, cost him the lives of truly beloved people whose absence was something he knew he might always struggle to recover from. It was too high a price—an entire life for nothing except the passing flush of hollow triumph. Having witnessed such decay of one's humanity, the prospect of suffering it himself terrified David. Some of the closest people to him, people who enjoyed wealth, power, and were mainly governed only by their own, faltering consciences, had revealed this malady. It was possible to spot it if you knew the signs. A lack of empathy, shallow emotions, irresponsibility, insincerity and overconfidence—those were some of the necessary ingredients in becoming a psychopath. They were seeds of the devil himself chewing at the spirit from inside out. Once he'd eaten away enough of a soul's goodness, there was no getting it back.

David's fingertips skimmed over Thierry's chest. The flesh trembled rhythmically as the boy's pulse and breathing quickened. Lingering to coax the fear and nerves, David watched his slave try to brace himself. Was the boy self-aware enough to realize he'd done wrong, and now expected David to lash out to enact a punishment? And was Thierry being filled with desire rather than dread? It was a fine line, really. A bead of sweat trickled down the side of Thierry's face, tracing the handsome edge of his jaw and dripping from the end of his chin.

Ever so softly, David heard his slave speak out of turn, begging, "Please, Master."

In reply, David delivered a firm, open-handed smack to the underside of Thierry's cock. The instinct to recoil only caused more pain due to the phallus lodged in Thierry's ass. Moaning, Thierry let his head fall forward.

David wandered away.

"You're too easy on him." Elet laughed threateningly, swirling his drink, eyeing their slave, strung up so nicely. "Come, put your feet up. Give me a turn. The slave he mocked has had more practice taking my cock than *him*. Look."

Standing, Elet walked to Thierry. Elet was taller than David, but there were other signs of difference as well, noticeable even if one was deafened with headphones and blindfolded as Thierry was—such as Elet's subtle cologne and the deep rumble of his baritone voice in laughter, vibrating from his chest, shivering the air. Thierry tensed visibly upon Elet's approach. His upper lip curled back in a sneer. His teeth were grinding together and his breath hissed through them.

"Now, now," Elet said in his eerie, low voice. The palm of his left hand stroked over Thierry's abdomen. Elet, who probably was the most skilled Master within their small circle besides David, pressed himself to Thierry's back and thrust gently against him.

Instantly, to David's fascination, Thierry's bravado evaporated. He trembled, his breathing too rough, too shallow. Small grunts and whimpers sounded from behind Thierry's clenched, pearly white teeth.

"He's terrified of you," David observed coolly, leaning back against the far wall and idly arranging a bullhide whip which hung from the wall. "I wonder why that is?"

"He's *weak*," Elet grinned, drinking in Thierry's apprehension like the sweetest nectar. The sadism in Elet had always captivated David. Since Elet was quite skilled at wielding it only against the proper targets, it was usually amusing to witness. Otherwise, it might have been disturbing how avidly Elet craved to cause another's torment. David had seen slaves piss themselves when faced with the prospect of submitting to the man, and Thierry was quite close to reaching that point.

Elet's hand moved to reach between his and Thierry's bodies, out of David's sight. A moment later, Thierry's cry pierced the air, his back arched slightly. All of his fingers splayed and his arms flexed within their bonds. Thierry's mouth worked as the shout faded away but still the anguish went on, though his breath had run out. Some clear fluid dripped from the end of Thierry's cock. A sob told David that Thierry was crying, yet he didn't use his safeword, nor speak again out of turn. He was learning.

With a sigh, David sank into the chair Elet had been sitting in and propped one foot up on the edge of the seat. Something eased in him when Elet shifted Thierry's headphones and began whispering to him. Though David couldn't make out the words, he could see their effect. Thierry's erection wilted as Elet grinned, slipping ideas, promises, or plans into his mind. Some of the color drained from his face,

5

as well. It didn't surprise David at all when a stream of urine began to drain from Thierry's cock, his body wracked with tremors as the stink of it filled the air.

"I've barely touched you, slave," Elet said more loudly. "And you piss on Master David's floor?"

"I'm sorry, Master David, Master Elet," Thierry pleaded in a thin, quavering voice. "Please forgive me."

"Should we bring Eric in here to see you now?" Elet asked. "Do you think he'd laugh at you, like you laughed at him? Or would he be smart enough to show respect?"

"Whatever you like, Master Elet," Thierry answered.

To the guard stationed on the door, Elet said, "Get the boy. Check the lounge."

"What are you up to?" David asked with a smile.

"Oh, you'll see," Elet replied, delighted and scheming.

At least the night wouldn't be boring.

An hour or so later, David was ready to retire. His thoughts were on other things, other places than the dungeon and the slave draped over a padded bench, his ass tipped up into the air. Eric was fucking him again and having a wonderful time from the looks of it. Though Eric wasn't as stunning as Thierry, and was also less wealthy, he had a much more pleasant spirit, though perhaps also a streak of sadism like Master Elet.

Thierry's groans were constant and powerful. He was too exhausted to move, so shackles were unnecessary. Elet used a towel to dry himself off, but was nowhere close to being finished.

David caught his eye and motioned him over.

"Time for me to call it a night, I think, and get some rest," David told him. "Victor will be in charge of closing up. When you're done here, show the boys out. Thierry is welcome to use the suite if he's too exhausted to drive."

"Bring someone to bed with you," Elet suggested. "Purge some of your troubles, friend."

"Not tonight," David smiled appreciatively. "But thank you.

Maybe tomorrow we'll go out? Find somewhere new? A change of pace might be nice."

"Whatever you like."

When Eric's cock withdrew from Thierry's puckered sphincter, the shaft was red, swollen, and wet with lube. Grunting, Thierry quivered. The stretched-loose, pink ring of muscle clenched shut briefly.

"What do you say?" Eric prompted.

"Please more, sir! Please fuck me, sir!" Thierry rasped, tilting his hips slightly in invitation.

Eric fed Thierry's hole his cock once more. Thierry moaned heavily.

"Glad to see they're getting along now," David commented with a small, wicked but pleased grin. He turned to go, but lingered long enough to add, "Message me which suite Thierry takes, just in case." The sight of him bent over and fucked delirious was too good to resist. It worked on all of David's weaknesses. Honest vulnerability was always an irresistible temptation.

"So you haven't given up on him after all," Elet noticed. "Of course, David. Good night to you."

"And you as well, my dear," David said, brushing his hand over Elet's arm as he left.

David wasn't sure of the time, but it was nearly dawn as he inched the door to the suite ajar with a hand. The hardwood of the floor was the same as in the rest of the mansion, the walls equally dark in color. Even the silk curtains which pooled at the baseboards had only a hint of shine. The night was too spent for anything resembling brightness. Wandering in the dimness, David appreciated how much closer everything felt when wrapped in so much heaviness. This was his world, in which he thrived. Give him passages to explore, secrets to discover, questions to answer with leisure and endless curiosity, and he came alive. He was the night's creature, hiding in the shadows, choosing the right moment in which to pounce.

Turning a switch on the wall, the sconces flickered to meager life, but stayed dim. David needed only a soft glow for his purposes.

A handsome male body was draped slantways across the huge, four-poster bed. It was naked, the muscles glistening with a flush of vitality, the curves and planes highlighted by what warm light the sconces threw out into the cave-like room. The figure lay undisturbed by the inky night's tentative withdraw. Exhaustion gripped him, binding him in invisible, invincible ropes.

Slowly unlacing the ties of his loose cotton pants, David walked to the bed. The wood under his bare feet softly groaned. On the bed, there was the faintest, beautiful whimper as Thierry shifted position, drawing an arm up in what seemed an attempt to ward off the faint light.

"Slave," David beckoned quietly.

Those fascinating eyes opened to gaze upon him, Thierry's expression carefully masked. Nevertheless, David attempted to puzzle out the boy's mood. Was he resentful of the disturbance? Harboring bitterness in the wake of his punishment?

"Have you slept?"

"Yes, sir," Thierry rasped, his voice worn down and huskier than normal. "A little."

Thierry turned his face away from David's scrutiny, but drew his legs up under him and spread them wide. Instinct, or sincere invitation, David wondered? Thierry's intakes of breath increased at a quickened pace. David was glad to see he inspired at least that much trepidation.

"Your safeword?"

"Red, sir."

The bed shifted as David rested a knee upon it. His posture mostly still hinting at his cockiness and coldness, Thierry whined softly in anticipation, his body tensed.

Climbing more fully onto the bed, David moved up behind Thierry. Slipping two fingers up the slave's ass, David said, "You should have enough lube in here already, I think, after the pounding Eric gave you. Not to mention the ways Master Elet used you. Practice, perhaps, for taking his huge cock? Now, that's something I'd *love* to see."

Thierry writhed, the tissues of his sphincter swollen up and tender, yet so very soft and yielding under David's touch. Prodding them, drawing rough little gasps, David couldn't help but smile. Thierry's toes curled. The harder David rubbed and pried, the wilder Thierry's cries became.

David slid his fingers back out and opened a condom.

"Did you learn anything tonight, slave?" David did have some hope left for Thierry—just a little. He hated to give up on anyone. But unless Thierry showed he was capable of some of the same compassion he elicited in his Master, David would have to safeguard the other slaves and ask Thierry not to return. And, for as physically and financially fortunate as the boy was, David didn't think he had many friends outside of their cozy circle at Manse. To lose their company, permanently, would be a punishment so cruel, David was prepared to go out of his way to avoid it if he could.

When Thierry hesitated in answering, it began to sadden David. Going from the boardroom to the bedroom and finding the same merciless disregard for others in both was beginning to make him feel like he was a fool. Maybe coming to seek Thierry out had been the wrong choice. Recently, many of David's choices had been turning out badly. Was the problem possibly with him? Was he seeing too much in the light of his own shortcomings? Maybe some time alone to reflect was needed, for him and Thierry, more than useless compassion. David had to stroke himself a number of times to become properly erect once the condom was on and he kept eyeing the door, suspecting he should just leave.

"Fuck, please," Thierry sobbed, panting. The break in Thierry's composure alerted David to some of the truth behind how his slave was feeling. Thierry had the fairly skilled ability to hide away his most private secrets. Elet was able to knock Thierry's well-crafted masks askew with fear, but David preferred other methods.

Thierry was holding his breath, fighting not to reveal much, if any, of his sense of weakness and dread of David's ability to do exactly what was seeming inevitable—banning Thierry from the club. There were signs of real inner struggle in the boy, but he was so good at burying his truths deeply, showing only enough to get him his Masters' leniency, David struggled to read him as clearly as he was able with others. It was what kept drawing him to Thierry—wanting to puzzle out exactly what it was he so fiercely guarded. "I, uh... respect.

Need to show — *ahh* — respect... to the slaves."

It was said sincerely enough that David was quickly decided. He entered the boy in a slow push, marveling at the heat of Thierry's over-used rim as it squeezed around his cockhead. Then he was through and Thierry shuddered, hard, as sensations quivered outward from the small place their bodies joined.

"Just the slaves?"

Sighing, David bottomed out and reached around to test the stiff-ness of Thierry's dick. It curved up snug to his belly, despite the pri-mal noises he was making, probably due to soreness. Getting fucked for hours would do that. It wasn't anything Thierry wouldn't recover from, though. David stroked him and began to work himself in the glove of Thierry's physically immaculate body. Like living granite, ignited within by a waning flame, Thierry was both hot and cold in perplexing ways which made it impossible to fall into the moment as David would have liked. Still, he found himself unable to withdraw. The night wound around them, a cloak pulling tighter with every passing breath.

For a second, Thierry couldn't reply, uncomfortable as he was, and he was barely able to keep still, though David was being fairly gentle.

"No, sir," Thierry managed before crying out into the bed linens in a deep, throaty voice. David grabbed him by the back of the neck and made sure his next drive inward rubbed hard over his slave's gland. "*Motherfucker*," Thierry growled, fucking David's fist. "Re-spect... everyone... every..."

Thierry began to move, rolling his hips, grinding against David with desperate need.

"Master, may I?" he growled.

David let go. Thierry shifted forward, pulled off.

Lying down on the bed, his head on the pillows, David let Thierry arrange himself, straddled atop David's lap. He fed his Master's cock into him with one hand, then stroked himself with the other, riding David almost greedily. When he leaned in and began to passionately kiss David, their tongues twisting together, Thierry moaned lustily against David's lips. More than anything, David wished he felt the same way, that his heart was engaged along with his body. But all

Thierry saw when he looked at David was the Master in him, not the man, and it wasn't nearly enough.

It should have been intoxicating. Thierry was exquisite and ripe with desire. Yet, there was something absent in his light blue eyes. The sex was spectacular, but so terrifyingly hollow, it left David feeling lost.

David's hands skimmed over flushed skin, feeling less than he needed to. The harder Thierry surged against him, the faster David receded back into the shadows.

Chapter 2

Dance with Fate

Shea Whittier barely glanced down at the small, two-person table he stood next to, his head spinning with all of the many things he needed to remember to do before returning to the kitchen. Like silverware. He couldn't forget the silverware for table six. Oh, and table three still needed to give him their drink order. He hoped they didn't take forever to decide. This day had been long enough without lingers clogging the flow. Wait, who needed the silverware again? Fuck, he couldn't remember. He wasn't a details kind of guy, unless you counted remembering extremely relevant information from the Captain America comics, Silver Age through the spinoffs involving the Avengers. Which he did think should count, since he always managed to impress the hell out of the other nerds at the local comics shop, and that was pretty much the only circumstance in his life in which he'd managed to impress anyone.

What was he trying to remember again?

Take the order of the people you're standing next to, stupid, he reminded himself when he realized the patrons were staring expectantly up at him. They were kind of good looking actually. Really good looking. Especially the one who looked like he could be Tony Stark's hopefully-less-arrogant younger brother.

Right.

He recited, with a sincere, sunny grin, "Hi, welcome to Teresa's! My name is Shea and I'll be your server. Can I start you off with some drinks?"

The music track changed abruptly and a heavy-thumping country song began to play instead. That meant one thing.

Nervousness fluttered in his stomach. That small but potent apprehension sent his thoughts reeling, his emotions spiking.

His beaming, professional grin faltered, turned crooked and awkward. Nearby, some of the other staff began to hoot excitedly, clapping their hands along with the beat and gathering in the aisles to dance. The two male customers seated at Shea's table were still watching him curiously, their full attention on him and not at all on their menus. He really wished they were looking at the menus instead.

"Oh God, no," was Shea's pained murmur.

"Is everything all right, Shea?" Stark's hotter brother asked. There did seem to be real concern behind the question, instead of impatience with Shea's admittedly chaotic social skills, which pulled his attention in quickly, helping him to focus.

"Oh, yeah. I'm fine, I think. Thank you for checking, sir. That's very kind and... observant... of you." He bowed his head and flipped open his notepad, pen poised ever-so-hopefully to take their orders. If they ordered something, he had a completely valid reason to not also be dancing. Wholeheartedly wanting his handsome customers to order something, he told them, "I'd be more than happy to tell you about our specials, if you're interested? I can personally attest that they're each spectacular and would love to give you a chance to try them."

Please look at your menus, he prayed. *Please.*

"We'd actually heard that Teresa's has gotten a lot of recognition in the press lately for the gourmet macaroni and cheese, which is why we decided to stop by."

"Oh, you're absolutely right about that, sir. They just reprinted the menus with the little award badge from the magazine contest right there next to where it's listed, see?" Shea pointed at the side of the menu in the customer's hand and got a strong whiff of an intoxicatingly masculine cologne. He also got a brief glimpse down the slightly unbuttoned neck of the guy's shirt, seeing tan skin and being really inappropriately unable to stop looking at it for a moment. "Would, uh, you like to order that now, or..."

"Yes," the customer smiled. "I would, actually."

"Let's take a little more time to consider the other offerings," the other man at the table interjected.

13

The hooting and cheering got closer, the clapping louder. There was a shout of, "Whitt! Come on!" and he was tempted to wave back at whoever had called, but continued, hoping against hope that the customers needed his attention. Making the customers happy was much more important than abandoning them in order to dance horribly in the aisles. *Please, oh dear customers of mine,* he thought silently, *save me from my inescapable humiliation? Please?*

"That's fine," Shea told them. "I can come back to take your orders but can I get you started with drinks first? While you look? We have freshly brewed peach tea which I highly recommend for its, uh... peachiness, or maybe something from the bar? I mean, it's lunchtime, but what the heck, right? I know I could use a stiff drink right now, not that I've ever had alcohol or can actually carry it to the table myself, since I'm not twenty-one yet—"

"Whitt!"

At Shea's table, the elegantly dressed, taller guy kind of had a Brother Voodoo vibe about him, since Shea could easily see him being able to hypnotize anyone into doing what he wanted, probably— hopefully—in a non-creepy way. He smiled coyly in his companion's direction but Shea was the only one to notice. The companion—or Tony Stark's less obnoxious, facial-hair-free sibling—was a disturbingly handsome, dark-brown-haired, light-green-eyed man seated across the table, and he seemed to have eyes only for Shea. The rapt attention from someone like him made Shea quickly lower his gaze and clear his throat, willing his face not to turn pink. He could only hope the staring was for a *good* reason.

Shea's skin felt too tight. *Like an overstuffed sausage,* he thought. *I've become a sausage. Dude, stop thinking about phallic things while there's a hot guy paying attention to you. He'll be able to tell. Your luck is exactly that bad.*

"We need another minute to decide," Brother Voodoo told Shea. "I think your co-workers over there want you to go dance with them."

Without acknowledging this statement, the other customer said, "You seem a little overwhelmed, Shea. Take a deep breath. Nothing else matters right now except addressing the needs of your customers, and you're more than capable of doing that, right?"

"Right," Shea responded. He took a deep breath, as instructed, focusing only on the green eyes of the man before him. The noise and chaos of the restaurant around them faded back, holding much less of his attention or concern. His hands stopped shaking and he smiled in thanks.

After winking at Shea, the guy's warm smile widened, drawing Shea in more. Then, the brunette's gaze swept downward from Shea's face, from his blue eyes and light brown, slightly shaggy hair, over his lean body and low enough that Shea did indeed start to blush. "There, you seem steadier. See how easy that was?"

Shyly, Shea bowed his head, dropping his gaze. "It's never usually that easy."

"It should be."

The certainty of the proclamation made Shea glance up again. The customer's smile was gone, as if he really was concerned about Shea's inability to get control of himself. Shea knew the feeling. "I'll give you two a moment."

In response, the guy said in a soft, supremely unhurried, enchanting and smooth tone, "Thank you, Shea. I apologize for delaying things. Everything just looks really good."

He's talking about the food, though, right?

Of course he is! This guy is way too sexy to even realize you exist on the same planet.

"Oh, no problem at all," Shea assured him, wanting nothing more than to stay right there and keep listening to the guy talk, the steady tone of his voice calming in ways Shea had never experienced before. "Take your time, sir. I'll be here to help with whatever you need."

"Thank you."

Shea was certain the guy could tell Shea was enjoying the attention in ways that went way beyond the customer/waiter dynamic. So much so, he felt compelled to apologize, which would have just been awkward.

"Whitt!"

"Fuck," Shea breathed. Brother Voodoo grinned.

With reluctance, heavy resignation, and even a small sigh, his volume getting lower with each word, Shea answered, "You're welcome. I'll be back, I guess, after completely humiliating myself in front of someone who I'd bet has never been embarrassed, ever."

As soon as the pad was back in Shea's apron and he turned away from the table, his arm was grabbed by another member of the wait staff—a vivacious guy named Bill who proceeded to drag Shea into the group of staff already line-dancing along with the music. Though Bill was a great dancer, Shea was less fortunate and he gracelessly fumbled his way through the steps, trying to hide in plain sight. Every bit of his mortification was reflected in his expression but he never stopped trying. Hopefully, effort counted just as much as skill. He clapped out of sync and he was a half-second behind everyone else with the steps; he felt like his dancing was so bad, they would probably have to dock his pay just to compensate the owners for all of the appetites he was currently spoiling.

A few minutes later, Shea was back at the table, trying again to take the order, though now he actually was physically unable to raise his gaze from his tablet and witness his table's horror at his dancing abilities.

"So, so very sorry about that. Are you ready to order or are you still deciding?"

The man who Shea had been so mesmerized by, said, "Shea, do you mind if I ask you something first? It has nothing at all to do with the menu, though."

The gentle tone of the request was too tempting to resist. He didn't understand what it was about this guy that seemed to cut right through all the bullshit and confusion, but it felt like everything Shea had been lacking for a long time, right there for the taking. "Um, sure. Go for it," Shea answered, as unable to hide his awkward, self-conscious state as he had been to mask his inability to perform a two-step.

"I really do apologize if this is presumptuous or rude of me, but why did you apply for this job if you don't enjoy dancing?"

"Well, uh, sir—"

"Please, call me David."

"Okay. David. To be honest, the dancing wasn't the biggest draw, but if I'm distracting you from having a pleasant meal I'd be happy to get another server to—"

"No, no. That won't be necessary," David cut in. "Please. Go on. I'm just curious. Pretend we've known each other for years. Why work at a job where the requirements don't suit your tastes?"

"Honestly?"

"Yes. Please."

"Well, I kind of have to take what I can get these days. There was a job opening here, and I needed a job. I'm sure you know how it goes. Or, maybe you don't, and that's fine too. I'm really just trying to make ends meet, not wind up homeless. I've experienced that a few times already and I'm trying to find ways to avoid screwing up like that again. Fuck, that's depressing. Sorry. And jeez, for the language. Christ, I'm probably offending the hell out of you right now... and I've added blasphemy to the list. Fantastic. Swell. Um. Starting over. Hi, I'm Shea. This is only my second? No, third. Third day working here and I'm feeling really flustered right now, mostly because of how calm and hot you are, and when I'm flustered I always say things without really paying attention to what's actually coming out of my mouth, and I'm a *terrible* dancer, as you've witnessed. But I excel at bringing delicious food to tables, so may I do that for you? Please? Making you happy would make me really happy, sir. David."

Oh god. Some of that probably shouldn't have come out of my mouth.

He was admittedly terrified to make eye contact after saying all of that, but he did and he was startled by the nonsensically captivated expression on David's face. David's friend was wearing an amused little smirk.

"Of course. I can see how you might feel overwhelmed and without many options, in that case. And after you've asked so politely, I'll speed this up a little for you and say that I'll have the peach tea you mentioned, and the macaroni and cheese. Elet? What have you decided on?"

Elet looked right into Shea's eyes, slouching back comfortably into his seat. His crooked grin grew as he stayed quiet and didn't respond.

"Please order before I'm tempted to start talking again," Shea began, pleading shamelessly, pressing his lips together as if to keep any more words inside once he'd said that much.

David's friend, Elet, began to look almost mischievous the longer the silence drew out, and Shea began to feel more uneasy.

"Fine then, he'll have the same," David said decisively.

"Oh, you're no fun," was the reply in an impressively deep voice.

"We're here for lunch, not to torment someone who's already under a lot of strain."

"David, it's like you don't know me at all," was the quiet, teasing reply.

"I'm, uh, going to go put in your orders," Shea told them, the urge to go and hide strong now that David's attention had been diverted and reality began to set in again.

David said, "Thank you, Shea."

Elet collected both menus, then handed them over. And then didn't release them once Shea had grabbed hold of the other end, while sputtering, "No, thank *you*, D-David."

For a moment, neither of them let go. Elet told Shea, "You know, if there's any *other* way you'd like to thank him, I can assure you, he wouldn't mind. Just speaking as someone who knows his... tastes." There was a deep, rich laugh from him and Shea's stomach fluttered again, and not entirely from nerves this time.

"You're out of line," David said to Elet, simply and quietly.

The menus were instantly released. David looked over at Shea in a way that was completely unlike the ways Shea was used to being looked at, especially by customers like David. To Shea, who was used to being ignored or written off, being on the receiving end of that look made him want to give in to it and anything else David might want from him.

"My apologies, Shea," Elet said.

An hour later, Shea was watching the pair walk out of the restaurant and went to clean up their table. The forty-five dollar check had been paid for by credit card but there was cash on the table for the tip. It was two hundred dollars in cash, to be exact, along with a note bearing his name folded around it, stating, 'I take what I can get, too. This is thank you for brightening my day. I hope the rest of yours goes more smoothly and that we'll see each other again. David.'

Chapter 3
Nature's Course

This is exactly what I needed! Maybe they won't kick me out after all, was Shea's main thought as he slung his messenger bag over one shoulder and went to unlock his bike. For the entire rest of the day, he had been daydreaming about how nice and alluring his customer, David, had been. The few things David said had made a great impact. It was impossible for Shea to stop thinking about their interactions, replaying them over and over in his head.

Passing Debra, another waitress, who headed in the opposite direction, Shea called to her, "Hey, Deb, tell your mom I hope she feels better! If she wants some homemade chicken soup, I'll totally come over and make her some."

"Thanks Whitt," Debra smiled, her cheeks dimpling. "You're such a sweetie. I'll let her know. Have a good night, okay? Get home safe."

"You too!"

Debra went on her way with a wave, turning a corner and heading to the bus stop.

He had chained his bike to a pipe near the back entrance to the restaurant, since the owner wouldn't permit him to keep it inside. His car hadn't been starting for a few weeks now, so it was either ride the bicycle or walk several miles to work. In the meantime, his car was gathering dust in a rare free parking spot a few blocks from his apartment building while he saved the cash needed to afford the repairs. He knew things would get better, that he just needed time and some patience. Being on his own without a real support system or a heck of a lot of resources kind of limited his options. There was no money to fix the car. No money to pay his share of the rent. No paycheck for another week and a half from his new job, which he was doing everything in his power not to lose. The goals were there. Baby steps would get him to them eventually.

He got the bike chain off and stowed it in his bag. He swung a leg over, sat on the bike's seat and began to pedal down the alley. His thoughts strayed back, again, to how amazingly happenstance it had been to meet David, who had been kind and curious, too, like somehow he'd known how much Shea had needed that little bit of extra encouragement to keep breathing and trust everything would work out. Those brief moments of surprising attention and insight had been helping to change Shea's whole attitude. He felt more capable and hopeful than he had in a long time.

But, of course, David had also been incredibly sexy. It felt like David saw Shea more clearly than anyone else had in a long time. That was probably just projecting, his overactive imagination filling in blanks that weren't really there. But there was something incredible about how David had lent support to Shea right when he had verbally and socially tripped over himself. There was always the chance David would make fun of Shea behind his back, especially after the remark Elet had made about expressing gratitude, and David was just being nice to drag out the Shea show a while longer. Even if that was the case, there had to have been some good intentions behind the gesture of tipping so generously. The much-needed cash was going to go a long way towards keeping a roof over Shea's head.

It was kind of magical, really. It was much rarer in real life than it was in the superhero stories Shea loved to have a gorgeous stranger swoop in to do a good deed without expecting anything in return. Those brief moments talking to David, somehow capturing the respectful attention of someone way out of Shea's league, was what he really appreciated. The money was just the icing on the cake. If Shea gave his roommates, Ryan and Mahendran, the two hundred bucks, even if it wasn't the full four hundred he owed them for the month, it was probably enough to get him by. They'd been threatening to kick him out. His inability to hold down a job, since he wasn't exactly bursting with any particular talent or natural ability, plus the fact that he was only eighteen and always the low man on the totem pole, meant his bank account hadn't seen any more action than he had.

As much as he wished otherwise, it was all a survival game, pure and simple. He'd been skating by for a while, trusting things would work out somehow. And now, right when he'd begun to think otherwise, that he really was screwed, his luck had turned. Shea had felt really bad about taking advantage of Ryan's willingness to help him out ever since Shea's family disowned him. Ryan just as easily could have let Shea crash at a shelter instead of his apartment. Not being able to cover his equal share of the rent had been an unshakeable burden Shea didn't know how to get out from under. If Ryan suddenly decided he wasn't able to help out any longer, Shea would just have to look for new opportunities elsewhere. None of it ever really got him down as much as it could have. The thing he was most thankful for was the way each day when he got out of bed, he was free to be himself and trust that absolutely anything could happen. He was independent; an adult, coping with his problems well enough to get by. Sure, he wasn't perfect, but things were slowly getting better and all of his really big mistakes were in the past. He could confidently walk away from them and leave them there. The whole world was out there waiting to be discovered, full of hope and adventure. He wasn't afraid to work hard to earn his own small piece of it.

It was probably dumb, but he'd always been inspired by Steve Rogers, Captain America. Steve had started out a lot like Shea—a scrawny, parentless kid with dreams much grander in size than he was. Steve followed his dreams even when no one told him he could do it, and look how he turned out. He became the greatest hero of all time.

Maybe Shea would become someone who mattered someday, too. Just thinking that that could possibly be true made Shea reach up to touch the good luck charm he wore around his neck. It was a silver Captain America shield.

Trying to stay on the shoulder of the road, but weaving onto the sidewalk now and then when traffic or obstructions made the road impassable, Shea slowly got closer to the place he was calling home for the time being.

It was late, dark, and kind of cold out. The neighborhood wasn't the best or the safest, so Shea knew to watch out and keep his head down.

A number of trucks were double parked to unload their contents, blocking the road, so he went up onto the sidewalk. It was trickier there to weave between pedestrians and avoid obstacles. When he got to a clear length of sidewalk, he sped up, pedaling harder.

It happened so fast.

It was just a glimpse of light glinting off of metal from the corner of his right eye. A long pole, which hadn't been there a moment ago, shot out sideways from the dark space between buildings to his right, sticking precisely between the spokes of his front tire.

They snagged violently, instantly.

Shea flew over the handlebars. Landing heavily on his shoulder, he scraped the skin down the length of his arm and over the side of his jaw on the jagged, pebbled texture of the pavement. A sour smell twisted up into his nose and he realized he'd landed in something wet, but it was too dark to see what it was.

There was a ringing in his ears. His vision was blurred from shock and the impact. The pain in his head was bigger than anything, even his ability to figure out what the hell had just happened. For a second, all he could do was stare blankly at the mangled bike tire, trying to focus on it. It was bent and twisted out of shape. A few of the spokes had snapped. He blinked, but the vision didn't shift or change, yet there was no way that could be real.

Without a car, without a bike, Shea was screwed. He would be forced to walk miles to and from work. He'd get there sweaty and likely be fired just for looking and smelling a mess. Shea could feel those breaks and twists in the tire like they were part of him, and it wasn't just a bike at all. It felt like his whole life was right there in those gnarled spokes, warped and pitiful, ruined by circumstance and bad luck.

Before his vision could clear, two shadows fell over Shea, emerging from the alleyway and swarming him.

Shea tensed up, grunting in fear.

A sharp kick from the toe of a boot connected with his left eye socket. He saw it coming a second before stars exploded in his vision. The pain punched deeply into his skull, then pushed outward. Grasping at his face, blocking any further hits, he tried to curl up into a ball.

His abraded skin dragged over the stinking pavement and his arm began to sting even more.

The others reached for him, and yanked his bag roughly from his shoulder. Their hands grabbed at his pants and he gave a wild, protesting shout, "No, please!"

They were digging into his pockets, pulling everything inside out. He got a quick glimpse of his wallet with the two hundred dollar tip inside some guy's hand. He couldn't make out features, or anything other than the general shape of him.

Shea knew that money was the only thing he had left.

He just let it go.

"Take it," he cried. "You can have it, just please don't hurt me!"

"Pussy," a gravelly voice taunted as a hard kick drove into his stomach, right below his sternum.

The air was knocked out of his lungs, and he gaped, his mouth working as he tried to draw in oxygen his lungs refused to swell to accept. Then someone else kicked him in the back, twisting him the other way, his spine arching as he spasmed in agony.

One of the men crouched down, grabbing Shea by the face, their palm covering his good eye. He screamed as they began pressing his wounded face against the pavement.

"We take what we want. Don't need your fucking permission."

Shea reached for the guy's arm with both hands, pushing back on it, trying to make them stop. His screams climbed when the movement only worsened the torment of the arm he'd landed on as he dragged it over the ground.

Instead of his face, the guy grabbed Shea's left hand, the fingers splayed in torment. He was yanked a few feet closer to the buildings, deeper into the shadows. He tried to roll to his back, needing to stop his damaged arm from touching the rough ground. The feeling in that arm went beyond pain. Shea was ready to do anything to make it stop.

"Stay down!" they yelled at him and kicked him again in the stomach. "Fucking piece of trash."

Shea coughed, wheezing. He covered his head and whimpered.

They kicked at him once more before sirens began to wail in the distance, getting steadily closer.

"Come on, let's get out of here."

He heard footsteps running away. The sirens grew louder as they passed Shea, then faded away again. Cars kept driving by.

Breathing hard, trembling uncontrollably, Shea didn't know what to do. Getting up would only mean facing what had just happened, but he couldn't stay where he was. The muggers could come back, keep hurting him for sport. He needed to get somewhere safe.

At first, the pain washed over him without sense. It was everywhere, in his throbbing head, the bones of his face, the side of his jaw, in his stinging, shrieking left arm, and in his stomach and back. He knew he probably had abrasions, cuts, and bruises, but Shea just folded his arms over his head and tried to calm down. He took a few deeper breaths, following the advice from David that had worked earlier that day. But, without the steady presence of the man who had so easy taken command of the situation at Teresa's, it didn't work nearly as well.

The little voice inside spoke up. It was the one which had once told him to run when his father had leveled a shotgun at him, letting him pretend he was escaping a villain instead of a parent. It was also the one which promised him that if he gave his crappy job his best effort, it would pay off eventually, just like when Steve enlisted. Steve's remarkable spirit had gotten him recognized and made him a candidate to become a superhuman. But Shea's voice now told him that Steve would have fought back. Steve Rogers would have tried to stop the thieves. Even before his transformation, he wouldn't have just sat there and took the beating without protest. It left Shea feeling disappointed in himself, but he didn't know what else he could have done.

When fear of more pain outpaced his desire to avoid reality, Shea slowly tried to stand. He got one foot under him, then the other, and had to lean against the wall as a dizzy spell hit.

He didn't want to look at his arm or see how bad the damage was. Anyway, what was done was done. His real concern was the ten block walk he still had ahead of him, now with a broken bike to drag along beside him.

The night was clear, the air crisp and the streets emptying out. It was March, feeling more like winter than it had all week, making him shiver and hunch forward to block most of the frigid breeze. Time slowed down and each step was a struggle but the aches in his body were blessedly overwhelming enough to keep any harsh reality check at bay for a while longer. Drinking in the hurt, breaking it down into fuel to keep going, pushing through it, he refused to let it kill his last remnants of hope—shriveled, torn, and mangled though they were. He could still get home okay. Ryan would understand. He would help.

At a red light crosswalk, he let an elderly man with a cane and a pronounced limp go ahead of him, but not before catching the expression of shock as the old man took in his appearance.

A block after that, a stray dog ran up to Shea, tail waving, and tongue lolling happily. Shea stopped to catch his breath and take a momentary break, giving the dog a scratch behind the ears after he rubbed against Shea's leg with a small whine. Shea crouched down, just wanting to rest. The dog licked at Shea's face, then sniffed and licked his left arm. The contact stung; Shea stood again, gently pushing the dog away and kept walking after the dog ran off.

Finally, he got to the building. He didn't think about the climb to the third floor, he just did it one step at a time, carrying the bike. It was hard to lament having an elevator to use instead, because it hadn't worked a single day since they'd moved in. If you never had something in the first place, it was impossible to miss.

The climb strained the arm he'd fallen on. Through jagged rips in his shirt, blood was caked with dirt and grime. Shea tried not to look at it and just kept moving. He was almost home. It was going to be okay.

Mahendran worked nights doing security at an office complex, so Shea knew it was likely just Ryan at home when he knocked on the door to be let in, his keys lost with everything else in his stolen messenger bag.

Five minutes after Shea began knocking, Ryan finally opened the door. He was holding a beer can, which he crushed and tossed behind him after looking up and down Shea's body. The television was playing behind Ryan in the living room of their apartment, showing a hockey game.

"Typical," was all Ryan said. He rolled his eyes and kept blocking the doorway. "Leave that piece of shit bike in the hall."

"Someone might take it. I'll keep it in my room like always. It won't be in the way, I promise."

Ryan barely stepped aside enough to allow Shea the space to get through and inside. He squeezed between Ryan and the doorframe, then wheeled the bike to his bedroom, leaning it against the wall there before going to talk to his waiting roommate.

He folded his arms loosely over his chest, not liking the way it felt when he moved his left arm, but liking the lecherous look on Ryan's face even less. "Look," Shea started, his voice sounding thinner and less forceful, when it wasn't very full or forceful to begin with. He guessed he was more shaken up than he'd thought. "I really was so excited to come back and tell you, I had two hundred dollars to pay you guys for the rent I owe, but I... I was mugged a few blocks from work. They grabbed everything I had on me, but I'll earn it back, okay? I'm doing everything I can to get the money."

"We're always cutting you slack," Ryan replied in an emotionless way, staring down his nose at Shea while he picked at a fingernail. "There's no slack left to give. Do you even know how much you owe us? Do you even keep count anymore?"

"I do, actually. I don't take that stuff for granted, but you know I make minimum wage, man. It's just going to take me a little longer to catch up. What are you... what are you saying, here, Ry? You're gonna kick me out for getting mugged?" Shea laughed in weak disbelief. "Do you have any idea how much bad karma that is?"

Ryan rolled his eyes again. Catching his bottom lip between his teeth, he tilted his head sideways, his brown eyes slightly unfocused. He walked right into Shea's personal space. Shea ducked his head and grew still as the closeness got uncomfortable really fast. After a sniff, Ryan mumbled, "Your shirt stinks. Take it off."

Without waiting, Ryan grabbed the bottom hem and pulled upward on it, stripping it from Shea who yelped when his injured arm was forced up at an angle, the shirt sleeve rubbing painfully over the wounds. Ryan tossed the shirt aside and grinned, smelling strongly of beer, slurring his words enough that Shea could guess he was pretty far along. A glance at the pile of empty beer cans by the couch told him he was right.

But then Ryan was pulling at the button of Shea's fly, getting it open before Shea could move to stop him, grabbing at Ryan's hand, trying to twist away. "Stop. Ryan, don't... please..."

Ryan was stronger, with a drunk's eagerness and Shea had barely enough energy left to keep standing. Ryan easily pushed his hand inside Shea's pants and grabbed at his dick, fondling it. Shea tried to pull away, to get out of reach, but Ryan slung an arm around him to keep him there. "You know, if you wanna work off your share in the sack, I told you, that's fine with me. I'll cover you. It's your choice. Don't say I never did anything for you."

Ryan didn't have much self-control when he wasn't drunk. When he was, all bets were off. It was one of the reasons Shea had broken up with him, but Shea had to guess that Ryan's anger at being stiffed out of rent payments had taken a nasty turn.

Shea might not have much, but he did have self-respect. Having sex with Ryan, who Shea had realized didn't respect him at all, would definitely have made it impossible for Shea to live with himself. He might not be a hero, but he did want to keep thinking of himself as a good person who deserved a lot better than what Ryan had to give.

"Ry, knock it off! We broke up months ago and I told you before, I'm not interested. You're drunk. Let me go." Shea managed to slip from Ryan's arm for a second, but after a flash of anger, Ryan grabbed him again, reaching down the back of Shea's pants as he was pressed up against the wall between their living room and the hall leading to the bedrooms. Ryan's fingers were rubbing into Shea's crease, poking at him like they wanted inside.

"Stop!" He managed to get hold of Ryan's wrist, breathing harder as his strength waned even more.

"Oh, come on," Ryan whispered into Shea's ear. "We've been through this, haven't we? Sometimes you've gotta do what you've gotta do. This is kind of the only thing you've got left to sell. Virgins fetch a high price. And after all of those times when you said no to me like a fucking prude, it'll be worth the expense to get first crack at ruining that tight ass of yours, and see the look on your fuckin' face while I'm doin' it. Of course, next time, you're gonna have to do a little *more* to work off the whole four hundred."

With a growl, Ryan yanked his wrist free of Shea's weakening hold. He pushed down into Shea's pants again, managed to find his hole after a firm, downward rub between his cheeks, and pressed at it with one finger.

"No," Shea gasped. He planted his hands on the wall and pushed against it as hard as he could. It made just enough space that he was able to lunge sideways, for his bedroom door. There was a tug at the back of his pants, so Shea grabbed the doorframe, using it as leverage to get free.

He fell forward as Ryan let go, laughing.

Shea scrambled up and slammed the door closed. He locked it.

After a minute of looking at it, he dragged his dresser a few inches to the right to block the door, too, just in case. Sometimes, with bad luck as with super-villains, you had to outsmart the problem instead of just wishing it away.

Heart pounding, trying to catch his breath and feeling unsure and unsteady in every possible way, Shea crawled into bed, pulled the covers up and closed his eyes. When Ryan banged on the door a few times, shouting, "Lemme in, Whitt! You know you will, eventually!" Shea grabbed his phone and headphones. He stuck them on his ears, turned on some music, increased the volume and told himself he would be okay, that Ryan would give up and go back to his game. Or sober up.

Hours slipped by as Shea passed out.

It was hours later when he woke, feeling like a miserable mess, but it was still dark out. Without bothering to look at his alarm clock, he told himself he had the day off, that he could ignore it all and hide as long as he needed to. Too tired and sore to be able to think his way out of his predicament, Shea knew the way Ryan was acting meant he wasn't safe there anymore. But Shea had been unsafe at home with his parents sometimes, too, and he'd stayed there a long time anyway. Maybe he could stick it out. Or maybe after sleeping more, the answer would come to him. He didn't want to look at himself, even to wash up, let alone go so far as to call around to see if anyone would give him somewhere else to sleep until Ryan cooled off.

His arm was throbbing, and he felt flushed and shivery; Shea went back to sleep.

It was midday when his heavy eyelids struggled to blink open, and he felt awful. Nothing had changed. His problems still had no answers. He couldn't stay with Ryan, but had nowhere else to go. He had to pay his debts, but he had no money. He had to get to work, but didn't have a functioning car or a bike. And, most of all, he needed to keep going, but all he wanted was to ignore everything he was feeling and pretend things would be better after some more rest.

Feeling parched, he drank some iced tea from a half-finished container on his nightstand, emptying it, then decided, shamefully, to piss into the bottle rather than venture out into the hall to find the bathroom. If he left the room, Ryan could be waiting for him, and even if he wasn't, Shea would still have to see himself and what a mess he'd become. That was something he just wasn't ready for.

His head was swimming and everything hurt. Once his bladder was empty, he returned to bed and stayed there all day, suspecting that once he did get up to go somewhere else, he wouldn't be able to ever come back.

Chapter 4
Unacceptable Conditions

"David? Darling, are you even listening to me? Penelope, fetch me another water. The Evian, not that filtered garbage. Over ice with a bit of fresh lemon. Thank you, my dear. Now, where were we? Oh yes. Your father expects you to begin attending board meetings. He won't accept excuses any longer, especially if they have anything to do with your little dalliances on the side. David? David!"

"I hear you, mother," David assured her. He was reclined back in his seat beside the patio table on the veranda outside of his parents' estate. It was all the same old nonsense—obligations to fulfill, appearances to keep up, more money to rake in and distribute to any number of overseas accounts. None of it meant anything. It wasn't helping anyone or positively contributing to the world. He was just going through the motions to please his father, when David really didn't care what his father thought of him in the first place. "You do know what I do at these meetings, don't you? He doesn't exactly give me room to speak. He doesn't want me to contribute. The only point of me being there is so he can parade me around like the family mascot instead of his heir. What was the point of all of that schooling if all he thinks I'm good for is to smile and nod at his suggestions?"

His mother, Marylyn Davenport, sighed dramatically, then glanced around for Penelope's imminent return with the damned Evian.

"It's all bullshit," he summed up, aiming a level look in her direction.

"Yes, dearest, but it's important bullshit, so humor your father, just this once," she said to him, reaching out with a limp wrist for the long-awaited glass of water as it was handed to her. "Thank you so much, Penelope. Remind George, will you, to give the dogs a vigorous run around the lawn today? They've gotten fat."

"Oh, just this once?" One of his eyebrows rose in question. She simply waved off his implied sarcasm. Penelope, in her carefully pressed, impeccable black uniform, hurried off to give George the word about the obese dogs.

"When you're older and you have real responsibility on your shoulders, you'll miss the supporting role you're currently playing. Go to the meeting. Have a party or two after. You'll be fine." His mother squinted out from under her elaborately over-designed mint green hat with its wide, dramatic brim, peering at the lawn like all of the dogs had just collectively shat upon it and the smell was wafting directly beneath her nose. Under her breath, she murmured, "Fuck, it looks like rain and they've just watered the new flowers from Peru or Argentina or some damned place. Where the hell were they from again? Oh, it doesn't matter."

"Mm. Parties do solve all of life's problems, don't they?"

Marylyn sipped at her water and glanced his way. "Well, your parties solve more problems than mine, I'll give you that."

"Not everything is about sex, Mother."

"Really? Is that what we've decided? When are you going to take a nice boyfriend, anyway? It's much more appropriate at your age to at least seem to be in a relationship."

With an amused smirk, he asked her with rapt attention, "And where am I supposed to take a boyfriend from, again? Is there a shop I haven't heard of? How is the selection process handled—by catalog or do they parade the candidates before you like they were show dogs on leashes, whistling and slapping their asses to make them go faster?"

"Mm, indeed," she hummed thoughtfully, with a far-away look on her face as she imagined it.

"Well?" he asked patiently. "I mean, it would make things much easier. It's not like I need anyone with a heart or brain or the ability to be compatible with my many endearing qualities and tediously boring, normal lifestyle."

"Oh please. How ridiculous to even pretend you have trouble

meeting men," she said with a roll of her eyes.

The afternoon was weighing on him. It was time to get out of there, away from the servants and employees, back to where normal people congregated and he wasn't treated like a regal envoy rather than a human being. As much as his father might pretend he was incompetent, David had been running his own company, without help, for a couple of years already. At twenty-five, he already had more responsibility than he could comfortably manage, juggling the running of his club, Manse, along with serving as C.E.O. of his real estate development corporation and board member of his father's firm as well. Sometimes he wanted to just escape from it all with someone he cared about, if only he could find someone trustworthy enough to give his heart to.

"Well, I suppose there's always George," David said, tilting his head in the direction of the immaculately manicured lawns where seven tiny, purebred Yorkies on leashes yapped and began to run before a grey-haired, stooped old man.

"George who?" his mother frowned. "What use are all of those pretty young men who are always draping themselves over your lap and your furniture if not to take as a boyfriend?"

"Ideally, a boyfriend is good for more than being a decent lay," David replied.

His mother just waved her hand dismissively.

"So you're still a true romantic, then?" she said. "How unfortunate. You'll spend your life looking for the perfect love and live a lonely, miserable existence in the meantime. Don't set such high standards for yourself. I said boyfriend, not spouse. What about the Evanswood boy? He's about your age and his mother always complains over tea about being saddled with a queer son who'll never give her grandchildren. Tiresome creature, she is. Her daughter may only be fourteen but with the way she dresses, I'm sure she'll have heirs before long."

"How about this," David proposed. "You don't try to fix me up with potential boyfriends and I'll do you the same favor. Unless you're interested in taking on Elet?"

"Please," she scoffs. "He's far too old."

"He's twenty-nine. How old are you again, mother?"

"Twenty-eight," she smiled.

"Are you absolutely sure about this?" Elet asked David, wearing the most put-out expression David had ever seen on the man's face.

Elet was dressed as he always dressed, in dark colors, with designer pants and an equally expensive shirt tailored perfectly to his trim, muscular frame. Though his skin was as dark as ebony, his eyes were a light, warm brown. They helped offset the constant intensity he exuded. The only times David had ever seen his dear friend relax and really enjoy himself was when his massive cock was breaching the rosy pucker of some pretty, young, male submissive. Not that David blamed him for his pleasure in those instances. Quite the contrary, though David did wish Elet found as much joy in more mundane things. Being easily amused did make the days more pleasant.

They were outside of the restaurant they'd eaten in two days earlier. To Elet, it was one thing to occasionally slum it with the commoners, but it was another to make a habit of patronizing such a gauche establishment.

"I am," David replied with a relaxed smile. He was dressed as simply as he could manage; in brown trousers which had been hand tailored solely for him and a shirt his butler vigorously insisted was not the color white but *iceberg*. "Do you suppose he might be here again?"

David couldn't stop thinking about their sweet, young waiter, Shea. He'd shown every sign of being a natural submissive. David had developed an eye for that sort of talent, and Shea had captured his interest, fast. After just a few minutes in his company, it was clear Shea was modest, adorable and respectful in ways Thierry could never dream of being. In fact, their manners were nearly perfectly opposite. Shea had been refreshingly unguarded while Thierry only closed up. Shea had responded to command not only with eager respect, but obviously drew comfort in the sense of control being taken by someone more powerful than him.

Thierry's secretiveness was his way of protecting himself and keeping some things sacred, following only the commands he wanted to follow. The difference with Shea, as tantalizing as his air of vulnerability was, only meant he was in more danger of harm from surrendering power to the wrong person. It made David want to intervene in order to safeguard. If Shea was at all interested, David suspected the boy could find fulfillment in ways that were likely completely unfamiliar to him. David was hoping to catch a quick, discreet conversation in order to offer Shea an invitation to visit Manse and see where things might lead.

"Would you like me to buy him for you?" Elet asked in all seriousness. In response, David instantly lost his near-constant smile and looked at his friend with an impassive expression.

"That's not funny."

With a sigh of surrender, Elet opened the door for David and ushered him in with a polite, "After you, Mr. Davenport, sir. Surely, Teresa's must regularly be visited by billionaires looking to chat with awkward, plain-looking, near-homeless waiters."

"A person's value should never be measured by such things," David said discreetly in reply, his tone making it clear they were dropping the matter, for now.

They were soon seated. Holly, the waitress who came to serve them, was certainly not Shea, which produced a distinctly uncharacteristic frown on David's typically elegant face. Elet handled the ordering of the food, as David scanned the busy restaurant for signs of the demure young man who'd captured his interest. There had been something about him — a freshness and forthrightness David hadn't experienced in a long time. Each time David had tried to gently press Shea for more, to draw him in a little or set him at ease, not only had it worked, but Shea displayed what David would characterize as the ideal submissive response.

Whereas Dominants like him drew pleasure from taking control of a lover who had consented to submit, the perfect submissive, in David's eyes at least, was one who gave of himself so openly and without hesitation; it was up to him, as Master, to keep each submissive safe and pull them back just before they gave too much. David wanted it all — total power over his slave with nothing but trust and affection reflected back at him.

Someone like Shea was capable of that. It was both a gift and a curse, because there were plenty of people in the world unworthy of that kind of surrender.

That wasn't the only reason David's interest had latched onto Shea. Yes, Shea seemed respectful and honest, but exceedingly polite. He'd also said David was attractive without seeming to realize it, which meant there might be some mutual attraction building there, too. There was more to it than that, but David had been unable to put his finger on what it was. He wouldn't be content until he figured it out.

As they sat there, David's thoughts spun on the matter, picking apart his memories of the other day to scrutinize them. That was probably why Elet spotted Shea first.

"David," Elet said severely, straightening in his seat and smoothing the front of his shirt.

David followed Elet's gaze instantly as Elet tensely murmured, "Don't do anything foolish. We don't need to —"

David was up and on his feet before Elet could finish his sentence with a resigned, "Draw attention."

David rapidly crossed the restaurant, threw the double front doors open and stalked outside to where Shea was sitting on the curb. His knees were drawn up to his chest, his expression forlorn and overwhelmed, but his appearance...

Crouching beside Shea, David demanded, "Who did this to you?"

Shea's face was swollen with a black eye, marbled in terrible colors ranging from yellow to crimson-black. His jaw was ringed on one side with a deep abrasion crusted with blood and dirt. He was holding his left arm against his body protectively enough that David had to assume it was also injured. Some of the light in his eyes had even been extinguished, replaced with a cringing look David had often seen in people who had been viciously mistreated.

At first, Shea just stared at him in utter confusion, looking lost. Inside Teresa's, people seated by the glass windows were gawking at them and the minor scene David was making, not that he cared one bit. Pedestrians on the sidewalks and in the parking area had also paused to observe. But none of this seemed to touch Shea's notice. He had eyes only for David and didn't once divert his attention. David breathed in the subtle submission and crowded further into Shea's space as if he had been invited.

"Oh my god, the hotter Stark and Brother Voodoo," Shea said, sounding incredibly bewildered. David hoped he hadn't suffered a concussion. "You're David. You left me that crazy tip the other day. This is so weird. Why are you here?"

"*Who did this?*" David quietly but firmly insisted.

"I-I don't know. I was mugged on my way home from here. It was actually the same day I met you. Never saw who did it. They took my stuff and beat me up, but when I got home, I..." Shea shook his head and seemed to draw further in on himself. "Never mind. I'm sorry if I'm upsetting you, sir. I'll go sit somewhere else if I'm disturbing your meal."

It was the way Shea sounded that was the final straw. There was much more going on here than a mugging, and if David was reading Shea correctly, the beating had damaged more than just skin. He looked like a broken doll, tumbled from his beloved's grasp, left to rot in the gutters, forgotten.

Anger like David hadn't felt in a long time suffused him. It didn't get the better of him, but only intensified his focus and need to gain control of the situation. All he could see were those wounds, the absence of any bandages, and the fact that Shea was at work, not at a hospital or, at the very least, at home resting. And not only was he not actively working, he was sitting on the edge of the sidewalk, like they'd...

"Did they kick you out?" David jabbed a finger at the restaurant.

Shea bowed his head, bracing his forehead against a hand and trying to hide his injuries. "The manager told me to go clean myself up, and I thought they'd let me use the sink in the restroom here, but he doesn't want me upsetting the customers, and I can't go home. I don't... I don't have anywhere to go."

Then, David did smile, with a murderous sort of wrath hidden in the hard sparkle of his eyes, as well as the glint of his teeth. He stood and Elet was right there, eyeing him and waiting patiently, knowing David well enough to back off respectfully.

"Okay, this is completely unacceptable."

"What?" Shea laughed a little, and it sounded hollow, thin, exhausted. "I don't know what to—"

"Come. Everything will be taken care of." David extended a hand to Shea. Warily, Shea took it and let David pull him up, wincing with pain as he did, hinting at other bruising, other wounds.

"Come where?"

"I'll have my driver bring the car around. Your injuries need tending and you need to rest. If you have nowhere to go, I'll give you a safe place. A good friend of mine is a highly respected doctor. He's at my residence now."

"I can't go with you, David. I'm sorry. I appreciate the offer, but I don't know you and you don't owe me anything, anyway."

Gently taking Shea's face in a hand, David tipped it up to catch the light, examining the damage. Elet had waved to their driver, who was pulling the car up to where they waited.

"What are you doing?" Shea asked quietly.

"Did you drive here?"

"N-no. I walked. I had a bike, but the wheel was broken when—"

"You were mugged," David supplied, putting the pieces together quickly. "How far did you walk?"

"Five miles, I guess? Look, maybe you could give me a ride to the free clinic on the other side of town? It's close to a shelter I used a little while back. I think they'd take me in, let me get some rest while I figure stuff out."

"No, the clinic and the shelter are for those who don't have the means to partake of better options. You do. And you deserve to have someone there to make sure you're taken proper care of. If you're uncomfortable coming back to my home, I'll get you a room somewhere and ask the doctor to stop by immediately."

Shea glanced around at the driver holding the door open, then at Elet, ready to get back in the car as soon as the matter was decided. Confusion still kept Shea frozen in place.

"Everything will be all right. I'll make sure of it. No strings. No conditions," David said. When Shea didn't move or reply, David added, "You've been hurt. What kind of man would I be if I turned a blind eye to that when I can do something to help? That's all I want—to help."

Shea smiled a little, and reached for a charm, hanging from a necklace he wore. It looked like a tiny, silver shield. He rubbed it between his fingers and said under his breath, "You sound like Cap. I've never met someone in real life who cared as much about doing the right thing, even if the right thing seems really crazy." He took a breath and nodded in something like surrender. "Okay. If you wanna be my hero, David, I'll play the damsel in distress, no problem."

Elet got in the car. Shea got in after him and David came in last. The door was closed and once the driver was settled, they sped away.

Chapter 5

Helping the Helpless

"I don't think I've ever met someone who had their own personal physician before. He is really a doctor, right? I mean, no offense, sir. You do look like a doctor, and act like one, and I'm not implying you're some sort of imposter or a guy who gets off on pretending to give medical care," Shea said, his voice wavering slightly. He looked a little uncomfortable to have had his shirt half-removed while in the presence of David and Elet, in addition to the aforementioned physician, Mark Wilkenson, who was busy examining the wounds along Shea's arm. With wide eyes, young Shea was following David's lead, trusting the help of a complete stranger. The doctor had already taken a medical history from Shea, before finally gloving up and beginning his examination.

"Shea, Dr. Wilkenson has excellent credentials. I'm always grateful when he's able to lend a hand to my friends. If it would set your mind at ease, I can pull up information about him on my tablet for you to read through," David offered.

"No, that's all right. I don't want to be more of a hassle than I already am. I'm just a little overwhelmed here. I can see how knowing a doctor could come in handy, though."

"It does," David smiled. "I'm just glad he was free and able to meet us here."

The hotel suite would suit Shea's needs. On the way over, David had sent a message to Violet Turner, his Chief of Operations, asking for any information she could pull up on Shea. There hadn't been much she could find. He was an alumni of a local high school. His address was linked to a married couple, also with the last name of Whittier. There were some police records tied to Shea's family from before his birth, but they'd seemed irrelevant to Shea's situation. There was no record of employment, no social media accounts. Shea had been slipping through a lot of cracks. David would need to be patient in order to learn why.

He had to first solve the problem of Shea's wounds before addressing his own reluctance to disclose everything about who he was. Bringing Shea back to David's residence would have made the situation more complicated than it needed to be, though David was most comfortable there, where he knew everyone and had complete control of what happened at all times. That was why he was a little relieved to be able to delay explaining who he was. He did feel slightly ill at ease over the small amount of loss of control over the circumstances. But what Shea needed was quiet, and safety. David intended to ensure he had it, rather than be counted as only one more on a seemingly long list of those who had failed the young man.

Shea hissed as the doctor swabbed the freshly washed cuts with disinfectant, prodding certain areas which were an angry red and looked slightly swollen.

"Well?" David asked Dr. Wilkenson. "How severe is it?"

"He needs antibiotics. Quickly," Dr. Wilkenson advised, peering up at David over his bifocals. "These wounds weren't properly cleaned and infection has begun to set in. If we were back at my offices, I'd have some samples to give him, but here..." He shook his head. "I can write the prescription."

"I'll get them," Elet answered. "Doctor?"

"Yes, good," Dr. Wilkenson said, retrieving his notepad and a pen. He scribbled out the prescription and handed it over to Elet, who hurried away with it.

Shea was docile; watching everything that was happening, staying mostly quiet.

David asked, "It's too late to stitch it up, isn't it?"

"Yes, we'll need to keep an eye on it. Change the bandages regularly, keep it clean. It will likely scar. Rest and those antibiotics are important, especially because of his fever. Maybe some ice for the eye. Acetaminophen for the fever, but we can have some of that sent up by the hotel staff. I'll take a look at him again in a few days to see how he's recovering. He may have gotten a concussion. Shea, do you have a headache? Feeling any nausea or sensitivity to light?"

"Yeah. A little of all of that, I guess."

"Yes, I'm not surprised. Ideally, I'd assign a nurse to his care, and have him stay in your medical suite. Will you be transferring him there?" The doctor began to put away his tools, the disinfectant, and the pad of paper.

David rubbed his bottom lip thoughtfully and said, "I'll do whatever makes Shea most comfortable." Seeing how the hotel suite was overwhelming Shea, David felt ushering him into the chaos of Manse would not be of any benefit just yet. "Thank you for coming by, Mark. You know how I count on you, and you never disappoint. You surely have other patients expecting you, so I won't keep you any longer. I'll arrange the follow-up visit and see what else can be done."

Clapping David on the shoulder, the doctor said to him, "He's lucky to have met you, sir."

David smiled his thanks with a brief pat on the doctor's back.

Dr. Wilkenson left the suite. When the door had shut softly behind him, Shea said, "Who *are* you? You have a medical suite? Like, of your own? For work or for fun? What kind of work are you in that you'd need your own medical suite?"

David's hand dropped from his mouth. "It's something I've found comes in handy. To explain the specifics would mean telling an exhaustingly long, complicated story, which I promise to do once you've gotten some rest. That's the most important thing right now. Shall we get you settled in one of the bedrooms? Do you need more water?"

"Can we... talk a little first? Please?" Hesitation and guardedness was written all over Shea's expression and body language. If some conversation would make it more possible for him to relax, David was willing to indulge him.

"Of course, if that would make you more comfortable. So... why didn't you clean your wounds?"

Shea sighed and fidgeted on the couch, drawing the shirt closer around him.

"Leave it," David said. "If you're cold, I'll fetch a blanket. The shirt is dirty and —"

"Sit with me?" Shea beseeched, sounding worn out and at his breaking point. "I mean, I know you're just trying to help, and I really appreciate that. I do. I can count on one hand the times in my life people have gone out of their way to help me in a substantial way, so this is pretty huge, but I have no idea why you care about my arm or that I was hurt and I would just really like to talk to you as a person talking to another person."

Wanting nothing more than to reassure, David went to sit beside Shea. He leaned forward, resting his elbows on his knees and glanced sideways at Shea, who was biting shyly at his lip and seemed slightly more at ease to have David next to him on an even level.

"It must be challenging to accept help if you're unused to being offered it, but everyone needs some support now and then. I know I couldn't get through a single day without the people I've come to rely on. If support is something you don't have, I'd be happy to offer it to you. If there's anything I can do to make you more comfortable, please let me know."

"I don't even expect comfortable. I'd just like to not be as afraid as I've been," Shea said softly.

"No one can hurt you here, Shea. I promise. Whatever is worrying you, I'm sure it can wait until after you've gotten a chance to take care of yourself a while. You deserve that."

"Thanks, David," Shea said with a tentative, bashful smile and a sideways glance. There really was something so unintentionally sexy about him. Maybe it was in his body language, or the intelligence behind his gaze, or simply in the ways he reacted. The natural ease of it was kind of wonderful and pulled strongly on all of David's weaknesses. Shea was clearly a young man who knew himself quite well—his strengths and his limitations. That sort of self-possessed clarity was, in David's experience, incredibly hard to find. But if David had a type, it would absolutely be someone who knew exactly what they wanted, who craved being in another's care and wanted to submit to a man capable of providing anything they might need. Shea was checking all of those boxes and it left David feeling stunned by this turn of fate. It felt too good to be true.

Shea hesitated, then said, "It's hard for me to talk about this stuff, especially to someone like you. I mean, you seem to be the kind of guy that has everything in life figured out, and it's embarrassing how little I have figured out right now. I think it's safe to say we probably have nothing in common, other than we both know hardly anything about each other. Maybe... we can make a deal? You answer one of my questions and I'll answer one of yours? That's fair, right?"

The boldness of the request was seductive. "Okay," David agreed. "That does seem fair."

"I don't understand why you came out to talk to me at Teresa's, let alone why you brought me here, and got a doctor and are letting me stay. You're even sticking around to talk to me when you could be anywhere else instead. And I'm... I'm no one, David. Why are you doing this? Why do you care about what happens to me?"

David's eyebrows rose. He gave Shea a soft, crooked smile and considered his answer before speaking. "I care because... I like you. I liked you the first time I saw you, because I sense something in you that I'm very rarely able to find. You might say I'm a difficult person to impress. But, you, Shea? You impressed me. So, I went back to Teresa's hoping to see you again. I was going to invite you to visit a private club with me, but... when I saw you'd been hurt..." He let the thought trail off for a moment, as something occurred to him, hitting him with powerful force. The slight frown of concentration on Shea's face had triggered the realization, along with the way Shea was turned slightly toward David as if seeking shelter from the openness of the room.

David had just figured out one of the reasons why he was so drawn to Shea.

Shea reminded David of a ghost from David's childhood—someone else who had been hurt, with nowhere else to turn, and, apart from the circumstances he'd found himself in, was good and kind. The similarities were fascinating, and now that he saw them, they were unmistakable. There was a vague physical resemblance as well as a similar temperament, too. Shea reminded David of Trent Cokely.

Breathing out a stunned laugh, David shook his head at himself.

"What?" Shea asked.

"You remind me of someone," David said with some difficulty, looking down at his hands as the memories came flooding back. He sighed and briefly touched Shea's knee. The physical contact was energizing and comforting, the heat of Shea's body beside him a counter to the cold, insubstantial forms of memory.

Turning even more toward David, Shea asked curiously, "Who?"

"Someone I was... really fond of. He was gentle, unassuming and... beautiful, in his own unique way. But I lost him, in awful circumstances." David lowered his gaze. The old grief, visions of what Trent must have gone through in his last days, utterly alone, the unfairness of it all... Clearing his throat, David pulled himself together. He looked Shea right in the eye and said, "Who knows? When I saw you were hurt, it might have triggered some unresolved feelings of helplessness. I couldn't help Trent, but I can help you, Shea. Or I can do my damnedest to try, if you'll let me. I realize you have enough to deal with without me adding complications. Hopefully, my strange ways of trying to improve your circumstances do more good than harm."

He could see the questions forming in Shea's mind, so transparent were Shea's emotions, and his thoughts. David suspected Shea wanted to ask in what particular way David liked him, though he didn't expect him to actually do so.

"I just want to do what I can for you. You seem to be in need of aid, and I'm fortunately in a position to provide it," David concluded. "Now, if you'd be so kind as to answer my question? Why didn't you clean the wounds?"

When Shea shyly averted his gaze, hesitating in answering, David pressed harder, "The truth. Please. I can tell something is wrong and—"

"I was afraid to leave my room," Shea confessed. "I, uh... I got back to the apartment where I'm staying, carrying my mangled bike half the way, bleeding everywhere, probably." He took a breath, then resumed, speaking quickly. "And when I got home, my roommate wanted my share of the rent but I didn't have it. He'd been drinking and didn't care that I was hurt. He just saw it as another excuse to cheat him out of the money I owe him. I get it. I've asked a lot of my roommates in being patient with me while I try to get on my feet, financially, so he had every reason to be frustrated. Still, some compassion would have been nice. He just wanted me to pay or get out. He's had enough of my excuses, I guess, and lord knows I've used plenty. But I honestly don't have the money. I'm flat broke, so..."

Shea laughed with self-consciousness so acute, David became certain he was on the brink of tears. Shea took a deep breath before continuing. "God, this is embarrassing to admit. Especially to someone like you. My roommate, Ryan... we used to date. But I never wanted to have... you know. Sex. I didn't mind doing other things, but he was kind of a dick as a person. Always has been, so I didn't want to give him that sort of leverage over me. He was honestly the last person I'd ever want to... you know... be inside me like that. And it bothered him. Still bothers him, actually. So, he got a little... pushy... and said he'd cover my share of the rent if in exchange I let him do whatever he wanted to me. I got scared, so I locked myself in my bedroom. And it's really, really embarrassing to admit it out loud, because now I feel stupid, but it's the truth. I got in bed and fell asleep. Didn't even want to look at my arm, really. It was just too much."

David briefly laid a hand on Shea's undamaged arm and said calmly, "You don't have to be scared like that anymore. You're safe now. I'll make sure of it."

"How?" Sounding lost and struggling with disbelief, Shea laughed a little. "I live with him. Or, I did, anyway. Maybe that was the last straw and they'll kick me out. Either way, I'm screwed. Either they'll evict me, or I don't go back just because of how Ryan's acting. But I have nowhere else to go. This job isn't the greatest but it's the only thing getting me by. It doesn't pay enough for me to be able to afford my own place. My only other option is to call around to see if anyone has a free couch they'd let me sleep on, and I feel like that's not much better than barricading myself into my bedroom at Ryan's place. They're all shitty options. Like I said, I take what I can get. This is all I can get."

"No, it's not," David argued. He looked around at the hotel suite, trying to sound logical while balancing between honesty and anything that would unnecessarily scare Shea. "Dr. Wilkenson has ordered you to rest and recover. This suite is simply a business expense. I'm not actually paying for it out-of-pocket and it's too big for just me anyway. Please, take the extra bedroom tonight. Get some rest. Put off any decisions until the morning, and I'll be here to make sure you're okay."

"David," Shea frowned. "I can't just stay in your hotel room with you. That's crazy. Actually, this whole day has been crazy."

David understood the argument, but Shea was visibly exhausted. He was flushed, his eyes glassy, his posture indicating extreme tiredness and he sounded slightly drunk with his elevating fever. Shea needed to stay. "Do you really want to go back there? To try to sleep in a room where you're scared to step outside the door? Is that really the better alternative?"

Shea sighed, running a hand over the back of his head.

"Do you even get how much of an ass I feel like for even telling you any of this? You're already doing so much for me. But... I mean... if I agree to stay, could I maybe go get some of my stuff first? Just the basics. A toothbrush. Clean clothes. My phone charger...."

Latching onto what seemed like progress, David brightened. "Yes, absolutely. To save time and speed things along, I'll arrange a car to take us there. I have some personal security under my employ. My man, Marco, is ex-military. He'll accompany us to ensure your safety."

Shea ran his tongue over the edges of his front teeth and gave David a look filled with bewilderment. He even laughed a little. "Personal security? Personal doctor? Dude, are you even for real? Are you, like, secretly Bruce Wayne or something?"

"Spend some more time with me. Maybe you'll find out," David smiled.

Chapter 6
Looking for the Catch

For Shea, it was surreal to pull up to his apartment building in a sleek black Lincoln. Even weirder was that the Lincoln was driven by an enormous pillar of a man who could totally have found work as a Colossus stunt double. In the back seat beside Shea sat hot, rich David Unknown-Lastname who was mystifyingly intent on saving Shea from his life. It all made Shea wonder if he was suffering some prolonged delusion. Maybe when the muggers had kicked him in the head, they'd rattled his brain so fantasy and reality were colliding. The heroes were out to save him, and Ryan, the token villain, was out to get him, while Shea was left being neither a good guy or bad guy, but only that poor bastard constantly getting himself into trouble and needing to be rescued. Soon, he'd wake up to his boring, normal existence and laugh about the whole thing.

"How are you feeling? Doing okay?" David asked.

"Yeah. So far, so good. I'd forgotten how much easier it is to get around with a car. I just hope Ryan isn't there."

"It won't be an issue if he is. You're not alone anymore. Whatever happens, Marco and I will handle it so we can get you back to the room and resting. Elet will have the antibiotics waiting when we return."

Shea was wearing one of David's shirts from a bag that had been delivered to the suite shortly before they left. David had insisted Shea wear it, along with a light sweater that still left Shea shivering in the warm car. Unable to shake the chills, Shea had attempted to leave the hotel room wrapped in a blanket, but listened to David's advice about bringing his fever down with the cool air outside. Even though he knew David had a point, Shea thought longingly of the fluffy blanket each time another uncontrollable shiver wracked his body.

The pillar in the front seat was Marco, and he was pretty scary looking, but in a nice, serious sort of way. It was kind of like meeting some guy who'd been the victim of some strange experimentation or a cosmic accident. It kind of made Shea feel bad that Marco had to go through life dealing with all of that bulk, like how The Thing had trouble doing normal tasks since he was completely made out of rock. The size difference between Shea and Marco, or Marco and any other human being, was enough to intimidate. That was probably good, because David said Marco worked security for him.

When Marco parked at a meter and walked around to open the door for them on David's side of the car — next to the sidewalk instead of rushing traffic — Shea saw Marco was wearing a gun in a holster under the coat of his nice black suit.

David got out first, extending a hand to Shea to help him out.

"Easy now. Take your time," he said when Shea stood up too fast and his head spun. Shea kept curiously glancing at Marco's gun as he stepped out of the car, gripping David's hand. He'd never been that close to a handgun before, and his only experiences with shotguns were incredibly bad ones.

David took off his jacket and quickly wrapped it around Shea's trembling shoulders instead.

"David, you don't have to," Shea told him quietly.

"No, but I want to," David replied. He gazed briefly up at the building like he was studying it, even though it wasn't that impressive.

With a very stark what-the-fuck-am-I-doing vibe, Shea fondled the spare key he'd borrowed from Mahendran that morning and followed Marco through the entrance with David at his side, one of his hands braced against Shea's back.

When the three of them got to the stairwell beside the non-functioning elevator, Shea opened his mouth to speak and turned to David. At first nothing came out, just because it was so bizarre to be bringing someone like David — who had his own bodyguard for fuck's sake — back to his apartment. Then, happily, the words started to flow again. "Maybe you guys should just go," Shea told them. "I kind of feel like I'm in a bad reality TV show right now or being pranked on hidden camera. I know you have better things to do than this. I'll just stay here and deal. That's what I do. I deal. It'll be fine, I'm sure. Ryan's probably not actually out to get me, he just acts like a jackass when he's drunk."

"I'm not leaving you here," David said. The reply was cool, composed, and very fucking confident. He ushered Shea forward, supporting him as they began their climb upward. "I'd never forgive myself if I allowed you to stay in this situation."

"Huh," Shea said thoughtfully. "I don't even know what to say to that. You totally get bonus points for sounding so sure of yourself."

"I'm always sure of myself," David replied, seriously, and Shea smiled.

"Must be nice."

They reached the third floor and walked down to his door. The key slid into the lock, he turned the knob and diligently ignored the two people waiting behind him, because if he didn't, he might just start laughing hysterically at the whole thing. His head was unbearably hot, but his body was cold enough to give him goosebumps. Maybe David did have a point with that whole 'rest' idea.

Marco stepped forward then, halting Shea gently with one hand. "May I, sir? Let me see if it's safe for you to enter."

"Sure, if you want to, I guess," Shea said with surprise.

Marco led the way inside.

"Who the hell are you? How'd you open the door? Get out of my apartment!" Ryan yelled from the living room.

Shea groaned and called, "Ry, it's me. They're with me. I'm just getting my things."

Stepping forward, he saw Marco standing between them and Ryan, who was dressed in his work clothes and looked incredibly pissed off.

"Who said you could get your things? You don't pay rent. Maybe I should sell your shit off to get some of the money you owe."

"Shea," David said calmly with a hand resting on Shea's right shoulder. "Go pack what you need." Turning his attention to Ryan, David walked forward, facing him. "It's Ryan, isn't it?"

"Yeah, and who the fuck are you?"

"A friend of Shea's. We're not staying and neither is he. Is this how you typically treat friends who've been mugged and beaten? You bully and upset them? You threaten them?"

Ryan sputtered, hands on his hips. Shea lingered in the doorway to his bedroom, eavesdropping. There weren't many people who were able to quiet Ryan when he was on a tirade, but David had easily managed it.

Marco stepped aside and let David slowly advance on Ryan. David was staring him down, exuding power.

"You... you don't know the shit I've had to put up with because of him," Ryan argued lamely. "What goes on between me and Shea has nothing to do with you."

Speaking low and steadily, David went on, "Like I said, Shea is a friend of mine. No one threatens my friends. You're going to stay right here, in this room, and not say another word until we've gone. It'll only be a moment. Marco? Keep an eye on him. Closely."

"Yes, sir," Marco said eagerly. Ryan's eyes widened slightly as Marco stepped up to be a human barricade between him and the rest of the apartment.

Shea walked to his room, amazed at how effortlessly David had handled Ryan. It set Shea more at ease than he'd have thought possible. All of the anxiety he'd felt the last time he'd been in that bedroom was gone... but for how long?

After a moment, Shea realized David was right behind him. Shea flicked on the light switch and moved further into the bedroom, scanning it for important things like clean underwear that didn't have comic book character logos stamped on them. Idly, he rubbed the charm around his neck, hoping it might hold some answers for him.

"You were great out there. You really were. But, look, David," Shea began, and even caught the look on David's face, which basically was a sexy, humoring sort of grin. He was clearly ready to counter any argument Shea threw his way. "I realize I already asked you this, but I'm still kind of baffled here, so... why are you doing this? Honestly. It's not like you're out to rob me. Am I a charity case? Is this all because of the guy you knew? Trent? You seem like an important person, someone that people care about, and who has others depending on him. I'm nobody. I'm wasting your time."

David shifted to clasp his hands behind his back, widening his stance. Slowly, diligently, he began to look around Shea's room, which was so small there was almost not enough room for them both to be standing in it at the same time. There were bars on the single window. The carpet was stained and old. There were childish posters all over the walls depicting Captain America, Wonder Woman, and Aquaman. There was even a plastic replica Captain America shield hanging above Shea's bed. David looked around at all of these things, then focused solely on the bed. When Shea followed his gaze, he saw why.

Drowning in embarrassment, moving quickly, Shea yanked up the blanket to cover the blood and dirt smears on the sheet. His face felt hotter than ever, his chest tight.

David let the moment breathe before speaking.

Softly, without any humor or condescension, David said, "Bad things shouldn't happen to good people."

It echoed in too many important ways. The longer the words stayed there, in the air between them, the more exposed Shea felt, like David could see right down into the core of who he was. He didn't want to let this good-looking, determined, fortunate stranger see him cry, but it felt like somehow David already understood what Shea had been fighting against—circumstances beyond his control, which were always overpowering his intentions and simple desires. Understanding, compassion, forgiveness and patience were the only things Shea wanted but had been unable to find. Seeing the possibility of maybe finally finding those things in David left Shea so weakened, he was utterly unable to do anything but give in.

David stepped a little closer, and gently pressed his hand on Shea's chest. The contact was nice, like a little anchor to reality, so Shea closed his eyes and let out a heavy exhale. It had been a while since anyone had touched him with nothing but caring concern.

"It's been a very long day," David said in that same, soft, soothing tone. "Let's hasten the ending, shall we?" He wasn't looking at Shea when he said it. It was almost like David had gone somewhere else in his head, was thinking of someone else.

That's what stilled Shea. As he reached up to touch David's hand on his chest, liking the feel of it there and the way it showed him he wasn't alone, that he was heard and seen, Shea wondered who else had captured David's thoughts. Was he still thinking of Trent, or someone else?

Shea knew he needed to stop trying to fight all of the rare good things David was so freely giving him. It wasn't because he didn't have any other choice, though that was true as well. Just being near David was helping Shea feel better, like maybe there was a light at the end of the tunnel, and trusting David was the way out. All he wanted to do was sleep, especially if David would be there, watching over him. In fact, he felt on the verge of passing out.

"Okay," Shea said in total surrender. He moved to gather some things into a duffel bag, keeping his head bowed until he felt a little more composed.

For a minute or two, neither of them spoke but it was an intimate, comfortable type of silence. Shea tossed things together, wondering what came next, and if one night away could make a real difference.

"I really am sorry if I've seemed ungrateful or suspicious of you," he told David. "As pathetic as it sounds, I've just never had anyone go this far out of their way to be nice to me before, and I'm having a hard time believing it."

"I know. I'd love to prove to you that there is kindness left in the world, for no reason other than because you deserve that. Don't worry about getting absolutely everything right now. If you're missing something later, I'll help you retrieve or replace it."

Shea zipped up his bag and just stared at David, trying to figure him out.

He really was gorgeous, like someone's idea of the perfect guy – a daydream given life and plenty of stubbornness. David's dark hair curved in an impeccable soft wave against his forehead. His lips were nearly always smiling in a soft, kind, alluring way. His eyes were bright and fiercely intelligent. David was the guy across the room at a party you fantasized about but never had the balls to actually make small talk with.

Yet, there he was, standing in Shea's shitty bedroom, looking at his bloody sheet without judging him for it, but trying to save him from the circumstances that put him there.

"One night won't change anything," Shea said, voicing his certainty, trying to pop the glossy bubble of hope forming around him. "I'll still have nowhere else to go. I'll still need to come back here, or beg my other friends for favors I haven't earned."

"Don't worry about tomorrow. It's not here yet. Are you hungry?"

Shea blinked at the abrupt change of topic. "I am, actually. I kind of skipped lunch. And breakfast."

David pulled his phone from his pocket, dialed a number and put the phone to his ear. "Yes, hello, Marie. Could you please have James send a selection of entrées to my room. Five or six of your most popular dishes, not just the ones I usually order, along with some non-alcoholic beverages and whatever soups are currently on the menu. Excellent. Thank you so much." He slipped the phone back into his pocket and smiled. Gesturing to the door, he said, "Shall we?"

Chapter 7

Intentions

David stared at his reflection in the bathroom mirror of the hotel suite, with Shea hopefully still resting in a nearby room. It was the morning after he'd first brought Shea to the hotel. The night before, Shea had taken antibiotics and eaten some of the food waiting for them upon their return, then quickly went to bed, his eyes barely managing to stay open. Some of David's staff had lingered, guarding the room and waiting to ensure David's needs were met. It had been early when Shea had gone to sleep. One of David's staff nurses had come by, and checked in on Shea every so often. David had word Shea's fever was down a little, which was good.

"What am I doing?" David asked himself. "How do I help him?"

David wasn't used to doubting himself. When he was a boy, he'd been sent to private schools, with only the best tutors as he learned self-defense techniques, several languages, business tactics, and every means of making a success of every endeavor he took on. The family legacy was resting on his shoulders. There could be no weakness, no doubt, only confidence and careful decisiveness. But what right did David have to insert himself into Shea's life? Yes, Shea looked a little like Trent, and had the same seductively sweet temperament that begged for tender loving care and fierce safeguarding. But Shea wasn't Trent. He was his own person. Just because he didn't have the means to care for himself didn't mean David should have the honor of filling that role.

At the very least, David was certain he'd done the right thing in providing medical care and a refuge for Shea. From what Shea had told him, it seemed he wasn't likely to get help otherwise and he could have wound up very ill, indeed.

But, what came next? David felt some responsibility for Shea's care and comfort, but wasn't sure of the solution. Also, David was all too aware of his attraction to Shea, which was a definite complication. Under no circumstance did he want Shea to feel obligated to return David's affections as some manner of payback. The gentlemanly thing to do was probably to admit to his feelings, then to bow out and let the shelter and sustenance be merely a means to getting Shea back on his feet.

Selfishly, David didn't want to have to walk away from Shea, not when he already liked him so much and saw such possibility between them for a good match. So what was the right thing to do? Did he stay with Shea to keep him company? Should he, instead, offer to visit now and then? Or leave entirely to give Shea his privacy, and let Shea be the one to ask David back? Perhaps the best way to help was to make more of an effort to find Shea a new, permanent home.

The answers were elusive. Instinct was David's main guide.

Once he was dressed in one of the fresh pairs of pants and a button-down shirt from the assortment of clothes delivered by his staff the day before, David emerged from the bedroom he'd slept in. He needed to head back to Manse to get the full report on how last night had gone at the club before heading to his office for work. It was going to be another long day. Maybe, though, there would be time that evening to have dinner with Shea at the restaurant off of the hotel's lobby. It would allow Shea more resting time, give David a reasonable excuse to see Shea again, and permit him something to look forward to.

Rolling his sleeves carefully back, David tried to streamline his restless thoughts somehow. Should he order breakfast? Now, or after he had word Shea was awake and ready to eat? Should he stay to eat with Shea or leave to give him some privacy? Was it best to try and pretend to be less well-off than he was so as to not scare Shea? Or was there more harm in lying?

"Oh, I don't know," David admitted quietly. His sleeves wouldn't roll smoothly. Frowning at them, he fought the fabric.

"Here, let me."

Startled, he looked up as Shea gave him an adorable, sleepy, crooked grin and took David's arm to straighten the folds. He was wearing the t-shirt and shorts he'd gone to bed in the night before. Though the inflamed side of Shea's arm was covered in a bandage, the bruising and wounds on his face were starker than ever. To think someone so young had almost nothing after being so brutally assaulted — no money, no family or support, maybe not even a place to live — made David resolve again to intervene and give Shea whatever comforts he could.

"Morning," Shea said amiably.

"Good morning," David replied, smiling helplessly. Something like gladness sparked, warm and invigorating, in his heart. There was nothing presumptuous about Shea. Just being near him made David want to drop his guard a little and leave his worries behind. "It's early, you know. You should have stayed in bed longer. Did you sleep enough? How are you feeling? You look well."

Despite the bruises and scrapes, Shea seemed stronger than before, which was a great sign of improvement. There was light in his eyes and joy in his smile. David had seen men with uncountable wealth greet the day with much less appreciation for it. If only more people could so easily overcome hardship with such grace.

"Oh, I'm great!" Shea said brightly, like it was Christmas morning and he'd rolled out of bed to find a mountain of gifts waiting for him. Only the mental image of those muggers beating him, and Ryan threatening to rape him, tarnished the rosy picture. David itched to get his hands on those men and make them pay for the pain they caused. "I think my fever's down thanks to the sleep I got and the pills I took. The bed was so much bigger than mine and so comfortable, it was ridiculous. You said something about being here on business, so I wanted to make sure I got up to see you before you left. Did you know there's coffee? There's totally free coffee and it's the good kind. It took me an embarrassingly long time to figure out how to work the coffeemaker, but, you know, persistence and all of that. So, yeah. Coffee! It's hot and smells amazing. I could get you a cup!" He stopped fixing David's sleeves and started to go but stopped himself almost instantly. Chewing his lip, he planted his hands on his hips and added, "Unless you're more of a tea guy. Are you a tea guy? Shit, you are, aren't you?"

David could only laugh. He was so glad to see Shea was acting more like he had at their first encounter, some of his lively spirit coming back after his ordeal. Smoothing a wrinkle on the right arm of Shea's shirt, David said, "Coffee would be wonderful, Shea, but I can't ask you to make it for me. It's thoughtful of you to offer."

"But I want to do something nice for you, David, even if it's just coffee. You're already doing so much for me. I need to return the favor somehow."

"Seeing you smile like that is the only favor I could want. I'd like to order you some breakfast. It's important to keep your strength up. Is there anything in particular you'd want?"

"Well, you already bought me dinner last night," Shea pointed out. "Most of it is still in that mini-fridge over there. I'll just have leftovers. I feel bad enough with you paying for this room and all."

"Please," David insisted. "It would honestly make me very happy to do this for you, so really, my motivations are completely selfish."

A beautiful flicker of shared humor ignited between them. Shea's smile grew. His gaze skimmed down, briefly and flirtatiously, over David's body and he was transformed before David's eyes. There was a natural sensuality to his body, a tease in his smile that lured David in. In all of these subtle ways, Shea begged to be taken, held tight, and kept close.

David realized, then, how much he enjoyed bringing that particular, complicated smile to Shea's lips. David was also powerfully attracted to Shea, who seemed too innocent to anticipate the heady strength of David's lust once it was fixed on something he desired. It was more of a challenge to lure Shea in, in an appropriately respectful way, given the strangeness of the circumstances. But David did love a challenge.

"How dare you, David," Shea teased. "The nerve of some people. Paying for hotel rooms and doctors and *food*."

David shifted a little further into Shea's personal space—just enough to be cozy. Then, he slowly, subtly, breathed in the clean, freshly-showered scent of Shea's skin and the perfume of soap lingering on him. With a cute, self-conscious smile, Shea wordlessly welcomed David in. Bowing his head slightly, losing some of his levity, David cleared his throat.

"I want to be honest with you," David said. Shea looked like he was paying close attention. "After what you told me about your room-mate, and his intentions for you, it's only fair, so there are no misunderstandings. I've realized that what I'm interested in with you is... more than friendship. You've been through so much. I won't pursue you if it's unwanted attention. And the medical care, the suite—none of it is contingent on you giving me anything, even your friendship or kindness."

Maybe the fate of his beloved sister, Donna, was a cautionary tale to stay away from Shea, who reminded David so much of Trent. But if David had learned anything, it was that total honesty, even when painful or possibly disastrous, was key. He had to trust that if he was direct and truthful with Shea, his instincts would guide him to the correct path.

"Wow," Shea said softly, searching David's eyes. "*Pursue*. That's a hell of a word. That implies what I think it does, doesn't it?"

"Most likely, yes," David agreed. "It would be dishonest to pretend I'm not attracted to you. Do you need me to back off?" He dragged the back of his index finger lightly down the center of Shea's chest, sensing his quickened heartbeat and the heavier rise and fall of his chest.

"No, I like when you're close," Shea replied, dropping his gaze as he grew shy. David's finger skimmed lower.

"Are you sure?" David opened his hand, wrapping it around Shea's waist. Shea's breath caught.

"Yeah."

"I know you've been hurt. It's in my nature to take care of the people I desire, to safeguard them and ensure they have nothing to worry about. I want to do that for you." David reached up with his other hand and lightly caressed the side of Shea's neck. "But I'm not only here to help. I want to *have* you."

Shea let out a soft sound, half moan, half gasp. When David pushed in, their mouths a breath apart, Shea tilted into David's approach, parting his lips, a slight frown line formed in his brow.

David was used to getting what he wanted, and having men fall to their knees before him. But Shea was a different type of person. It evidently wasn't in his nature to fight back, even to defend himself, so when pursued by a dominant man, Shea was left helpless. Imagining what could befall him in the wrong hands told David he needed to try to step in. Yet, in yielding to David, Shea had no idea who he was playing with, who he was dealing with. David suspected his desire, abilities, and resources were well beyond anything innocent Shea had ever dreamed of facing. David needed to tread carefully.

"Say the word, and I'll go. I'll leave you alone."

In response, Shea took hold of David's arm and closed his eyes as he pushed toward David's lips, his warm, minty breath ghosting over them. The primal need in David, the Master used to claiming and consuming, surged to the surface. With a growl, his teeth scraped over Shea's lower lip, barely biting it.

Shea's hand tightened its grip on him.

"I'm so fucking tempted," David breathed.

The warm silk of Shea's lips skimmed nervously over David's mouth, trembling against him. Right away, David's fingers found the back of Shea's head, palming it as he pressed in, taking the kiss deeper. Shea's hair was soft between his fingers. After sucking on Shea's upper lip, David licked firmly into the heat of Shea's mouth, over his tongue, tasting him with a moan. Shea yielded so easily, opening to the kiss no matter how deep David went, arching in his arms to let David surge in as much as he needed to. Shea rocked against David's body, moaning softly.

Let him go, David's mind warned him, as he realized how easy it would be to keep going.

David ended the kiss. He pulled back slowly until Shea's lips, parted around his quickened breaths, brushed very lightly against David's, barely touching them. Bowing his head, David took a backward step and licked the taste of Shea from his bottom lip, savoring it. His gaze measured every detail of body language, expression, and sound.

"Take today to think about whether you want this or not," David told him.

"Well, you're kind of convincing. I'm pretty sure I don't need to think about it," Shea said, still breathing hard. David tried to collect himself, straightening up, becoming more professional, and less the lover or the Dom. After one last caress of the skin beside the wounds along Shea's jaw, David let go and stepped back.

"Order whatever food or drink you'd like and have it charged to the room. Unfortunately, I need to get to work, but would you have dinner with me tonight at the restaurant just off the hotel lobby? We could learn a little more about each other. Talk some more. You need to know more about who I am before you make this decision."

"Dinner would be nice. I'd like that," Shea replied with a hint of a smile. Every signal his body was giving off asked for David to come at him again, to grab hold and not let go this time. It was dangerously enticing. David imagined stripping Shea down in order to map all of his bruises, kissing each one away for hours. He'd show Shea exactly what it meant to be with a careful, talented Dominant, testing his instincts, giving him overwhelming pleasure rather than pain, tasting, and teasing to hear how he would beg for more. "Maybe today I'll call around, see about somewhere I can go, since it doesn't seem like a great plan to go back to Ryan's."

"I'd rather you rest than worry about that yet. Stay here as long as you need to. I'd feel better having you here instead of sleeping on someone's couch, but we can discuss that later. Sleep. Take care of yourself," David urged. "Please. I'm very much looking forward to dinner with you tonight."

"Me too," Shea murmured.

David walked to the desk, on which there was a pad of paper with the hotel's logo and a pen. David wrote down his personal phone number.

"If you need to reach me for any reason, that's my direct line. Very few people have it. Don't hesitate to call."

Shea was touching his own lips, still bewildered. The dark bruising around his eye and down his jaw echoed the pain he must have been feeling, and his fatigue was there in every glance and movement.

Checking his pockets, David did a quick mental tally to ensure he wasn't forgetting something. With a nod of satisfaction, knowing his bodyguard was waiting for him just outside the suite's door, David smiled fondly at Shea.

"You have the antibiotics, correct?"

"Yep."

"Good. Take them. Order breakfast. Have a bath. Get a massage.

Indulge a little," David grinned. "I'll see you soon."

On his way out, he lightly kissed Shea's cheek. Shea reached for his hand, giving it a squeeze, unable to raise his gaze.

"Thank you, David. For everything."

"Certainly, sweetheart."

Chapter 8
Dinner with David

"David, this is incredible. Thank you for doing this, and having dinner with me. I have no idea how I'll ever be able to pay you back for all that you've done," Shea confessed.

They were in a secluded area of the restaurant, the French doors were closed to give them a little privacy. Two of David's bodyguards stood just outside those doors, letting the designated pair of waiters serve them and holding the door as they came and went. The room itself was cozy, with modern artwork decorating the walls. Soft candlelight lit the room with a romantic ambiance that left Shea feeling a little out of his depth. Date night usually meant renting a movie or walking around town, window shopping. He'd never had the money to go out to dinner at such a nice place. Two enormous, thick, juicy steaks had been set before them, along with an assortment of side dishes. The food was of a much higher quality than what he was used to serving at Teresa's. He would have felt impossibly nervous having to bring such carefully and artistically presented dishes to customers, let alone have any right to actually eat it. He couldn't even remember the last time he'd had steak. Maybe at his cousin Meghan's wedding to a lawyer when he was fifteen.

"Well, I forbid you to even attempt to pay me back, so that's one problem solved," David said, smiling handsomely with an upward glance at Shea. He carved off a piece of steak and ate it.

"Do you do that a lot? Forbid people to do things? Because you just said that like it was a totally normal thing to say. I don't even have the balls to forbid my neighbor's cat to piss in the hallways." Shea carefully began to carve up some of his meat, expecting someone to come over at any moment to yell at him to get the hell out of there and to stop touching the real customers' food. The elegance of their surroundings and the soft music being piped in through the stereo system only added to his need to not screw things up somehow.

"Well, I do run more than one company, and I've lost count of how many people are employed at my residence, not to mention the power dynamics I prefer in my sexual and romantic encounters, so yes, I do actually forbid people to do things quite often." He topped all of this off with a charming smile, so Shea couldn't tell if he was just being a smart-ass or if he was being honest.

"Wow," Shea said with awe. "I have... so many questions right now. Where the hell do I start? I mean, for one, you can't be that much older than I am, and you run more than one company? And you called it a residence, not a home. I don't even know what that implies but I do know it's way, way, over my head. Like airplane flight path level above my head. And I don't even know where to start with the sex thing."

David opened his mouth to reply, but then his phone rang. "Shit. Excuse me one second, please."

"Sure."

David pulled out his cell phone and answered without leaving. "Yes."

Shea noticed David's good humor leaving the longer he listened to whoever was on the other end of the line. "I'm actually at dinner with a guest right now, so no, it's not at all a good time. Yes, I'm serious." David sighed soundlessly, rubbing his forehead like a headache was forming. "The Marquis on Main Street," David said, which was the name and location of the restaurant they were in. "Surely this can wait until— Fine." He hung up, jaw clenched as he bit down on his back teeth.

It was probably not a good sign that even when David was angry, Shea thought he was unspeakably hot.

"If you have to go, I totally under—"

"No. Don't be ridiculous, I'm not leaving you. We made plans to have dinner. Anything else is less important than that. It's not at all a problem. I'm sorry for the interruption, Shea. Where were we?"

"I'm not sure, actually," Shea answered. His suspicions told him he was in exactly the wrong place but he had no idea how to find the right one.

"How old are you, Shea?"

"Eighteen. Why, how old are you?"

"Twenty-five," David said, his gaze dropping to the table and his glass of wine. Reaching for it, he took a sip and appeared thoughtful. "You're a teenager. You should still be with your family, but you're not, and whatever the reason for that is, it's probably nothing good. I'm so sorry, Shea."

"Don't be. It's fine. Well, not *fine*, but it is what it is."

"Bad ending?" David guessed, looking so regretful over something that had nothing to do with him. It made Shea wonder how David, with so much else on his mind, could possibly have the energy to worry about Shea's bad luck.

"Yeah," Shea admitted. "It's not a nice story."

"Okay." David seemed to digest this, and accept it. "And this is why you were staying with someone as potentially dangerous as your roommate, Ryan?"

"Yeah. Limited options. Minimum wage job. Non-impressive skill set. Connect the dots." Shea looked down at himself, at his Neil Young t-shirt, his Captain America shield necklace and old jeans. Embarrassed that he didn't have nicer clothes, especially when eating at such a nice place with a man like David, Shea folded his hands in his lap and slouched down a little. "David," he sighed, "I don't even know your last name. You have me staying in a hotel suite that probably costs more for one night's stay than I make in half a year. I don't deserve any of this, and I definitely don't deserve your attention."

"Stop," David said firmly, sending a shiver through Shea. After a deep breath, he said, "I'm used to managing things, Shea. People. Businesses. Financial holdings. Situations. Sex. I like control. And everything that's happened to you... there's no control over any of it, so instinctively I feel the need to try to bring it all into order for you, when it's not nearly my place and..." He took another sip of wine, then made and held eye contact with Shea. "The person you remind me of, Trent, suffered a similar loss of control. There was nothing I could do to help him. I was too young. I didn't know better. But now I do, and... the last thing I want to do is scare you off. Or maybe I just don't want you to look at me like everyone else does. When people see me, Shea, they don't see *me*. They see my name, my profession, my money, my reputation. I absolutely adore how when you look at me, my history isn't getting in the way. But that's not fair to you, so I apologize for holding back."

"That's why you haven't told me your last name? It's like... a secret identity sort of thing, isn't it? David, I don't really know you, but I would never think less of you for being honest about yourself. I know how hard it is to be honest with people you think aren't going to accept you if they know who you really are."

"I believe you, Shea. I really do," David promised.

"David," Shea coaxed. "You can trust me. I swear you can."

There was a commotion beyond their little room. People rushed around and a moment later, several men in suits strode quickly toward them. The bodyguards opened the doors and Marco announced, "Mr. Davenport, your father is here."

A chill shot up Shea's spine and he didn't even know why. The room filled with more men who were just as intimidating as Marco, if not more so since they didn't have Marco's friendlier qualities. Suddenly, David was by far the only comforting thing about where Shea found himself.

Davenport, he thought. *His name is David Davenport. Who's David Davenport?*

David stood up, and Shea became even more unsettled. Should he stand up, too? He wasn't sure, then cautiously got to his feet and continued to look to David for guidance.

An older man, an older version of David, with similar features and a similar build, entered the room.

"Father," David said in greeting, circling the table. "This is my guest, Shea Whittier."

David's father looked Shea up and down in a manner Shea was quite familiar with. He understood distaste when he saw it reflected back at him.

"I hope you're not dating this pathetic boy, David."

Shea felt it like a slap, knocking the wind out of him. He dropped his gaze and the hand he'd offered for David's father to shake, folding his arms around himself instead.

"That's quite enough," David said sharply. "I won't tolerate you being rude to my friends. I'm not a dog, Dorian. You can't expect me to heel at your every call. If I say I'm too busy to discuss business, then I'm too busy. Period."

"He looks like you found him on the street!" David's father retorted. He took another look at Shea, then appeared to do a double take and stared. Shea squirmed when David's father began to scrutinize his features.

Quickly, David took Shea by the arm and maneuvered him into place behind him.

"What did you say his name was again? Whittier, was it?"

"Shea is not your concern."

"Where do you know him from?"

"I'm not doing this. I'm not subjecting Shea to this. Leave, Dorian. Now."

Ignoring David's command, Dorian asked Shea, glancing around his son, "You don't have an older brother or cousin named Trent, do you, boy?"

"*I said, get out.*"

Dorian straightened up a little, smoothing his tie and looking down his nose at his son. "You do remember what happens if you associate with trash, don't you? Your sister sure as hell found out. Have you learned nothing?" Dorian made eye contact with Shea, who peeked out from behind David, and the look was chilling. Dorian then turned his back on them and left.

David was breathing hard. Shea wasn't breathing at all.

To Marco and the other guard, David said, "Keep that son of a bitch away from us."

"Yes, sir. You won't be disturbed again."

"Good." The guards closed them back inside the room, alone, and stood sentry.

Running a hand over his mouth, David seemed to be quickly calming down. He growled softly, then turned to face Shea. He gripped Shea's shoulder with one hand and held his gaze. "I am so sorry for that, Shea. None of what he said is a reflection on you. My father is... disturbed. His issues stem from old arguments between us and if I had known he was going to behave that way... He usually barely looks at people I spend time with and he's never spoken to my friends like that before."

Maybe it hurt more because Dorian's words only cemented all of Shea's doubts about why David would care about him in the first place, not to mention the trauma of the mugging and confrontation with Ryan. Dorian was right. Just like the muggers had said, Shea was trash. He had nothing. He really was using Dorian's son. It was all wrong.

"Look, I'm gonna go, okay?" Shea said stiltedly, averting his eyes when David came closer, into his personal space. David exuded the warmth and steadiness Shea craved more than anything, which made it feel impossible to follow through and walk out. Shea bit at the inside of his cheek to keep from crying. He needed to go, no matter how much he wanted to stay. Maybe the shelter would still have an opening for him if he left now. Maybe tomorrow he'd have more luck finding a place to sleep.

"Like hell you are," David said defiantly.

"It's not as bad as it seems," Shea shrugged. "Even if I don't know where I'm going to be sleeping, at least I won't have people talking to me like that."

With a pained expression, David gently caressed the bruised side of Shea's face, then slowly drew him into a hug. "I'll fix this," David swore in a whisper by Shea's ear.

"You can't, and you don't even have to."

"I do." He stepped back.

"I know you ordered all of this incredible food, but I don't think I can eat it right now."

"That's okay. Let me walk you back to your room. Stay, just one more night. Please. I'll help you find a more permanent solution tomorrow. The night is already paid for, and I can't have you out on the street because of my jackass of a father. You need rest, and a chance to heal. You've been through too much."

Shea wanted to argue, to be freed from the sinking suspicion that he was taking advantage of David's kindness in the same way he'd been taking advantage of the kindness of other friends since the day his parents kicked him out. But he was just so tired. A warm bed was something he couldn't pass up.

"Please stay," David murmured, kissing Shea's un-bruised cheek and holding his hand.

"Okay," Shea relented.

Chapter 9

Suspect

Lying in bed, alone, with early morning's sunlight streaming through gauzy white curtains in the luxurious hotel suite, Shea enjoyed the peaceful quiet.

It probably wasn't the biggest suite in the world, but comparing it with every other hotel room Shea had ever personally seen, as well as his admittedly shitty apartment, the thing was enormous. It had two bedrooms, each with a connecting bathroom that were each bigger than his entire apartment. They had Jacuzzi tubs, walk-in showers, and mirrors so huge and gleaming; he was tempted to leave the light off when going in there for the toilet just so he wasn't accidentally blinded by the glare or risked becoming bladder-shy due to his own, un-ignorable reflection. There was a kitchen area with a bar. There was a lounge which looked like it was designed for swanky parties or important business meetings. The enormous glass windows over-looked the city and the balcony allowed you to go out and chuckle at the puny little humans crawling around like specks far, far below.

He had no idea what he was doing there, or how to exist in that place without feeling like he should be spit-polishing all of the shiny objects to help earn his keep. It was out of the question to stay long on the balcony. He kept experiencing that moment where you think, *I should jump over this railing*, just because the worst thing he could do was jump over the railing. The devil was out there, whispering insane thoughts in his ear. It was equally impossible to spend time in the lounge. He felt like an imposter in there. It only served to highlight how much lower on the social spectrum he was than everyone else.

Though the bed was big enough for three or four of him, so far he'd mostly settled on lingering in the bedroom. That morning, he resisted getting out of the bed and having to face impossible decisions. It was so much nicer to doze off a little, thinking of the fairly chaste goodnight kiss David had given him the night before, right there next to the bed. It had sent shivers down to Shea's toes and up through the top of his head. He loved lying there, remembering the softness of David's lips, the woodsy scent of his cologne and the smooth, crisp texture of his carefully ironed, tailored shirt as Shea had lightly grasped David's back, letting the kiss go on as long as David wanted it to. After that sweet goodbye, David had left to take care of business, though he'd still stationed a guard at the door for reasons Shea couldn't figure out. He'd promised to call Shea in the morning, to begin planning what came next.

Shouting shattered the peace, coming from a few rooms away.

Was it coming from the hallway? The next suite? The floor below? Perking up his ears, Shea froze there on the bed, not knowing what to make of it. The shouting was quickly followed by heavy, running footsteps that seemed to be getting closer. There was the bang of a door violently thrown open, and more running footsteps from right down the hall, *his* hall....

Before he could react or even sit up, the bedroom door burst open and five armed men poured into the room.

Terrified, Shea got very still. He was naked under the sheet, staring dumbly at them all. He had no idea who these guys were, what to do or what to say. Two of the men—armed guards—stayed by the door, their guns drawn and ready. Two more guards and a man in a plain grey suit approached the bed.

"Get him out of there," the suited man said, pointing to Shea. The remaining pair of guards swooped in and yanked Shea out from under the sheet by his arms while Shea's heart pounded hard enough to threaten to burst from his chest and flop around on the floor.

"What's happening? I didn't do anything! David—"

The back of someone's hand knocked, hard, across Shea's mouth. Pain flared up his aching jaw and into his skull, rattling his senses. He tasted blood on his tongue.

"We'll let you know when we want to hear from you," the man in the suit told Shea. "Search him."

Where were David's staff? Where was the guard David had left behind to guard the door to the suite? Who were these people?

They ripped off all of Shea's bandages, exposing the painfully sensitive, reddened wounds along his arm. One of the guards stood behind Shea, holding Shea's arms spread out at his sides and kicked his feet apart. The other guard was just finishing up pulling on a pair of latex gloves, the sight of which made Shea's balls try to climb back up into his body. Latex gloves in place, the guard began roughly running his hands over every inch of Shea's naked body, from the soles of his feet, between his toes, up the insides of his legs, behind his balls, around his shaft, through his pubic hair, then up his chest. When they rubbed, hard, down his arms to his fingers, Shea shouted with pain. Ignoring him, the guard ran his hands back up to Shea's neck, behind his ears, and through his hair.

The man was handed a tongue depressor and a flashlight.

"Open!" the guard shouted in Shea's face. Shea was too scared not to obey.

The tongue depressor was shoved far enough back into his mouth to make him retch as the flashlight clicked on and was shone down his throat.

The guard behind him laughed, "Well, what do you know? Guess this faggot's still got his gag reflex. That won't last long."

The stick of wood moved around, to pull at the inside of his cheeks, lifting his tongue.

"Clear," the guard said, turning the flashlight off.

"Over the table," the suited man ordered, indicating the small set of table and chairs by the window. The table was rectangular and only a few feet wide. The legs scraped loudly over the floor as they yanked it away from the wall. The guard holding Shea, who was somehow even larger than Colossus-sized Marco, dragged Shea over to the table and manhandled him over it, on his stomach.

Holding him down by the shoulders, he called another guard over with a gruff, "You! Over here. Keep him from squirming."

The guard from the door got to the table and took one of Shea's arms while his other arm was held by another guard, each of them pressing their full weight down on Shea's shoulder blades. Shea was barely breathing, taking tiny gulps of air, panting and crying out in terror, his vision swimming and tilting with the severity of his panic.

The guard wearing the latex gloves moved up behind him.

"NO! STOP!" Shea screamed, just before two thick fingers were jabbed up his ass, dry. They pressed in farther than Shea could have thought possible, and he kept yelling, thinking of Ryan and all of the worry of being taken by force, worry he thought he'd escaped by being in David's bubble of safety.

The fingers rooted around inside him, searching, making him hurt in places he'd never thought he could hurt while he tensed, clenched, and grunted hard at the violent, humiliating probing. He wanted to pull some magic words out of the air to make it stop. The ache inside his ass and his mortification grew exponentially by the second, trying to outpace each other.

"Bet he's *loving* this," the one guard chuckled. He leaned down and whispered to Shea, "Got a big, tough man with half his hand shoved up that ass to the last knuckle. Moan for us, faggot! Beg us for more! Bet you want it rougher, don't you? We're being too easy on you! You do this all the time, right?"

Shea realized he was crying, the taste of salt mingling with the metallic flavor of his own blood. In his beloved comics, Captain America would have come to the rescue before things got this bad. It was just another reminder that not only was Shea not man enough to save himself, but there would never be any real life heroes to help when he really needed them. People like him didn't get rescued, and if they escaped, it was only to more dire circumstances than before. He tried to block out what was happening, somehow, the way he'd blocked out Ryan for so long.

When the fingers finally pulled out, leaving him throbbing inside, they flipped him over onto his back. He was held down just as tightly, by shoulder and forearm, as well as by his upper thighs, and he understood things weren't nearly finished.

"Urethral swab, then the blood sample," the suited man instructed, pulling a plastic baggie from his inside jacket pocket and handing it to the gloved guard.

"No. No, *don't. Don't,*" Shea pleaded, whimpering in mind-splintering terror as the guard removed a vial with a screw top and a long, metallic swab from the baggie. His whole body began to tremble violently. The guards gripped him tighter as he fought, trying to throw them off and failing completely.

The gloved guard set the vial aside on the table by Shea's hip and took hold of his flaccid penis.

"*No*," Shea sobbed.

The guard stuck the metal swab into Shea's urethra, slipping it through the tiny opening of his slit and pressing it deeply into the organ. Shea's shrill yell of agony filled the room, echoing the shrieking within his body as such a sensitive part of him was so roughly impaled. The pain was a throbbing, growing force, taking apart his ability to hold himself together in any sense. He just needed it to *stop*. The metal stick was pressed even farther into his penis, a few centimeters at least. His whole body shook. His mind tried to deny what was happening, what he was feeling, his sore ass clenched tight as he tried to close off the pain and the shame.

He kept yelling, "No!" Nobody listened.

The swab twisted slowly deeper inside his penis and Shea pulled as hard as he could to get free, somehow finding more breath to scream, his voice cracking under the strain. Nothing could ever hurt more than the ways that swab was hurting. He had to make it *stop*.

Slowly, the stick was withdrawn. The metal swab went into the vial, the cap screwed on and stuck back into the baggie. Next, a syringe was retrieved. Shea would have done anything to cup his aching genitals, to curl into a ball in the corner, to hide, to go back to his old life and Ryan and all of it, just to be somewhere else, *anywhere* else.

The needle was jabbed roughly into him like the guard took particular pleasure out of making everything as painful as he could. Shea stared at his arm as the plunger was released and his blood began to fill the syringe, the room spinning slightly, giving him faint hope that maybe he'd pass out for a while.

When they'd gotten his blood, adding it to the baggie with the metal swab they'd raped his dick with, the whole thing went back in the suited man's jacket pocket.

But, they weren't done with him yet.

The gloved guard held down Shea's legs, leaving the others to focus on keeping Shea's arms held straight out, perpendicular to his sides, gripped at the shoulder and wrist. The worst one, the one in charge, wearing the suit, strolled over with a nightstick in hand. He was running it through his palm, stroking it like it was a cock and Shea bucked.

"We ran your records, Mr. Whittier. You've been in Mr. Davenport's life for... what? A couple of days? We contacted the people at the address you have listed on your driver's license and they denied knowledge of your existence. There's barely a record of you online. It's like you don't exist, so I've got a few questions for you. The first is the *most* important, so listen carefully."

The club smacked in a light staccato against the suited man's palm as he tested its weight. Everything about him was calm, composed, and merciless, while Shea cried and tried not to piss himself.

The club swung, too fast for Shea to track it, and it connected with shattering force against the sore, scabbed flesh of the arm on which he'd landed during the mugging, connecting with a meaty thud. Some of the scabs ripped off, leaving his blood to flow again. That arm hurt even when nothing was touching it. The blow left Shea reeling, wiping out all thought.

Shea's shriek of pain was loud enough to drown out the suited man's question, so he repeated himself. "I said, WHAT IS YOUR INTEREST IN MR. DAVENPORT?!"

Chapter 10

In Distress

"We're not finished, here, David," Dorian said with a patronizing chuckle. "You made quite the scene last night, but we have actual business to discuss. My meeting with the Watkins firm is in only a couple of hours and..."

David was only half listening. He'd just tried to phone Anthony, the guard stationed that morning outside of Shea's room, for a status update on him. The call hadn't been picked up. He tried again, putting the phone to his ear.

"Hang up the damn phone!" Dorian snapped. "I'm talking to you, boy!"

That was the last straw. David stood, turning his back to his father and made to head to the conference room's exit. From the corner of his eye, he saw Dorian gesture to his staff. The security guard moved swiftly to block David's path.

Dropping the phone to his side as it rang and rang, David gave his own malicious chuckle and said to the guard, "Get the fuck out of my way. Now."

"I'm afraid I can't allow you to leave, Mr. Davenport," the guard explained without making eye contact, just staring over David's shoulder in Dorian's direction.

"Mm," David hummed thoughtfully, shifting his stance casually. Catching the guard by surprise, David grabbed hold of the man's head and slammed it back against the wall in a well-practiced move. Immediately, the guard crumpled to the floor. "Right then."

"David, you don't understand!"

"What have you done *now*, Father?" David said through gritted teeth.

"I'm just trying to keep you safe! He could have diseases or be related to that murderer!" Dorian snapped, and it sent awful chills racing down David's spine.

Shea.

David immediately bolted, racing through the top floor of the Davenport Corporation headquarters to the elevator, his own guards posted outside of the conference room, Marco and Andrew, jogging after him. Once they were down on the first floor and in lobby, David ran hard, his arms pumping, his feet flying over marble. Marco got on the phone with the driver, then began trying to call hotel security.

Precious moments ticked by as David jumped into the car waiting at the curb and the guard piled in after him.

"There's no answer from Anthony," Marco said. "The hotel is going to send people up to check on Mr. Whittier."

"My father's people," David sneered. "Ex-CIA, soulless motherfuckers, bought and paid for. We need to get Shea out of there, *now.*"

It took forever to get to the hotel. As they pulled up, Marco's phone rang.

After an all all-too-brief conversation, Marco ended the call and told David, "The elevator isn't working and in the stairwells, the doors to the fourteenth floor are blocked from the inside. They've just now called the police and are trying everything they can to get in there."

"Fuck," David groaned, tensed and ready to fight his way to Shea, trying to figure out how.

They got out of the car and raced into the hotel.

"Stairs are our only bet," Marco told David.

"Fine," David nodded. Then, they began to climb.

At the last flight of steps, they saw hotel employees gathered around the doorway. David saw they were removing the doorknob entirely and were almost finished. He waited impatiently, and was glad when Marco stepped up. He asked the others to get out of the way and rammed the door with his shoulder.

It flew open, ricocheting off the wall.

"Let's go!"

Faintly, from down the hall, they heard a muffled scream.

David was moving instantly. A short sprint brought them to the closed door of the suite. The guard David left wasn't in sight. Marco held David back with a hand to his chest.

"We need to be smart about this, sir," Marco whispered.

"I'll fucking kill them," David seethed. The scream had come from Shea. They were hurting him. There was no time.

Andrew passed David a gun, finger raised to his lips. David took it and nodded.

"Stay at the back, let us clear the way, then we move in," Marco said. "Keep it silent."

David nodded again.

Marco and David were on one side of the door, Andrew on the other. Andrew knocked lightly on the door.

A moment later, it opened, and a confused guard peered out, looking for the knocker. Marco had him by the throat, then brought the butt of the gun down on the back of the guard's head with a sickening crack. The man crumpled like a rag doll. Andrew dragged him out of the doorway and used zip ties to secure the man's arms behind his back.

The second guard wandered out while this was going on and received similar treatment. When the pair of guards were both restrained and unconscious, the three crept through the main living space toward the short hall where the bedrooms were located, which was where the more experienced, reliable guards would have been stationed. They found Anthony in the lounge area, restrained, gagged and unconscious.

A fresh, earsplitting cry from Shea's bedroom made David want to rip off the fingers and toes, one by one, of whoever was touching him before stuffing them up their asses.

David needed to move, to get to Shea, but Marco hissed to him in warning, with a tight shake of his head as they approached the open door to the room.

From inside the room, David heard, "Don't let him squirm! Hold him down! Spread his legs wider!"

Needing to intervene, to stop them, David felt his foot take the first step. Marco had his arm again, pulling him back, whispering, "Let us handle this, sir. Please."

"Like hell I will," David snarled, yanking his arm back.

"Calm, sir. Nice and calm," Marco soothed.

They forced David to the rear again, their guns cocked and ready, hugging the wall.

The hall was clear. Andrew peeked into the room, then drew quickly back. He held up five fingers. That meant five were in there, doing Christ knew what to Shea.

He motioned to Marco and David, holding up one finger, just behind his other hand, then sliced the air. Marco nodded. Andrew hurried in a crouch, along the wall to the open bedroom door. It was barely a second, a flash of movement. Andrew cracked a tranquilizer capsule and attempted to shove it up the guard's nostril with one hand, using the other to cover his mouth. Fighting back, the guard was pulled by Andrew around into the hall and held down while the drugs knocked him out.

That left four of Dorian's men. Three against four was better odds, at least.

Marco gestured to Andrew and David, wanting to move around David with Andrew to take out the farthest targets while David stayed as close to the exit, and the cover it provided, as possible. They nodded. They did a silent count off to three, then moved.

David didn't let himself look at Shea, not yet. He had eyes only for his target. Aware of Marco and Andrew flying around him, ahead of him, David raised his gun to the back of the suited man's head, the hammer cocked, his finger on the trigger, and said smoothly, "*Please* give me a reason to kill you."

Marco and Andrew had their weapons pointed at the three guards, who raised their hands in the air, letting go of Shea who slid off the table and tumbled to the floor.

"Mr. Davenport," the suited man explained with more fear than he probably wanted to show, "you have no idea who this person is, what he wants, what his intentions for you are—"

"And you do?" David countered.

"Toss your weapons. All of them. Now. Unless you want me to *accidentally* shoot you in the balls?" Marco asked.

Guns, nightsticks, tasers, and knives clattered to the floor.

"Lie down, face to the floor, hands behind your heads."

While Marco and Andrew secured the guards, David patted down the suit. He'd barely started when he found a large baggie filled with a blood sample and a used urethral swab, damp with fluid.

It was one step too far.

His knee connected with the suit's balls, driving up into them with as much force as he could find. It almost doubled him over but he was too experienced with torture to be much phased, so David fed him the barrel of his gun, sliding it far enough to touch the back of the suit's throat and said quietly, "You think Mr. Whittier is unclean, do you? Who are you to judge? Have you been similarly tested? Had a team of guards hold you down while someone shoves a metal rod up your cock?"

Marco and Andrew finished tying up the guards and came to David's side.

"You shouldn't have touched him," David warned.

"What's the call, sir?" Marco asked. "We need to get Shea to a doctor."

David considered the despicable man currently eating his gun. "Make sure he keeps his hands to himself for a while."

"No problem."

Marco took hold of the suit, who fought uselessly, and dragged him back a few feet to the doorway. After stretching out the man's right arm so that the hand was set against the doorframe, Marco nodded to Andrew who was holding the door. As the door slammed shut, the suit's shout burst from his tightly sealed lips. While Marco and Andrew shifted the man around to the other side, to get at his other arm. David turned his attention to Shea.

The door slammed again, followed by a rise in the suit's yell.

Shea was lying unconscious and naked on the ground, on his bleeding, injured arm. There were fresh bruises and who knew what else they'd done?

David gathered Shea into his lap. "I'm so sorry. It's over, you're safe," David told him, even though he knew Shea likely couldn't hear. Shea's nose and mouth were bleeding. New bruises were forming along his battered jaw. The scabbed-over flesh of his injured arm was broken and bleeding freely.

A glance back showed David that Andrew had the suit on the ground and was hogtying him by the door, his crushed, mangled hands splayed. Marco was putting his phone to his ear. "This is Mr. Davenport's security. What's the status?" He looked at David, relaying, "The elevator's working now, sir. The police are on their way in. Should I request an ambulance?"

"No. The hospital isn't safe enough, not if my father went this far to get to Shea. Shea is coming back to the house where his security can be ensured. Andrew, once you've finished with him, please warn Dr. Wilkenson and his team that we're coming. They'll evaluate Shea, and we'll bring in whatever specialists he'll require."

Andrew brought over a blanket. They wrapped Shea in it carefully. Marco lifted Shea like he weighed nothing and they hurried from the suite.

Chapter 11
Waking Up

The hazy feeling kept pulling Shea back into sleep. He stirred enough to shift position in bed, but not quite enough to open his eyes. The light shining on the other side of his eyelids bothered him at first. Then it dimmed and ceased troubling him.

Sometimes his hand was held by someone else where it lay limp on the bedspread. Sometimes the soreness in his head and arm ached enough to provoke groans of complaint, but every time it started to get really bad, he'd feel the prick of a needle, and everything would dull, fading way, way down again. Then, he'd sigh and sleep.

Some of his dreams were of being held down and struck with a nightstick, or he'd see some eyeless, nose-less creature leaning down over him, and it would smile just before drawing its knee up into his unprotected scrotum. Then, the pain was so intense; he'd struggle in bed and fight. The hands holding him down in the dream would become real. His eyes would open and there would be people—nurses, uniformed staff members, David. The prick of the needle would help him let go, cease his struggles, and drift back down, down, down.

An uncertain amount of time later, he opened his eyes and was able to make sense of the shapes around him. The delirious feeling was finally subsiding, but what he saw wasn't helping him figure out where he was. It seemed too quiet and refined to be a hospital. There were no people pacing outside the room, hurrying here and there. Everything was still and seemed brand new—the walls, floors and furniture spotless—like no one had ever stayed there before him. It also didn't smell like one. There was a clean scent to the air, but it wasn't overpowering. He was in a white room, with white walls, white curtains, white blinds, white sheets, and a white ceiling.

Daisy was there. He relaxed a little upon noticing her. She was his most trusted friend, though he tried not to go to her for help too often, since he knew she already felt bad about her own situation. She lived with her grandmother and younger sister in a small, two room apartment. Daisy had been born of a Jamaican mother and a heavily-freckled Irish father, both of whom she rarely saw. She had been tall and skinny since they were kids and had her mother's curly hair, as well as her father's freckles. Daisy's real name was LaTonya, but since she'd grown out an impressive afro, she'd been known to everyone as the cheerful flower her silhouette resembled.

The familiar outline of her hair, her slender body beneath, was so comforting; he stared without really processing the vision of her for a long time.

He wanted so badly to go to sleep again, even if it came with nightmares. It was a good place to hide. He knew as soon as he started to ask questions, he'd be expected to answer them too. Looking with unfocused eyes at Daisy, Shea felt instinctively that he was in danger, even if the facts escaped him. If only he could sleep some more, he could forget, and hide, for a little while.

More details caught his notice.

There was a guard by the door, standing just outside the room.

His cheeks were damp.

Daisy leaned forward, a crumpled tissue in her hand, and dabbed the wetness away.

"It's not safe," he told her, voicing his biggest instinct, but it wasn't his voice that came out of his mouth. It was someone else's. His voice wasn't hoarse and broken like the one he heard.

Daisy glanced up, across the bed at something he couldn't see, and frowned with worry.

"The infection?" she asked, but not Shea.

"No, the fever's finally down. Possibly the dreams again."

"It's not safe!" He tried to sit up. Daisy was out of her chair, backing away, as figures hurried into the room, bracing Shea's legs and his arms and carefully forcing him back down to the bed. "Daisy?" he cried. "*Please, help me.*"

Daisy looked across the room again, bringing a hand nervously up to her mouth to cover it.

"S-shea? Shea, can you see us?" she asked.

"He's waking up," a familiar voice said. "Let him go."

"Sir —" one of the figures holding him down argued.

"I said, let him go!"

They released him. Shea scrambled up into a seated position, drawing his knees up to his chest, folding his arms over his head to block them all out.

"Leave us. Miss Brown, you may stay."

Footsteps over wood. Not running, but too many. Too crowded. Too white.

"Daisy, you're here... How?" Shea asked from his cocooned position.

"I called to check on you," she explained. "It had been a few days since I'd heard from you and there were rumors about you and Ryan having some kind of fight, and that you weren't staying there anymore. When I called your phone, David answered. He introduced himself and brought me here to see you. I've been spending time here over the past couple of days while you recovered."

"Shea, do you know where you are?"

"David," Shea murmured, not looking up. A weight settled on the bed.

"Yes. Look at me, Shea. Please?"

Shea shook his head. His whole face hurt, but not as badly as his arm. His arm....

He looked at it, the thick, white bandages covering it.

"The infection came back," David was saying. "So did your fever. The effects of that, coupled with your severe concussion and... bruising... led the doctor to recommend we keep you sedated so you wouldn't hurt yourself. This isn't the first time you've been awake, but you would fight, violently."

Some of those memories tried to come back. He didn't let them, and closed them out.

Shea ran a hand lightly over the pristine bandage and said hoarsely, "Hey, at least when I'm delirious I know how to fight. How long?"

"Five days."

For the first time, Shea looked up at David. There were purple shadows under his eyes and signs of stress in his expression. Strangely, Shea felt better having David there. He might not know much about David yet, but what he did know was that with David came calm control, which was what Shea wanted most of all. David had been there for Shea during the nightmare at Teresa's, when there had been no answers, nowhere to go. He'd easily kept Ryan civil at Shea's apartment, against all odds. He'd been there in the hotel after Dorian called Shea trash, soothing and keeping everything from falling apart. Now he was here after...

Shea didn't want to remember, or understand what was happening, he just wanted David to tell him it would all be all right.

"You look awful," Shea heard himself say in that stranger's voice.

"Likewise, sweetheart," David answered.

"Thank you for bringing Daisy."

"You're welcome. She's been very concerned about you. I felt you should have a familiar face here when you woke."

"I've been screaming, haven't I?" Shea realized, guessing at why he was so hoarse, his voice so thin and weak.

David tensed up, clenching his jaw and replied, "Yes. You have. How are you feeling now?"

Shea shrugged.

Daisy touched Shea's leg. He looked at her, feeling so confused.

"Hey, girl," he said.

"Hey Whitt. It's good you're awake," she said. "Been worryin' us, you know."

"Am I in a hospital? It doesn't really seem like one."

"You're at my main residence," David said. "Those men who attacked you are ex-military. Ensuring your safety has been just as important as providing medical care. Having you stay here instead of a public place means you stay out of their hands."

"You really think they'd come after me in a hospital?"

"It's not a risk I was willing to take. I hope that's okay with you."

"This is a pretty sweet place, Whitt," Daisy told him. "I don't think you need to worry about anything besides getting better."

Shea held his head in his hand. "Everything's just so foggy. It does seem really nice here. Peaceful." He saw a pitcher of water on the bedside table and reached for it.

"Let me," David offered, guiding Shea back to lay down. He poured some water into a cup and passed it over.

"Thanks. My mouth is dry."

"Is there anything else you need? We don't need to talk about things until you're ready. If you're tired, rest."

"Yeah. I think I'm just tired."

"Sleep, then. We'll be nearby if you need anything at all."

"Thanks."

Daisy stood and kept looking to David as if for guidance. With a hand to her shoulder, David led her gently from the room. Daisy gave him a smile and a wave as they slipped out the door.

Chapter 12
Give and Take

Hours slipped by as he slept off and on. Sometimes he just lay there, trying not to think about what had happened or what came next, and just enjoying that he was somewhere clean, away from threats, where he wasn't bothered or even had to work to take care of himself. Other times he watched TV and let it distract him a while. By the time David came back to check on him, Shea was more prepared with some questions and ideas about what he wanted.

"How are you?" David asked right away, as soon as he slipped through the door, closing it behind him. Shea spotted an armed guard out there, standing sentry.

"Better. My head's clearer. The painkillers are kicking in. Mostly I just don't know what to do with myself. Can we... talk, a little?"

"Of course." David pulled up a chair.

"You can, you know, sit with me, if you want," Shea offered, feeling an urge to have someone near enough to touch if David was willing. It had always been distressing for Shea to have his mother be standoffish whenever he most needed someone to hold him. Growing up that way ingrained in Shea a need for comfort that he felt might never be sated, not that he wasn't willing to try.

Leaving the chair, David came to sit on the bed, facing Shea.

"Thank you. Hi," Shea smiled. "It's good to see you."

"You too. I've been so worried. Your fever spiked so high, but the doctor has assured me you're doing much better now, that the infection is finally receding."

"You said we're at your residence, but where exactly is that? What kind of place is this? This is really your house? Because it doesn't look much like a house."

"Mm, part of it is a house. But it's also an office, a club... it serves several purposes. It's a large building with four floors and excellent security. When you were first brought here, directly from the hotel, you were staying in the medical suite you heard mention of before, on the third floor. We're on the fourth right now. Dr. Wilkenson has been treating you, along with a team of nurses."

"The guy from the hotel."

"Yes."

"Okay. But... I'm not in the medical suite? It looks really... medically... in here."

"Well, yesterday I had you brought up to my private quarters because that means additional security and easier access for me to check on you. No one gets access to this floor without my say-so. Are you okay with being here rather than the hospital? The security is much better here, and you don't run the risk of further infection, like you would in a hospital setting. You can rest and be cared for, and I have plenty of extra room."

"Yeah, no, that's fine. I don't have the money to pay for treatment anyway, so they'd probably just kick me out. At least with you I can try to charm you into letting me stay."

"You already have," David smiled, though it looked regretful. "Shea, I'm afraid this is all my fault. Those men... my father sent them because he was afraid you were out to hurt me."

"I figured it was your dad behind it, with the kinds of questions they asked. It's strange to hear that's actually true, though."

"It is, unfortunately, but I have experience dealing with them. I know how they work. I can head them off better than anyone else. My father..." David sighed, shook his head. "Suffers from paranoia, and I'm afraid you fell victim to that. It won't happen again. He thought you might be a relation of that boy I told you about, Trent. He intended to run your DNA and also test you for STDs."

"He really thought I was trying to hurt you? I mean... I know we're both young and all, but I think we both know what sexually transmitted diseases are, and how to avoid getting them. Plus, he way overestimated my ability to get someone like you into bed with me."

"Don't underestimate yourself," David retorted with a sly, raised eyebrow and a brief, heated glance. "Your sex appeal is part of what drew me to you right away."

"I have sex appeal?"

"You do," David smiled. "And my father has always acted like I can't take care of myself."

"Has he even met you? I think you're more capable of self-management than any other human alive."

"I guess you just need to understand that people have tried to hurt members of my family in the past, and succeeded. My father's trust is hard to come by when it applies to his children. It's no excuse, but it's the truth. Don't worry. My father will be held completely accountable for all of this. You have my word." Seeming to hesitate, David reached out and took Shea's hand, holding it. When Shea gripped David's fingers, David softened a little and gave him a smile.

"Thank you for being so concerned about me, David," Shea told him with bare honesty. "Just the fact alone that I can tell you really care about my health is a big deal. You're not just saying it, are you?"

"I've been sitting with you as often as I could," David confessed, "whenever I could get away from the office. Knowing what you went through, because of me, and after everything else you were already struggling with... The only way I can deal with all of this is to make sure I'm able to see you're okay whenever I want. Maybe that's too selfish of me."

"Where else would I go, David?" Shea asked quietly. "Like I said, I don't have money for medical care and the clinics don't let you stay for days on end. Friends like Daisy are all the family I have now, and their lives are challenging enough without expecting them to take care of me, too. If you really don't mind letting me stay, I will. Plus, being able to spend time with you makes me want to get better."

Looking concerned, David caressed the side of Shea's face, then smoothed some of the hair off of his forehead. "Good. I'm honored to have you stay with me. And relieved," he added with an apologetic grin.

Shea nodded. "Promise to tell me if I'm asking too much."

"You could never ask too much."

"And I keep hearing you say that this is your fault, but it's not. You're not responsible for what your father does. I know what it's like to have Dad go off the deep end. I wouldn't ever want to be held responsible for what he's done either. Don't worry about it. It's just nice to be sitting with you again."

"I agree," David said, and it really didn't seem to be an act. There was every sign that David was being genuine and his focused worry specifically for Shea began to generate a specific response. It made Shea want to set David's mind at ease, and to do nice things for him too, somehow. But really, Shea was just purely grateful to be treated like someone who was worth caring about for once.

"Thank you for watching out for me. You're kind of incredible like that, you know. I've always had this love for superheroes, probably because they're capable of such amazing things, and are such good people. Sometimes, they started out just like me, as just a normal kid. Things were never really great at home, so those stories were my escape. But that's all they are. Stories. Real life is a lot different. But... the way you've stood up for me when you really had nothing to gain? I never thought something like that could happen. And I know you've forbidden me from trying," Shea said, "but I'm going to pay you back someday."

David didn't say anything; he just kept caressing Shea's hand. It drew Shea's attention and he realized that David was holding his hand in a romantic and not just a friendly way. A thrill chased through Shea's body, David's touch was electric, charging Shea with renewed energy and want.

"Is this part of your pursuit of me?" Shea asked, just to be sure.

"All I want right now is for you to be well. I have you here," David glanced around the small room. "I have you safe. I'll have you in... other ways... later. We have time."

The allusion to sex brought back Shea's sense memories of the attack. He found himself confessing, "I don't remember all of it, you know."

"You don't need to talk about it if you don't want to," David told him.

"I know. And it's nice to not have to explain things to cops or anything, but you were involved. You got me out of there, didn't you?"

"Yes. Marco, Andrew, and myself stopped them as soon as we could. The police have all of the men who attacked you in custody."

"I'm glad. You really are a hero, aren't you?"

"No, I don't think I've earned that. But I do agree that my father has been acting like a villain."

Though Shea wasn't ready to talk to strangers about what he'd gone through after he'd been pulled, naked and terrified, out of the hotel bed, he wanted somebody safe to share his memories with. When he woke up screaming with nightmares, maybe David would hold him and understand his fears. "You must be wondering what happened. I'm sure Dr. Wilkenson wants to know, so he knows how to treat me."

"You were evaluated. They took x-rays to check for breaks and... other injuries. No one will pressure you for information."

"That's what they were doing," Shea said, struggling slightly to get the words out. "Trying to get me to t-talk. They held me still, searched me everywhere. One guard had gloves on. Latex gloves." Shea sat up, curling forward slightly but not letting go of David's hand. "He searched me for... something. Inside. He wasn't careful. Then the guy in the suit told them to flip me over again, said he'd use the, uh... the s-stick to make me talk."

David frowned heavily. "Oh, Shea. I'm so sorry."

"They hit me, David. With the baton, they hit my arm, my face. They kept asking me what I wanted from you, what I was after." Shea laughed a little, humorlessly. The memories, the motives, they were too big to wrap his head around. "They were so suspicious about why they couldn't find much information on me online, but come on, why would there be? My family doesn't want anything to do with me. I haven't accomplished anything. I don't have anything. I'm nobody special."

"No. You're a survivor, Shea. Seeing how you've come through all of these terrible things? You're stronger than you think, especially because you haven't let unfortunate circumstances change who you are. You have every right to push me away, but you're not. Quite the contrary." He reached up and caressed the unhurt side of Shea's jawline. Closing his eyes with pleasure at the gentle, soothing touch. Shea couldn't help but lean into it, loving the way David's hand felt. "Thank you for trusting me enough to let me touch you like this."

"Feels nice."

Shea sighed deeply, his heart beating harder as David's hand slipped down the side of Shea's neck, then down the front of his chest, falling to rest on his thigh. Playing bashfully with the sheet that covered him, Shea looked at the IV line running into the back of his hand, hooked up to a bag on a stand. It wasn't the only tube hooked up to him.

"Daisy's not still waiting out there, is she?"

"No, I had a driver taker her home once she got tired. Call her if you'd like. If she's available, I can have someone pick her up again."

"Maybe later. Look, David, I don't know what happens next, and I'm fine with just waiting to see, but can I ask you something?"

"Anything," David told him.

"It's something I've been trying really hard to ignore. It's been bothering me for a while and now I know I just can't pretend it away. I need to actually do something about it. This is really difficult for me to talk about, but..."

"What is it? What's wrong?" David asked.

"Why is there a tube stuck up the end of my dick?"

David was surprised into laughter, which he quickly stifled. "It's a catheter."

"Oh. How do you know? You haven't even seen it."

"Well, I may have supervised its insertion just to make sure it went smoothly and you weren't harmed."

Shea laughed in astonishment. "Jesus, David, you really are a control freak, aren't you?"

"You were in my care and I take that very seriously."

"I can tell," Shea grinned. "So. You've seen my dick, huh? You didn't even trust your own doctor to handle my dick?"

David swallowed thickly and sat up a little straighter. "It's not that I don't trust him. It's more that I feel better if I'm aware of situations in which harm could come to people I care about."

"I think that was the most difficult way you could possibly have said that."

David shot him a look, like he thought Shea was trying to pick on him, which he was, just a little. "Fine. I didn't like him touching you. I don't like anyone else touching you."

"Wow. That's... you really care about me that much, huh? You even care about my dick. Don't roll your eyes. I saw that."

David chuckled and shook his head. "Yes, I really care about you. Every part. I would've inserted the catheter myself if I'd been able to ask your permission first. I've been trained to do so, but I didn't want to presume."

"You're even a gentlemen when I'm passed out."

"Especially when you're passed out," David added softly.

"Could you take it out? I really want it out."

"I could, yes, if you were comfortable with that."

"Better you than someone I don't know or trust."

David looked into his eyes in a way that made Shea's stomach swoop. There was heat there, and plenty of desire, carefully held back behind well-fortified, deeply instilled manners. "I'll be very gentle," he promised.

"I know."

David nodded again. He squeezed Shea's hand once, then went to a sink in the adjoining bathroom to wash his hands.

When David's hands had been washed, he came to the bed and peeled back the sheet. Shea felt a whole cloud of butterflies begin to do loop-de-loops in his stomach. Shea was naked. David could see everything. But then, Shea had to remind himself that it wasn't the first time he was seeing it.

"Lie down."

He only glimpsed it, the tiny tube running into the end of his penis, taped in place.

"Does it hurt?" David asked, sitting on the bed's side. He began to gently peel the tape away.

"No." Shea shivered with excitement to feel David touching him there, cradling Shea's cock in one hand. It felt like they suddenly crossed a few different lines, with dizzying speed.

"I've been a little crazy while you were sleeping, Shea. Overprotective of you. I'm sorry."

The gentle movements of David's fingertips, holding Shea's dick, removing the tape, then tugging gently at the catheter tube started to create a horrible reaction in him. Slowly, he was starting to get hard.

"Fuck, that's embarrassing," he groaned, telling himself not to watch, helpless not to as David, with torturous slowness, extracted the tube. It was fascinating to watch as more and more of it was pulled from inside his penis like some perverted magic trick.

Once it was completely out, David wiped him down with a swab of cotton, dipped in cool liquid, and that only made it worse. By the time David was finished, Shea was almost completely hard.

David's gaze was directed at Shea's crotch, not his face, as he tenderly brushed the inside of Shea's hip. He looked like he wanted to brush something else.

Moving to stand, turning away, David said, "I should give you some privacy."

"Why?" Shea said lightly, with plenty of embarrassment. "I think it's kind of too late to worry about that."

David paused, then sat back down, measuring Shea's expression with a scrutinizing gaze.

The backs of David's fingers brushed, feather-light, along Shea's stiffened shaft. It made Shea shiver, his cock twitching into the touch, eager for more. With a soft gasp, Shea let his head fall back and his eyes close. His lower lip trembled as David did it again, proving the touch was deliberate. His hand opened, and David used his palm, instead, pressing Shea's cock upright, letting it slide through his fingers. It drew a whimper from Shea. He felt the instinct to spread and offer himself take hold. Not understanding why he wanted that, or why it felt like the correct response, he turned his face to the side, covering his eyes with a hand.

"You're so beautiful," David breathed.

His hand slowly closed around Shea's erection, then moved against it with a more steady tugging, and somehow Shea could feel all of David's want for him in it. There was such carefulness and gentleness as he tested the waters of their mutual desire. He was giving Shea every chance to pull away, or say no.

Breathing shakily Shea reached out for David with his right hand. Briefly, David wove their fingers together, brushing the side of Shea's hand with his thumb, then let go to caress up the inside of his arm, up the side of his hip to his waist. Each little touch felt so good, like David understood without Shea having to explain just how wonderful it was to be seen and appreciated by someone who made him feel safe and understood.

David shifted to face Shea more directly, laying an open hand on Shea's stomach, rubbing lightly up to his chest, searching Shea's face as Shea couldn't help but let his hand fall away to watch David. For a moment, neither of them moved. Then, David *tugged*.

With a desperate frown and a sigh, Shea moaned, arching his back and rolling his hips into the tug. He let his legs fall further open.

"David," he whispered, begging.

David moaned then, and it was a shattered, desperate, primal sound. He leaned over Shea, watching him avidly while Shea could only manage a shy glimpse now and then.

Shea rocked into David's grip, each pull on his cock getting him quickly closer to release and whispered, "*Please* don't stop."

"Shea," David said gruffly, a rasp of need. Leaning down lower, David's lips dragged lightly over Shea's, which quivered with his gasps. Reaching up to hold on to David, wrapping a hand behind his neck, Shea kept him close.

"Please," Shea cried in an urgent, anguished plea that overtook his ravaged voice. David pumped him faster, tighter, and Shea whimpered with orgasm against David's mouth, shuddering and giving in to the pleasure, letting it wash over all of the pain.

Chapter 13
Instinctive Reactions

David stayed nearby as Shea used the adjoining bathroom to wash up. Shea was careful not to get his bandaged arm wet. He just worked around it. A couple of times Shea got lightheaded, but gripping the wall or fixtures helped him wait out the dizzy spells. After he had showered and brushed his teeth and hair, he felt much better.

Dressed only in a towel, he emerged from the bathroom. Right away, David came over and helped steady Shea as he crossed to the bed where David had laid out a clean set of what looked like white scrubs. Shea didn't question it. Who the heck knew where his clothes — or any of his other possessions — were at his point? It was just nice to be wearing pants instead of a gown that opened in the back.

A small table and chairs had been moved into the room, and there was food and drink waiting on it. David guided Shea into one of the seats and began to serve him coffee.

"I'm pretty sure you've got that backwards," Shea murmured.

"The coffee pot?"

"No, that I'm supposed to be serving you, not the other way around." David finished filling Shea's cup and made sure the cream and sugar were easily reachable for him, then sat down as well.

"Not today, sweetheart," David said tenderly, averting his gaze as he said it and looking like he had a heck of a lot on his mind.

Shea's heart swelled, hearing the endearment come so effortlessly from David. "Is that what I am, now?" he asked quietly. "Your sweetheart?"

"I hope so. But you'll always be a sweetheart, Shea." It wasn't said bravely, but in a small, private way, meant for only Shea to hear.

"I've never known anyone like you. So many people and facets of my life make me feel like I need to close up and fill a predetermined role instead of just being who I am, and a normal human being. But, with you? You open me up. When I'm with you, it's like I can breathe again, like I haven't really breathed for years."

David shifted his chair, straightened up and let out a deep exhale. There was so much they needed to learn about each other. It was keeping them apart. Shea could feel it.

There was a lot of vulnerability in David in that moment. So far, he'd always seemed so strong and self-assured. Shea realized there were many more layers to this mysterious man who was currently acting the part of Shea's hero and pursuer. He was letting Shea see some of the weight threatening to crush him, and how, amazingly, this quiet, secluded morning conversation with someone he felt comfortable with was helping David cope.

"You've helped me so much," Shea told him, his heart going out to David in new ways. "I want to help you, too. Can we sit together a little longer? Do you have time for that?"

"Absolutely," David smiled, his green eyes shining with undisguised affection and gratitude. It was the type of smile that peeled back a few of those layers, leaving David looking younger and closer to his actual age. He gestured to the food, "But, please. Eat. You need your strength. I had a message while you washed up. Daisy called, hoping to come by again today. Over the past few days, she's been doing some schoolwork in my library in between sitting with you whenever the doctor allows."

Shea smiled at that, shaking his head, "A library, too, huh? David, who *are* you? How do you have all of this?"

David was fixing his own cup of coffee, but began explaining, "I come from old money. Generations upon generations of Davenports building upon the wealth of their ancestors. A few generations back, my family lived in England rather than America. I was bred into this world, and I've never known differently. With the help of private tutors, I graduated from high school at age sixteen, then moved to London to attend University as well as studying... other pursuits." He grinned, giving Shea a good idea what those other pursuits were even before he explained. "Do you know anything about BDSM?"

"Just a little."

"Well, I only mention it because of how big a part of my life it is, and if you want to know me—"

"Which I do," Shea smiled.

"Then you need to know about that part, too. London is also where I studied the art of Domination. It's become an important part of who I am. Being a Master is just another way I enjoy more control, but in my personal relationships."

His imagination running wild, Shea admitted, "Yeah, I can see how you'd like that."

"After finishing my... studies, I moved back to America, using my trust fund to invest in real estate development up and down the East Coast. I built my company using all of the knowledge gained from watching my father run his business in the same field. Establishing my company apart from my father's was always one of my primary goals. Now, I manage things, and I'm the acting C.E.O. of Davenport Properties, but my true passion lies in other areas."

"So, that means you're, like, a child genius and you've got Money with a capital M."

"Capital B, actually, from what I'm told," David said, like it wasn't a big deal at all, taking a tentative sip of his coffee.

"Jesus," Shea gaped. "Seriously?"

David shrugged. "I don't mean to sound ungrateful, or unappreciative of being so fortunate, but some days I'd trade it all in a heartbeat. Attaining and keeping wealth isn't exactly my life goal. But it's important you know all of this about me. My name, my connections, they're both a benefit and a burden. My father has enemies. Right now, my father *is* my enemy. This... ugliness... between me and him, it goes back a long way. What he did to you, Shea, was simply my breaking point. There's no excuse for what he did. But he has incredible resources at his disposal, so now it falls to me to ensure you stay out of his reach. Unfortunately, perhaps, that means I need to keep you very close."

"Oh, well, that sounds awful, I said sarcastically," Shea commented, taking a bite of eggs.

"I'm glad you don't mind. I got you into this mess. Until it's cleared up, it's my duty to ensure your absolute safety and comfort."

"David," Shea laughed a little, "This is all so, so far beyond my understanding."

"That's just because you don't yet have all of the facts. It's a deficiency I intend to correct, because you're not just my friend, now. I want to be with you, Shea, in whatever ways you'll have me, for as long as you want me. I'm just afraid that the closer we are, the more danger there will be for you. That's why it's crucial you have the option to change your mind. If this is..." David briefly bowed his head, his jaw clenched. "If this starts to become too much for you, tell me. I can still protect you even if you're not interested in being with me. It's just... you make me happy. And I know it's selfish to want you the ways that I do, and not only for your benefit. But even just seeing you enjoy some real food, having you look at me the way you are, and how you can make me laugh... this is already the best day I've had in a long time, despite everything that got us here."

"Same for me, David," Shea beckoned, letting his feelings show in his words and expression. David looked up, into Shea's eyes. He could tell David wasn't just saying all of those things to be flattering or polite. Even just compared to how he looked when he'd first come into the room, David seemed steadier and more content. It was invigorating for Shea to know he was helping David, too, without even needing to try. "I'm yours if you'll have me."

"Why?"

The question hung there.

"My parents disowned me when they realized I'm gay," Shea said matter-of-factly. "I've been on my own for a while now, and it's really hard just to do all of the day-to-day bullshit of going to a job you don't really like and aren't really suited for, when there's no one who actually cares if you make it or not. I have some great friends. I really do, and I owe them a lot. But it doesn't make it hurt any less that my family hates me for something I can't change." He laughed a little, needing to dispel the tension and push past the feeling of wanting to cry. Blinking rapidly, sniffling, he waited for it to pass. David reached across the small table and took his hand, weaving their fingers together.

The physical connection helped. Shea blew out a breath. "I don't usually talk about it," he confessed. "I mean, I haven't talked about it. The friends who count know, but they've never asked, and..." He stopped again. He still wasn't past it. He took a drink of coffee and gave it another moment while David gently stroked the skin on the back of his hand and waited patiently. "I want to belong to someone again," Shea whispered, tearing up too fast. "I want to belong somewhere, and not be just a throwaway anymore. I'm better than that."

David came around the table, crouching by Shea's feet and pulling him into a hug. The comfort of that went a long way toward helping Shea feel steadier. Stroking Shea's hair and his back, David held on like he was offering himself as an anchor to keep Shea from drifting off into more pain. "You're *so much better* that that," David said urgently. "They're ignorant. Cruel. But they don't get to be part of your life anymore, so just let them go."

"I'm trying."

He pulled back, just a little, tenderly touching Shea's face. "Shea, I look at you and all I want to do is touch you. I see so many good things in you and I'm scared I'll hurt you somehow again, but... I can't help it. I want you anyway."

Shea sighed, leaning forward to let his forehead rest against David's, his eyes closing as he did try to let go of more of the past, and just be in the present. Sometimes he became so aware of it—the bad things that had happened, like they were something dragging along behind him, of which he would never be absolutely free.

David kissed each of Shea's closed eyelids, and tried to smooth away his frown with little brushes of his fingertips. "I hate seeing you so upset. But anytime you need to talk about any of this, or anything else that's bothering you, I'm always here to listen, all right?"

Shea nodded.

Winding his arms behind David's neck, he drew him into another embrace, liking that connection and that feeling of understanding David gave him. After a moment, Shea found David's lips and kissed him, slowly.

With a small growl of need, David responded, kissing him back passionately. It lifted a lot of Shea's fret, feeling how easy it would be to yield to all of that passion and let it consume him. To be desired that strongly was powerfully alluring after so many people in his life only seemed to want him to disappear.

David's hands were on Shea's thighs, his breathing roughened. He broke the kiss with a gentle nip of Shea's lip, nuzzling his neck. "Every time I kiss you or touch you, it's so hard to stop. I could kiss you for days, but you should eat. There'll be plenty of time later for this."

"Oh yeah?" Shea grinned.

David growled again, plunging back into the kiss. When Shea whimpered and shifted forward, legs spread in a wide stance, trying to press his body against David's, with David's hand palming his ass through the thin scrubs, David let out a trembling groan. It seemed quite a struggle when he made himself pull back and stand, disengaging. He looked wild, like he wanted nothing more than to rip the clothes from Shea's body and move against him, kissing and touching until there was nothing between them to keep them apart. Shea felt it, then, how David's passion came from such a deep, primal place. Getting lost in it would mean surrendering in a way he never had before.

"We need to talk more before we do that," David said apologetically. "It's crucial you understand what I want to have with you, first. I won't pressure you. I'm not very good at going slow, but I'm trying my damnedest right now."

"Okay," Shea replied. He ran a hand through his hair and tried to get back to his breakfast. David paced a little before he was able to sit and relax again. It reminded Shea of the way tigers paced in their cages at the zoo, watching the people on the other side, ready to pounce. It was intimidating, but it was sexy as hell.

"You're a virgin?"

"Yeah."

A few flashes of memory of the attack hit him. He felt the nightstick pressing at him, and the hands holding him down as he screamed. Closing his eyes against the recollections, he willed them away.

"Are you all right?"

"Yeah. Yeah, just bad memories." He drank some coffee, then said, "You mentioned liking control with your relationships, and it's funny because that's always been a big deal for me too, because with Ryan, the things he wanted always seemed way out of control. Saying no was the only way I could deal with it. But maybe there are other options. What do you mean, exactly, by taking control?"

"In my world, there are Masters, and there are slaves," David explained. "As a Master, I like to have complete control over my relationships. That means my partners are submissive. I respect, honor and cherish them. If you, Shea, were to consent to be my submissive, you would have complete control over your ability to say no or yes to anything that we would do together, but you would also trust me to know the best way to meet every single one of your needs."

"That sounds kind of good," Shea said, biting at his lip.

"I've never had a boyfriend, only submissives, and never someone I truly felt a connection with, like I do with you."

"So, you'd want me to be your submissive?"

"Among other things, but yes. That too."

"What does that mean? How is that different than normal relationships?"

"Between Dominants, like myself, and submissives, sex is based on trust, respect, and power. The trust and respect have to go both ways. But the power?" David licked his lip, his gaze slipping down Shea's chest in a way that made his dick twitch. "A submissive surrenders all power and control to the Dominant, finding pleasure and freedom in being able to let go and trust he'll be cared for in ways that respect his boundaries and understand all of his needs. The Dom's duty is to anticipate and provide whatever is needed."

"That's why you offered me that suite, isn't it? And the food, the doctor... everything."

David nodded. "It's instinctual, I'm afraid. And you, Shea, you seem to be a natural submissive, to have these instincts of your own, moving you to want to yield and be taken when you encounter a dominant man. That's a beautiful thing, but it can be dangerous, too. When someone like Ryan meets someone like you, it can go terribly, violently wrong, very quickly. Your submissiveness, it's part of who you are, and how you naturally react. No one should get to take advantage of that, or you, without full, expressed permission beforehand."

Shea was trying to focus on eating, but he could feel the way David was looking at him, and all the ways it was making Shea want to respond.

"I've never done anything anywhere close to any of this," Shea confessed. "It kind of makes me nervous."

"I know," David acknowledged tenderly. "I want you to carefully think about this before deciding anything. Taking you as my submissive would be a huge responsibility that I would not at all take lightly. I'd train you, teach you about how everything works."

"How what works?"

"The protocols and proper behaviors. We would establish rules we'd both agree to."

"What if I break a rule? Would you punish me?"

"Yes."

"Wow, really? How?"

"Have you ever been spanked?"

Shea laughed with embarrassment. He ran his tongue over the edge of his teeth and considered his reply. "Not like that, no."

"But if the submissive obeys and pleases his Dom, there are *rewards*."

"Oh, I can only imagine," Shea murmured, reaching for his coffee. David was smirking in a kind of dark and dirty way, which didn't really help, especially since Shea's cock was evidently really interested in the conversation. His face felt really hot with the heat of his blush. "I thought BDSM was bondage and stuff like that. A handcuffs on the headboard type of thing."

"It is," David assured him.

"You would tie me up?"

David flashed a heated look in Shea's direction, still chewing on his lip like he wanted to bite Shea instead, which made it difficult for Shea to breathe normally.

"To start with," David answered eventually. "If you were okay with that. I would never do anything you weren't interested in trying."

Shea weighed his internal responses, and finally said, "Okay."

"Okay? Okay to what?"

"To what you were saying."

"Does that mean you're interested?"

"Yeah. I'll be your submissive."

"Shea, this is a big decision and we're still getting to know each other. Take some more time to think about it. Don't give yourself over so lightly. Like I said earlier, you're worth more than that."

"But how am I supposed to think about something without really knowing what I'd be getting myself into? Can't I try it and see if I like it?"

Shea had trouble reading David's expression. He didn't reply, he just watched Shea closely.

Then, he stood and walked around the table. Shea stayed where he was, eyes downcast as a bout of nervousness hit hard.

David circled around behind him, his hands on Shea's shoulders, guiding him to sit back in his seat, his chin up. David's fingers carded through Shea's hair, then David's right hand caressed down the front of Shea's body, down his chest, down to his crotch. He palmed Shea's cock, then grabbed a tight hold of it when he found it hard. Shea gasped, letting his head fall back to lean against David's body. David's left hand caressed around Shea's jaw to his neck, hooking around it just under his chin.

Maybe being held by cock and throat should have only made Shea more nervous, and he *was* still a little apprehensive, but he was shocked to find himself relaxing, trusting David to be gentle, and not hurt him. He felt like if he kept letting go, looking for safety and comfort in David, things would only get better.

So he did. Sighing, he let David tug his chin higher, his breathing evening out. The hand gripping his cock squeezed and his legs only fell open wider.

"Fucking gorgeous," David breathed.

Chapter 14

Puzzle Pieces

Gradually, David began to release Shea, his thumb stroking back under Shea's chin to his throat, and the hand on his cock shifting from a tight grip to a caress. When he was about to break contact, Shea reached up and grabbed hold of David's left hand, keeping him there. There was so much need in Shea's sweetly anxious, slight frown.

"Once you're rested and feeling better," David began. "And after you've had time to think this through, then we'll discuss it again."

"I'm fine. I feel fine," Shea countered, sounding eager to persuade and afraid of David letting go.

"I'm glad you do, but you're not fine, sweetheart." David's left hand moved across Shea's chest, his hand flattening there to hold him back against David's body. Shea's arms overlapped David's, completing the embrace. He just looked so very sad, which only strengthened David's convictions that Shea needed more time to adjust. "Your fever hit one hundred and six. The antibiotics you'd been taking weren't strong or effective enough. Your head wounds from the beating you sustained could have been very dangerous, and—whatever else those monsters did to you—you're not alone anymore. I swear it. We can ease into this. There's no cause to rush."

"I feel better when I'm being held by you," Shea said shyly. "I haven't had someone hold me like this in a long time. Forever, actually."

David's other arm wound around Shea. Then he didn't want to let go, either.

"You need to eat," David heard himself say. "Afterward," Shea asked, speaking hesitantly, "would you lay with me, just for a little while? Can you?"

"I'd love to."

David took his seat once more. Shea dug into his food, like he was hurrying to finish.

David smoothed his napkin, listening for movement outside the door, or voices, but there were none. That was good. Quiet meant peace. "Once you're feeling better, I'll take you on a tour of the building, so you can get a better idea of the place. That's probably the best way to understand it, since it's not a normal home by any means."

"I can tell. This looks like a hospital room. A really frickin' nice one, but still."

David glanced around at their surroundings. "Yes, this room is kept sterile for medical emergencies, but because it's on the fourth floor, it's even safer than the medical suite below. No one gets up here without passing through multiple levels of security."

"You know, when I first met you, you reminded me of Tony Stark a little. Or, well, Tony's younger, hotter, brother, minus the questionable facial hair. I'm not really a facial hair guy, hence the Captain America fixation." His hand reached up to search for his necklace, which David had made sure stayed around Shea's neck, even when he was recovering. He touched it then, as if he didn't even realize he was doing it. "And I'm realizing that sounds a lot more embarrassing than I thought it would when I actually admit it out loud in front of you. But anyway, too late now, I guess. I didn't actually think you owned Stark Tower or anything. It was more because you have this whole classy, disarming *thing* about you."

David smiled helplessly and told Shea, happily, "You're sounding more like yourself. Good."

"The rambling is a sign of health? Really? Huh."

"The last, big, piece of the puzzle in understanding who I am," David explained, "Is that I run a private gay club, called Manse, out of my home. The entire first floor and the basement level is the club. The second floor contains semi-secluded spaces for consenting adults to play, and engage in BDSM scenes if they wish. My security staff is always present, monitoring things. The third floor contains offices and the medical suite. This, the fourth floor, is only accessible by private elevators which you need a special badge and security code to operate."

"That's why I was in the hotel, wasn't it? You thought it would freak me out. Be too overwhelming."

"I did give you the option of coming here, if you remember," David argued gently, teasing Shea a little. "After what my father did, though, I saw you weren't safe enough at the hotel. That was a major oversight. It won't happen again. I promise. But I had been ensured the hotel staff were properly aware and their security team was up to par."

"Wait. You told the entire hotel staff to take care of me?"

"Of course. I own the whole chain."

Shea laughed weakly and took a sip of orange juice, raising one eyebrow at David. "David, you're insane. This entire thing is insane. You own a hotel chain? And a gay, sexy club? You know how I said before, at my shitty apartment, how I felt like I was on a hidden camera show? That feeling isn't going away. What's the punch line, here?"

Clearing his throat, David smoothed a wrinkle in his napkin, losing most of his smile. "That there's a price for knowing me, obviously," David admitted, with more than a little regret. "I've been torn, Shea. Meeting you is the best thing that's happened to me in so long, but you would have been better off, maybe, without me. I don't know." He paused, silently debating with himself again. "I feel I've hurt you by trying to help you."

"You don't have to apologize to me," Shea insisted. "You really don't. I wouldn't want to be anywhere else, and that's the truth."

"Okay." David just watched him for a moment, feeling so thankful for Shea's understanding. "But it is very chaotic downstairs. There are always people there, day and night, either preparing for the club to open, running and filling the club when it is open, or cleaning up after. I'm the head Dom of the local BDSM community, which gathers here as well. This... This is my world. I love it. I revel in it. It's everything my real estate business is not. It's the pleasure facet of my life, and if you're going to be with me, that means I need to familiarize you with the way it all works." Clearing his throat, he focused his gaze on Shea to gauge his reaction. "Is it too much? Does it scare you?"

"No. It is a lot, I'll give you that, but it's actually so much, I can't even comprehend it. But I think I get you now, David. You're all about control, all the time. Running your company, running the club, running the BDSM community—that's just part of you. Ever since I started to suspect that..." a cloud passed over his face, darkening his sunny spirit for a moment. "That my parents wouldn't accept me, I've craved some sort of order and normality to my life. Seeing how you have everything figured out to such a ridiculous level? I don't know." He shrugged. "I like it. It makes me feel like I don't have to worry so much now."

"I'm glad," David said with relief. "And you don't. I'll take care of you, in every way you can imagine, and even a few you can't."

"Are you seriously doubting my powers of imagination? My favorite people wear spandex and have magical abilities."

"My favorite people wear leather, collars, and have a massive array of sex toys."

Shea burst out laughing, then composed himself and said in a mock-serious tone, "Okay, you win."

Shea took another couple of bites, and David could see his energy fading. Regretfully, David said, "You look so tired, sweetheart. You need some more rest."

Shea drank the last of his coffee and wiped his mouth with his napkin.

"But you're not leaving, are you?"

"Not if you need me to stay."

Glancing up at David with wide, hopeful eyes and a plaintive, subtle pout to his soft, dark lips, Shea was irresistibly opening himself up in ways that only made David eager to gather him close. The various hurts Shea had endured, they were right on the surface, begging for soft kisses and soothing caresses to ease them back to the point of tolerance. He was just a teenager, but he'd been expected to endure too much, too fast, all on his own. Astonishingly, there was nothing in him that tried to mask his vulnerability. He was the child that crawled quickly into your lap, throwing himself into your open arms, nuzzling against your chest as if believing you could save him from all of the bad dreams and nightmares. There, David had gravely failed him, and there was no way to undo the harm caused.

That was only a piece of it though. As David stood and Shea followed, getting to his feet as well, David noticed the way Shea moved.

There was a natural sensuality to the way he came close, hesitating a little out of bashfulness. All of Shea's desire was right there in the soft parting of his lips, the heat in his eyes, the language of his body, but there was no motive behind it. None. He just craved, and hoped that what he needed would be given kindly.

David wrapped a hand around the side of Shea's jaw, hooking his hand around his ear. Shea leaned into the touch, turning a little to kiss the inside of David's wrist. Nothing on earth in that moment could have pulled Shea from David's arms. The stars themselves could come crashing down around them, and it wouldn't matter, David had everything he could ever want, right here.

"I'll lay down first, all right? I don't want to accidentally press on any of your bruises or wounds."

Shea nodded without looking up.

David lay down on his back, his head on Shea's pillows. Reaching out for Shea's hand, David drew him down, helping hold him as Shea eased down to lay on top of David. He settled atop David's chest, straddling his legs, propping himself up a little on his good arm.

Knowing what Shea wanted, David let him move at his own pace, leaning in, bit by bit, towards David's lips. Caressing up under Shea's shirt, David savored the warm softness of the skin of his back, the firm muscle beneath. The skin to skin contact caused Shea to sigh and close his eyes. A flicker of a smile moved over his lips.

"Kiss me, beautiful," David invited.

"You make me nervous."

"Good," David teased. "You're adorable when you're nervous."

Shea's smile grew, then faded as he watched David's mouth. Finally, he came in close enough for their lips to brush together lightly. David's hand slipped underneath the waistband of Shea's pants, his hand palming Shea's ass. With a moan of want, Shea pressed into the kiss. He opened up as wide as David wanted as David's tongue teased the tip of Shea's, then tasted him, took him. Holding behind Shea's head, David kept him there to be kissed long and slow. He squeezed Shea's ass, which made Shea thrust in a slow drag against him. He began moving in a steady rhythm, working himself against David, undulating in such a sexy way, it made David want to peel all of the clothes from him just to watch his body work and to have access to touch it everywhere.

With a firm grip on Shea's right butt cheek, David nipped gently at Shea's lower lip and looked into his eyes. David pushed a little at the elastic waist of Shea's pants, inching them down. There was no protest, but Shea's breathing did get heavier, his thrusts firmer.

"I want to feel you against me," Shea asked shyly by David's ear, a whisper of sound. "Is that okay?"

David nodded, trying so hard to hold back, not wanting to take advantage or hurt Shea more than he'd already been. Letting go, he reached for his belt and fly. It took a few moments to get it opened, especially since he didn't let Shea pull away much. David shifted his pants down, freeing himself, smirking a little at Shea's apparent determination to not try to sneak a look, his eyes focused on the bed's headboard, breathing like his heart was beating at a frantic pace. Then, David pushed Shea's pants farther down, too, grabbed under both cheeks, and pulled him into a thrust.

Shea's cry split the air, full of ache and honest reaction. Their bare cocks slid against each other. Shea shuddered, goosebumps rising fast. David's hands were all over him, scratching lightly, squeezing. Shea's thrusts became quick snaps of his hips, determined drags right against David's hard shaft. He was wet, but so was David. Shea's blush soon overtook his neck, his chest, his gasping breaths becoming intertwined with small whimpers that threatened to bring out the animal in David, driving him to want to flip them and pin Shea if only to make him cry louder and with even more passion. He didn't dare though, not until he was sure Shea had properly healed.

Palming behind Shea's upper thigh to spread his legs wider, kneading the muscle of his ass as roughly as he dared, David urged Shea on, pulling him firmly into each grinding rut. He felt every tremble, caught every aching gasp as Shea got closer to release. David's lips hovered by Shea's, and Shea's eyes were mostly closed though David was trying to see everything. This was Shea. Underneath his self-deprecating jokes and banter, beneath the awkward laughter and shyness, this was the part of Shea he fiercely hid from the world out of self-preservation, and it was breathtaking in its frailty. He disguised nothing, and was completely invested in the moment. David had never witnessed such transparency in a submissive before. There was no goal behind his actions. He wasn't using David or trying to prove anything. He was simply giving, completely, of himself, even if it meant getting hurt. Already, he trusted David. It was unbelievable, and David felt truly blessed.

He knew, then. He felt it—how everything had suddenly changed, irrevocably. David pulled Shea down more completely against him, kissing just below his ear, his own breath catching as he came seconds before Shea. With a sweet cry so purely erotic, Shea climaxed, quivering. Their spend mixed on David's stomach, but he barely felt it. It only added to the warmth between them.

Exhausted, overcome, Shea melted into David, his head pillowed on David's chest. Drawing the blanket up over Shea, David soothed him with caresses from head to tailbone.

His voice slightly roughened, David told him with barely any sound, "I'm afraid I'm falling for you."

Shea reached up, brushing his fingers over the underside of David's chin, the side of his neck, the shell of his ear. "I'm not afraid. I'll fall with you, okay?"

Catching Shea's hand, David kissed the knuckles, then held it loosely, sighing a heartfelt, barely audible, "How did I get so lucky?" Shea's body relaxed even more and soon he was asleep.

Chapter 15

Formal Introductions

After a few calm days had passed, Shea felt much better. His head was clearer and his strength was returning. David and his staff seemed to offer food constantly, which helped reinvigorate Shea. His fever was also gone. Mainly, it was the little aches and pains and his arm bothering him, but he had painkillers to deal with those.

When David paid his morning visit, Shea asked if he could have a tour of the building.

"I don't know, your strength isn't what it should be," David said doubtfully, rubbing his lips with his arms folded across his chest, looking at Shea like he was something precious to safeguard, not some annoying houseguest. It was a difference profoundly noticeable to Shea, who'd so far only been the latter.

"You're incredible, you know," Shea said affectionately. He pushed his hands into the pockets of the scrubs he was wearing, feeling really awkward to pay the compliment just because of how much he was starting to care about David.

"For what?" David said with distracted confusion, his thoughts clearly somewhere else.

"Just for you."

Reacting noticeably to the sentiment behind the words, David was coming at him and kissing him before Shea knew it. His hands wound around behind Shea's lower back and neck. "I just don't want to take any chances with you."

"Can you just walk me through the club? Just to see it?"

"Of course," David relented. "I owe you at least that much. You're sure you're up for this?"

"Mm-hmm."

"All right." He glanced over a shoulder. "Marco?"

"Yes, Mr. Davenport?"

"Mr. Whittier would like to see the club. We'll need a full team. Please make sure the entrances are all closed and guarded before we descend. No one gets in until he's back upstairs."

"David," Shea protested. "You don't need to—"

"I do. This is my condition. My peace of mind, if I'm going to be your Master, and... as someone who cares about you."

"Well, shit," Shea breathed. He rested his hand on David's chest and he could feel the steady beating of David's strong heart beneath the immaculate black fabric of his button-down shirt. "No argument here. I care about you too."

David groaned and kissed him, frowning. He caressed Shea's cheek. "A quick tour. Then, I want you all to myself for a little while."

"Okay," Shea agreed.

Beyond Shea's white, sterile room, and down a short hall, the space opened up considerably. The hardwood floors were blonde, like farm boards. The walls were white with lavish moldings and trim. Paintings hung on most of the walls. Most of the furniture and carpets were also light in color. There were a few sitting areas, the furniture gathered in cozy arrangements, as well as a stately dining table with a gourmet kitchen barely visible beyond. Hallways led off this space in various directions and Shea could only imagine the floor they were on—David's living quarters, as he'd called them—were about the size of the main floor of his old high school. It was gigantic.

An elderly woman with a kind face and her white hair pulled back in a loose bun hurried toward them. She was dressed in a uniform and apron.

"Mrs. Tinsley, I'd like you to officially meet Shea Whittier, a beloved companion of mine. Shea, this is Mrs. Tinsley, who manages the house for me."

"The house part of the house anyway. The rest of it is left to Mireille," Mrs. Tinsley grinned warmly, shaking Shea's hand. "It's so good to see you're up and about, Mr. Whittier! Very nice to meet you." Mrs. Tinsley chuckled. "Can I get you two anything? There's homemade stew and soup on the burner, but if you'd like coffee, I can brew a fresh pot."

"Thank you so much, but we're off to take a quick tour of Manse. Lunch will have to wait until later."

"Certainly," she nodded, stepping back.

Pouring out of a side hallway, men in suits quickly surrounded them on all sides. Shea counted five, including Marco. Shea was led to some elevator doors. One of the guards pressed the button to open the doors and they all stepped inside. A short ride saw them delivered to the first floor. When the doors opened, it was like they were suddenly in another building entirely.

A staff member in a crisp black suit, with what appeared to be the logo for Manse embroidered on the front, came rushing forward. "Welcome, Mr. Davenport," he said, his hands folded around a clipboard.

"This is Mr. Shea Whittier, my personal guest."

"Of course, sir. If it's not too much trouble, may I just ask Mr. Whittier to sign the waiver and consent forms?" He flipped a few pages on his clipboard and turned it around for Shea to read, producing a pen as well and handing it over.

"Is this really necessary, Miguel?" David asked.

"I'm sorry, sir. Legal will be up my ass unless we cross the I's and dot the T's."

"As usual," David commiserated. "All right." To Shea, he said, "If you would just sign here, sweetheart... And here... I'll have copies of these sent directly to your room upstairs for you to examine in detail when we return. It's just a waiver of responsibility for the club, which everyone signs before being admitted. It's the same type of thing you agree to when visiting amusement parks. And the other paperwork is confirming you're of legal age and agree to the conditions of admittance. Since we're not staying but just passing through, we won't need to worry about that just yet."

"Yeah, that's fine." Shea signed in each place and handed the pen back to Miguel.

Once they were completely inside, it was almost too overwhelming for Shea to comprehend what he was seeing. Mazes of rooms interconnected, leading this way and that, surrounding them. Some had occupants, sitting on luxurious couches, sipping drinks, barely glancing up as the group passed by doorway after doorway. A large staircase led upward. Dark wood was everywhere, on the floors, the walls, the ceilings, lending the cavernous space a sort of unlikely coziness. They were passing by a space which looked most like what Shea would call a "club", with a dance floor and a huge bar lining one wall, when a nearly naked young man began to hurry past. He was wearing a pair of boxer shorts, but nothing else. The young man stopped, startled, when he almost ran right into the front of their group and the burly staff.

He had caramel-colored skin but startling light blue eyes which skated over the staff members, one by one, until they fell on David.

"Master," the newcomer said on a relieved exhale of breath. The staff let him past, much to Shea's amazement, as he fell to his knees directly at David's feet. Bending down as low as possible, the young man touched his forehead to the floor.

That was when Shea noticed his back.

"Jesus, Thierry," David groaned, wiping a hand over his face. To the nearest staff member, David demanded, "Where the fuck is Mireille? Get her down here. Now."

"Yes, sir," was the gruff reply as the man began to speak at a low volume, holding his earpiece to relay directions.

"On your feet, slave," David said severely to the barely-dressed Thierry.

"Mercy, Master. Please," Thierry begged, not moving, only lifting his head to kiss the toe of David's shoe.

"Don't make me repeat myself." The sharp, abrupt tone from David was jarring.

"Yes, sir. I'm sorry, Master," Thierry apologized, scrambling to his feet. He brought his arms behind his back, clasping his hands together, bowed his head and took a wide stance.

"Turn," David ordered.

Thierry spun slowly in a circle, showing David his back. It was crisscrossed in welts and what looked like fresh, open wounds, as if he'd been viciously whipped, but Shea thought that only happened to people in third world countries, as barbaric punishment. The lashes covered Thierry's upper back, the backs of his arms, and the backs of his thighs. The loose pair of boxer shorts he was wearing hung from his narrow hips.

"Face me."

Thierry turned back, avoiding eye contact, keeping his gaze turned downward.

"Why are you down here, slave?"

Thierry's gaze shifted upwards, to Shea for the first time, but he didn't look at Shea's face. He only seemed to see his body, the way he was standing just behind and beside David, wearing only scrubs, and paled slightly. Shea couldn't even pretend to understand why. When Thierry kept staring at Shea, David commanded, "Eyes on me."

"Sorry, Master," Thierry apologized, looking like he was on the verge of tears. He blinked rapidly and bit at the inside of his cheek.

"You don't look at anyone but me," David said with quiet, steely power. The only other time Shea had heard such a tone of voice from him was when they were faced with his father in the restaurant. Shea had forgotten how startling it had been at the time. Witnessing it made Shea want to fall in line, too, just to avoid being spoken to like that.

A tear slipped down Thierry's cheek and he didn't move to brush it away, but kept his head bowed, his chin almost touching his chest.

"Answer my fucking question. Now."

"I, uh... a cigarette... I just wanted... Leftovers at the bar, found a-a pack on there, and..."

Thierry was terrified, Shea realized. Terrified of *David*.

A woman in an elegant plum-colored suit and heels hurried their way, her brown hair blowing backward with her speed as she was followed by two other female staff members dressed more simply in black suits with skirts.

"Mireille, what is this?" David said. "He has open wounds and he was in the bar, *smoking*."

Mireille spared Shea a brief glance. When she did, David took notice. "This is him?" she asked David under her breath, nodding toward Shea. Softening his mannerisms slightly, David put his arm around Shea, bracing a hand against his back and said, "Yes. Shea, this is Mireille, she manages the rest of the house, including Manse and the medical suite."

"A pleasure, Mr. Whittier," Mireille smiled charmingly, shaking hands with Shea.

Rapidly, she turned her attention back to David and asked him quietly, "Sir, if I could just speak to you privately for one moment—"

"No, just tell me. It's all right," he assured her, seeming to brace himself for bad news. Looking like she wished the conversation was more private, she explained, "He punched Eric last night. Broke his nose. Elet handled punishment in your absence. Thierry had been resting upstairs in medical but it's not like he's a prisoner there, David. Aftercare had been handled hours ago."

"Who's on duty today, in medical? Nurse Petrecz?"

"Yes," Mireille nodded.

Of Thierry, David asked, "Is this true, slave? You punched Eric?"

"Please, Master, he was laughing at me with his friends, he—"

"*Enough.*" David stalked up to Thierry, looking down his nose at the younger man. "It's obvious you haven't learned your lesson when it comes to respect and humility. That's a serious problem if you expect to continue to be allowed to visit here. I think some time spent submitting *completely* to Master Elet will help."

"No! Please! *Mercy,*" Thierry sobbed, his shoulders shaking and tears streaming from his striking eyes, which were bloodshot now. He gazed up pleadingly at David.

"We've avoided it too long. It'll be taken care of tomorrow. Clear your schedule for the next several days. You'll need the recovery time. I'll be on hand to supervise, as will the doctor."

"Yes, Master," Thierry murmured in defeat, sounding broken. Another tear dripped from the end of his nose.

"You'll be seen back to the medical suite, where you will stay until discharged." To Mireille, David said, "If he tries to leave again, call in Elet; have the boy shackled to the bed."

"Yes, David," Mireille nodded. "Low protocol, slave," David said. Thierry relaxed, his hands unclasping to hang at his sides. He stepped forward and kissed each of David's cheeks. David held him there, for a moment, his hand clasped around Thierry's jaw. Turning into the touch like he was starved for the comfort, Thierry brazenly nuzzled David's palm.

The hand fell away. David said, gently, tenderly, "Go. Rest. Master Elet has been your staunchest advocate. Trust in that."

"Yes, Master. Thank you."

"I trust I'll see you again soon, Mr. Whittier. Glad to have met you," Mireille said, turning to leave.

"Thanks. Likewise," Shea replied.

Thierry spared one last glance at Shea before he was ushered away by Mireille.

"There's one more thing I want to show you. It's waited long enough. I'm sure you've been wondering," David explained.

David took Shea's hand and led him down a corridor. They were back upstairs in David's private quarters. Two guards followed. The rest had been dismissed at the top of the elevator. Down one hallway and into another, they came upon a metal door which spanned floor to ceiling of one wall.

"This is my vault," David said. He placed his thumb on a screen, which scanned it. The door's locks disengaged and a staff member pried it open, pulling on the handle as if the door itself was incredibly heavy. Inside, in front of anything David might have had stored, were piles of boxes marked with Shea's name and descriptions of their contents. "Your things. I had them retrieved from your apartment by my staff, supervised by the local police, immediately following the incident at the hotel. Since it appeared you would be staying with me for a while, I assumed it would be more of a comfort to you to have everything at hand rather than left behind where you couldn't be assured of its safety. If I assumed incorrectly, I apologize."

"No, I appreciate it," Shea told him, feeling stunned. "Thank you. It's one less thing to worry about. I'm sure since I basically vanished, Ryan might have started to sell some of it off to pay my debt."

"This area is only accessible by three people right now. Myself, the head of my away team, Marco," David gestured to one of the staff members behind them, the Colossus stunt double who had seemed to be in charge at the hotel and in the car. "And the head of my home security team, Ivan. The police have been notified of this arrangement, and of my taking temporary responsibility for the storage of your possessions. I thought it important for your sake that it be public record.

If at any point you'd like to arrange your own storage instead, I'll facilitate that."

"I-I don't even... sure? How you could possibly find so much time to look out for me, David?" Shea replied, his head spinning with it all. "It's really generous of you to do all of this and bring my things up here. But... this vault? It's not like I have priceless items in there, you know. It's pretty much my comic book collection and some video games."

"Nonsense, these are your things. They're priceless to you. That's all that matters."

"Did Ryan give them a hard time at all?" Shea asked, wincing a little just imagining David's people swooping in and grabbing Shea's stuff.

"No, from what I understand he was fairly quiet and kept to himself until everything was cleared out."

"Hmm," Shea grunted, folding his arms. It was so weird to see his stuff in David's fancy vault. "I guess that was because of cops being there, or because of how scary your staff is. No offense, Mr. Colossus, sir. Or maybe Ry was just glad to be able to rent out my room to someone who can afford it. I should probably at least give Mahendran a call. But, what the hell do I *say*?"

"You have my full permission to ignore the issue for now," David said, running his hand lightly down the side of Shea's arm. The touch felt so good, it moved Shea forward, closer to David. He ran his fingers over a few of the buttons on David's shirt, feeling weighed down by everything surrounding them, waiting just beyond the bubble of peace David seemed to create so effortlessly around them.

"Thanks."

"Let me take you back to your room. You look a little overwhelmed."

"No, I'm okay. I mean, yeah, this is overwhelming, but being with you helps."

"Would you like to see my office? It's a little more... private."

"Yeah. Show me where the magic happens, Mr. Davenport," Shea grinned. David laughed despite himself, his eyes crinkling happily at the corners in a way that was so cute, Shea's stomach did a little loop-de-loop.

David took possession of Shea's hand again and, with an incline of his head, said temptingly, "Come on." The way he said it, and the look on his face, made Shea suspect David had more on his mind than business.

Chapter 16
Workplace Submission

The office was grand, but much cozier than some of the other wide open spaces in David's home. Marco and the other guard stayed at the doorway, facing the hall, the office door open as David led Shea inside. There was a huge desk with one chair behind it but several in front of it, leading Shea to believe David regularly conducted business there. The windows, like most of the others on that floor, showed mainly the tops of trees budding with new leaves and blue sky. There were no buildings in sight of a similar height to block the view. There was a whole wall of built-in cabinetry across from the windows. Framed photographs of countless buildings decorated the wall behind the desk. A comfortable-looking couch to their left was placed a couple of feet away from the wall of cabinetry.

"Those are your properties, right? You developed them?" Shea asked, pointing to the photos on the wall.

"Some, yes," David agreed, pushing his hands into his pants pockets.

"Are they just yours, or your father's too?"

"Just mine." His tone changed slightly, becoming more introspective as he said, "You know, a lot of people haven't understood why I've been so driven to build my company apart from my father's. After all, I'm the sole heir. It would have been easier to simply prepare to take over for him, once he was ready to step down. He's been grooming me to take over for him since my mother found out I was going to be a boy. But I think, maybe more than anyone else who's passed through my life, you might really comprehend the complicated motivations behind wanting to stand on my own two feet, financially, practically, and permanently."

"That's all I've ever wanted," Shea agreed, with all of the terrible circumstances in mind that were forever getting in the way of that goal. "Being able to establish your own life, your own source of income, and set your own rules... yeah. I can see why. But, David, you're only twenty five years old. Why the rush?"

David let out a heavy breath. "The things my father is capable of, the things he's done out of fear, jealousy and grief... My independence and personal security have been the distance keeping all of that away from me."

"Hmm," Shea let out a mirthless chuckle. "Maybe we're not so different after all, huh?"

"Shea, are you sure you're interested in being with me? Submitting to me?" David asked, the hint of doubt plain in his voice. Shea moved closer, into David's personal space, and right away David started to touch him, like he couldn't help the impulse. His finger trailed over the back of Shea's wrist, over his hand. Shea was hyperaware of the guards only a few feet away, able to overhear everything.

"Yes. I've had a lot of time this week to think about it, like you told me I should, and I have. This feels like only a good thing. Why?"

"Just making sure it's not going to be another complication you don't need," David replied. Shea decided then, that he liked seeing David worrying about him, if only because it gave Shea an opportunity to set David at ease over something. David worried far too much about too many things from what Shea could tell.

"This is who you are," Shea assured him. "I understand that. And you... the ways you take care of me, it's incredible, so I'm in."

"But is it something *you* want?"

Pressing his lips together, Shea pushed down on a surge of self-consciousness. "I guess because of my family life, suspecting they would hate me for being gay, which they do, I've avoided my sexuality in a lot of ways for a long time. I just had so much else to worry about. I didn't know where I was going to sleep some nights, how I would eat, what I was going to do. Not having sex, not screwing around more than I was ready for with people like Ryan—that was the only way I could take control of my life. It was literally the only thing completely under my control."

"I can see how that might be true. Your body, your heart—you protected them," David guessed.

"Yeah. And now I'm ready to let you protect them. Obviously you do a kick ass job at taking care of stuff, whether it's a building or some punk kid." He hesitated, then asked, "That guy downstairs, Thierry—I wanted to ask, but also wanted to wait until there was privacy—or more privacy, I guess," he added, glancing toward the guards. "Is he okay?"

"Absolutely," David said, giving Shea's hand a gentle squeeze. "All of that with Thierry has been going on for a while now. I like him. I really do, and not just because he's submitted to me more than once. But I don't know if he has the right temperament to be a slave. I can't say more without violating his privacy, but please have no doubt that we're handling the situation. I've been distracted with everything that's happened over the past couple of weeks, but Elet has stepped in and will continue to do so."

"Okay," Shea replied, "And a slave is the same thing as a submissive, I guess?"

"It is."

"So that's what I would be? Your slave? That sounds kind of weird."

"The terminology is less important than the meaning behind it, but yes. You'd be mine. I'd be yours. Master and slave. Dom and sub."

"But Thierry... he was whipped. His back looked..." Shea shuddered. "Would you whip me like that, because—"

"No, understand that Thierry's misbehavior has been a constant issue for his Masters. He's been warned, and punished in less severe ways. It's had no effect. Thierry wouldn't keep coming here if he didn't want to be here. A submissive would never be whipped that severely against their will. Not by me."

"You're saying he wanted that?" Shea asked with disbelief.

"He did. In his own ways, for his own reasons."

"Interesting."

"Submitting is sometimes the best way to receive things you'd not be otherwise able to ask for. Once consent has been given, the Master explores everything within the slave's personal boundaries. That's why rules and clear communication are important."

"Makes sense." Shea glanced again at the guards by the door, thinking about everything David had said.

"If this doesn't feel right, I understand," David began to say.

"No, it's not that. I'm just trying to get it all. But talking it through is a lot different than doing it. We could talk about it all day and what it actually is still might not really sink in."

"Does that mean you'd like to have a bit of a trial run at submitting to me? Just to see if you like it?"

"Yeah," Shea nodded, already starting to become aroused in anticipation. "You mean now?"

"Right now," David smirked. "We'll have as much privacy here as anywhere else."

"Can we... shut the door?" Shea asked hopefully.

"Don't worry about the door. All you need to focus on is me, okay? It's my job to decide what ensures your safety and enjoyment. Can you trust me with that? If so, the proper, respectful way to answer is, 'yes, Master', or 'yes, sir.'"

"Yes, Master," Shea said, trying it out. It wasn't as awkward to say as he had expected.

"Good. You are to address me while submitting as Master or sir, only. The proper stance is with your feet slightly apart, your back straight, hands clasped behind you, chin up and eyes down. Can you handle that?"

Shea shifted into the position.

"Good," David said warmly.

It wasn't that different than following orders at work. It was just more specific. Usually, the more something was explained to him, the better Shea was able to perform — though in this case his performance was going to be of a much more intimate nature.

"Now, I've noticed you tend to get quiet during sexual situations, probably out of nervousness, and that's completely understandable. Just remember your manners while the scene is happening. Please and thank you. Always using the honorific of Master or sir afterward. Speak when spoken to. Are we good so far?"

"Yes, Master," Shea said with a little smirk. Good manners were already something he was comfortable with using habitually. Earning the respect of the people he served — and showing it in return — had always been important.

"I'd like you to choose a safeword now. As soon as you would say that word, I would stop completely, no matter what."

"Can't I just say stop?"

"Of course, if you prefer. But, sometimes things are said in the heat of the moment, things the submissive doesn't actually mean. It's like role playing, only... getting carried away with it. A safeword is something you would never accidentally say. It indicates to me that things need to stop, abruptly."

"Okay. Master."

"It can be the traditional safeword of 'red', or something else you associate with comfort and has no connections with any negative memories or feelings. Do you have one in mind?"

"Yes, Master. I'd like to use 'Captain' if that's okay."

Sounding like he was smiling, David replied, "Yes, that's fine. Now. Let's see if you really do trust me..." It was a tease, but a good one. Right away, Shea's heart started to beat faster in anticipation.

"Oh no," Shea quietly groaned.

David chuckled softly. He reached out and hooked a finger in Shea's waistband, pulling on it to stretch it out, sliding the finger side to side as he inched the pants down very gradually.

"Please remove your shirt, slave," David commanded in a tender, softened tone.

Feeling shivery, Shea did as asked, pulling the white shirt, borrowed from David's medical supplies, over his head, then tossed it over onto the couch.

"Back in position," David reminded him.

"Oh. Right." Shea stood up straighter, putting his hands behind his back, even though he was apprehensive to do it with the way David was inching his pants down. They were quite low on his hips. Half his ass was already exposed and his dick would be next.

Slowly, David got the pants down past Shea's thickening cock, then past his balls and down to mid-thigh. Leaving the pants to hug there, David watched Shea thicken even more, swelling due to David's focused attention.

It was so quiet in there, it seemed Shea's breathing and the thudding of his pulse in his ears were obnoxiously loud. At first David wasn't even touching him, just watching, but that was enough to get Shea going, it seemed. Maybe Shea was more sexually desperate than he'd first thought. When Shea was almost at full mast, David finally moved to stroke the underside of Shea's cock with the back of his index finger, brushing it as if encouraging it to attain its rigid, upright position.

"Beautiful," David breathed. He gave Shea's cockhead a little pinch, grabbing hold just above the ridge on either side with his thumb and index finger, then squeezing. Shea's breath stuttered, his thighs and stomach reflexively clenching a little. "Good, deeper breaths whenever you feel discomfort." His thumb swiped over the end of Shea's cock, through the fluid collecting there. Then, the edge of his thumbnail dug into his slit a little, prying at it. Shea grunted, his face suddenly hot. He bowed his head to hide his startled expression.

"Chin up. Eyes down."

David's nail played there a little longer and Shea felt himself get wetter. Frowning against a little shame at that, he struggled to stay still. Another hard grunt was startled out of him. "Sorry," he muttered.

"Don't be. I want to hear you. Don't censor yourself on my account, please. The sounds you naturally make, your breaths — all of it's exquisite, slave. There's beauty in honesty. I'd hate for you to stifle that out of bashfulness."

Rubbing firmly through the pre-come, David trailed his thumb down to just under Shea's cockhead, then rubbed back and forth there. Right away, his cock jumped and a surge of sensation caused him to whimper, just a little.

"Fuck, I could do this for hours," David moaned.

Shea surprised himself by laughing. He closed his eyes, frowning just a little, gritting his teeth. The harder David rubbed, the wetter Shea got and the more impossible it became to not hump David's fingers. He lost control, thrusting once.

"Steady now," David warned. "If I wanted you to move, I would give you permission to do so."

"Sorry, Master."

The effort to stay still was so overwhelming, though, and in seconds Shea was crying out roughly, growling back in his throat. Only then did David change tactics.

"On your knees, slave."

"Oh thank fuck," Shea said on a heavy exhale.

"What was that?" David teased, playing dumb. Probably smiling, though Shea didn't look.

"Nothing, Master."

Shea got on his knees, hyperaware of his hard, dripping wet dick jutting up from between his legs, his butt clenched tight and the damned guards still standing *right there*. He told himself he should be embarrassed to be as turned on as he was, but it seemed his dick didn't care one bit about the guards.

David's hands were on his fly, opening it, and Shea's eyes grew wide, realizing what was about to happen. His mouth watered at the thought but his heart rate kicked up even more.

"Open wide, tongue out."

Shea moaned but complied, staring at David's dick as it was freed. It was thick, red, long and hard as hell. More than anything, Shea wanted to taste it.

"I was tested this morning, slave. I'm clean. You are as well. Would you prefer I use a condom, or go without?"

"Without, Master. Please," Shea answered, then opened wide again. He was almost, but not quite able, to hold in a heavy moan of pure want. It was so loud when it came out, he winced.

"I want you to want this, slave," David assured him. "I want to hear you. There's no shame here."

Breathing harder, practically panting, Shea watched David shift closer and angle his cock down, sliding it onto the tip of Shea's tongue. It was warm and thick, the weight of it tempting Shea to lick and taste the skin. Shea's next moan broke into an aching whimper.

"So fucking sweet," David sighed, caressing the side of Shea's face as he eased himself in. "Okay, close your lips."

They sealed tightly around David's tip and Shea sucked at the taste of him, greedily, rubbing his tongue against David's flesh and swallowing the taste. Shea's cock twitched in delight. He started to push forward to take more into his mouth, wanting to, but David held him up, his hand clamping under Shea's chin.

"Be still. Patience."

Shea's frown deepened. He heard the low voices of staff members down the hall, was reminded again that the pair of guards were within a few feet of them, and there he was on his knees, mostly naked with David's dick between his lips. A subtle shudder raced up his back and outward through his body. He licked some more at David's cock. The more he did, the more he needed to thrust against something and get off.

"Thank you for being so obedient, slave," David said in a gruff, low voice. "Your cock is soaking wet. Do you enjoy holding my dick on your tongue?"

Shea moaned brokenly, then grunted his agreement.

"Should I let you suck on it?"

It was so fucking hot, Shea humped the air, his hips rolling briefly forward. Chest rising and falling heavily, he grunted his assent again.

"Stay still. Keep your throat open and relax. Show that you trust me."

David thrust very slowly, pushing back into Shea's mouth. His hand was hooked around Shea's ear, his fingers wrapping around to the back of Shea's head to hold him steady. When David's cock pushed back to fill Shea's throat, a small, helpless grunt escaped him, but he bore it, his eyes squeezed shut. Buried balls deep, David didn't hold there long but pulled right back out until his cock sprung free of Shea's lips.

Staring at it, wanting it back, Shea tracked it with his mouth open and ready.

"What do you want, slave?"

"Your cock. Please let me suck it, Master."

David moaned and fed it to him again. Shea took it with a hungry groan. Building a rhythm, David rode Shea's lips. His cock, wet with saliva, was stretching Shea's mouth out in a wide O. Shea chased it with his tongue, letting it wrap the shaft. He fought not to push into each inward thrust but to let David control the movements. The more Shea relaxed and let it happen, the easier and faster David moved and the more comfortable Shea became.

Soon, Shea was panting and David was fucking his mouth with

shallow, quick thrusts. With a growl, gritting his teeth, David pulled out, stroking himself. "Open wide. Tongue out."

He came over Shea's tongue, his lips and chin. Small, pleading sounds escaped Shea on each of his exhales. When David seemed spent, Shea swallowed what he could. David rubbed the come from his lips with a hand, then found a few tissues to clean him off with.

"On your feet. Over to the couch and strip off the pants . Lie on your back, lengthways."

Shea got in place after removing the last of his clothes, wondering what came next, hoping it was him.

"Draw your legs up and keep them as widely open as you can. Hold your legs under the knees."

Watching David move into position, Shea saw how incredibly red and swollen his dick was. Now David knew how exactly much he got off on giving head.

David knelt below where Shea lay. With one bent knee braced on the couch, the other leg planted on the floor, David sat back on his heel and reached for Shea. One hand wrapped Shea's cock. The other, wet with his own come, rubbed through Shea's crease.

Gasping audibly with a rough, nervous cry, Shea felt David tease his hole with his fingertips.

"I would never hurt you, slave."

"I know, Master," he said shakily.

"Let's try one finger, okay?"

"Okay."

It pushed at him, feeding the finger through his rim. Clenching down on it, Shea felt David push it deep. His head falling back, Shea panted, trying to get control of himself, feeling like he didn't have any. His body quivered and he swallowed thickly.

"Just relax. You're safe. It's just me," David reminded him. He began stroking Shea's cock. Shea had been so close to coming, but the small, private fear of that finger up his ass pushed his orgasm away again. His deflating cock slid easily through David's fingers as the finger pumped shallowly in his ass.

It was terrifying. The finger twisted around and Shea whimpered more sharply, his back arching. He knew he was only scared because of those men and the nightmare of what had happened at the hotel. It wasn't because of David, but it was hard to keep the two apart in his mind. It started to overwhelm him, and he thought of his safeword, almost ready to say it.

That's when David started to jack him, furiously.

Shea gasped violently, his hips bucking. The finger inside him tapped something that caused Shea to shout, and the sensation was a bombardment. Rational thought failed him. All he could do was feel the explosive reactions to David's touch. Shea's hands tightened their grip on his legs, his feet flexing, his back arching, body straining; he felt David tap that oversensitive spot inside his ass again and again while tugging hard on his cock.

Without warning, Shea came all over his stomach, shuddering hard, still crying out and panting for air. David kept triggering him, though stroking more slowly now.

"Fuck," Shea whined, convulsing slightly.

"Easy, beautiful. Ride it out."

There was one more spasm, another smaller jet of pearly fluid. He was aware of the sounds he was making, and couldn't do a thing about them. But then David was leaning down over him, braced on one arm on the couch, his finger moving slowly in and out of Shea's ass. David kissed him, angling his head to lick deeply into Shea's mouth, swallowing his moan.

He pulled back, just a little, whispering, "One more. A little pressure."

A second finger pushed in along with the first. The stretch ached and Shea muffled his small cry against David's cheek. David was biting his lip with concentration, looking so focused. All Shea could feel was pressure and ache. David's lips brushed by Shea's. "Thank you," David murmured, then kissed him lightly while Shea gasped into his mouth. "I know that's not comfortable."

He kissed a trail back along Shea's cheek, pumping the pair of fingers, burying them completely. Then he palmed Shea with the rest of his hand.

David kissed Shea's earlobe, the edge of his jaw. Time slowed down. Slowly, Shea relaxed again.

"It's hard to get used to," Shea admitted in a whisper.

"I know, sweetheart," David said with a look of concern, then kissed his lips again. "I'm so proud of you. The more you get used to it, the easier it will be. Stretching is really important."

Shea nodded. "Can I... can I touch you?"

"Of course."

Shea caressed the side of David's neck, taking a few deeper breaths to calm down. Touching David helped, his body warm and strong under Shea's hand. David's fingers pulled out, rubbed his rim, then pushed in again with only a shiver from Shea in response.

"Thank you, Master."

"You were perfect, Shea. I hope you enjoyed it as much as I did."

"I did," Shea said shyly, trying a smile. With a hitching sigh, he kissed David's lips.

It went on a little while longer, and the ache disappeared entirely. Instead, Shea felt a little swollen, and definitely oversensitive. When David rubbed over his opening for the last time, Shea was shocked at how sensitive he was there. His fingers tightened a little around the side of David's neck, not really wanting it to be over already.

"Let's cover you up and take you back to your room for a shower and a nap, okay? I'll have Mrs. Tinsley deliver you a tray of lunch options in a little while."

"Okay," Shea replied. Though he didn't want David to go, with how busy David was, Shea knew he couldn't keep him forever, and he was a little sleepy. Telling himself there would be more time for them to be together later, he decided to trust David's judgment, and obey.

Chapter 17

Secret Talents and Fears

David asked, "Are they still out there?"

It was evening. Shea was in bed, resting. David was worrying.

"Yes, sir," Ivan, the head of the home security team, answered while standing at attention inside David's office on the third floor. Ivan was head of security at Manse and within the home, a former Marine and, David suspected, physically incapable of smiling. He took everything *very* seriously, which David appreciated. "The vehicle is parked just beyond the edge of the property and the main gates. They're using telescopic lenses to watch the building, as well as everyone who comes and goes. Somehow, they're anticipating the drive-bys the police are doing. They clear out, then come right back."

"Lovely," David murmured.

"Ms. Turner reports that your father continues to attempt to reach you and is becoming steadily angrier about being denied your new personal number."

"Yes, I'm aware of that. Thank you, Ivan, that'll be all. I'll be occupied for the next several hours, so please handle anything that comes up. Mr. Whittier is still the priority."

"And Manse, sir?"

David pushed back the edge of the curtain, gazing down at the small gathering outside the main entrance to the club. The parking lot down the hill, inside the main gates, was already partially full as hopeful guests began to gather. There were about fifteen young men, dressed to impress in clothing that barely fit, smoking or chatting at the end of the path which led from the parking lot at the bottom of the hill. Since the club's doors were locked, they'd been waiting a while for entrance, and would, unfortunately, be waiting even longer. David hated to keep them out, but until the area around the building was more secure, and the threat Dorian placed more thoroughly understood, it wasn't safe to invite in company.

"It stays closed for the night, I'm afraid. Just tonight. We'll re-evaluate again tomorrow."

"Sir," Ivan nodded with a small bow, then left the room.

Violet Turner, David's Chief of Operations, handled all of David's business concerns, and at the moment, was Dorian Davenport's biggest obstacle in reaching his son.

There was a good reason why David controlled his own investments and had made his own money, apart from his trust fund. He wasn't counting on the inheritance coming through, not anymore. The money itself didn't really matter to David, but practical security did, not only for himself but those around him. He also wanted to ensure no one in his employ lost their jobs because of one of Dorian's fits. Even though he remained his father's obsession, David wasn't interested in living up to expectations if that was the path to the cash. Dorian could keep his billions. David would gladly, instead, take everything he'd worked for on his own, if it meant independence and the ability to safeguard everything most important to him — like Shea, for instance.

David's phone rang. It was Mireille.

"Elet and Thierry are ready for you, sir," she told David.

"Thank you. I'll be right down."

Detouring past Shea's room, David nodded in greeting to the door guards. Their hands were folded loosely in front of them, inches from the guns sitting in holsters on their hips. Logically, David knew it was overkill, that anyone who'd get this far into the building would have had to pass through five other levels of security to do so, but it still helped him breathe easier to see those weapons there, loaded and ready. Especially after what Shea had been made to endure because of David's lack of foresight in anticipating Dorian's capability for maliciousness.

Lying in bed, Shea's head had fallen to the side, his cheek against the pillow. His injured arm lay above the sheet, wrapped in fresh bandages to help speed the healing process. The last time David had seen it uncovered, the area had looked much less inflamed. Thankfully, Shea was healing. The IV line David had gotten used to seeing, delivering powerful antibiotics, was no longer there. The television was off, the room quiet.

He looked deceivingly healthy. The wounds on his arm were covered. The bruising elsewhere was hidden from sight as the initial injury to Shea's jaw continued to heal faster than his previously-infected arm. The straps they'd used to hold him down and keep him from re-injuring himself were no longer there either, but David remembered in heart-stopping detail each time they'd needed to use them.

Shea was just so very young and helpless. With his eyes closed, resting peacefully, he was little more than a child, yet he had no one watching out for him. It was a role David was determined to fill to the best of his ability. Too many times, Shea had been hurt, as if fate was doing its best to crush him. That stopped now — David was making sure of it. More than anything, David wanted to do the right thing. David had already failed Donna, and Trent. There was no getting them back. But he'd be damned if anyone or anything hurt Shea again.

Standing just inside the doorway, thinking of his failures and his fears, David's gaze locked onto Shea. David ground his teeth together and controlled the urge to hit something. To not know how many times they'd hit Shea, or where, or what they'd said or what else they'd done was maddening. The doctor's examination could only tell them so much. The whole truth was Shea's alone and only time would set it free. It left David feeling agonizingly unprepared to comfort and help as thoroughly as he'd like. Piecing the attack together with what facts he had, he kept filling in the blanks with the worst things imaginable.

Closing his eyes, expelling a breath, David tried to acknowledge the helplessness of his position in order to process it and move beyond it. The last thing he wanted to do was ask Shea to relive his ordeal just to get more information about the crime, not when they'd finally made real progress with his recovery. Shea was safe, and healing. He seemed comfortable with David, and there was such a strong pull of real affection between them already. It had to be enough.

That's what he told himself, anyway. He wore the resolution to abstain from acts of vengeance like a coat, easily undone and discarded, if things heated up beyond his tolerance.

"The stoic guarding of the sleeping patient is very Steve Rogers of you," David heard murmured.

"Hmm?"

Shea opened his eyes without moving. David hadn't realized he'd been awake.

"Never mind. It's the meds and hunger pangs talking. I'm just not used to waking up to find handsome, seductively intimidating guys watching over me."

"If you're hungry, I'll let Mrs. Tinsley know. She'll arrange for whatever type of food you're in the mood to eat."

"Thanks, but I'd kind of rather just get something myself. I don't think I could tell someone I'm not paying to make me food. It seems kind of bossy."

"Yes, well, get used to it. You're not allowed to cook for yourself. You need rest. Allow me to be bossy for you."

"Yes, Master," Shea said, smiling only with his eyes. "You're going to see him, aren't you? Thierry?"

"Oh, are you clairvoyant as well, now?" Wandering to the bedside, David let the backs of his fingers run down the exposed skin of Shea's left forearm, from just below the bandages' edge to his wrist. After all of the pains David had taken to ensure Shea's safety in the hotel suite, safeguarding him from Ryan and the dangerous neighborhood between where he worked and lived, it had come to this. It had all been for nothing, because as soon as Shea had entered David's world, he'd suffered more pain than Ryan had ever inflicted. Maybe David was the real danger to Shea.

"You're not the only one with secret talents," Shea smiled. "Besides you know, how good I am at getting fucked over like a champ."

Visions of Trent hanging by the neck from shoelaces in his jail cell, because of Dorian and bad luck, hit David hard. They were immediately followed by mental images of sweet, virginal, unassuming young Shea being held down and raped by Dorian's guards while he screamed.

Rage on their behalf froze David, for only a moment. He was blind, deaf, and mute to everything but how much he needed to make his father and those other men pay.

David wasn't sure how to fix things. All he knew was that he wasn't going anywhere. Being near Shea, thinking of him, touching him, kissing him, it caused a twisting tension in David's chest. Shea already had David's heart. His fingers still lightly touched Shea's arm. Suddenly, his hand was taken up and held.

Lying naked, crumpled on the floor, passed out from shock, the scent of blood in the air, dripping from Shea's skin, the echoes of screams lingering, refusing to fade away.

"I'll kill them for hurting you," David whispered.

"Hey, David," Shea beckoned, tenderly, drawing David's gaze back into focus. Shea seized and held David's attention, refusing to let go. Peering across the distance, a chasm of beatings, rape, and betrayal, Shea was there, waiting for David to find a way to lead him back. They needed to talk about this. They had to try. "You're already a superhero to me. You don't need to do any more. I'm okay. Promise. Your dad loves you so much, and is so afraid of something happening to you that—"

"*Please*, don't," David protested. "Don't defend him for this."

"I won't have you keel over from a damn aneurysm from stress or doing something crazy just because you're upset right now."

Doing his best to look stern, Shea was only able to pull off the ferocity of a terrier puppy. Yet, David admired Shea's ability to stand up for himself. It wasn't often that David came across someone willing to talk back to him. But, if Shea was to be more than just David's submissive, it was quite an important trait to possess.

The urge to apologize again was so strong, but David knew he could never undo what his father's men had done. Only time would allow David the chances to prove himself to Shea again, and it was up to Shea whether or not David deserved that time. It was out of David's hands entirely.

"I'll be with Master Elet and Thierry for a while," he said. "If you need to reach me, do. Tell the guards, the nurse, Mrs. Tinsley—anyone that's nearby. I won't have my phone on me, but they have ways of getting my attention during a scene."

Shea lowered his gaze, chewed his lip. There was a simmering of confusion and frustration behind his vulnerability that David didn't know how to dispel. "Can I watch?"

"Not this time. But, next time, maybe."

Shea gave David's hand a squeeze. "Take care of him, okay?"

Chapter 18
Master Elet

The suite smelled clean—notes of lemony cleanser and disinfectant lingering in the air. The space wasn't large, but it didn't need to be. There was a small room with slate floors, dark walls and a mirrored ceiling. Beyond it was the black tiled washroom. In the main room, everything had been cleared away with the exception of a small cart, on which sat a large bottle of lubricant and extra large condoms, and an inclined metal table, the top of which was thickly padded, the sides ringed with shackles and chains of adjustable length. Sconces gripped tightly to the walls, casting a warm glow. The heat had been raised to compensate for the nakedness of the participants, so the air was thick, filling the lungs like liquid, drawing perspiration quickly to the skin.

The soft, flattering lighting was the only welcoming aspect of the suite. The darkness, the cold, hard edges and intimidating fetish furniture were used to maximum, intentional effect. David and Elet wanted their slaves on edge, prepared for anything.

David walked through the room into the washroom. The floors, the walls, the countertops and the toilet were all a glistening, spotless black. There was an open shower in the far corner with a drain in the floor, but no walls, no privacy.

Thierry was there, seated on the toilet, straddling the tank, his arms folded atop it. Though his head was bowed, his back was almost perfectly straight, curved beautifully at the base of his spine where his ass pushed out slightly. His thighs were clenched, his feet flexed with only the balls of his feet making contact with the black tile floor. There was a long tube leading from a large bag of fluid on a stand and into Thierry's anus.

"Clench!" Elet ordered sharply, then slowly pulled the nozzle end of the tube out of Thierry's body. Grunting softly with effort, Thierry turned his face slightly more away from their sight, tensing visibly from head to toe.

Elet glanced up at David, and smiled wickedly. Elet was bare-chested, his muscle-packed chest glistening. His snug trousers hinted at the size of the flesh contained within. On his feet were heavy, black boots, laced with straps.

"Release!"

David heard the fluid draining from Thierry, who trembled and breathed unevenly.

Covering the end of the nozzle with a fingertip, Elet brought it back over to Thierry, holding it slightly above his ass and moving his finger away for a moment in order to rinse him down. Then his finger blocked the flow once more. Tilting the tube upward, Thierry plunged the nozzle through Thierry's sphincter, feeding it inside him quickly.

Thierry let out a shuddering, open-mouthed breath as fluid moved through the tube and filled his insides once more.

"Slave, you haven't addressed Master David," Elet scolded.

"Forgive me, Master David," Thierry said in an uncharacteristically timid voice, without glancing around or raising his head.

"You've broken him already?" David approached the boy and ran his fingers over his head. Thierry yielded to the touch but squeezed his eyes closed.

"He's likely to piss himself again," Elet chuckled.

"You've been on a liquid diet, slave?" David asked.

"Yes, Master David," Thierry answered obediently.

"How many times have you washed out his ass?"

"Several," Elet answered with amusement. "I'm afraid his tender little pucker is already sore from the nozzle. Clench!"

Thierry whimpered, but obeyed.

The nozzle fucked him shallowly for a moment before pulling free. Somehow, Thierry bowed his head more, breathing in small gasps.

"Release!"

More fluid, more rinsing. Elet soaped his hands until it was covered in suds, then scrubbed them over Thierry's cheeks, through his crack, over his balls and cock. Two soapy fingers twisted up his asshole, making Thierry whine. They thrust in and out, then were replaced with the tip of the nozzle as Elet washed the soap away before it could aggravate the tissues too greatly.

"Crawl to the table, slave!"

"Yes, sir," Thierry murmured, avoiding their gazes, his chin tucked nearly to his chest as he slid from the porcelain throne and crawled away.

"He's truly afraid," David said under his breath to Elet.

"Indeed."

They followed Thierry to the table. Thierry stopped at the edge, then turned slightly when catching sight of Elet's boots beside him.

"May I, Master?" Thierry asked quietly, with absolutely none of the bravado he liked to display around those smaller, weaker, or poorer than him. In fact, David saw the tear tracks on his cheeks, the glassiness of his eyes.

"You may, slave," Elet replied. Humming with pleasure, he watched, avidly, as Thierry bent even lower to kiss Elet's boots, one, then the other, with reverence. With his lips pressed lightly to the second, Thierry held there, eyes closed, as he breathed and attempted to draw courage. "Stand!"

Thierry lingered a moment longer, seemingly wary to rise and leave the security of his place on the floor. Getting slowly to his feet, he stood with his arms clasped behind his back, chin up, eyes down, lips sealed tightly as he took jagged, shallow breaths through his nose.

"Do you trust Master Elet?" David asked.

"Yes, sir," Thierry replied with enthusiasm.

"Mmm. Then why are you crying?"

Thierry's jaw worked. His eyes blinked rapidly. One more tear got away from him as he sniffed. There was still so much pride there, David marveled to see it. There was potential. So much of it, if only....

"I'm, uh," his voice failed him, breaking off with a sigh. He tried again after clearing his throat. "I'm scared, sir. And...."

"And what?"

Thierry rolled his eyes, then closed them, muttering silently to himself. "Ashamed," he managed, quietly.

"Ashamed of the way you hurt Eric, or ashamed of what I'm about to do to you?" Elet challenged with a growl.

Thierry seemed to grow pale.

"It's an honor to take your Master's cock," David reminded their slave. "One that young Eric has already enjoyed, happily. Of course, that's not the only honor you'll be enjoying this evening, so you'll be staying with me, as we've discussed, during your recovery. You'll receive the very best treatment by my staff of nurses and Dr. Wilkenson. Master Elet and I will remain here to ensure your comfort."

"Yessir," Thierry replied. "Thank you."

They got him in position on the table, lying on his back. His ankles were shackled, the chains pulled tight enough that his legs were bent sharply back toward his head, a spreader bar keeping his thighs far apart. With his legs immobilized, unable to move in any direction, Thierry next had his arms shackled loosely above his head. A strap wound across his chest, pinning him down. A collar around his neck was chained loosely to the table as well. The position pulled his ass wide open, tipped up as if eager to get fucked. His balls and cock were equally exposed and vulnerable, lying softly against his pelvis.

Elet undressed while David spoke with Thierry.

"What's your safeword?"

"Sarah," Thierry answered somewhat shyly.

Sarah was Thierry's cat. It was one of the little discoveries about him that had warmed David to him. David thought it was quite an endearing choice. Thierry switched off between Sarah and Red as his safewords, depending on how afraid he was, and who was watching.

"I won't leave you, okay?" David assured him, leaning in to kiss Thierry's forehead. Closing his eyes with a sigh, Thierry frowned and nuzzled against David's face when he lingered, getting closer. David rested a hand on the underside of Thierry's right calf, caressing gently.

"Thank you, Master David," Thierry said.

Two fingers, thickly coated with lube, entered him, smearing around. Thierry grunted, then expelled a heavy breath, his mouth working soundlessly around the fear, like it was strangling him. The fingers reached deeply, pushing in to the hilt, pulling out for more lube, then pressed back in, corkscrewing around to pry him loose. Thierry, David noticed, was avoiding looking at the ceiling, so that he didn't see Elet, or his huge cock, as he was prepped to receive.

The more Elet worked his hand in Thierry's passage, grinding it into him, the more Thierry's cock responded, twitching with interest despite his nervousness. Taking hold of it, Elet began to stroke Thierry hard and added a third finger. Moaning heavily, Thierry clenched briefly around the fingers nestled in the pink ring of his hole, rolling his hips into Elet's tugs with closed eyes and a small frown.

Once his fingers were moving steadily, Elet buried them completely. His hand, wrapping and tugging on Thierry's erection, quickened its pace, going faster and faster until Thierry cried out, his thighs, his arms, his stomach all tensed up, the muscles clenched. He smacked his head back against the table once, his eyes rolling, hissing between his teeth as he fought it.

It sounded as if the orgasm was ripped from him against his will the way he gasped. Semen shot from his slit, slicking Elet's fingers, dripping onto Thierry's abdomen.

David glanced up. Elet was already wearing a condom, his cock coated in lubricant. Before Thierry had even a moment to come down, Elet touched the tip of his cockhead to Thierry's opening, then spread it wide with both hands palming Thierry's cheeks. The sight of such a dark, heavy, steely cock, the size of a small arm, aligned with the paler ass of the boy on the table was captivating. It didn't seem possible it would ever fit inside.

Before Thierry could anticipate it and tense up again, Elet thrust the bulbous head through the tiny ring of muscle. It parted reluctantly around the thickness pressing hard for entry. Suddenly, it was through and Thierry yelled roughly. The sound was thick, raw and frantic, coming from way down low. His chest heaved, and he managed to pull his legs even further back as if he could ease the ache that way. Elet was firmly lodged in him, their bodies joined, the entire length of his shaft left to take possession of young Thierry's slim body.

With the thickest part through, Elet slowed down, giving Thierry time to adjust. While Elet smeared a handful of lube around Thierry's stretched-smooth rim and up his own shaft, Thierry begged, hoarsely, *"Take it out. Take it fucking out!* I'm sorry about Eric!!" The pitch of his voice climbed, became shrill.

"Slow your breathing," David said soothingly. "Fill your lungs.

Hold the air. Bite down."

He placed a leather strap between Thierry's teeth. Instantly, Thierry bit down as hard as he could.

Elet thrust just firmly enough to begin to go deeper. Thierry's eyes grew wide. He made a choked sound.

"Exhale. Now, slave."

Elet paused as Thierry finished exhaling. When he drew in a new breath, Elet pulled back a little, the thick, dark, wet shaft expelling slightly from Thierry's body.

"Hold it."

Elet thrust again, going further, getting a few more inches inside. He caressed the undersides of Thierry's thighs, then up past his hips to his sides, back down again. Humming with pleasure, Elet tugged back and did it again, working to claim.

Thierry kept practicing deep breathing, and it seemed to help him. The inward thrusts made Thierry frantic each time, yelling sharply and straining against the bindings. This was likely due to the drag of Elet's cock over Thierry's oversensitive gland so soon after his orgasm. Elet continuously caressed Thierry's lower half, soothing him. David stayed in Thierry's sight but now kept his hands off so that their slave was focused solely on the Master in charge. Then, hesitantly, Thierry's gaze slid from David to the ceiling, just as Elet was pulling back. The subsequent inward thrust saw more than half his length sheathed.

Thierry grunted hard, bearing down, red-faced, shaking his head back and forth.

"Mmm, better than I hoped, *chéri*," Elet hummed. "Is this why you've been playing shy?"

He pulled back, then thrust the deepest he'd gone yet. With a keening cry, Thierry arched his back, tossing his head backward, as much as he could in his bonds. He breathed heavily through his nose, in little panting gasps. The leather strap was still between his teeth, and David saw him grind down on it. Reaching out, David caressed Thierry's jaw. Instantly, Thierry turned toward the touch, seeming to need it.

Covered in a thin layer of sweat, Thierry lost focus on everything. His eyes glazed over as Elet burrowed the rest of the way into him, then held there, caressing, kneading the muscle of Thierry's ass. His penis was soft, but when Elet wrapped a hand around it, Thierry moaned thickly, frowning, almost fighting it as Elet coaxed him stiff again.

Slowly, Elet drew back, pressed in, did it again, taking longer strokes each time. Thierry receded even further into himself, mouth slack, grunting thickly on each push, his body loose but trembling. David removed the leather strap, kissed Thierry's cheek. There was no reaction. All he knew was Elet, and the massive thickness taking him apart in very real ways.

It went on and on. When Thierry was once more stiff, swollen, and red inside Elet's grip, his moans grew more powerful. He fought the pleasure, writhing and tensing in his bonds. He pushed down against Elet but, strapped down and spread as he was, Thierry was unable to affect the steady, slow movement of the huge cock sliding easily in and out of him. He couldn't stop it, change it, do anything but take it. The only thing that would end the ache and humiliation was a single word.

His cries grew more animalistic. Subtly, he began to rock into every thrust, meeting it, urging Elet on. Elet squeezed up tightly, stopping just under the ridge of Thierry's cock, shaking it a little. Pearly white semen erupted in an arc from the flushed skin, leaving Thierry gasping, unable to catch his breath.

David fetched a cool cloth and held it against Thierry's brow.

Elet pulled out completely and walked around to catch his slave's gaze. Thierry stared at Elet's stiff cock, jutting up in the air and colored a deep, dark purple. It waved around in front of him with each step like a mast. Captivated, Thierry moaned softly.

"What do you say, *chéri?*"

"More, please, Master." It was soft, weak, beaten down.

Elet walked back around to the foot of the table. He pressed a button to raise the angle. Thierry gazed down between his legs, now with a better view of what was about to happen.

He made a sharp gasp, his lower lip quivering sweetly as Elet slid back in, parting the pink, wet, loose muscle gripping it. The cock fit back in him like it belonged there, was always meant to be there. Thierry's feet were flexed, his posture inviting as Elet bottomed out with the first thrust.

Elet took him harder, with growls and more force, pounding Thierry's ass, not holding anything back. It made David so hard, watching that, aching for Thierry, but drinking down each sign of his struggle to bear it like the sweetest wine.

Buried, Elet slammed in, in, in, and sighed heavily with his climax. Thierry could only breathe and lie there, whimpering softly.

Elet pulled out, removed the condom, and wiped himself down. It only took a moment.

Next, David helped Elet put a latex glove on his right hand, which Elet then slicked with lube, all the way up to the elbow.

A tear slipped from the corner of Thierry's eye. David went to him and held his hands, pressing a kiss to his temple. Thierry's fingers wrapped tightly around David's hand.

"What do we say, *chéri*?"

Thierry grunted, too far beyond words to speak.

Elet slid his tapered hand through the swollen, flushed, stretched-loose opening. It went in easily until his knuckles caught on the rim.

"Bear down, *chéri*," Elet coaxed, tenderly. "Harder now. Push through the pain, I know you can do this."

Two more tears slipped down his cheeks. He gripped David's hands tightly.

The knuckles passed through, the rest of the hand breaching him. David stared as Elet's whole hand disappeared into Thierry's ass, passing into him to the wrist. Thierry cried out roughly.

Elet caught David's eye, nodded subtly.

David squeezed Thierry's hand, leaned down to press his lips against Thierry's head and braced himself.

The scream was raw; a ragged scraping of vocal chords, as Elet formed his fingers into a fist, then began to pump. Fucking Thierry with the fist, Elet bared his teeth, moving steadily, but carefully. Affectionate caresses from Elet's free hand moved over Thierry's body. They were a reward that had been hard-earned, but clearly worth quite a lot to Thierry, who gave a faint, honest smile despite the pain. With pleasure and relief, David watched the exchange between them.

Thierry was knocked up the table with each inward push, pulled slightly down it with every withdrawal. He never stopped yelling, even when he had no voice left, and it was only wheezing, desperate sighs. They found a rhythm. Thierry melted into Elet's touches, both rough and tender. Unable to hold off any longer, David opened his pants and worked himself at speed, coming with a relieved sigh. Thierry extended his tongue to catch as much of it as he could, turning his face toward David and opening his mouth widely. David aimed for his lips and tongue, and Thierry moaned, licking it all away, then sucked the taste from his lips.

The shackles were undone by David, the spreader bar removed as well. He held Thierry's legs, limp in his hands, as Elet finally removed his arm from Thierry, who shuddered intensely, then lost consciousness.

As David wiped Thierry's sweat-speckled brow with a cool cloth, Elet leaned in to kiss his slave's flushed cheek. A gurney was wheeled in. With help from two nurses, they shifted him over, then accompanied him over to the medical suite, leaving the room behind for David's staff to clean and sterilize.

In the medical suite, Thierry's vital signs were checked. The doctor did a brief examination of Thierry's rectal muscles. There was no tearing, but it would be a few days until the muscles recovered from the trauma they'd endured and tightened back up. Elet and David helped the nurses wipe Thierry down, then dressed him in a diaper. David suspected that was what Thierry had been dreading most—a severe blow to his precious pride—so was glad for him that he slept through that part of the process.

He was tucked in a bed, attached to monitors, just in case, and left to sleep. Elet insisted on taking the first shift, settling into a chair by the bedside, holding Thierry's hand while he rested.

Chapter 19
Playing by the Rules

Days bled together while David immersed himself in the tasks of managing his usual workload. The last breath of winter was lost in the drenching rain of spring. He oversaw his property holdings during the day and Manse at night. This was coupled with the additional stress of communicating with his father via messages relayed staff member to staff member in a professional whisper-down-the-lane type fashion, rather than humoring any sort of notion of talking with the man directly. Added on top of all of that, surmounting all of it, was the need to continue monitoring Shea's healing process and safety at all times, twenty-four hours a day, seven days a week.

There was little energy left over at the end of each day — which tended to fall somewhere in the middle of the night — for any sort of sexual escapades with David's usual cadre of slaves, or for romancing Shea the way David knew he deserved. The frustration of trying to do too much in not nearly enough time set him on edge, but there was nothing on his plate of responsibilities that he could relinquish. David's staff assumed as much of the burden as he would allow in order to lighten his load, but being busy also helped him avoid facing some difficult decisions and hard truths.

One afternoon, while thinking he was overdue to pay a visit to Thierry, David emerged from his private elevator onto the third floor of his home. Loosening his tie, then running his fingers through his hair, he tried to shrug off some of the invisible but sizable weight on his shoulders which was causing him to feel exhausted. His carefully polished shoes tapped softly against the wood floors as he walked toward the kitchen, his pace slowing steadily, then quickening once he realized what he was seeing.

"What are you doing out of bed?" he asked with concern, his voice thinned slightly by the degree of his tiredness. "You should be resting."

Shea laughed, smiling crookedly as he tapped a handful of playing cards against the tabletop. Clearing his throat and raising an eyebrow, he tried on a serious expression and said solemnly, with dripping sarcasm, "Of course, Mr. Davenport, sir. I'll continue to seclude myself in my chambers if that's what you wish." Then he bowed as deeply as he could manage while sitting on a chair pulled up close to the kitchen table, so that his forehead almost touched the table's surface.

David worked hard not to laugh, his mood instantly lightening. Logically, he knew he shouldn't encourage his fledgling submissive to behave like a smartass, but it really was funny. Mrs. Tinsley bought David's stern act, though.

"Oh, give the poor child a break, sir," Mrs. Tinsley encouraged, getting up from her chair and setting her stack of cards down — face down. "He's had no one to talk to — "

" — I've had *no one* to talk to," Shea agreed heavily.

" — And he's lonely," Mrs. Tinsley finished.

"I'm *so* lonely."

"Please don't start singing," David begged, barely stifling a laugh.

"Not likely to happen. I'm a dancer, not a singer."

"If you say so."

"Hey!"

"Have a seat, sir," Mrs. Tinsley said, pulling out a chair for him. "Let me get you a fresh cup of coffee."

She hurried away, giving them their privacy.

David found himself evaluating Shea's condition. The scrapes along his jaw from the mugging were disappearing. The bruising from the attack at the hotel was also fading. There was still the bandage on his left arm, hiding the most severe damage. He looked well enough; though maybe a little too thin, too pale, and tired.

"Look, can we talk?" Shea asked with a bowed head while fiddling with the cards. Sometimes David forgot Shea was barely an adult at all, just a teenager. There was a maturity beyond his years about him, beneath his usually persistent lightheartedness. That was why, despite the slight age difference between them and the exceedingly different lives they'd each led so far, David could relate to Shea remarkably well.

Shea's gaze flicked around to the various guards. There was one stationed at the elevator doors, another nearer to them. That would be the guard assigned to Shea's room, following him rather than sticking with his post.

"Of course," David agreed, finally sitting in the chair across from Shea. "What's on your mind?"

"It's just that," he chuckled a little nervously, resting his head on one hand, "you know in movies how the hero secludes the civilians in some safe bunker type place out of the way of all the action? And kind of just leaves them in there until after he's fought the evil villains, the dust settles, and he's handled everything himself? I'm in the bunker, David. It's making me kind of nuts." He held out a hand, palm out, to David, explaining, "I know why you're trying to protect me, and I appreciate it, but I don't even know who you're protecting me from. I'm pretty much the least important person in the whole world."

David masked his expression carefully, thinking of the unmarked cars, which Shea had no knowledge of yet. They had been constantly present at the perimeter of the property.

"Yeah, I got in the way with your dad after he saw us together," Shea continued, obliviously, "but it's over, and I haven't set foot outside this... mansion... since you had me carried in, unconscious. I don't even know what the outside of the building looks like, or where we are, exactly. Daisy kind of described the drive to me, but I'm stir-crazy. And, you know, what happened to my *life*? I used to have an apartment, a job, a car that didn't run, friends. I can't stay in the bunker forever. When I leave it, is there going to be anything left? Or is it all rubble? And I don't have anything of my own. I just need to know what's going on, because you've had me staying in that room, under guard. I don't get to be with you very much, or sleep next to you. I know you've been busy, but I feel like even so, if you really wanted to be around me, you would. But you haven't, so I'm taking the hint, okay? I'll get out of your hair if you don't want me around, but, I mean, I don't have anywhere to live, or a way to support myself, and having at least one of those things covered at all times has been the only thing getting me through the rough spots. And let me tell ya, there have been one hell of a lot of rough spots."

There was a contained, frantic energy to the way he'd explained himself. Shea glanced around at the guards he could see from where he was sitting, but security was trained and selected for their discretion, so there was no eye contact, no sign that they'd heard anything.

David said slowly, "I see."

Where could he start? There was so much to say. But, as with all of David's important conversations, he was aware there was a correct order in which things should be explained for maximum clarity and efficiency. The last thing Shea needed was more worry.

"I'm feeling better," Shea added more quietly. "A lot better. So, can I go? Visit some people I haven't seen in weeks? Get some fresh air? Daisy relayed a message to me the other day, when you were out. One of my friends from high school has a couch I can crash on, and she'd only charge me like three hundred a month, since it's not an actual bedroom. She's an EMT, and has a dog, so I could help her take it for walks when her hours are weird. Seems like the best choice for me right now. I also need to stop by Teresa's and speak to the manager, probably do some groveling. Maybe I could have my job back, if—"

"I should have explained earlier," David interrupted, gently. "And that's my fault. I've just been so busy. I want you to live with *me*, Shea. I want this to be your home. It's one where you will always be safe, and it will always be here for you. There will no longer be any need to wonder if you'll still have a bed, or food, or any other basic need."

"Oh," Shea said quietly, sitting up a little straighter.

"This isn't something I've ever done before—asking a lover to move in with me. I don't think I've ever *had* a lover before, actually, only slaves. You're so much more than that." Shea didn't say anything. He just chewed on his lip, his eyes wide with his rapt attention, watching David carefully. So, David plowed on, taking a page from Shea's book and over-explaining himself to cover a sudden surge of nervous certainty that Shea would refuse the offer.

"You mean a lot to me, Shea, and when something or someone means a lot to me... Look at my businesses. I purchase land, develop various types of properties on it, watch them grow, fill with life, and hold them. They're investments. And Manse — my passion — is my way of giving back to my community. Now that I've established this place, I intend it to be here for a long, long time. I know you're very young to be moving in with a lover. I'm not surprised that you're restless. But think of how old I am. I'm twenty-five, Shea. At my age, most people are still figuring out what sort of job they'd like to do, or are still in college. And, meanwhile, I have —"

"An empire," Shea answered softly. "Am I one of your investments now?"

"I don't give my heart away lightly," David told him, imbuing the words with as much emotion as he felt. "I... I believe I'm falling in love with you, Shea. I want to have things with you I've never considered before. Yes, you need a safe place. I would love to offer you that. All I ask in return is for your trust and patience as we figure out our way, together. I'm not convinced that I deserve you. Not after what I've put you through because of my negligence."

"David," Shea breathed. He sputtered a little, then said, "I don't know what to say. I know you don't say things without meaning them. You do really mean that, don't you?"

"I do," David answered, letting Shea search his eyes for the truth.

"I told you I'd fall with you, didn't I?" Shea said. "And I am. I have. It's just... I feel like you're over-thinking this. I get that you're very formal about everything, which by the way is the polar opposite of me, because hello — I've never been formal once in my life. I kind of understand what you're saying here, but — can you explain it to me a little more? As simply as you can?" Shea asked. "I swear I'm not an idiot, but... Do you want me to be your sex slave? Your live-in boyfriend? Both? Am I your kept boy now? I can't just live off of you and hide away behind enormous, armed guards at all times. I'm sure for some people that would be an *awesome* way to live, but it's not who I am. I'm a normal kid. I love to work, and have a reason to be proud of the job I've done. I love having responsibilities and paystubs. I *dream* of getting my car running again, and going grocery shopping with more than five bucks in my wallet. If I'm with you, do I have to give up that stuff?"

"Privilege comes with conditions, and so does a relationship with me, I'm afraid. But I would never ask you to be anyone other than who you authentically are. If you're my lover, my partner, people will find out. They might try to get to me through you, and I can't allow that. I won't risk you like that."

The word 'partner' seemed to make Shea shy or uncertain for a moment, dropping his gaze again to his hands, which David took up, and held.

"Please keep telling me what you're thinking," David asked. "No matter what it is. What do you think?"

"I think I probably don't deserve to be your partner, David, but I would love to be that. I just..." he sighed. "I don't know how to do this."

"That's why I hesitated in having this conversation with you earlier, but this is good. All I want is to take small steps, deciding together what is best for both of us as we progress. This is an adjustment period. Please, bear with me a little longer. If there's any way I can make each one of your wishes come true, I will."

"Wow. I never had anyone offer to grant all of my wishes for me before. The crazy part is you could actually do it, couldn't you? But..."

"What?"

"Am I in danger?" Shea asked.

"There will always be danger."

Shea's head fell forward, between his outstretched arms, his hands still in David's grasp and he laughed a little. "That's not exactly the straight answer I was looking for, you know."

"Do you trust me?" David pressed.

"Yes. Of course I do. I passed that submissive test you gave me, didn't I? I'm totally up for doing that again anytime you want, by the way."

"I'm glad you are. Shea, I'm not interested in changing you," David said emphatically. "I want you to be your own man. All I'm asking is for the privilege of living with your company. Clearly, it's important to you to retain your own identity, and I respect that. Of course you're free to make your own decisions about your life. However, as I've said, being with me has already saddled you with burdens you would not have had to carry otherwise. All that means is that, for the time being, I'm asking you to clear it with me first when you want to leave the premises, so that arrangements can be made."

"Even for a walk around the grounds?"

"Yes. Even that."

"How long is this particular condition of yours going to last?"

David was reading every hint of body language Shea was giving as rules were established. The slightly bowed head, the reluctance to make eye contact, the slumped posture, the softened tone of voice — it all helped ease David into the role he was most comfortable with, that of Master.

"I can't give you a specific answer." David glanced up as Mrs. Tinsley silently walked in, carrying two cups of coffee. She set one down in front of each of them, with the preferred amount of sugar and creamer already added. With a slight bow, she took her leave. David slid his cup closer and savored the warmth of the porcelain heating his palm. "Being my lover is quite dissimilar to any normal situation, and not only because of my wealth, and my family. In love, with sex, there are rules and roles to play."

"You're my Master," Shea supplied, chancing a brief shared look.

"And you're my slave. We urgently need to continue exploring what that means, for your comfort. It's one of the reasons why I haven't yet moved you into my bedroom. I didn't want to pressure you intimately that way. It wouldn't have been fair to you."

"What're the other reasons?" Shea asked, low undertones of anxiety touching his words.

David took a sip of coffee, glanced at his watch. He had time. "Would you be all right with moving this conversation into the bedroom? It would give me a chance to change and I could show you around —"

"David, what are the other reasons?" Shea pressed, sounding tense and maybe even a little upset. David guessed Shea knew the other reason; he just needed David to admit to it.

So be it.

They were essentially as alone as they would ever be, surrounded by staff and guards standing ready to intercede should there be any trouble.

But still... David hesitated.

"Come with me, bring your coffee," he said, standing.

For a moment, David thought maybe Shea would refuse. Then that innate submissiveness in him won out, fascinatingly. He got up, took hold of his coffee with his right hand, favoring his injured arm slightly and tucking it against his body. David watched as Shea faced his pushed-out chair and moved his bad arm slightly, almost pushing the chair back in, before biting his lower lip and bringing his arm even closer to his body than before. David walked around the table and pushed the chair in for Shea, then braced his free hand against the small of Shea's back, guiding him forward and into the hall.

It was a short enough walk to the bedroom, down one hallway to another. Three sets of footsteps echoed off the walls and heavily-varnished floors as Shea's security detail followed along behind.

The bedroom itself had a double-door entry. A member of the house staff had hurried along ahead of them, and threw both doors open, bowing slightly with a muttered, "Mr. Davenport, sir."

The guard stayed in the doorway, facing toward the hall rather than the suite. David watched Shea glance around, taking it all in. There was a sitting area to their left with plush, antique couches and footstools, and a small bar. To their right was the sleeping area, which was quite large. Though the bed was huge and king-sized, it was dwarfed by the space surrounding it. The floors were a dark wood, the linens a crisp white, the furniture and walls done in muted tones. Always one to favor good lighting, David had the space ringed with wall sconces which alternately used real candles and electric ones, depending on his mood. Directly in front of them, beyond the vast sleeping area, was the terrace, outfitted with ornate furniture for lounging or eating, or simply admiring the view. On the far wall to the right was the entry to the washroom.

David set down his coffee, then moved to take Shea's from him as well, setting them both aside on a granite countertop running along the wall, atop a long series of cabinets.

Shea glanced around at all of the various bolts and rings in the walls, ceiling and floors, some with chains and shackles attached and at the ready.

"Well, it's not cozy, but it's definitely impressive," Shea said.

"What's through there?"

He pointed to a set of closed double doors to their left, beyond the bar.

"You'll find out soon enough," David answered. It wasn't the time or place to introduce young, virginal Shea to David's assortment of personal bondage furniture, stored nearby in a large walk-in closet through the doors he'd indicated.

"These guards—I know you've had someone keeping watch for me because of things with your dad, but I thought that was an exception. Are they *always* watching? Even when you're sleeping and, you know, gettin' it on?"

"Always," David agreed. "I urge you to take comfort in that."

"Oh, *so much* comfort," Shea said doubtfully.

"Safety is a key aspect of BDSM," David told him. "The guards in my employ are trained to safeguard not only me, but my submissives as well. They're here not only to protect us from outside threats, but also to ensure BDSM scenes are carried out under supervision. That ensures another layer of protection for both the Dom and the sub.

"I was trained as a Dominant in London, with an organization called the Master's Circle. They taught me everything I know about dominating, submission, bondage, discipline, masochism, and sadism. As I've explained, the key to any relationship between Master and slave is trust and respect. It has to work both ways, at all times. You trust in me, I trust in you. I respect your needs and preferences, and you respect mine. It is my duty, as your Master, to take the best of care of you: mind, body, and soul. I interpret your needs and make decisions accordingly. Your duty as my slave is to obey me, explicitly, and to submit to my will. You let go, in every sense, so that I'm better able to hold you. Control gives me peace, Shea. Orderliness, and a clearly defined set of rules to play by, allow for the greatest freedom.

"Tell me your safeword."

"Captain."

"Good." David moved closer, into Shea's personal space. "Now, having heard that, my security team knows it. Again, if you use your safeword, it is either a withdrawal of your consent to participate in whatever is going on, or a warning that things are getting too intense. If you say the safeword, your Master will stop what he's doing. Security will intercede if necessary to verify that you're okay."

"Okay," Shea said, sounding like he was doing his best to understand and follow where David was leading. He did look a little overwhelmed, though.

David peered into Shea's blue eyes, wanting to touch him, to be with him. He wanted the whole world to fall away and leave them an oasis of peace to get lost in together.

"You're doing so well with all of this, especially since it's all so new to you, but you're not ready. That's the other reason why I didn't move you into my bedroom. You hesitated in pushing your chair in, out of fear for your arm. That's normal, and healthy. You know you're still healing, that you're sore."

David let the words hang in the air between them, giving them a chance to sink in.

"It's not just your arm that was hurt," he continued. Shea dropped his gaze, bowing his head with embarrassment and closing his eyes tightly. "Taking you to bed when you've so recently been sexually abused would have been wrong. Your comfort and safety is more important than my libido."

"I know you're not gonna rape me," Shea said, sounding hurt.

"You experienced a trauma. You were held down, made to yield to things that were...." David couldn't get the rest out, the anger on Shea's behalf choked him. He couldn't bring himself to give voice to imagined acts that played nearly constantly in his mind, uncensored. "I won't encroach upon your space before you're ready."

"What if I say I'm ready?" Shea challenged. "Don't I get to decide that? Being in this place, alone — it's eerie. To say I've never slept someplace this massive is kind of an understatement, so I haven't been sleeping well. Maybe if you...." He struggled, fidgeting slightly. "Maybe if we did that together, it would help. I'm curious and I want to do it. I want to make you happy, too. You're promising to share so much with me, to make me part of your life. I don't have anything to give you in return. I don't even get to see you at the end of the day anymore. If, at least, we could be together like that, it would be something. I'm ready to have sex. I want — *need* to give you that."

"You don't owe me anything, especially not sex."

"But I want to be with you!"

"You are with me, but you're *not ready* to have sex."

"You can't decide that for me!"

Holding Shea's face in both hands, David touched their foreheads together. Sliding a hand down the front of Shea's body to clasp his waist, leaning in to breathe in the scent of his neck, David savored the feel of him, and the fragrance of his natural state. Both were things he'd barely allowed himself to enjoy lately.

Shea's arms hung at his sides, unmoving, not returning the embrace, but he yielded to David's touch.

"I'm trying to tell you," David said in a whisper, lips moving against skin. "*It hurts.* It *always* hurts, but especially the first time. I know from personal experience, and I *won't hurt you* that way. Not after what you went through, because of me."

"You're not going to break me," Shea pleaded. "You keep asking me to trust you, but I do! Just because bad things have happened doesn't mean I need you to protect me from everything, even *you*. I told you I trust you and I meant it. I'm ready. I want you like that. I want to feel you inside me, and give you something that important. *Please.*" "You want to sleep in my bed, be my submissive in more than just name?"

"Yes!"

"You're ready for that?"

"*Yes*," Shea answered urgently.

David let him go, stepped back. Raising his voice, he said, "Then kneel. The scene has begun."

Chapter 20
The Master's Weakness

Shea knelt on the hardwood, his head bowed but eyes wide with a heady rush of adrenaline. He had no idea what was about to happen or what David was thinking, intending, or planning. After mentioning his wariness to hurt Shea, it wasn't really clear how he would try to get hot and heavy, especially in that ridiculous bedroom of his. It was bigger than all of Shea's bedrooms, ever, combined. It might even have been bigger than all of his houses and apartments combined. It was the opposite of intimate, at least from Shea's embarrassingly limited experience.

David wandered over to the cabinets where their coffee had been abandoned to sit and cool, unconsumed. Opening a door, pulling out a drawer, he retrieved something shiny which Shea couldn't quite make out, running it through his hands almost reverently before closing things up again. Then, slowly, he brought whatever it was to where Shea was kneeling.

David held it out for him to see. It was a smooth, circular band of polished, platinum silver metal, with a D ring and a engraved tag attached to it.

"What is it?" Shea whispered, still feeling out of the loop or like he was merely pretending to understand pretty much everything that was happening.

"Manners, slave. We are in a scene. Address me as Master or sir."

"Oh, right. Um, what is it, *sir*?"

"It's a collar. One made specifically for you."

With the edge of his thumb, David lifted the engraved tag for Shea to read. It had David's name etched into it, along with an ID number.

David made no move to put it on Shea. He was just watching Shea look at it, and Shea was glancing between David and the collar, still trying to understand.

"Is it for going out? Like you collar a dog for walks? I swear I'm not going to run off chasing squirrels or anything, but I'm pretty sure if I got lost I could tell whoever found me how to get me home again. Well, once I have a better idea of where we are, I could. Sir."

David cracked a smile, then cleared his throat and attempted a serious expression. He wasn't quite successful.

"Have I told you how much I adore you?" David asked.

"Yes, I think so. Sir. I'm supposed to keep saying, 'sir,' right? Sir?"

At that point Shea suspected he heard the guard at the door stifle a chuckle, which wasn't entirely appreciated. Shea frowned at him from over a shoulder.

It took David a few attempts at a serious expression before he managed one.

"It's not like a dog collar," he explained. "When a Master collars a slave, it's a sign of how committed they are to one another. It's a high-ly respected bond. Of all of the Masters who visit Manse, I know of only two who have collared slaves, and I have never claimed a slave like this. If you would wear this, everyone who sees you will know that you're mine, and fall under my protection." He took a breath and softened a little, turning his face slightly away. "It's a little selfish of me, too. I want them to know you're mine. I don't want them touching you without my permission. I don't even want them looking at you without understanding you're off limits."

Shea raised his hand in the air.

David grinned. "You don't, um — Yes, slave?"

Shea put his arm down. He was a little excited that he'd started to get a handle on it all, and it came through in his rambling questions. "So, it's like an engagement ring, sir? In a commitment sort of way? Or, like a letter jacket? Do they still make letter jackets? But, you know what I mean. The jock asks the cheerleader to go steady and lets her wear the jacket. I realize that makes me the cheerleader, but I'm okay with it. There are male cheerleaders. Sir. Did you know President

Bush was a cheerleader? That totally blows my mind."

Perking up attentively, he waited for David's answer. Behind him, the guard coughed suspiciously, like he was trying not to laugh again.

"It's much more meaningful than an engagement ring," David explained. "An engagement ring is given with the understanding that there will, someday, be a marriage or commitment ceremony. It's a placeholder. A collar is a vow. It's me, swearing to you, that I'll protect and care for you, with all of my heart, all of my being, and everything I have. And, just as a marriage carries a certain weight in public society, when a slave is collared, that carries a significant amount of weight in the BDSM community, and with the Master's Circle. It's respected, and honored. If anyone disrespects you, as my collared slave, there will be consequences and repercussions."

"Huh."

"I'm sorry, I don't understand, 'huh.'"

"Sorry, sorry. Right. Sir."

"Will you wear my collar, Shea?"

Shea smiled. David really was cute when he was being earnestly romantic. There was a vulnerable sort of hopefulness in his green eyes that was completely irresistible.

"Yes. I will," Shea agreed.

David smiled back at him, bashfully. "Fantastic," he replied, trying not to appear as happy as he seemed to feel, which, in turn, made Shea happy to cause such a reaction.

Stepping forward, David opened the collar to gently fit it around Shea's neck, closing and locking it once it rested comfortably there.

"Some other collars have several rings to allow for bondage. But you're new to all of this, and your collar is more for symbolic reasons than practical ones anyway. This collar also contains a tracking device, so my staff is aware of your location at all times. That's why it will be essential for you to wear it whenever you leave this floor, for a little while, anyway."

That part was a little spooky. Shea tried to interpret David's expression and the determined look in his light eyes while he arranged the fastened collar on Shea. He really did think Shea was in danger, then. As much as the evidence was right there, in David's words and actions, Shea couldn't help thinking it was all paranoia from living under such heavy security for so long. In a way, it made Shea feel bad for David, to worry so constantly about things that were not even really a threat. It made Shea yearn to bring David into *his* world for a little while, and live as a normal guy, just to see what it was like, how the possibilities opened up before you.

As Shea drew in a more filling breath, though, and the metal pulled tight around his throat, inhibiting his ability to breathe as deeply, he was reminded of how improbable that dream had become. He truly was in David's world. There was no going back.

And that made him sad, yet more resolved to add normalcy to David's everyday life as often as he could manage.

David finished with the collar and stood before Shea, exuding power and beauty. It seemed to shine from him, coming so effortlessly that it only enhanced Shea's feeling of weakness. Or, instead, maybe it just enhanced Shea's awareness of how much he wanted David to take control of him.

"Go lie on the bed, slave," David said in command, though his gaze was filled with affection and love.

As Shea stood, then walked to the bed, it struck him, again, how improbable it was, to belong to such a man as David. Shea was a cast-off, an unwanted failure of a son, a near-homeless, talentless nobody, yet there he was, in David Davenport's mansion, with David's name against his throat, lest anyone get any *ideas*.

He would have laughed, but as he lay down on his back, his legs hanging over the edge, instinct urged him to fight.

Hands on my wrist and shoulder, spreading my arms, pinning me down, then pain, then fear...

Breathing hard, Shea sat up again, tucking his left arm against his body protectively. His head was swimming a little, as though someone had spun it like a top. But then David was right there, standing in front of him, his legs straddling Shea's knees. David was holding Shea by the jaw and the shoulder, kissing the top of his head. "Shhh. Easy now, sweetheart. Try to control your breathing. Slow it down. Remember where you are. You're safe."

"I could *feel them* holding me down."

"I know. That's why there will be no bondage for you. Not today and not for a little while. All I ask is that you trust me to understand your limits and boundaries, and do your best to follow my instructions. Would you like to try that?"

"Okay," Shea murmured, calming down thanks to the breathing exercises.

"Take off your shirt. Be careful of your arm."

When Shea had managed to get it over his head and off, David took it from him and tossed it aside.

"Lie down. Arms tucked against your sides. I don't want to strain the muscles yet."

Shea tried lying down again. Keeping his arms down helped lessen the panic.

"Eyes on me at all times, slave," David instructed. "I need you to know who's touching you and why. Stay out of your head. Stay in the moment."

"Yes, sir."

"Good," David smiled. He leaned down over Shea, his hands planted on the bed at Shea's sides, and kissed his lips gently. It was skin brushing skin, lightly enough to make Shea shiver, goosebumps pebbling his skin from head to toe, making it feel tighter on his body. The nearness of David and the heat radiating from him warmed Shea at the same time, making his blood rush a little harder, flushing the skin. He glimpsed the bare, tan skin beneath David's partially unbuttoned shirt. It made his breathing quicken, his mouth watering, wanting to kiss, to taste him there, too.

But David held Shea's jaw in a hand, keeping Shea's mouth where David wanted it to be. The tip of David's tongue teased at the center of Shea's lower lip, and a hot spark of want shot down the center of Shea's body, stiffening his nipples, tensing the muscles of his stomach, stirring his cock.

"I want you *hard*, slave," David ordered in a wicked whisper right before he licked into Shea's mouth, opening him wide for a deep, probing kiss. It made Shea moan into David's mouth, his jaw working around David's tongue. Like his dick had just been waiting for David to say those words, it swelled, growing fuller in seconds, heeding David's wish. "When we're together, I prefer you to be hard and wanting. Do you understand?"

"Yes, sir," Shea gasped between delving strokes of David's tongue, nips of his teeth at Shea's lips.

There was a breath of space between their bodies, the only contact being at their mouths, and David's hand on Shea's jaw. Like it was trying to bridge the gap, Shea's cock only got harder, straining upward, tenting his thin, loose pants. He wasn't wearing underwear. There was nothing to contain him, and the thin cotton fabric slipping against the hot, aching skin of Shea's cock, the friction tickling lightly, only made it feel better.

David's lips dragged backward along Shea's jaw to his ear. They closed on his earlobe in a kiss, then he bit down with teeth.

Pre-come wept from Shea's slit, dampening the fabric. David bit down harder and the wet spot grew. Shea's hands flattened, palms down, against the bed, grasping, trying to be still, not really wanting to be still. The urge to thrust and to embrace David was strong. But Shea knew David expected him to do only what he was told. David was *trying* to arouse him, and it was working.

David mouthed downward from earlobe to neck and teased the skin there with the tip of his tongue. Shea's neck was bared to allow him access. The tease of the hot, wet muscle against skin was followed by the scrape of David's teeth, the press of his lips. All of the blood in Shea's body funneled down to his cock, pooling there, filling it so completely that it felt like all of him was just straining, pushing up through his balls and shaft.

But David wasn't touching him there. The teasing at his neck, directly above the new collar, went on until Shea grew dizzy, panting, "*Please.*"

"Is your cock hard, slave?" David asked, pulling back to look Shea in the eyes.

Shea chuckled weakly, embarrassed by how easily David turned him on. Quietly, he answered, "Yes, sir."

"No, *show me*, slave."

"Fuck." Shea untied the pants, then hooked his thumbs in the waistband. Pulling it away from his body, then down, he stretched it out around his erection, getting the fabric down below his balls. He was privately a little glad David was on top of him, blocking the view of the guard by the door and anyone else who might come by.

He didn't really want to glance downward, but did, quickly, and groaned behind sealed lips. It was so much worse than he'd thought. His dick was so hard, it was a purplish red, the head slick, his balls drawn up tight to his body, feeling swollen and heavy.

David said nothing, just scrutinized Shea's expression, the blood close to the surface under his skin, turning it pink. He stared at Shea's cock as he straightened, then got off the bed, leaving Shea there, exposed.

Wordlessly, David took hold of the white pants and drew them off of Shea, leaving him naked.

A hard shiver worked its way through Shea's body while, simultaneously, somehow his dick got harder. It was an intolerable rigidity between his thighs, an obscene exclamation point punctuating how easily manipulated he was. Shea closed his eyes rather than witness David staring at his genitals.

"I didn't give you permission to break eye contact, slave. I told you, I need you to stay in the moment. You look at me. Eyes open."

"Sorry."

"Sorry, what?"

"Sorry, *sir*."

"Bring your legs up onto the bed, bent at the knees, that's it. Now let them fall open. All the way. More than that. Good."

The pose completely exposed him — his balls, his cock, his hole — and on that field of white that was David's bed, it was like being under a spotlight. It became suddenly almost too difficult to maintain eye contact. His face was so hot with shame it was like he had a fever again.

"There's no reason to be shy, here, slave," David told him. "You should *want* your Master's attention. Your body is so sexy, and being displayed like this only reminds me of how lucky I am. Seeing you, completely exposed, wanting me, waiting for my touch, is everything I'm asking of you. It makes me *very* happy. You *want* your Master to be happy, slave."

"Yes, sir." It felt like one of the most difficult things he'd ever had to do, to lie there like that while David examined him, and not even be able to look away or block it out. Shea had always needed to hide this part of himself. His desire for men, his body, and sexuality in general were what troubled him most. It had caused *all* of his worst problems. It had lost him his family, and gained him unwanted attention from cruel people. It had deprived him of every chance he had at being normal, and robbed him of every possible advantage.

Except for David. It *had* gotten him David.

Cloud cover was robbing them of sunlight, so David wandered a few feet away and found a remote which he used to light the sconces around them. They cast a warm, golden glow, lighting up Shea's body in new ways. Next, David retrieved a small bottle from the cabinets. Pouring some of the contents onto a hand, he approached the bed. He stood at the foot of it, between Shea's spread thighs. His wet palm wrapped Shea's aching cock. Stroking it with slow, complete tugs from root to tip, the head vanished into David's closed fist. Then he stroked back down again only to repeat the process. David hummed with a faint, pleased grin, watching his hand work. It made wet squelching sounds as the lubricant was squeezed between David's fingers and Shea's cock.

Shea pushed upward into David's hand, grunting thickly, shuddering.

"No, lie still," David scolded. When Shea didn't obey quickly enough, David gave Shea's cock a firm slap.

All of the air left his lungs at once.

"I said, lie still."

Shea growled through the ache, thighs quivering as he fought to stop moving and not close his legs.

He needed to come so badly, he was pretty sure if he even just kept looking at David looking at his cock, he would come. It was that hot. The pose made it feel like he was presenting his dick for servicing, which Shea guessed was the truth.

After two more strokes, David let go. Shea let out an exasperated whine through gritted teeth, riding the razor-thin edge separating him from climax.

"*Don't stop,*" Shea begged, nearly sobbing.

"Quiet."

David fondled Shea's balls, then rubbed behind them with two fingers, from the patch of skin there, down through the crack of his ass, over his hole, up the rest of the way and back.

"Are you experiencing any soreness?"

"Yes!"

"That's not what I meant, and you know it," David retorted with a glance up at Shea's face before resuming his focused scrutiny of Shea's dick and balls.

Then, the pad of David's middle finger came to rest on Shea's hole, pressing at it. He rubbed back and forth a little to tease open the muscle. Shea hummed, biting at his lip and frowning. The sense memory of being fingered by those thugs came back.

"Look at me, slave," David said sharply.

Shea hadn't realized he'd closed his eyes. Holding his gaze, David slid the finger up Shea's ass. Self-conscious, Shea clenched on the finger in flutters, not familiar enough with the sensation of being breached to know what to do or how to be comfortable enough with it to endure it without reaction. Immediately, he was breathing roughly, chest rising and falling heavily. That pressure inside him, from David's finger filling him, overpowered everything else.

David held it in him to the hilt, then began working it in and out of him, pumping the finger inside the snug ring of muscle.

"You don't like that very much, do you?" David observed.

The finger rubbed at him and twisted around, feeling him out. In his peripheral vision, Shea saw the guard at the door witnessing him getting finger fucked.

He opened his mouth to reply, to argue, but all that came out was a keening, breathless whimper.

David leaned down over him, closing the gap and kissing him lightly, lingeringly, like the sounds of Shea's whimpers lured him in. "I love to listen to you. So fucking gorgeous," he moaned.

He buried the finger completely, rubbing with the rest of his hand, gently, over the underside of Shea's groin and the side of his ass. He placed a gentle kiss to Shea's gasping mouth, nuzzled his cheek. "That's it. Clench on it. Take a deep breath. Steady yourself."

He filled his lungs with the faded scent of David's cologne, tensing up on the finger inside him, focusing on David's trail of feather-light kisses over his jaw.

"Better?"

Shea nodded. The finger resumed its pumping. Shea moaned

against David's cheek.

"This is why I haven't pressed you for sex," David told him, staying close, allowing Shea to bury his face in David's heat and solidity. "You're still recovering. There's more fear than lust. I want you to *need* it. I want you so desperate for my cock, you can't think of anything else, and you're willing to do *anything* to get it. I want you begging and shameless, not afraid and uncomfortable. Okay?"

"Yes, sir," Shea murmured.

"Should I try to guess what you want, or would you like to tell me?"

Shea licked his lips, panting softly against David's cheek, frowning against the feel of that sliding, constantly probing digit. Strangely, as much as it disturbed him to be touched like that, he didn't want David to stop. Every inward pump, filling him up again, also seemed to fill his cock, causing it to twitch and jump, begging for attention.

"Guess," Shea said on the exhale, adding, "Master."

David slipped the finger out and reached for his fly, crawling up Shea's body. Moaning heavily as David freed his cock from his pants, Shea begged, "Please let me touch you, Master."

David pressed his cock downward once it had sprung free, arching up in a tight curve to his belly.

Feeling greedy, Shea brought his right arm—the one that wasn't sore and aching when he lifted it—upward, using the hand to steady David's flesh. Shea stroked it, loving the slide of the silken, steely cock, thick and long and gorgeous, between his fingers, over his palm. He wanted nothing but to pet it and fondle it for hours, for *days*.

David leaned down over him, bracing an arm on the bed, curling his body around Shea. Eagerly, Shea nuzzled David's cock, sighing heavily when it slid against his cheek, leaving a trail of wetness. Kissing over the shaft, then taking a lick, Shea shivered and thrust against air, wanting to stroke himself, too, and get off while mouthing David.

"I want to come, touching you," Shea moaned.

"No. Not yet."

So, he shifted the alignment of David's cock, taking the head into his mouth. Sucking the slightly salty taste of it, wrapping his tongue around the head, Shea moaned, stroking the shaft with his hand. The tighter and faster he stroked, the more pre-come coated his tongue.

David thrust shallowly, breathing heavier now, too. Shea lifted his head off the bed, chasing into the thrust. Each inward slide over his tongue, filling his mouth, went deeper than the last. Shea struggled to take it all, wanting to make it good for David. When the head lodged in Shea's throat, he grunted, trying to stay relaxed. David pulled back, caressing Shea's head with a sigh, letting him take a breath, then did it again. He rode Shea's tongue that way, and Shea stayed open, letting David love, take, and use him as needed. The saliva-soaked shaft slid in Shea's hand, still steadying it by the root. Shea's nose and eyes watered from being so thoroughly, deeply face-fucked, and he struggled to keep breathing whenever he got the chance. Though he might not have had any experience with anal, he'd given his share of blowjobs. He used everything he knew to make it good for David, wanting him to feel like he hadn't made a bad decision in including Shea in his life.

Fondling David's sac with his hand, Shea felt the testicles draw up. David's cock stiffened even more as he prepared to unload. Moaning, wanting, needing, Shea tugged on David's sac, then palmed David's bare ass, drawing him in completely as he reached orgasm. The whole load went right down Shea's throat and he swallowed it down. David cursed and thrust, twitching, pushing hard, tensed up from head to toe.

Pulling out, David let Shea breathe. Shea stroked him through it, kissing the inside of his hip, the root of his cock, anywhere he could reach. Breathing hot against sweaty skin, smiling, laughing gently, Shea held David close, needing the moment to draw out as long as David would allow.

"I love you so much," Shea whispered, so happy he couldn't stop smiling.

But David was quiet. He'd stopped moving. Shea continued to embrace and kiss him, even lifting his aching left arm to clasp David's calf.

Then, Shea heard a sniff and a sigh.

"David?"

Finally, he moved, slinking back down Shea's body until they were face to face again. Wearing a somewhat embarrassed, crooked grin, David wiped his bloodshot eyes dry and sniffed again. A couple of fat teardrops escaped him anyway and David averted his gaze. Shea wiped the tears away with the pads of his thumbs, trying to understand.

David shook his head, burying his face against Shea's neck and letting out a quaking exhale.

"Did I do something wrong?"

David pulled back again, searching Shea's eyes, glancing quickly between them. His expression changed, becoming anxious, bare, overwhelmed. Frowning heavily, he kissed Shea, hard. It went on, became rough, possessive, as David gripped him tightly, and took him deeply.

They broke, with Shea's lips throbbing, his body still thrumming with need for David — *all* of David. Whispering by Shea's ear, David said, without an ounce of pride or power, "I never thought I'd find this, or be loved so honestly. *I never....*"

His forehead pressed hard against Shea as his breath hitched and he hissed between gritted teeth. His hand came up to caress the collar, then gripped ferociously under Shea's ear, holding him.

"I won't let them take you. *I won't let them hurt you.*"

David was so angry, he trembled with the force of it in Shea's grasp. Giving in to instinct, Shea soothed, kissed, and let David ride out the emotion.

"Yes, Master," he said softly, obediently, without understanding the reason for David's fear and anger. "I'm here. You have me."

When David was able to pull back, let go, the fire in his eyes astounded Shea. He was sure, then, that David was capable of anything, when it came to safeguarding what was most important to him. He'd do it with teeth and claws, blood and screaming. All of the grace with which he moved and lived, all of his elegance and composure would fall away like the thinnest, gossamer-like film, to reveal the manic beast within.

He slid down Shea's body, hooking his arms under Shea's knees, clasping hands to Shea's thighs. Lovingly, he kissed the soaked, reddened end of Shea's cock, then exhaled heavily, nuzzling it, breathing against the fevered skin. There was so much raw gratitude and pure affection in that kiss, and Shea was so captivated by the plain devotion in his pale, sage-hued eyes, that there was nothing left to do but surrender. David brushed the shaft with his cheek, his eyes closing over with delirious pleasure. Sucking kisses to the head, the side, the root, David let Shea begin to thrust, just rutting, pushing against David's lips, his cheek, his jaw, and the backs of his fingers as they caressed. As soon as Shea was close, David reared up, clamping his hands down on Shea's thighs to hold him still, sucking him down to the root and burying him in his throat.

Shea let out a shattered, raw cry as David swallowed, then growled through his climax as he shook, bucked and came. Pushing all of it down David's throat, Shea grabbed fistfuls of the bedding and fought through it. He felt claimed, owned, possessed. David had gotten inside him, down in Shea's darkest, most unexplored places, and was unraveling key ties holding him together.

Coming down slowly, Shea stared as David hummed with pleasure, letting Shea's dark, wet shaft slide between his stretched lips in slow, long strokes. His hands cupped Shea's ass, kneading.

Finally, Shea was allowed to slip free of David's mouth, leaving him gasping against Shea's inner thigh. For a little while, lying quietly, they had peace.

Chapter 21
David, Powerless

Night fell, hours spun away and David sat at his desk, in his office, behind a locked door. The phone was at his ear. It was a few hours before dawn, but he knew his call would be answered. Maybe Brennan would already be awake, figuring in the time difference. He'd always been an early riser.

On the other end of the line, a wonderfully familiar voice whispered, "Yes?"

"Master," David replied, unable to hold in a fond, vulnerable sort of smile. There was a soft exhale through the phone, a quiet hum, and that's all it took. It was like they were back there again, in the dungeons of the Master's Circle headquarters. The cameras were on; people were watching — important people. There was no privacy, but there had never been any, had there? Of course this would be the same.

Only it wasn't.

Master Dom Brennan had always understood more than David ever expected him to. That's the only reason why they worked so well, and why David had stayed so long.

"I've collared my submissive," David admitted. "He's living with me, and he's been through hell. He's counting on me in every way imaginable."

There was a lot David wasn't saying, but Brennan was one of the few who knew how to read between David's lines. In fact, that's where Brennan lived, on the other side of all of David's order and formality, down in the dark where it was dirty and wild. Every time they spoke, or locked eyes, David felt instantly transported to someplace safe where only Brennan could reach him.

None of this was new. Brennan had seen war. David's small troubles were nothing compared with that. The perspective was good to help David find a way through.

The soft scrape of Brennan's voice and the gentle tumble of his British accent was tempting as he asked, "Do you need me to get on a plane?"

How to reply? David did want Brennan there. He'd easily correct the problem, but this was David's war. Calling in Brennan would be as much of a copout as Dorian calling in his hired thugs. No, they had to do this the right way. And David had called for other reasons than to look for a hero to save him from problems he'd created for himself.

"You know I always need you, but now is not the time. Later, perhaps. You should meet him."

"Tell me. What's he like?"

"Hmm," David hummed fondly, chuckling. "Young. Vulnerable. Pure. He makes me laugh."

"How young?"

"Eighteen."

"David," Brennan said, scolding.

"I know. It wasn't planned. None of this was."

"How much danger is he in?"

"Plenty. Most of it is my fault."

Brennan sighed and David slipped backward in time, back to that dungeon where he'd been stripped of all of the power he'd grown used to. Ropes wound around him, tied in knots, immobilizing his naked body completely. They were down on the cold ground and Brennan was behind him. Two fingers were pressed into David's body as the cool flat of his Master's exceedingly sharp blade slid over the skin of David's bound and vulnerable testicles. One slight twist and it would cut.

'Do you feel powerful, now, slave?' Brennan asked in memory, with all of the dark willingness of someone who had survived horrors, and knew he could again. The blade had already kissed David's skin, parting the top few layers in various places where gaps in the ropes allowed access. It was enough to make him bleed, but not enough to

171

scar. Brennan was an expert at wielding every weapon he handled. Feeling the metal of that knife against his most fragile organ, the hot blood already slicking his skin, and the rigidity of his bonds, encasing him from ankle to jaw, David knew Brennan had every bit of the power. There was none left for his pupil. Money and titles meant nothing when it was just two men, figuratively alone with their sweat, lust, and blood.

Brennan had then set the blade aside, choosing a different, more fearful weapon instead. Sheathing it in David swiftly, completely, despite the terrible, desperate sounds David was making, as pain overtook the panic his bindings had provoked, Brennan asked, *'How powerful are you now, David Davenport?'*

In the present, David's Master asked, "Yet you expect him to trust you?"

"He does trust me," David admitted, not proudly, just feeling the weight of responsibility heavy upon him.

"And you trust *him*, as much as you do me?"

Brennan sounded doubtful. There was blatant warning in his tone, urging caution to his student and former lover.

David had never forgotten how it had felt that first time, submitting to Master Brennan as completely as he did, in order to appreciate what he would be asking of his own submissives. The intimate ache of being fucked for the first time was magnified by Brennan's infinite patience and calm, resolute nature. Held fast and taken apart on a basic level, David had been wild. Never had he cried out like that before, or needed so badly to feel his Master's gentle, comforting touch, after. Because that's what kept David there, on his knees for Brennan. David's Master knew the key to David's heart was simple, honest affection. Few men could kiss like Brennan had kissed David, and no one had ever taken him as thoroughly.

They were parted by an ocean now, but David knew Brennan would always be there for him, in every sense, and that was precious.

"Your lack of a response is not a comfort," Brennan warned.

"Just reminiscing," David told him, carefully. "I trust him. It's not about that. What if I'm not enough for him?"

Brennan breathed out a laugh, then said, quite seriously, "Then he doesn't deserve you. Be frugal with your trust. Remember what I taught you. Power can be taken away. It doesn't take money or resources, just willingness and want. You are a target and *you need to be careful.*"

"Yes, sir."

Brennan had taken David many times, and was the only man to ever have done so. He'd shown David how to dominate and opened up doors to him that he hadn't even known were there. They were valuable lessons David intended to pass on someday, as well. He would never have known himself as well as he did without his Master's help.

Feeling Brennan inside him again, if only in memory, David remembered how safe it had made him feel. Once the ache had faded and his Master's arms still held him tightly, caressing lovingly, there had been nothing better than how possessed he'd felt by someone he adored so much.

David said, "It would be good to see you again, once things settle down."

"Say the word and I'll be there."

"Thank you, Master."

"Take care, David."

They slept together in David's bed that night, for the first time.

Before sleeping, and following a hot bath Shea had taken at David's insistence, David had turned out all the lights and asked if Shea had a little energy left.

"Yeah, are you kidding?" Shea grinned, happily, greedily enjoying every moment he had with David, in his own space. Now, he guessed it would be *their* space.

"Ready to follow some orders?"

"Yes, sir," Shea answered, feeling a stir of arousal already. He chuckled softly as David pulled Shea's pants off again, then manhandled him over onto his stomach.

"Bend your knees, draw your legs underneath you but spread them as wide as you comfortably can."

Shea got in the pose, his ass in the air, his legs spread.

"Good. Fold your arms above your head, shoulders down, hips up. It's okay, your arm will be fine. Perfect."

David's hands caressed over Shea's ass, grabbing handfuls of his cheeks. He spread them, then kept them spread. Shea moaned, desperately, drawing a growl from David. His fingers dug in just beside the edges of Shea's rim, pulling at it to pry it open. Suddenly, something soft, warm and wet stroked directly over Shea's hole.

His gasp was sharp, frantic. He realized it was David's tongue. First, it licked up through Shea's crease, drawing a hard shudder of pure, raw pleasure. When it plunged through his rim, filling it, licking up through it, Shea keened, gasping against the bedspread.

David pulled out and said roughly, "That's it. Let me hear you and how much you love it."

"Fuck," Shea cried. David's tongue slipped back into him and Shea couldn't stop or hold in the sounds it provoked. He convulsed, fucking air, his cock dripping fluid.

David grabbed hold of Shea's balls with one hand, and tugged downward and back a little. It moved Shea to arch his back even more, exaggerating his position to relieve the pressure. David's tongue withdrew. Gasping, panting, Shea felt David's eyes on him, and his hole.

"This is mine now, slave."

Shea's cries climbed in volume and urgency. David twisted his balls and began to give light little licks directly across his rim.

"Please, *fuck*, oh god," Shea begged. The need to come, to get off against something, was maddening, but he couldn't. He was held fast. All he could do was undulate, reacting strongly, reflexively to little licks over his hole, clenching briefly after each one. Then David would wait for him to relax and would do it again.

Gradually, David began to squeeze Shea's balls. The pain made Shea grunt, then try to pull away, which only stretched the skin of his sac and added additional pressure. But David kept licking. The combination of pain and pleasure was unlike anything he'd experienced before. It kept him thrumming, hovering right on the edge of orgasm.

A finger slid all the way up his ass. He cried out. The finger pulled downward and David licked again, above where his finger was nestled.

Strangely, Shea felt himself craving more pain to counteract the pressure in his ass and the thrilling stimulation from David's twisting, restless tonguing. So, he pulled forward. David squeezed harder.

"More. Please," Shea asked, his voice ragged.

David let go of Shea's balls entirely, rolling them firmly in his hand, then letting go. He slapped them once, twice, again. Shea flinched each time, twitching, but the finger inside him kept him in place. A second finger entered him and they spread apart. David grabbed Shea's balls in a fist, pulled hard.

Shea hummed, rocking a little, testing his range of movement, loving the fact that at least his expression was hidden. It made him feel free to respond without inhibitions.

David let go of his sac, just for a second, then grabbed only one of Shea's balls. He pulled down, squeezed harder than before.

Whimpering, Shea twisted away from the pain. When that didn't help, he pushed back into it, and the fingers began fucking him.

"Breathe, slave. You're doing so well. I know it hurts. Push down on it."

He stuck out his ass as far as he could and the fingers slid easier, in and out to the hilt, riding his passage, prying it open. They twisted inside him.

"Please fuck me, sir," Shea rasped. The pressure on his balls eased tremendously.

"You want my cock?"

"*Yes*," Shea whined at a fresh bout of pain as David squeezed.

David let go. The fingers pulled out. Shea got very still, waiting.

Hands spread his ass out wide, then kneaded the muscle of his cheeks. After a moment, David's tongue was back inside him, licking as deeply as it could reach, his lips kissed around Shea's rim.

Unable to restrain himself any longer, Shea reached for his cock. He'd barely touched it and he was coming, clenched so tightly around David's tongue, shouting with the force of his climax as he came all over his hand.

David pulled out and massaged Shea's rim. "I didn't give you permission to touch yourself *or* to come, slave," he warned.

"I'm sorry," Shea pleaded, his voice ravaged. "It was just so fucking good."

"Mmm. I'm glad." Gentle kisses trailed over the curve of his ass to his lower back as the fingers moved against his hole in a tight circular motion. "Next time, we'll work on your *obedience*."

"Yes, Master."

"It didn't hurt too much? You liked it?"

"Yes, Master," Shea said.

"Good." He guided Shea upright, then back to sit on his heels. After a small peck to Shea's neck, David said, "Give me a minute to wash up. I'll bring you a washcloth. Then we'll sleep."

"Thank you," Shea smiled shyly. He watched David climb off the bed and go into the bathroom, counting the seconds until he returned.

Soon, they slept. Shea lay curled up on his side, tucked in David's secure embrace from behind.

Chapter 22
Indulgences

It must have been near dawn when David left, excusing himself with a gentle kiss to Shea's forehead, in order to attend to business downstairs with the club. Unable to fall back to sleep without David, Shea wandered over to the windows to peer down at the activity below.

It was packed, from what Shea could determine from his limited view. Tree branches with the buds of new leaves blocked most of it. The guards, under David's instruction, wouldn't let Shea out on the balcony. Part of Shea wanted to make a joke about David being afraid of snipers or an air strike, but he didn't because he was partly afraid of what the response would be.

It seemed ridiculous, too weird to be true, but maybe it wasn't a joke at all. Shea knew David had real fear of what his father, Dorian, was capable of doing. Shea still didn't know how far Dorian would go to ensure David wasn't harmed by the 'trash' he'd taken to bed.

He tried to push the thoughts away. Worrying never solved anything.

Absentmindedly, Shea rubbed the charm on his necklace, the only piece of his old life keeping him company in his new one.

It was kind of amazing how many people had showed up to hang out at the club. It was all men, from teenage-looking guys to ones who had to be in their forties. The parking lot was so full; cars had been forced to park along the road leading to the property as far as the eye could see. Guys were walking up the street to the property's gates, then through the parking lot to the path to the house. They spilled out onto the grounds, rolling around in the grass, making out, goofing off, smoking, laughing, dancing, and drinking. Lights along the paths and the front of the building transformed the night, welcoming the club's guests in with a warm glow. It looked like paradise.

Shea had never seen such a spectacle. He'd never gotten around to finding the balls to actually visit a gay club. He was barely legal anyway. He'd figured he had time to get around to that later. The priority for him had been on maintaining a steady source of survival needs like clothing, food, and shelter. Paying for a cover charge to hook up when he wasn't even ready to get laid was just stupid.

But in the safety of David's bedroom, it felt like a chocolate fudge ice cream type of indulgence to peer out of the windows and people watch. It was funny, to remember how intimidating clubs had seemed only weeks ago. Going out late at night to dance or flirt or drink—it was something only more glamorous people did, people with more time and money on their hands than Shea, and freer spirits. Shea had been too normal and bogged down in daily struggles just to get by to fit in somewhere like Manse. So, how in the hell had he gotten into the bedroom playground of the head Master and owner of the fucking place? Why was he, out of everyone down below, the one David chose to take to bed, and share his heart with?

Shea still didn't really know, but the memories were real enough. He could even feel the dried teardrops on his skin from when David had gotten too emotional to contain them. There had been no elaborate explanation. But, up in that white tower on the hill, under guard, and carefully secluded, Shea could guess at the loneliness that would give such simple shared affection powerful meaning. He wasn't stupid, after all. Naïve maybe, and inexperienced, but he knew what it was to crave the sort of connection with another human being where you felt *seen* and *heard* and loved even after they'd realized you were far from perfect.

Grateful for his sharp eyesight, Shea marveled at the beauty of the patrons of Manse. They were of all ethnicities, and everyone had dressed to impress. From the weather reports Shea had been seeing on his phone, Shea knew the evenings had been chilly, though the days were warm. The cold temperatures didn't seem to be dissuading the men below from showing skin. It seemed like every face he studied was more attractive than his own, their bodies perfect, the product of hard labor in the gym, tanning salons, and barber shops. Their clothes were immaculate, designed to show off tight, fuckable asses, broad chests, bulging arms, trim waists, powerful thighs, and sizeable packages.

Without exception, everyone was hot.

Or, maybe Shea's standards just weren't as high as other people's.

He kept glancing back at the bedroom doors and the guard there, checking that someone wasn't hurrying in to tell him he was in the wrong place, that there'd been a mistake. He wondered if over time he could get used to being in such surreal surroundings, then laughed aloud and kept chewing at his lower lip, pensively, while eye-fucking the sea of sex gods below.

It occurred to him that David must have fucked some of them, and tried to decide who they might be, who would appeal to the improbable man who'd been so respectful of Shea's virginity. All Shea had to go by was himself and Thierry, and Shea didn't think he really had anything in common with Thierry, so it didn't help him from any sort of helpful mental image.

His thoughts stayed with Thierry for a little while, as handsome, outgoing men laughed and flirted below, in an entirely different universe than the one Shea was occupying. He wondered if Thierry was okay, and what had gone on in that scene Shea wasn't allowed to know details about. According to David, it was between Master and slave, and would betray Thierry's privacy to tell Shea anything, but Shea was curious how he was ever supposed to get a clue as to what it meant to be a submissive without some other examples to go by. Surely, some of the men below were also part of David's BDSM community. They were secretly Masters or slaves. He tried to guess just based on appearances, but then felt like an asshole for labeling people with no context.

Maybe David would let him visit the club when things calmed down. Shea hoped so. Maybe David would even include him in the meetings of the BDSM community which happened downstairs, regularly. Then, he tried to envision himself, wearing his collar, being led around on a leash or something by David while other men led around *other* men on leashes, and laughed aloud.

The guards probably thought he was losing his mind, laughing to himself for no reason and peeking out the windows.

"I swear I'm not going crazy," he called over his shoulder, for whoever might be listening, then felt even crazier for having said it. "What the fuck is wrong with me, anyway?" he chuckled, spying some muscle-bound guy with his hand down the pants of a much skinnier guy. He promptly forgot what he'd been thinking about as he stared, mouth agape.

David wandered in and out of rooms on the first floor. He didn't like dramatic entrances and, in fact, typically asked security to stay back at a discreet distance so it was easier for David to blend in with the crowd and get a better feel for things. Most of his guests had no idea who he was, and he liked to keep it that way.

So, if someone grabbed his ass, or started dancing with him, or slung an arm around his neck and kissed him out of the delirious heights of joy, David went with it. He would kiss them back or linger to dance for the rest of the song before continuing on. It was perfect.

The wait staff was likewise trained not to acknowledge him. David found it to be the much smarter cover to pretend to be no one of particular importance than to announce his identity with constant, heavy guard. He was a ghost, slipping in and out, disappearing down hidden, private hallways and chambers, but always followed, always watched.

It would have to be the same for Shea, at least on the busy, general admittance nights. Shea would be watched and assigned bodyguards, but would need to be taught how to move around, escaping the tighter presses of humanity or unwanted advances. No one outside of the staff would know who he was, and especially who he was to David. The most dangerous thing David could do to Shea, he'd come to understand, was to publicly own up to how much Shea meant to him.

Of course, exception would have to be made, eventually, in the case of BDSM play parties. Then, Shea would be collared and very, *very* closely guarded. David hadn't thought any farther than that, though. Truth be told, he felt some anxiety whenever he considered the idea of exposing Shea to anyone, even those David trusted. He'd trusted his father, after all, and look what had become of that.

Once he was satisfied with the way things were running with Manse, David took his leave and ascended to the second floor, passing the door-less rooms where patrons could escape for a little more privacy than the dance floor could provide, though voyeurism was encouraged, no matter where you were on the property. It was a condition of attendance.

Through a secure entry and up another flight of stairs, David passed into the medical division of the building, in order to seek out Thierry and Elet.

A few days after the scene in which Thierry finally submitted completely to Master Elet, David had visited the same recovery suite which he was approaching now. Thierry had been biting back hard grunts but yielding readily to Elet, whose sizable cock was buried halfway in Thierry's ass.

On his hands and knees, Thierry had chanced a look backward at the door when he'd heard it open, when David slipped in to join them. Flushing redder once he'd seen it was David, Thierry then faced forward once more. Jostled forward with each in-stroke, tugged bodily backward on the withdrawal, knees planted widely on the bed, Thierry growled through the ache. David walked to the bed and retrieved a pair of latex gloves from the container stuffed with them at the bedside. After pulling them on, David reached beneath Thierry's rocking hips. His cock was fully erect and wet. As soon as David's fingers closed around it, Thierry bowed his head and swallowed a moan. David felt the battle in the slave to control instinct, to bear the touch without seeking relief for his own sake.

"How do you feel, slave?" David had asked.

Elet thrust inward, pushing Thierry forward, his cock sliding inside David's grip. At first, Thierry could only moan in reply, on the edge of delirium. Struggling for coherency, he managed to grunt, "Fucked, sir."

David laughed. Glancing at Elet, who was smiling fiercely and evidently enjoying himself quite a lot, David asked, "How is the delicate little rose faring?"

"He's taking it easier. The swelling is down."

With his free hand, David rubbed around the stretched, lube-slick opening through which Elet was forcing his cock. It felt hot to the touch, and still a little swollen. Thierry hissed through gritted teeth at the prodding and hung his head.

Stepping back, David had watched Elet work. When Elet took firm hold of his slave's cock, jacking it hard, Thierry cried out, "*Oh fuck yes.*" David could tell there was still pain. It was there in Thierry's frown, the anguished tilt of his eyebrows, the small whimpers between the rougher cries. But, he came with a tremble, pushing into Elet's hand, begging for more.

"Oh, you will get your wish, *chéri*," Elet purred, riding him with slower, longer strokes. Thierry shifted his position once he was spent, collapsing onto the bed, letting his arms and shoulders rest there, circled around his head as Elet held Thierry's hips, his ass tipped up and knees planted solidly. Watching Thierry take the full length of his Master was like a magic trick — it didn't seem possible. But, there was a small, almost peaceful smile on Thierry's face, beneath the slightly furrowed brow.

That's when David knew he'd be fine, and left him to Elet's care.

How would things have progressed since then? David was eager to find out. Pushing through the suite's door, after spying the room's occupants through the glass of the small window, David willfully intruded on the examination underway.

Elet and the doctor looked David's way briefly but Thierry didn't bother. He was too distracted by his Master's presence at his side. Elet's expression was intent. He had a hand cupped under Thierry's jaw, the fingers wrapping the top of his throat. Thierry was bent over the side of the bed, his arm braced on the footboard. The doctor was busy probing him with two fingers, and Thierry appeared to resent it. He was scowling unhappily, his jeans pushed down to mid-thigh.

"Clench again," Dr. Wilkenson instructed. A moment later, he removed his hand and then the glove covering it. "Good. Everything seems fine to me." He was speaking directly to Elet. "Give him a few more days' reprieve before resuming normal activity."

"That means keep your cock out of him," David added with a smirk.

"Is that what you want, *chéri*?" Elet asked in a whisper by Thierry's ear. Thierry's eyes slipped shut and he tilted his head slightly, as if inviting more, exposing more of his neck. Elet scraped it with his teeth and a low, pleasure-filled moan sounded from back in Thierry's throat. "Or would you spread yourself for me right now?"

"Yes, Master." Thierry sighed heavily, starting to get hard, his cock twitching the longer Elet teased him with his teeth and words.

"But you *won't*, will you?" David said, sounding like the disapproving parent.

"Not yet. Soon," Elet said with a hum filled with anticipation.

David and Dr. Wilkenson stepped back. Thierry stayed in the bent-over position until Elet gave permission for him to move, with a murmured, "Cover yourself, *chéri*."

Thierry straightened, pulled up his pants and set to work on fastening them. David caught Elet's eye. Motioning to the hall, David communicated wordlessly with him. "Slave, will I be able to see you again in a few days? Will you visit me?"

"Of course, but... just you, sir?" Thierry inquired with a sly expression. He slipped his belt through the loops of his pants and bit at the edge of his lip. There was an alluring mix of sexiness, brashness, and obedience in Thierry that continued to draw David to him.

"That's for me to decide," David answered coolly. "I'll send for you, then."

"Yes, sir. May I?"

David had taken a few steps toward the door. He paused and nodded, smiling.

Thierry approached. For all appearances he was nothing but reverent and humble as, with lowered gaze, he kissed each of David's cheeks.

"Glad you're looking well," David told him.

"Master," Thierry said with a small bow.

In the hall, David pulled Elet aside. "Well?"

"Physically, he's fine, like the doctor said. I've visited him nearly every day, and have been here during all of the doctor's exams. He is... changed. He may try to act like he hasn't, but he has. He's much more trusting of me," Elet explained.

David caught hints in the recesses of his friend's gaze as to what may have gone on in those visits, as well as Elet's own increased protectiveness toward the boy.

"Shall we proceed as planned, then?" David asked. "Could you tolerate it?"

At first, Elet frowned, as if insulted, and scoffed. But then he faltered and understood his own feelings on the matter, possibly for the first time.

"I can tell you care for him," David said gently. "I won't betray that. This is your decision."

"Perhaps... concessions might be made," Elet murmured.

"His issue has always been with the other submissives. As much as he may have grown to trust you, it's still possible he hasn't learned how to move beyond pride and selfishness when challenged by *them*. Do you think he trusts you that much?"

Elet had no reply.

"You know I'm fond of him," David explained quietly, apologetically. "But I can't have him here if he's a danger to their safety."

"Yes, Master," Elet replied with a bow of his head. "I understand. Would you permit me to take full accountability for his actions? I'll attempt to persuade him, privately, to accept the other submissives and respect them as he should. I know he can. Instead of the public scene we'd planned, I'll incorporate the other subs in our scenes, regularly, to train him. If he misbehaves again anyway, he's gone."

"You'd agree to that?" David asked doubtfully, knowing the bond that was already there between his friend and his newly devoted sub.

"I would. Give me this, David. Please."

"Very well," David relented, hoping Elet would be successful.

Chapter 23
Activity

David and Shea sat facing one another over the dining table beside tinted windows overlooking a spectacular view of the grounds. The leaves on the trees were growing in, the landscape a more vibrant green with each passing day. A lush spread of breakfast foods had been placed before them, along with mugs of coffee made to suit their particular tastes. Shea's leg bounced restlessly. He felt like his eyes were open too wide, but when he forced himself to close them a little more, he realized he was squinting weirdly and causing David to feel concerned for him. Being cooped up in David's room, constantly trying to anticipate what would happen the next time they were together, and guessing at what David was trying to protect him from was fraying Shea's nerves and making him feel even more awkward than usual.

"Are you all right, sweetheart?" David inquired before popping a piece of toast into his mouth.

"Mmm. Yeah, about that," Shea began. "Not that I'm not grateful or anything, because I'm super grateful, but I'm feeling awesome. My arm doesn't even hurt anymore. My fever hasn't come back. However—"

"You're still feeling stir crazy?" David guessed, trying to hide a grin behind his coffee mug.

"Yes," Shea agreed adamantly. He laid both hands flat upon the table in front of him and sighed in relief in seeing David understood, letting his head tip back. "I keep apologizing to the guards for being weird. Please save me."

"Well, perhaps now is a good time to ask if you'd like to safely, covertly, look in upon the BDSM community's play session this evening? Boys only," David smirked. "I thought maybe you'd be interested in seeing how other Doms and subs behave and enjoy themselves, to get a better feel of —"

"Yes! I'm in. A thousand times, yes. Sorry, I totally just interrupted you and that's rude. I swear I'll stop talking now and let you finish. But yay! I'm excited to go. No, really, I'm stopping. I really am." He pressed his lips together and sincerely tried to shut up. He did bounce a little in his chair though. That seemed safe enough.

"Are you sure?" David teased.

"No," Shea confessed. "I could start talking again at any time. It's what happens when I get excited. See? It's happened."

"But, you are comfortable going with me? Because this is all so new to you, I think it's better if you play the voyeur this time, unless you change your mind and want to join the others, but you will be able to see everything that's happening."

"Okay. I think that seems a safe way to start out with it. At least I'll have the option to break out of the bubble if it's all not too overwhelming."

"Yes, that's the idea. I'm trying to ease you into it, sweetheart."

"Okay. Let's do it. I feel like there are conditions though, aren't there? You have that conditions look on your face."

"You'll find out more about that later," David winked, wearing a really wicked little smirk. Then he took another sip of coffee and glanced over the morning paper.

"Wow," Shea breathed. "It's even more intimidating when you won't tell me what the conditions *are*. I'm not too worried though. What's the worst that could happen? There's already a no touching clause, and a no bondage clause, and a no sex clause. I feel pretty secure."

Smiling in a way that was somehow more worrisome than reassuring, David said, after a pause, "Good. I'm glad." For a few minutes, they both ate in relative silence. Further into the home, there were softened voices as the staff performed their duties as unobtrusively as possible. It made Shea want to yell for everyone to relax and stop pretending they might offend by talking at a normal volume. The strangeness of it all was still like an itch under his skin. He couldn't get rid of it. But he didn't even really want to get rid of it. Imagining what kind of person he'd have to become to not be bothered by such coddling and kowtowing by hired servants made him resolve to always be bothered by it, at least on some level. As much as he was growing to love David, and he was, Shea more than anything wanted to remain the person he felt he was, at heart. He swore to himself he would always try to be his version of normal, no matter what. It had endeared him to David, after all, so he couldn't be that bad, because David was pretty incredible.

Deciding that enjoying the moment was more important than enjoying breakfast, Shea set down his fork. He rested his right elbow on the table, propped his chin in his hand and smiled fondly in David's direction. After a few bites, David stopped pretending he wasn't aware of Shea staring at him, and set down his fork as well. Wiping his mouth on the cloth napkin which had been spread across his lap, he folded his arms on the tabletop and asked with raised eyebrows and an amused twist of his sexy, kissable lips, "Something on your mind, sweetheart?"

"Maybe," Shea answered, smiling a little more and drumming his fingers against the side of his face.

David pressed his lips together, looking pensive as he attempted to puzzle out Shea's behavior and motives.

"...and that would be?"

Pushing his chair away from the table, Shea walked around to where David was sitting, tracking his every step oh-so-carefully. When Shea grew closer, David inched his chair backward as well. The napkin was set on the table. Shea lowered himself onto David's lap, straddling him, and slung his arms behind David's neck. Pressing a soft kiss to his lips, Shea said, "You. Just you."

David chuckled, winding his arms around Shea's back, and returned his kiss eagerly.

If Shea was so moved to beg for more from David, it was a great sign he was becoming ready for David to test his boundaries in new ways. It also gave David great hope for what the evening would bring. But why wait when he had Shea in his lap right now?

"Mmm, I love you like this," David said, grabbing hold of Shea's ass, pulling him in. "Showing me exactly what you want, what you need..."

"I know you're busy, that I should let you eat, but I can't help it. I want you. Being close to you just feels so good."

"Likewise," David grinned. His hands slid greedily over his prize—his handsome, willing slave. David caressed roughly over Shea's thigh, squeezed his ass. Shea pushed into the touches, rolling his hips against David's crotch. It made David hard, fast, to see Shea's sex drive so awakened and all the little signals that he was enjoying David's attentions.

"I should let you eat," Shea sighed, trying to lean back a little. David just pulled him in harder.

"Don't you dare." He reached for the drawstring of Shea's pants, yanking the tie loose. "You started this. I intend to finish it."

"What if I finish all over your breakfast?"

"Who said I was going to let you?"

Pushing his fingertips into the sides of Shea's pants, David yanked again, pulling them down past his ass, getting them down to the top of his thighs.

"Fuck. And now I'm naked."

"I prefer you naked."

"Of course you do. Even if there are people around, obviously."

"Exactly. That's the nice thing about being in charge. I make the rules."

"I don't think people usually strip their lovers in front of their employees."

"Happens all the time here," David shrugged. He'd pulled Shea's cock into his hand. Massaging it lightly, teasing it to encourage the blood to flow, David sat back in his chair. "Hands behind your head, slave. Lace your fingers together. Sit up straight." He waited for Shea to obey, then added, "Besides, your body is delicious. It would be self-ish of me to not show it off properly."

Shea was blushing fiercely, a distinct pink heat spreading over his skin. His cock was perfectly erect. David pushed Shea's thighs farther apart, his thumbs stroking firmly over Shea's sac. He noticed immediately when Shea glanced toward the guards, who faced them given their proximity to the windows, but the guards' gazes were politely averted.

"Consider it part of your training," David told him. "Stay absolutely still, now."

Parting his own legs, atop which Shea sat, David created a gap between his thighs, beneath the junction of Shea's legs. Balancing there, thighs tensed, Shea fell quiet, surrendering to a submissive, compliant mindset.

After sucking on his index finger, David reached behind Shea's balls and fed it to him slowly, watching him quake as he was breached.

"I have every intention, slave, of displaying you to the most respected Doms and subs of Manse and the Master's Circle, whenever it's convenient and desirable for me to do so. I want you naked, spread, hard, horny, and begging. I want you desperate to come, focused only on me, your Master, because I'm the only one who can give you what you need. Isn't that right?"

"Yes, Master," Shea answered, breathing hard, his voice scraped raw already with lust and nervousness. There was such bare timidity in the furrow of his brow, the quiver of his lips and the subtle undulations of his body. He obediently held the pose, but trembled with each touch, his eyes downcast. Nothing in him tried to keep David out or at a distance. If anything, the more David stimulated and exposed Shea, the more closeness and protection he appeared to crave. He truly was the most exquisite creature.

David's finger moved steadily; twisting, rubbing, and sheathing itself in his claim. Very subtly, Shea began riding it, pushing into each penetration.

"I didn't give you permission to ride my finger, slave."

"Sorry. Sorry, Master," he winced, stopping.

"You may ask permission, if you'd like. Politely."

Shea's head was bowed, turned slightly, modestly, away from the guards. Watching the tip of his swollen erection, David saw precome drip down the head as he pulled the finger completely out, then popped it quickly back through Shea's clenched rim. With the sweetest purring gasp, Shea thrust a little, rising up slightly at the inner pressure as he was filled.

"I'm sorry. Please. Please may I... May I move and... ride your finger, Master?"

"You want to?"

"Yeah," Shea ached, begging, "Please."

"All right. You may. But you may not move or lower your arms. Understood?"

Shea nodded, "Yes, sir."

They began slowly, at an easy pace. David pumped his finger deeply, enjoying the incredible tightness of Shea's ass, gripping him with its soft, yielding heat. And Shea started to move, pushing down into each inward stroke, pulling up when David withdrew. His breath caught. Swallowing hard, then biting at his lip, Shea showed every part of his inner struggle to relax and let go.

"How do you feel?"

"Embarrassed."

"Why?"

After a low groan, Shea said, "Because I like it. Because they can see. Because I'm hard."

"You just don't understand, yet, how impressive you are, slave. You'll learn." David was careful not to touch Shea's prostate. He wanted him to focus only on the sensation of taking and staying open for it. "These guards won't watch when you submit, but others will. They'll stare and become enraptured by all of the ways you open up to me. Would you let me finger you while Elet watched? Would you take my cock in front of a room full of Doms? Don't answer. Just think about it."

Trailing the thumb of his free hand through the sticky fluid dripping along Shea's head and down his shaft, David collected some. Raising the thumb to Shea's lips, David said in command, "Lick."

Following a trembling exhale, Shea touched the tip of his tongue to the pad of David's thumb, licking away his own taste. His full lips kissed around the fingertip and he swallowed, still rocking gently on David's other hand. Shea was frowning, with ache and his reticence. Yet, he obeyed, he persevered.

"Can I tell you about my favorite aphrodisiac?"

Shea nodded slightly, breathing hard, maybe not trusting his voice any longer.

"It's anticipation." He feathered his fingers over Shea's cockhead, which twitched and followed the touches, seeking more. "You're not permitted, slave, to climax until you have my permission. Today, I don't want you to come until our appointment this evening. That means no touching yourself. If you jerk off after I leave, I'll know. I'll be able to tell. Do you believe me?"

He nodded again.

"It was very generous of you to offer yourself to me this morning. Thank you." He leaned in and kissed Shea slowly, thoroughly. Whispered against his lips, David said, "I want your mouth again. May I take it?"

"Yes. Please, let me suck you, Master," Shea beseeched so tenderly, brushing kisses to David's mouth.

"Okay. Relax," David urged, smiling. "Let's switch to low protocol. That means you may do what you wish. The only rules are you don't cover or touch yourself."

Shea smiled back, looking happy and eager. He wasn't focusing on the guards as much—another good sign.

He pulled free of David's finger, then slid gracefully off his lap and sank to his knees. Shea began to free David's cock. In no time, he had pulled it out. Using his hand and his mouth, he began to work David to a quick orgasm. Humming and moaning as he sucked, mouthing the tip, tugging gently with his hand, Shea proved how good he really was. The hot, tight wrap of his tongue, the intense suction, the hug of the insides of his cheeks when he took David farther back, the perfect fit of the inside of his throat when David was allowed to slide all the way in—it was incredible.

Shea eased back when David started to orgasm. Opening his mouth, Shea let David watch as his come shot over Shea's tongue, coating it. Stroking him through it, Shea swallowed some, then licked David through the aftershocks.

When David moaned a soft, "Fuck," Shea looked quite proud of himself, giving David a cute, wicked smirk and the briefest upward glance. "Impressive," David praised breathlessly. He grinned, biting at his lip as Shea helped cover him up.

"Thanks," Shea replied, glowing with heat, energy and unique beauty.

He pulled Shea close, kissing him as he gently, carefully, covered him, too, drawing his pants up over his noticeable, impressive hardness. Moaning again at the taste of himself on Shea's tongue, David took the kiss deeper.

"You're killing me," Shea said between gasps for air.

"Good."

David was still kissing Shea when Ivan stepped from the elevator and moved in their direction.

Reluctantly, David was forced to excuse himself, saying, "I'm so sorry, love. Give me just a moment to see what this is about, all right?"

"Sure," Shea replied with a soft, sexy smile. It just made David want to tumble back into bed with him, pull the covers up over their heads to hide from the world and stay there for hours.

He sat back and let David up.

David let his fingers brush against Shea's cheek as he walked away, then composed his expression as he approached Ivan.

"What is it? Has there been activity?" David asked quietly so Shea would not overhear. He walked Ivan out of the main living area and into a more secluded room.

"Yes, there has," Ivan told him gruffly. "Last night there were three separate attempts to enter Manse with false identification. When efforts were made to apprehend the suspects, they fled. Security lost track of them in the crowd. We got a few shots of their faces from cameras at the perimeter of the property but no hits on facial recognition scans when crosschecked against the database of known felons."

"Damn," David sighed. "You're certain no one was able to get inside?"

"Absolutely, Mr. Davenport. We did a full sweep at the time of the incidents and after closing. No suspicious activity."

"All right, well I want an extra man on Mr. Whittier. Don't let him leave the building under any circumstances or linger near the windows. I'll have to, uh, have a talk with him. Bring him up to speed. I have a board meeting off-premises today. I'm going to take the copter as an experiment, see if our friends beyond the property line stay or attempt to follow me. That should tell us if they're after me or Mr.

Whittier."

"Yes, sir."

"Fuck. I suppose now is as good a time as any to do this. Better to keep him in the loop if I'm leaving. Come with me."

They returned to the main living area, walking into the dining area adjacent to the kitchen where Shea was back sitting in his own chair, swirling his coffee in its mug. He brightened upon seeing David, though his smile subtly faltered when Ivan continued to tag along. David could hear Ivan relaying instructions discreetly in his earpiece to the rest of the security team.

"That's not a good sign. That's the head guy, right? Igor?" Shea guessed.

"Ivan," David corrected. "I, uh, have to fill you in a little more on what's been going on, Shea."

"Really? I'm glad. I mean, I've been wondering but haven't wanted to ask, since I know you're dealing with a lot. Is it bad?"

"Hard to say," David confessed, sliding his hands into his trouser pockets. He took a deep breath, then shifted his chair closer to Shea's. Sitting in it, a cozy amount of space between them, David leaned forward, elbows braced on his knees, hands folded, and began to explain. "Since I brought you here from the hotel for treatment and care, there have been people watching the building. Professionals. Likely my father's men. They've eluded the police and my security team, but we've seen them nearly every day at the edges of the property. My guess is they haven't given up suspecting you're here with me."

Instantly, all of Shea's levity was gone. "They want to finish the interrogation, don't they?" Sitting up straighter, his gaze shot to the windows. "They're not going to leave until I answer their questions."

David took hold of Shea's hand, folding it between both of his own. He brought it up to his lips and kissed the back.

"I'm sorry I didn't tell you earlier. I thought it more important you focus on recovery and adjusting to living here rather than making you worry about something I can handle entirely, on your behalf. You're protected here. I'm assigning you an extra guard for the time being. I do have a board meeting today, off premises. Usually, under these circumstances I'd telecommute, but today I'm going to take the copter and attend in person. They won't be able to tail me as they would on the ground, but they'll try if I'm the one they're after. But if they stay here...."

"I don't want you to leave," Shea said softly, frowning with worry. "Is it safe for you to travel like that? You can't be sure who those guys are, or what they want."

"Don't worry about me. I've had years of training in self-defense tactics, at my father's insistence, ironically. My security team is made up of some of the most talented people in the world. They've proven themselves to me, over and over again. I'll be fine. And you'll be safe. I just wanted you to know why I haven't given you permission to wander outside the building or return to town to see your friends. Stay away from the windows. Stay with the guards."

"Why do I have to stay away from the windows? You really think they'd shoot me or something?"

"No, I don't. The danger isn't that extreme, but they do have telescopic lenses on their cameras. I don't want to give them any evidence you're here if I can help it."

"Oh. Okay. That's not as bad. But there's something we can do about these guys, right?" Shea asking a little fearfully, his irresistibly earnest, deep blue eyes shining with hope and faith in David's abilities. "I don't have to keep hiding in here forever, do I?"

"Of course not," David promised. Soothing him with a kiss, David caressed the sides of Shea's face when he pulled back.

"I have a plan. We're working through our options carefully. Meanwhile, you're in very good hands. I know it frustrates you to be stuck in here. It severely frustrates me as well, and I'm holding Dorian responsible for every bit of the trouble he's causing. We'll get past this. Once we do, if you would prefer to keep a job, or to not live with me, then that's of course your choice to make." He tried to say it as evenly as possible, though he feared his sudden sadness at the idea of Shea wanting to leave showed in his expression, especially when Shea frowned and shifted closer toward David.

"Neil is on his way up, Mr. Davenport," Ivan told them.

"Thank you, Ivan."

"Could you send me a message when you get to your meeting? Just so I know you got there okay?" Shea asked.

"Absolutely," David replied, warming at Shea's display of concern. "Think of our night tonight. The club meeting. Let my men worry about the rest."

"I'll try."

"No movement, Mr. Davenport," David was informed the second he stepped away from the helicopter and could hear properly again. Marco looked as aggravated as David felt. Who would have thought it possible to be so irked by *not* being pursued by hired thugs?

David pulled out his phone and sent a message to Shea to say he'd arrived.

"So that's it then." David let Marco and Andrew lead him into the building. "It's not like we could have made a more obvious exit, if I'm the one they were after."

"And they would have been certain Mr. Whittier was not accompanying you," Marco agreed.

"Damn."

"There's been no pursuit of his family members," Marco informed David. "It's him they want, and they're smart enough to rule out blackmailing him into appearing."

"Right," David agreed with a heavy heart. "His family wouldn't care of his plight and they know I'd never allow Shea to cave to threats of that nature anyway. At least this narrows our options."

"Let us handle things for now, sir."

"Thank you, Marco."

Chapter 24

Ready or Not

Luckily, the meeting ran shorter than expected. Just a few hours later, David was back at home, where Shea wanted him to be. He walked into the bedroom, loosening his tie and wearing a wicked grin. He popped open the top button of his shirt, then the next, and the next. "Are you ready for this?"

"Uh..." Shea stared as David advanced upon him while continuing to undress. God, but he looked perfect, like he'd stepped right out of a sexy cologne commercial—dim lighting, immaculate, masculine features, sickeningly hot body, and with a gorgeous, lush room surrounding them. Shea closed his eyes and counted to five. Aloud.

"Why are you counting?" David whispered, touching Shea's thighs, jolting him a little at the sudden closeness. He caressed upward and Shea laughed nervously.

"Sorry. I thought I'd completely lost it for a second there and I was full on hallucinating. The counting was to see if you were going to disappear. There's no way this is really happening. I'm probably spaced out watching TV back in my old, shitty apartment and this past month or so has been a prolonged wet dream. But, nope, you're still here. And touching my balls." His laugh became breathless and more bashful. He bit down on his lip, the intimate touching making him fall quiet in order to devote more attention to paying attention to what David was doing to him. It was so hot; he expected to melt into the bed from the heat David was stirring in Shea's crotch. "So I guess you're real," he finished in a breath of sound before David kissed his lips. "Um, ready for what?" His voice cracked over the last word as David rubbed between Shea's legs.

"Sensitive?" David grinned devilishly, giving Shea's balls a gentle squeeze.

"Yeah," Shea answered, trying not to whimper. "Yeah, my, um, *balls* are kind of sensitive."

"You seem nervous," David observed, right before he began to slowly open Shea's pants.

"God, I'm *really* trying to believe this is actually happening, but the weirdness factor of my life is kind of reaching monstrous proportions. Maybe those guys who mugged me rattled my brain when I hit the pavement and I'm hospitalized and in a coma somewhere."

David slid Shea's zipper down. Shea had finally found a pair of actual jeans. It was pretty much his greatest triumph of the entire day.

David wasn't looking into Shea's eyes any longer. No, he was looking right at what his hands were doing, and it was kind of unsettling to see such focus in David on Shea's crotch.

"You're really here. I promise," David told him. "Maybe this will convince you."

David's hand slid into Shea's opened pants, inside the waistband of his boxers, and wrapped around his shaft. He pulled Shea's cock out and began playing with it.

"What do I expect of you, slave?" David whispered by Shea's ear, his lips brushing the shell in a way that sent a shiver right down Shea's spine which flared outward into his dick, which twitched inside David's grasp. "Mmm, almost. More than that."

Shea couldn't speak. Words had ceased to form in his head, as well. There was no connection between his overloaded senses and his mouth. With a shudder, he could only feel how specifically David was running the pad of his thumb along the ridge of Shea's cockhead. Everything else in the universe had ceased to exist.

He knew what David was asking. He knew the answer.

David expected Shea to be hard and hot for it. Luckily, Shea was already there, and his dick was catching up, fast. With embarrassing speed, he attained a full erection and felt David caressing with a fingertip over Shea's slit as a few glistening drops slipped free. David's lips were still brushing against the side of Shea's neck, his gaze directed precisely at the work of his hand. Shea shivered again with a rush of lust and tried, somehow, to find his voice.

"H-hard," he whispered timidly.

"Manners."

"Hard, Master," he corrected.

"Are you ready to obey? We won't be in full attendance of the party—if you're still interested in going—but you will still be acting as my submissive. That means you follow my every command, address me accordingly when I ask you direct questions, and have the use of your safeword to end the scene, if needed."

Parting the opening in Shea's pants, David spread the fabric farther to reveal more of his body. "So, are you ready to obey?" David pressed.

Shea couldn't imagine that anyone, ever, had said no to David. This was a man who was used to getting what he wanted. And now, he wanted Shea.

"Yes," Shea answered, with some reservation just because of how out of his depth he felt. He added the honorific, "Sir," after a pause. It still didn't come entirely naturally to him.

"In the future, you will be nude during our scenes. Tonight, however, I'll permit you one article of clothing, which I'll provide. You will wear your collar, of course. Did you follow the cleaning ritual?"

There had been an actual printed-out instructional document in the bathroom for him, specifying how David expected Shea to clean himself in preparation for the scene. It had been too formal and specific to ignore.

"Yes, sir."

"Let's check, shall we?"

"Are you serious?" Shea laughed, then stopped abruptly. "Oh fuck, you are."

"Stand. Drop your pants to your ankles."

Anxiety was a fist squeezing the air from his lungs. Feeling slightly dizzy, Shea did as ordered, even as his heart pounded.

He stood, then pushed the pants and boxers down. Straightening, he avoided making eye contact, preferring to keep his gaze lowered to the floor in front of him. He was completely unable to ignore the guards at the door, overhearing this whole thing.

"Hands behind your back, slave," David commanded gently.

Shea shifted his hands behind his ass, clasping them there.

"Feet slightly apart."

Shea adjusted his stance.

David went to his knees before Shea. "Are you breathing?"

Shea blew out a heavy breath and forced himself to inhale. "Not really."

"Please do," David said, being a smart-ass.

"Yes, sir."

David cupped Shea's balls, lowered his mouth to them. After inhaling Shea's scent, he licked over the sac. Making a hugely embarrassing trembling sigh, Shea shivered at the intimate scrutiny and soft, wet pressure of David's tongue, which then licked up the underside of Shea's straining, massive erection.

Breathing. Focus on breathing. Oh god.

"Turn around."

Shea hesitated, and David looked up at him, knowingly.

"I'm not going to hurt you," he said.

"I know. I know," Shea murmured, as if repeating a mantra, then turned. His heart rate skipped up even faster, his breathing quickened.

"Bend over. Hands flat on the bed."

For a second, Shea had to make the effort to gather his courage.

"If you're to be my submissive, you'll need to trust me enough to do these things," David reminded, gently.

It's a test, Shea realized. Somehow, that made it easier to go through with it. He reminded himself how much he wanted David, and wanted to please him.

He bent forward, planting his hands on the duvet. Two hands spread Shea's cheeks. He felt warmth near his crease, and between his legs. When the tip of David's tongue touched him, Shea quivered and made a soft, plaintive sound.

David moaned, curling the muscle of his tongue in a lick over Shea's opening. Then, Shea felt it touch him again, though this time it pressed at him. He made another small cry as the muscle parted and David's tongue was fed into him. Gasping soundlessly, Shea bore it. He was sure David would stop and pull out, but he kept pressing deeper. The hands on his cheeks strengthened their grip, pulling him open even more.

David pulled out, licked over Shea's rim, then plunged back inside.

"*Oh fuck,*" Shea quivered, his arms feeling unsteady. The tongue darted in and out of him, and he could only press greedily back into each in stroke, tipping his hips in invitation. It was easier, better than asking with words.

Then, he remembered what David said. If Shea wanted David to go through with sex, he needed to show it, and beg for it. As the wonderful feeling of David tongue-fucking him overpowered Shea's reservations, Shea realized he needed to stop being so shy if he wanted to get anywhere.

And he did, he realized, want to get somewhere. Even if it hurt. David was worth it.

"More please, sir," Shea said gruffly.

"Mm, maybe," David replied. He ceased touching Shea. Shea was astounded by the force of his disappointment. "Turn back around. Show me your cock, slave."

He straightened, feeling self-conscious of the wetness between his cheeks.

"Lace your hands behind your head."

"Oh god," Shea moaned, doing as asked, but glimpsing the extent of his arousal, dripping wet, his balls drawn up and swollen. His dick was a deep red and thick.

"Step out of your pants," David urged, helping him do it. Naked, Shea reminded himself to try to gather his pride and not feel ashamed. It was good he enjoyed David's touches, or so he told himself.

David rose to his feet. With one hand, he toyed with Shea's cock, knocking it side to side, dragging a finger up the underside, then lightly pinching the head. "Very nice," David told him. He gave Shea a darkened, briefly upraised glance before returning to staring at Shea's dick. "You're to be proud of this, is that understood? When you're this aroused, it makes me incredibly happy, and you want your Master to be happy, slave. Nothing else matters. Not your shyness, not what other people think or say or do. Your goal is to please me. Mine is to give you absolutely everything you didn't know you wanted. Answer if you understand."

"Yes, sir. I understand."

David walked over to the cabinets, returning a moment later with what he retrieved. It was a small—very small—pair of silk, black shorts with a drawstring waistband.

Holding them up, David told Shea, "This is your wardrobe this evening. It doesn't hide much, which is why I chose it."

"Yes, sir."

Shea stepped into the shorts with David's help, and remained in the pose as David secured the drawstring at the waist. The shorts were tented obscenely at the front with Shea's arousal, but they were so short, the fabric rode up his crack in the back.

"Perfect," David said, admiring his work and teasing his lip between his teeth with a hungry expression.

An overwhelming certainty settled upon Shea, then. David's hunger for him was the most powerful lure Shea had ever experienced. It gave him so much fulfillment to be wanted as David wanted him, Shea would happily endure any ridiculous situation David would throw him into—or any pair of humiliating *shorts* David would throw him into. It suddenly didn't matter where they were or what might happen, or how they'd gotten there. All Shea wanted was to be wanted and needed the way David wanted and needed him. He wanted to be the man David saw when he looked at Shea, and he wanted to make David as happy as he possibly could.

"Ready?" David asked, gesturing toward the door where their guards waited.

"You'll protect me, right?"

"And treasure you," David admitted, with heart-stopping tenderness. It decided Shea. He would follow David anywhere, obey any order. He was ready. "You're doing an incredible job. I'm so proud of you. This is all so new to you, so of course you'll be tempted to feel overwhelmed. I order you to be honest, all right? Tell me as soon as it becomes too much. If you've had enough, we can always come back here and spend the rest of the night alone. But, if you enjoy being out, we'll stay out."

"Okay. Thanks, um, sir." Shea glanced toward the door and resolved to trust himself, as well as David. "Yeah, let's do it."

David stepped forward and kissed Shea, grinning with pride and joy. "All right then. Hands behind your back as we walk. Stay a step behind me, at my side. The guards will flank us."

Shea positioned his arms, fell in step behind David, and prepared himself for anything.

Chapter 25

Enslaved

The farther they got from the bedroom, the more Shea's doubts crept in. Reality, something he'd managed to avoid for weeks, came crashing down around his ears as he stepped into an elevator wearing pretty much nothing, surrounded by enormous guards and David 'The God of Sex' Davenport by his side.

When they got to the first floor, there were people around—people who could see him and mostly all of his naked body, including the steadily wilting erection between his legs.

Heart pounding, trying diligently to not make eye contact with anyone, for any reason, Shea followed David and began deeply questioning his ability to make even the most basic decisions, like whether or not to put on clothes before going out.

They approached a doorway in a long, narrow hall. The walls were a dark wood, with elaborate moldings and no windows in sight, only sconces. Shea murmured to David, "I'm going to need to you to reassure me again that everything is fine, and I'm not making a complete ass of myself."

Men and women in nondescript uniforms, that Shea was pretty sure were David's staff, passed them in the hall. Everyone averted their eyes, but that didn't help calm Shea. The fact was that not only was he there, visibly, actually enslaved—everyone around him was pretending they didn't notice.

The well-polished wooden floorboards were cool and slick under his feet. The dim light made him feel like he was just a shadow slipping by in the night, and not really there at all. The guards, the procession of their movement, it made Shea feel like he was being led to

203

something he'd be better off avoiding.

"Sweetheart, please just have faith in me," David told him. "We're here. Come inside and I'll get you settled."

The guards opened the door by punching in a code on a keypad. One remained beside the door on the outside, taking it as his post. The rest proceeded inside with David and Shea, who was ushered along with a hand to his lower back. The room was little more than a pitch-black corridor, maybe ten to fifteen feet wide. Shea couldn't tell how long it was, as the other end vanished into darkness. Another guard remained standing directly on the inside of the door they'd come through.

"Do a sweep, then circle around," David told the guard.

"Yes, sir."

The guards disappeared into the corridor, leaving David and Shea where they were.

The only light came through an opening in the wall to Shea's right, but he refused to look at it, choosing instead to keep his gaze fixed to the floor at his feet. From the edge of his vision, he could see bodies moving, and hear the murmur of voices and music.

After all of that time spent hiding away upstairs, Shea's first instinct after coming out in public again was to hurry back to where he knew he was safe. He'd take the cabin fever over this level of uncertainty.

He didn't want to look around, or move, or speak. He just wanted to stand there, pretending he wasn't where he was, in the condition he was in.

"Look at me, slave," David commanded, too severely for Shea to be able to ignore him. Shea slowly lifted his gaze from the floor, letting it skim over David's body as it rose to meet his eyes. He really was so startlingly handsome, Shea realized again. David stood directly in from of him, his expression composed and controlled.

"Do you trust me?" David asked.

"Yes," Shea answered instinctively, then remembered the rules. "Yes, sir."

"I'm the only one you need to worry about. You're under my control. Nothing touches you. Nothing hurts you. Everyone here respects you in ways you can't imagine. I've never taken a collared slave before. You hold a cherished, coveted role in this household. Is that understood?"

"Not really, but I'm trying. Sir."

"You look upset," David observed, as Shea resisted the urge to look toward the light beyond David, shining like a beacon.

"I'm feeling overwhelmed," Shea admitted.

"What would help more? Distraction? Comfort? Or, would you prefer to go back upstairs?"

Shea tried to figure out his answer. But, while he debated, David gave him a kiss to his lips, then his cheek, holding there for a long moment. Maybe it was against the rules, but Shea touched David's arm. David's steadiness helped Shea feel steadier, too.

David nodded to their left and pointed to a spot on the floor. "Stand right there," he said in command, using that tone of voice Shea found he couldn't ignore.

His thoughts and emotions were in turmoil, but he obeyed, and moved to stand where David wanted him. There was a post right next to him, which reached from floor to ceiling.

"Grasp the post with both hands. Lean against it."

The window—he didn't want to look but caught glimpses, since he was now facing it directly. He tried to focus only on the post. He held onto it, as David told him to, but it was far away enough that he had to lean slightly forward to manage it. Then, David drew Shea's hips farther back. It forced him to grasp lower on the post, putting Shea in a sharply bent over pose. David nudged Shea's legs slightly apart. Suddenly, it was taking much more effort to maintain the position, which eased the worry over what was happening nearby.

When Shea felt David shift closer to him, his body heat warmed Shea, making the hairs on Shea's arms stand on end. He felt David untying the drawstring on the already insignificant shorts, and Shea's breathing roughened.

"Long, slow breaths, slave," David said from inches away. He slid the shorts down past Shea's hips, then down his thighs. "Step out of them, then return to the position."

"Fuck," Shea said softly, swallowing the word as he did as commanded. Then he was really naked. The air of the room, moving softly against him from down the long, dark corridor to his left, tickled the hair on his body. There was a weight in the pit of his stomach. His balls drew up, protectively. He felt the presence of the guards, projecting their imagined judgment of him like he used to do in high school and with his family.

"Look at the glass, slave," David ordered.

"I don't want to," Shea whispered.

Something struck his bare ass, right across the thickest part of the muscle, and he gasped loudly, flinching and clenching up. It struck again, even harder. Blood rushed to the spot, the skin stinging, the muscle aching.

It shocked him.

"Ass out, slave!" The order startled Shea into obedience. He stuck his butt out, bracing himself for more. There were three more lashes, and Shea saw it was a leather strap David was striking him with. Where he'd gotten it, Shea didn't know.

Maybe he should have tried to get a better look at his surroundings.

He was hyper-aware of his cheeks jiggling with each slap of the leather, and of the gruff, gasping sounds he made after each lash.

"That was for talking back and for disrespect," David explained. "Look at the glass."

Shea was panting a little, the stinging in his ass only getting worse. The discomfort wasn't really that bad, he just didn't really like the reminder that he was completely naked and vulnerable. Finally, he shifted his gaze from the post to the glass, right as the door a few feet away opened.

Two more guards came through. One remained at the side of the door, flanking it with the guard who was already there. The other crossed to the corridor, standing to face the darkness as if he was protecting them from it. Shea guessed he was, actually.

But the sudden presence of more men to stand witness to his spanking and nakedness eased his dread of looking at what was right in front of him. It was better to turn his focus outward than to think about everything those guards were about to witness.

"It's one-way glass," David explained.

The room on the other side of that window, the other side of the wall, was filled with men either nude or with only straps of leather to cover them. Some wore collars, most didn't. There were guys who looked even younger than Shea, though he knew that was impossible. There were also plenty of men who were much older — their size, strength, and stature intimidating even without the thick cocks swinging between their legs, or the fierce lust and determination in their eyes.

Pretty much everyone in that room looked shockingly comfortable being there. Men were draped over couches, pressed up against walls, tied to large wooden crosses, bent over tables or benches, or kneeling on the floor. There was a massive, broad-shouldered and dark-haired, bearded man seated on the couch, with his cock buried to the hilt in a young slave's plump-lipped, rosy mouth, and his enormous hand wrapped the swollen, red shaft of another toned and slim slave, with tousled auburn hair and freckled skin, kneeling on the cushion beside him The kneeling slave's arms were bound behind his back, his mouth fitted with a gag as he was steadily stroked.

There was a young man with buzzed-short hair, colorful tattoos and several piercings in his ears and nose, lying on a horizontal x-cross, his wrists and ankles bound to it, spreading him wide as his ass was stuffed with the cock of one man, his mouth filled with the cock of another as he was taken from both ends at once.

A pretty slave, whose heart-shaped face was framed in loose, blond curls was being whipped in the corner. Hanging from shackles fastened to the ceiling, even from a distance Shea could see the boy's long, pale eyelashes that fluttered in pleasure with each red stripe appearing on his golden skin.

Two men at once fingered another slave with caramel skin and dark, seductive eyes, who seemed eager for more, pushing back impatiently onto the wriggling fingers.

Everywhere Shea looked, there was sexual decadence and things he shouldn't be seeing, but was.

"They all *agreed* to this? They're all fine with doing this in front of everybody? Oh my god, David, this is — "

The leather cracked against Shea's ass, causing him to cry out wildly in surprise.

"Manners, slave," David said coyly.

Shea growled with the small pain and humiliation.

He dropped his gaze. It was too much.

I want to keep watching. I'm actually enjoying *this. What's wrong with* me?

This was the biggest reason why he couldn't continue to indulge the desire. The shame of facing that truth was huge.

Chapter 26

Surrender

"I didn't give you permission to look away, slave. Eyes on the window. Now."

Chest heaving, digging his fingers into the wood of the post, Shea battled through his conflicting instincts to both heed David's command but also to avoid looking at all costs. In the end, he realized he was more intimidated by David than he was by himself. So, he looked.

David walked to the wall, pressing an intercom button. "Send Joshua over," David said before returning to Shea, smiling deviously.

Joshua? Send him where? Shea thought, afraid more strangers would be joining them in their darkened corridor.

Joshua had dark blond hair, pale skin and shy eyes with thick, black eyelashes. His black-ink tattoos encircled both of his arms from wrists to shoulders. He had a few long scars laced across his chest and could not have been more than eighteen. After being led by a collared leash to the window, he was urged to climb up onto a piece of furniture, which was mostly beyond Shea's range of sight. It gave them an up-close view of the seemingly timid slave's nakedness, right on the other side of the huge window. The large Dom holding Joshua's leash moved to stand behind him, and carelessly thrust two thick fingers up Joshua's ass. The sub was positioned, then, so his bottom was turned slightly more toward the glass, allowing them to see everything that was happening. Shea was close enough to see the wet lube shining on Joshua's pink rim, and the wrinkled knot being stretched wide around the invading fingers which twisted and slid deeper on each inward push. Panting and rolling his head on his shoulders, Joshua's initial act of subtle hesitation melted into restless delight. His back arched slightly as he writhed. His tattooed arms flexed with tension.

Shea was staring with such rapt attention, he was quite startled when a wet, warm hand grabbed hold of his own dick and began tugging on it, the sounds squelching loudly in the quiet. Grunting with surprise and shame, Shea felt David quickly make him hard. He didn't dare look away again, but continued to stare at Joshua. Something shy lingered in his expression, just around his eyes and furrowed brow. A third finger was added, stretching the slave's opening wider, causing his parted lips to quiver. The Dom slapped the boy's ass, which clenched briefly around the fingers buried within it.

Shea was breathing hard and starting to sweat. David rubbed down over Shea's balls, then gave them a hard tug before rubbing up behind them at the same time as his other hand pulled Shea's cheeks apart. He could feel David looking at him, examining his ass. Without hesitation, a finger pressed at Shea's rim, then slid smoothly through it in a long, wet slide up to the last knuckle.

With a thick, desperate grunt, Shea felt his arms tremble — his legs too, as he fought to stay still. The urge to close his eyes and focus on one thing at a time was strong, because it was intense to say the least, to have to watch Joshua get brutally fingered as Shea was simultaneously, more gently fingered. When Shea felt David rub, hard, over the patch of skin behind his balls, a jolt of sensation drew a strange sort of whimpered cry from him, of which he was instantly self-conscious.

"That's it," David said with encouragement, doing it again and rubbing even harder. Shea's cock was suddenly, completely rigid, straining upward and dripping pre-come. The finger up his ass pumped steadily, going deeper than seemed possible. "No need to be quiet. They can't hear you, but, believe me, slave, *I* really want to hear you. Do you like what you see?"

The finger rubbed over the inside of his ass as if David was trying to touch every single part of him, staking his territory, knowing Shea in ways he didn't even know himself. With David, there was no shyness, no hesitancy. He simply knew what he wanted, and took it.

"I guess so, sir," Shea managed to answer. A hand wrapped loosely around Shea's cock, weighing it.

"Would you like to see that slave get fucked in the ass with a big, meaty cock?"

A subtle shudder shook him as the finger explored him from the inside and his dick twitched eagerly inside David's hand.

He couldn't admit to it, though. Not right away, so David added, "You're wet, slave. I can tell you like it, even if you don't want to admit it. There's no lying here."

A fourth finger was squeezed into the sub's tiny opening and Shea thrust helplessly against David's hand, needing relief, too turned on to hold back any longer. And, after he'd thrust forward, it was only natural to rock backward against the finger, taking it more deeply into him again.

"No, be still. Answer the question."

The finger pulled out of Shea. Three fingers rubbed back and forth over the surface of his rim, stimulating the sensitive area. He felt the urge to push back onto them to take them into his body and was instantly shocked at himself. David's hand played at his dick, and it felt so damned good. Shea's balls were full and heavy. His dick was so hard it grew painful. Meanwhile, tickling, light touches from the pads of David's fingers skimmed over the head of Shea's cock, tracing the ridge, teasing the slit.

"Yes, sir," Shea answered gruffly, between heavy breaths.

"Yes, sir, what?"

"Yes, sir, I want to see it. But...."

"But what?"

The fingers rubbing Shea's opening teased at it, pulling the outer ring apart with two fingers, wriggling a third through the middle, slowly.

"*Oh god,*" Shea moaned, brokenly. The pitch of his cry climbed, twisted into a hum.

"But what?" David insisted, continuing his slow, thorough torture. Shea almost couldn't think past it, the deliciously filthy touches lit up nerves which had never been awakened before.

"B-but... *ahhh*... won't it... won't it hurt?"

"Does *this* hurt?" David asked smoothly, teasing a finger just barely inside Shea's opening.

"*No,*" Shea moaned.

"How does it feel?"

"*So fucking good,*" Shea sighed, biting off the end of the confession as his voice broke. He turned his face away from David's scrutiny.

"Does it look like that slave is in pain?" Fingers squeezed lightly around Shea's cockhead and he thrust again, helplessly, letting out a stuttered, throaty cry. Then his hole was pulled open wider, and the finger slid smoothly into him again.

He shuddered with pleasure.

"*Fuck,* please. I can't... need... I need..."

"Does it look," David said slowly, with plenty of determination, "like that slave is in pain? Answer me. Focus on my words."

Shea tried to do as asked. Arching his back, he fought to be still. He clenched up as hard as he could on David's finger. Even more fluid pulsed from his dick when he liked the way the finger felt inside him.

The slave on the other side of the window had his mouth slack with what seemed like exquisite pleasure, his back bowed, his ass out and up in invitation. He was pushing back onto the hand with little movements, riding it.

"No, Master," Shea said in a wrecked, pleading voice.

"Give the word," David called to one of the guards, who pushed the intercom button and said only, "Proceed."

The hand on Shea's dick fell away, but he still had one long finger buried in him. He felt David reach away for something without removing his finger. On the other side of the window, the Dom took his massive cock in hand, aligning it with Joshua's asshole, now unfilled. Fascinated, Shea watched the rim spread around the Dom's tip, hugging it as it was slowly pressed through. Thrusting reflexively against air, seeking relief that he wasn't going to get, Shea felt David slip something slender up his ass. It was cool and hard.

When it breached him, Shea got very still, too surprised to know whether he liked it or not, initially.

A hand flattened against Shea's lower abdomen as the object was rocked against him from inside. That sensation alone was strange. But then it hit something inside him that made Shea shout and flinch, jerking away from the thing sheathed inside him which now pressed against something intensely sensitive. David's hand kept him still as the object was rocked the other way and an extension pressed against that patch of skin behind Shea's balls where David had rubbed. He was jolted with the direct stimulation to the same spot, only from outside his body instead of within. Head falling forward, panting for breath, quivering from head to toe and unable to stop crying out, Shea felt like he was coming apart.

"Stop," he pleaded in a whimper.

"Easy," David hushed. "We've done this before, that's your prostate gland. Tense your arms but relax the rest of your body. Focus on that, and the sound of my voice. I'm going to milk you while you watch that slave get fucked. Do you remember your safeword?"

At first, only grunting low in his throat, Shea felt like he was going to swallow his tongue or try to pull that thing out of David's hand. After a sharper keening cry, Shea managed, "Y-yes, sir." His cock was dripping wet. Each rocking press of that toy made Shea come up on his toes, blowing out his breath, biting back harsh, broken gasps as he became desperate under the bombardment.

"Good. You're doing really well. Watch that slave. Try to relax your body."

"Can't."

"You *can*. Try." David's hand pressed at Shea's abdomen, forcing him to take each precise rub of the toy against his gland, steadying him as he quivered.

Joshua now had the full length of the Dom's cock in him, and Shea stared because it didn't seem possible it had fit inside there. When the Dom withdrew until the head caught on the sub's rim, his shaft was wet, dark, and as nearly as big around as a baseball bat. He simply thrust it back into the sub, momentarily knocking the breath from him. Shea could see how hard Joshua was, though, and the quicker the thrusts came, the more the sub pushed back to meet them, impaling himself on the Dom. When the Dom's hips were slapping regularly against Joshua's butt cheeks, the sub smiled happily and sighed.

"Oh fuck," Shea moaned.

A hand was sliding through the fluid soaking Shea's dick. He tried to twist a little into the contact and away from the toy he couldn't escape.

"Be still," David commanded. "I wish you could see how exquisite you are right now, slave. I absolutely love all of those beautiful little cries you're making. I can feel how close you are to coming, but you're not allowed to, do you understand?"

Shea grunted.

David's wet hand came up to Shea's mouth, painting the warm, tangy fluid he'd milked from his dick over his lower lip. Then he slipped his index finger into Shea's mouth for him to suck on. Tasting himself, Shea felt caught between being more uncomfortable than he'd ever been in his life and, at the same time, just as strongly, willing to do anything to keep David from stopping.

"I'd love to lick your rim right now," David said quietly by Shea's ear, sending a shiver down his spine. "It's warm. I can feel the blood beating right under the surface. Do you want that, slave? My tongue petting your hole while I rock this toy against your gland?"

"Fuck me," Shea heard himself cry, brokenly, in a plea. "Fuck me, Master."

He knew he wanted it, to be able to have David the way that slave had his Master. The pain he'd been afraid of wasn't a factor anymore, not if that submissive loved it as much as Shea could see he did. He didn't want David's toy. He wanted David.

"Please give me your cock, Master," Shea implored with a raspy, breathless voice, between keening little hums as the toy kept stimulating him, making him wild. The hand flattened on his stomach again and the rocking quickened until Shea made a wordless, sobbing sound, fighting it. His cock jumped and the fluid dripped from him. On the other side of the glass, the slave was being fucked hard and quickly, bouncing forward with every movement of his Master. Briefly, the Dom pulled out, as if showing them his impressive, darkened cock, then sheathed it again, with a grin, in his sub.

"*Please!*" Shea cried.

"Are you still feeling shy?" David asked calmly, ignoring Shea's pleas. "Would you let me bring that slave and his Master in here to fuck for our pleasure? I'd let them watch the way your hips chase the air, your cock dripping wet and jumping with every press of this toy. It would make their mouths water, wanting to taste you, to pet your cock and balls with their tongues, the way I want to use mine to pet this unspoiled, virginal hole."

214

"Yes! Fine! Anything! *Please...*"

So slowly, Shea wasn't sure it was actually happening, the toy was removed.

"Shift your grip lower on the post. Spread your legs wider. Even wider."

He was bent at a ninety degree angle, his ass up and spread. Gently, he felt pressure against his opening, and thought David was really going through with it. But the pressure became ache, then a feeling of uncomfortable, intimate fullness.

"That's two fingers, stretched slightly apart," David told him. "Does it hurt? You're frowning."

"No, sir, just...." He let out a shaky breath, letting his head hang between his arms as he steadied himself mentally and physically.

"Just what?"

The fingers began to move, in and out. He tried pushing back on them, pulling forward, counter to their movement. The more natural it started the feel, the more he trusted himself to continue, until he was riding them. David's other hand clasped Shea's hip, guiding his pace. Soon, Shea was panting, moaning almost constantly as he fucked himself onto David's hand.

"Please. I need to come... please... Master...."

"No," David said shortly.

Shea stopped caring about the window, or the guards. There was only David, controlling every movement, each feeling, connecting them and driving Shea on. He listened to the sound of his ass slapping lightly against David's hand.

"I want you, David," Shea heard himself say, with more honesty than he could have dreamed. "Please. I'm ready."

David caressed Shea's ass, sighing. His fingers pulled out, rubbing briefly over the tender opening. Shea tipped his hips in invitation.

"*Please.*"

Already, he felt empty, and there was only one thing he wanted to be filled with, the only thing he could think of.

"Once you give this away, there's no getting it back," David warned.

"I know. It's my choice. I've chosen."

"Turn and face me, slave."

His heart beating faster with the force of his own bravery, Shea stood, then turned around.

"Kneel."

He went to his knees in front of David, head bowed, his body crying out for more. He was shocked by how wet and red his genitals were.

"I won't pretend I don't want you, just as much if not more," David said softly, caressing Shea's hair and the back of his head. "Would you like to return to the bedroom together?"

"Yes, please, Master."

"Should we end the scene now or will you submit to me in bed?"

Shea looked at the state of himself, at David's polished shoes, feeling the effects on his body, knowing what was still happening next door. There was only one choice, really. Recognizing it, he felt lighter, and more at peace than he had in a long time.

"I want to submit to you, Master. Please."

David sighed, and stepped closer. He hugged Shea to his body, and Shea mouthed over David's hardness, trapped within his pants, while David's fingers combed through his hair, greedily.

Chapter 27
Sacrificial Virgin

David knew it all came down to trust. Trust, in the face of imminent hurt, was all Shea had. Considering everything, that he had any trust left at all was quite a miracle. So many people had hurt him. His family had abandoned him when he needed them most. Friends had betrayed him. The job he'd hated was the reason why he had been attacked and robbed. Even David, who liked to think so highly of himself, had inflicted bodily harm and potentially mortal danger upon Shea just by associating with him. Without family, or a solid support system of friends, without money, shelter, skills, or even luck, here Shea was, giving irreplaceable, priceless pieces of himself, freely.

No one had ever trusted David so much. Shea gave everything, and he did it with a light heart and a charming smile. He had possibly the purest soul and the best intentions of anyone David had known. There was nothing selfish in him, no motive, no judgment or expectations. Instead, there was gratitude, bravery, humility, and even love.

Shea was kneeling on the bed, his head bowed, and his body naked. He was gifting all of himself to someone who, perhaps, did not deserve such a treasure or leap of faith. David had, after all, failed Shea once.

If the tides were turned, would I be able to give so much? Even if there seemed to be no other choice, would I dare?

There were men beyond the walls who wished Shea harm. Perhaps, even now, hired soldiers, trained assassins and criminals were plotting ways to get closer in order to pry Shea from David's sanctuary. Because Shea was the unknown—a threat. They would eagerly, happily, torture Shea for information, confessions, or simply their own satisfaction, until there was nothing of him left.

There had been other threats, before. Now, David knew Dorian saw Shea as a return of everything that had torn their family apart. Years ago, Dorian had allowed his daughter, Donna, what had seemed a harmless favor, a show of respect. She'd had a boyfriend whom they allowed into their home. Trent had been so unassuming, so gentle and respectful. He had also been poor. The similarities were there.

So, David understood. He was paying for the sins of the past, of which he'd only been a spectator. He'd taken no part, held no fault, yet here they were. The circle had turned and it was his lover who was being asked to pay for Donna's life.

His *lover*. His Shea, who knelt there, willingly, giving his whole heart, his whole body, and everything he had in the world, to David.

David knew what Shea had been through, all of his secrets they had not yet discussed aloud. In the interests of protecting his clients, as well as himself, and being more able to safeguard Shea, David had delved into his past. He'd seen the police records, the death certificate, everything. When David looked at Shea, he saw all of him, and could only wait patiently for Shea to be ready to open up and let David in.

Now it seemed Shea was doing just that, and there was no choice — David had to be more reliable and take much more care than those Shea had dared to trust before.

Inspiration struck. It came to David then. Clouds parted, and a shaft of brilliant, shimmering revelation shone down.

He knew what he needed to do, had found a possible path out of their nightmare.

And it made it easier to accept Shea's generosity, as he resolved on the actions he would take. He might not have been able to go through with it, otherwise, since the idea of taking advantage of Shea made David feel like a monster. The bruises and scars were still there on Shea's body, proof of David's guilt and collaboration in an innocent's suffering. Who was he to punish a slave for laughing at another's misfortune when he was placing the man he loved in the path of torture and death?

Unable to stay away a moment longer, David walked to the bed. There was a guard by the door, within the room. At least two more were standing just outside. They were as safe as they would get. And

Shea... he was beautiful. His deep blue eyes glimmered with the most intimate, understandable, private sort of fear. His body glistened with a light sheen of sweat, the muscles tensed. His abdomen flexed slightly with each breath, his chest rising and falling gently. His hands rested upon the tops of his legs, one thumb moving restlessly, tapping as he glanced up so hesitantly, almost making eye contact, but not quite. He was the self-conscious, sacrificial virgin, and he was breathtaking.

Cupping a hand under Shea's jaw, caressing with the pad of his thumb the overheated skin, charged with the electricity of a teenager's entirely warranted fears, David savored him.

"Will you submit to me?" David asked in a whisper that moved between them, secret but not. Secrecy and privacy were indulgences for the un-pursued.

"Yes, Master," Shea answered on a tense sigh. His breath began to come harder. Certainty turned like a screw, winding him up.

"Lie back," David said. He was also naked, his body ready and eager to claim. When his hand twisted up his own shaft, spreading the slick to ease the way, Shea's gaze fell upon it. With a soft sound of fret, he arranged himself on his back. "Let your legs fall open. All the way."

A little restless with anticipation as he bore David's scrutiny, Shea kept his legs bent but ever so slowly forced his knees to fall open, showing the man who would take him exactly what his prize was. Gazing down through mostly closed eyelids, through thick, dark eyelashes, Shea watched David stroking himself and moving onto the bed. The heaving of Shea's chest, the tightness of his nipples, the rigidity of his cock—it lured David in, intoxicating him. He felt, more than he ever had, like a predator—the cat in the night, stalking prey with no hope of escape, or the snake in the grass, creeping in, fangs bared, jaws wide and ready to devour.

The bed shifted only slightly as David knelt between Shea's opened legs, seeing everything.

"Touch yourself."

Shea didn't want to. That was clear. An endearing expression of fleeting reticence moved across Shea's face. He squeezed his eyes closed, gathering courage, and reached down between his legs. His hand trembled as he took hold of his cock and began to stroke it while

David watched.

"Shy?" David smiled.

Shea made a soft, sweet whimper as his cheeks flushed pink. The longer David watched Shea's hand work, the more plaintive Shea's groans became. His thighs tensed as though he wanted to close them, more than anything else.

"Okay," David said. "Spread yourself. Use both hands."

Shea breathed out a word, which might have been David's name. He was frowning, looking scared. Drawing his legs back, Shea palmed his cheeks and pulled. He let his head fall back, choosing to look at anything other than David, or himself. David considered the sight of him—the flushed, stretched, wet ring of his hole, and his cock as it twitched, almost softening, but not quite, as well as the anxiousness in his body's tension.

"How does that feel, slave?"

"Weird, sir." Shea murmured. "Humiliating. Scary."

"Do you want my cock?"

"Fuck," Shea exhaled. His frown deepened. His anxiety grew. Yet, fascinatingly, he pulled harder at his cheeks and angled his hips slightly upward as if offering himself. "I mean, yes. That's the whole point, right?"

"Slip a finger in. Just one."

Shea sighed heavily. For a second, he refused, frozen. Then, he moved. The tip of his index finger of his right hand shifted over fractionally, touching the over-sensitized rim gently. It held there, then pushed through. Shea's chest heaved, his feet flexed.

"To the last knuckle, then hold it there," David said patiently, still stroking himself, greedily staring at the delicious show Shea was putting on.

The finger sank deeper. Shea swallowed a heavy moan. His jaw was clenched, his eyes shut.

"Very nice. Now, fuck yourself with it."

Shea whimpered, but the finger moved, pulling out, pushing in again, over and over. His face was very flushed now.

"Rub your rim. Use three fingers."

"Oh god," Shea groaned softly, but obeyed.

"What do you want, slave?" David asked, leading Shea with intent.

Shea opened his eyes. He glanced down at David, kneeling there, his gaze roaming up and down, then up again. Once more, Shea spread himself, tilting his hips.

"You," he answered, bravely bearing David's stare. "I'm ready."

"Okay. Bring your hands above your head."

Shea complied.

Letting go of everything in a heavy sigh, David moved swiftly into position, hooking his arms under Shea's knees, bending them sharply and folding Shea in half. Coming in close, he felt his cock nudge between Shea's cheeks. The heat of Shea's body washed over him, charging David's resolve.

David shifted slightly and adjusted his angle. Shea was panting and grimacing with the force of his anxiety now that the moment was at hand. He was so resolved, bare and open, it took David's breath away.

"Just do it, okay?" Shea begged in a whisper.

"I could never. Look at me, Shea," David implored. When he'd caught Shea's gaze, David kissed him, tasting his heat and flavor, chasing every tremble of his lip. "I love you."

He thrust, the movement slow and steady but firm. David's body wrapped Shea, holding him and taking him with building pressure. Little quivers he felt in Shea were soothed away with gentle caresses. The more David pushed, the more Shea opened.

Shea made a startled, fragile cry that could not have been heard by anyone but David. Pressing through, being squeezed maddeningly by the natural tightness of Shea's body, David took his time as he entered Shea. Using his full body weight, David held himself still, moving only his hips as they pressed into his lover.

He would never forget the scared, soft sounds Shea made, his trembling lips brushing David's temple, his body trying to push back instinctively, futilely. It was the crossed line. Shea's pain was David's in every sense. Shea's hands gripped David's side and his arm, clawing at him. His expression twisted with the ache David knew he was feeling, so he sank deeper. A wild, jagged gasp rent the air as David gave one last, firm push so they were fully joined.

"It doesn't feel..." Shea said with barely any sound at all. "David, it doesn't feel good."

"I know," David promised, dragging kisses over Shea's jaw to his lips. Touching them with his own, David drank down Shea's gasps. "I know. It gets better. I swear it."

He withdrew slightly, then rocked back in, setting a slow pace, giving Shea a little more each time. Shea's eyes flew open, his hands grabbing at David, his breathing stopped entirely. Then, he grimaced and exhaled heavily, crying out a pained groan.

"Relax your body. Stay open," David panted, becoming quickly delirious with the extent of his pleasure. The grip of Shea's ass was matched only by the earnestness of his yearning to break through the pain and the gentle hug of his muscles around David's cock — it was worth the wait, the effort, and the sacrifice. It was worth everything.

The more steadily he moved, the more he felt Shea give over to it. His mouth was fallen open, his body nudged slightly upward with each inward thrust. A soft moan accompanied each withdrawal.

David felt Shea turn his damp face towards him, nuzzling his cheek, gasping against his skin. Taking Shea's arms, guiding them upward, above his head, David held them there and kept rocking, getting off on the grip, heat, softness and, most of all, the way Shea held his Master's gaze. David saw everything reflected there — every sensation, every shame, all of the trust and hope.

For Shea's sake, David didn't draw it out, but let the forbidden pleasure sweep him away that much quicker.

"Will you take my seed, slave?" David asked, fiercely holding Shea's gaze.

A flush of pleasure, then, "Yes, Master," Shea grunted, gritting his teeth against the bombardment and steady, ceaseless nudging deeper, deeper, deeper. Feeling his slicked, steely cock sliding within the hot glove of Shea's ass, David moved to kiss him. His tongue licked into Shea's mouth, tasting the delicious heat of him. Holding him down, David came, unloading deeply within Shea, holding there until he was spent.

"I love you," Shea whispered against David's lips, their salvation and damnation.

"I'm not done with you," David warned with a growl.

"*Seriously?*" Shea groaned, which only made David laugh. "My ass is throbbing and really sore in very embarrassing ways I didn't know were possible, but you're not done?"

"I'm absolutely serious," David promised. "You thought this was it? The culmination? My love, I haven't even *started* yet. You're going to be mine in every conceivable way, in every position, with every technique, in every circumstance, as long as we both shall live."

"You're incredible, you know," Shea smiled, looking happy, of all things. It tugged at David's heartstrings so strongly, they were kissing again, quite suddenly.

"Not *nearly* as incredible as you," David groaned. "But I'm still not done."

"Fuck," Shea groaned.

"*Fucked*," David corrected with a smirk. "Keep your hands there, above your head. Don't move them until I give you permission, or you'll be punished."

"Yes, sir," Shea answered with a crooked hint of a smile.

David sat back on his heels, so that he was looking down at Shea's body below him, arranged perfectly there on the bed with his arms loose, wrapping his head, his torso long and lean, and his ass stuffed full of David's cock. Shea's cock was being seriously neglected.

After filling his palm with a dollop of lube, David twisted it up Shea's shaft, then back down again. He rubbed it over his balls, then down around his stretched rim, and back up again, all the way up his dick. Shea's groan was rolling thunder that deepened with the arch of his back, trying to push into David's tugging.

"You're going to associate taking my cock with *nothing* but pleasure, slave," David warned. "You will come. You'll beg me to allow you to come, and make you come. You'll think of *nothing* but getting fucked and how hard I can make you orgasm, every single fucking time. Do you hear me?"

David thrust against Shea's ass, letting him feel the slide of his softened member nestled there. He pumped Shea harder, faster, jacking him. With his free hand, he rubbed Shea's rim and balls. Soon, Shea was crying out roughly, and loudly, quivering with the imminent approach of his orgasm.

"What do you want, slave?" David asked, demanding an answer.

"More. Fuck, more, don't stop. Don't...."

David let go, grabbed Shea's upper thighs and began to move, fucking him shallowly.

Shea moaned harder than ever, his brow furrowed, his eyes squeezed shut, his cock desperately fucking nothing but air. He ground down against David's cock, like that might help.

"Feel that?" David asked, darkly. "You're *mine*, Shea. And I'm going to keep you, as long as you'll let me."

"Yes, Master," Shea choked out.

For a while, they just kissed and breathed, savoring the closeness. Once David was hard again, he was sliding easily. His hips beat a steady rhythm against Shea's ass and the fingers of his left hand brushed feather-light over Shea's tip.

Frantic sounds purred from Shea. He was beyond words, or sense, pushed hard into primal need.

"Say please," David teased.

"Please, Master. *Please*, Master. *Please, Mas—*"

David gave him one tight, complete squeeze. Shea's entire body clenched with climax as hot semen poured through David's fingers. He growled and fucked. Shea continued to shiver and beg nonsensically, thrusting against David's hand, riding his cock.

"*More, Master. Please, Master. Fuck, Master...*"

David came with a gasp and a subtle convulsion. He was embracing Shea tightly, their bodies entwined, clutching to one another desperately. Nothing else mattered.

Chapter 28

Belonging

Shea's sleep was broken only by the aches in his body, distant reminders of the tangible world and the things he'd done with a man who had been such a mysterious blessing and catalyst. When he woke the next morning, David was spooned up behind him, one arm slung around Shea's mid-section, the hand loosely palming Shea's stomach. Held like that, so gently and lovingly, Shea thought about where he was, how he'd gotten there, and where he'd been. There were still so many questions. At the moment, he felt like he belonged with David, *to* David, but everything in his life kept changing, over and over again. Sometimes it was hard to believe anything was permanent anymore, as much as he wanted that to be true. The quiet moments before waking always brought the doubts back.

He thought about the bag of his things that sat in David's dressing room, still unpacked, and really, just the fact that he was dating someone who even had dressing rooms was pretty mind blowing.

I'm dating David. We are dating, aren't we? Can you call it that, when I live with him, act as a sex slave for him, and we never go out?

There was no other word that made any sense, though. He had to use it. So, he was dating a man who had dressing rooms. Plural. It was something Shea couldn't wrap his mind around, just like so many other things. But in that entire room, which was just really a fancy closet, sat the most important possessions in Shea's life. There were a few of his most prized comics, his sole photo of his entire family posed together, an old journal of his deceased grandfather's, and a few mix tapes given to him by old boyfriends. They were all tucked in a ratty, navy blue duffle bag he used to bring to high school on days he had gym class. Now, he had real life mercenaries trying to kill him, and was being held for his own protection in what was basically his very own, personal, fortified secret lair. David was acting like the superheroes that Shea had always dreamed about, knowing he would never become one himself.

Things needed to change, but he wasn't sure what, or how to change them. He didn't even know how to start. David was giving him so much, but it was all basically a stepping off point. It was really up to Shea to figure out where to go next and how to get there. But Shea had never felt powerful, unlike David, who had power over so much—his company, his staff, his properties, his money, his future, and his lovers.

It did help Shea find some inner peace when he glimpsed behind David's power to the normal guy he was underneath. Shea knew how to relate to the real David. Even with all of the things money could buy, David needed things from Shea he hadn't been able to find elsewhere, even with all of the resources he had available.

Maybe Shea didn't have a team of intimidating bodyguards, or years of training in self-defense, but he did have other sorts of strength. That's what he had to give to David, and that's what Shea knew would get him through.

David's lips pressed to the back of Shea's neck, over his spine. It sent shivers down his back and pebbled the skin along his arms.

"What's on your mind?" David whispered, a soft rumble of sound against Shea's neck.

"Things that have happened to me, I guess. Where I've been. Who I've..." he sighed. "Is it okay if I talk to you about stuff? I usually keep things to myself, but I... I want you to know me."

"I want that too. Please. I'd love to listen."

"Okay. I just think you should know more about me."

"Like what?" David asked, in a patient, unhurried sort of way that made it easier for Shea to keep going.

"Like why I want to belong somewhere. Why it's important to me," Shea began, then paused, unsure where to go next. Hell, it was the story of his life. "My things are all in boxes. My pathetic, ratty old gym bag is sitting in your closet like the trash the maid forgot to throw out, and my whole life is in there, David. I wear clothes that aren't mine, eat food I didn't earn, sleep in a bed that's — "

"Please don't be so hard on yourself," David interjected. "What's wrong?"

Shea breathed out a laugh, then paused thoughtfully. He caressed over the back of David's hand, which was clasping Shea's bare abdomen. He'd been trying to tune it out, but he could feel it, the intimate soreness caused by having sex for the first time. It was just so real, and final.

"My, uh," Shea started, choosing to focus on the warm solidity of David's hand, touching him, instead of the silk sheets, or the sprawling room around them, or anything else beyond it. "My dad was always angry, and I could never figure it out. It was just part of him. It had to have been caused by something. I mean, it's only logical. People don't just get born pissed off. Toddlers are naturally happy, aren't they? But if there was a reason for it, I never knew what it was, and he never explained. There were entire groups of humanity he didn't like, because of their religion, or their race, or their political affiliation. That's why we lived so far out in the middle of nowhere. He wanted to be as far away as he could from all of these groups, like whatever he thought was corrupting them was going to rub off on him, or us.

"TV was bad. Popular culture was bad. For years, I had to cart around my comics in my backpack instead of leaving them at home, because if Dad found them, he would have tossed them. Some I kept with friends, but my favorites lived with me. Kind of funny that even before they kicked me out, I was already living out of a packed bag.

"My friends from school were suspect and pretty much not welcome at home. I don't know how to explain it. It was like he saw poison everywhere that no one else could see. And as a kid — as *his* kid — it was really confusing and frustrating. All I wanted was to make him happy. I figured it couldn't be *that hard*."

Shea blew out a breath and shook his head. David moved his fingertips in a gentle arc against Shea's abdomen, and it tickled a little, making Shea smile and grab hold of David's fingers to stop the tickling touch. He folded their hands together instead. It felt nice.

"Anyway, my mom was... different. I couldn't figure her out either. I mean, when I was little, I never questioned the way they were, but the more I saw other people's parents, and visited them at their homes, I started to compare and contrast. And no one else had parents like mine. But mom... it was like she wasn't all there, like there was a piece missing. You'd talk to her, try to get her to understand something or a point of view, or anything really, and her eyes would glaze over. She wasn't listening. She would nod and smile and make sounds like she was listening, but she wasn't. Maybe she was tuned in to a different frequency than the rest of us, or maybe it was just her way of dealing with Dad. Who knows? She was personable, and polite, and pretty, but there was just never any real connection.

"It wasn't until I found a photograph packed away in the attic that I finally had some answers."

Falling momentarily quiet, looking at the fine texture of the pillowcase under his head, Shea remembered how it had felt, going into the attic like he was on a mission, a hero with a cause. He'd been so hopeful.

David caressed Shea's hand and kissed the back of his neck.

"I got this idea in my head, and once I had it, it seemed to fit so perfectly, like this big plot twist I should have seen coming from page one. And I was really relieved! It was like, wow, this would explain everything. I had to have been adopted. My parents were really these totally normal people, people just like me, and the people I'd always thought were my mom and dad were just not the right fit. I mean," he laughed at how stupid he'd been, "There aren't that many pictures of me growing up, especially from when I was a baby. That was my first clue."

"Shea," David sighed with what sounded like heartache, like somehow he knew the punchline already.

"So I would imagine what my real parents were like, and how happy they'd be to finally see me after I'd found them again. I'd daydream about it constantly. It made so much sense. All I needed was proof. That's why... why I..." He started tearing up. "Fuck," he cursed, rubbing his eyes, his breath hitching.

"It's okay," David promised, palming Shea's chest, right above his heart. "I've got you."

"I went through the stuff shoved into corners in the garage, anything that had lots of dust on it. I went through the attic, but I waited until they weren't around to catch me, and I..." he blew out a breath and rubbed his eyes again.

"It wasn't you in the photo, was it?" David said quietly.

Shea shook his head. Hearing David say it first made it easier to keep talking.

"I was so stupid," Shea whispered painfully.

David held him, wrapping him in an embrace and said, "No, sweetheart. Far from it. Hope may be foolish, but where would we be left without it?"

"I went looking for a photo of two parents with a baby, and that's what I found. But, you're right, David. It wasn't me, but it was them. The picture was of a baby boy with my parents, but the baby had dark hair, brown eyes. It was someone else, and my parents were really young in the photo. Too young. I dug some more, found two other pictures of that other boy, but that was it. There was nothing of me, nothing that helped it make sense. So, I called my uncle. He's kind of hard to pin down, like me I guess, but he does keep a cell phone. He told me about Isaiah. He was born ten years before me, and died when my mom was pregnant with me. Isaiah was on his bike. There was a drunk driver, a hit and run accident. Gotta say, it explained a lot. That's where the anger came from, for my dad, and why my mom just couldn't connect anymore. That was why there weren't any pictures of me and why they'd never treated me like they..." He blew out a breath, waiting, then when he felt steadier, said, "I guess I wasn't living up to my brother's legacy, in their eyes."

Shea got choked up again and had to stop. It felt so good to have David holding him, easing him through it.

"I'm betting you haven't said his name aloud often. But it feels good, doesn't it?"

"Yeah," Shea replied hoarsely. "After all, he didn't ask for that to happen. I'm sure he would want to be remembered in a nice way and not..." He let the sentence fade off and backed away from it. "They really are mine. My parents. But all I've brought them are reminders of what they don't have anymore. They're in pain and I did that to them, so no wonder, you know? No wonder they always treated me like they wished I was someone else."

"It's their problem, Shea," David told him urgently. "Not yours. You did nothing wrong. You're this sweet, loveable person and for them to not react to that the way they should have is inexcusable. Think about what I've been dealing with regarding Dorian. Don't take their actions onto yourself."

Shea murmured a soft sound and covered David's encircling arm with his hands, the touch and tender connection even more comfort than he'd dreamed possible.

"They kicked you out for being gay?" David's lament changed his tone and made Shea flush with appreciative warmth for the sympathy.

"Yeah. It either pushed them over the edge or just gave them an excuse to do what they'd been wanting to for a while. Dad saw me kissing Ryan and that was it, I guess. I ran after him to explain, but he just grabbed a box from the garage and started to go through my room, throwing armfuls of clothes and random crap from my shelves into it. Mom was there somewhere, but she didn't get involved. He filled the box and took it outside, dropped it on the driveway. He told me to get out and never come back."

A painful, shaky breath escaped him, then, and he shook his head at the memory. Closing his eyes, holding David just a little tighter, Shea said, "When I didn't leave fast enough, he came out with his shotgun. I hadn't wanted to believe he'd really meant it. I was hoping it was momentary anger and he'd realize he'd gone too far. But, when I saw that gun, I knew."

David became very still. There was no sound of breath for a long moment.

Then he said, "Look at me, Shea."

A command. It was kind of funny, that David was always on like that, always in control.

Shea turned and made the effort to lift his gaze. It didn't seem possible at first. He was caught in that memory, standing in the road, staring at his dad like maybe the love in Shea's heart would be able to melt all of the ice between them. Shea had loved his dad so much. He couldn't wrap his head around the fact that he wasn't loved in return. The more he stood apart from the situation, he was able to see it was all because of Isaiah, and it really had nothing to do with Shea at all. And that helped a lot, but it didn't make the ache go away.

Shea guessed that his parents did love him, but their own grief and regret were too big to allow them to show it.

David clasped the side of Shea's face, holding him there to be seen, making sure Shea knew he was seen, even though Shea wanted to close himself off and hide.

David's eyes were so vibrant, the sage of a lush field or the bloom of spring; they sparkled with intention. Strangely, it felt like the unimportant things were falling away. David knew his way down some path Shea couldn't see, and on the other side, it would all be open and the possibilities would be endless.

"You didn't deserve that," David said. "He was wrong to act that way. It was his job to take care of you and he failed."

Shea didn't know what to say, so he just looked into David's eyes, liking how they held him so closely.

"You sound so sure," Shea replied with disbelief, eventually.

"I am," David agreed. "I owe you an apology, sweetheart. I've been so overwhelmed by things lately, that I haven't paid enough attention to what you need."

"No, David, you've already done so much. You don't need to do anything else for —"

"I do," David countered, firmly. "I'll have my staff clear ample room for your things in my dressing room. Drawers, cabinets, whatever you need. As far as this space is concerned, you're welcome to add your own possessions, however you see fit. This is your home. I want you to make it yours. Put your stamp on it."

"David," Shea sighed. "That's really generous of you, but it's still important to me to have something of my own. When they threw me out, I swore to myself I'd never feel like that again, like I have nothing and no way to take care of myself."

"I can provide you with your own apartment instead, if you'd like, or in addition to you staying here. Someplace with adequate security, and not too far away."

"David," Shea cut in. "Please. You don't need —"

"No one is ever going to make you feel like you don't belong anymore. Do you understand? You'll have property in your name. No matter what happens, you will have a place to go."

"You can't —"

"I *can*. Tell me again I can't," David dared, eyes blazing now. Shea felt a strange heat bloom low in his gut and dropped his gaze, bashfully. He hugged David, pressing his lips to his shoulder while David caressed the back of Shea's head. There was no way he could defend a position or argue in the state he was in. His ass ached from getting fucked and David's sternness was arousing him, dismantling Shea's ability to do anything but yield to David's every demand. "I have a plan to deal with my father, for good. There are a few calls I need to make, people to see to make the necessary arrangements, but it will be taken care of. I'd also like to introduce you to my mother, who would be delighted to know you. She's much more sensible than my father."

"I don't know what to say," Shea admitted quietly.

"Do you know how much you've given me?" David asked softly. "Just by holding me like this? Just by loving me as honestly as you do? By trusting me so much? I know how difficult it was for you to be with me this way, and to talk about these things. Keeping you secure is the very least I can do, in return."

Shea caressed David's back, then felt David kiss Shea's jaw.

"You deserve more than you know," David said conclusively. "And now I know why."

David moved to sit up. Self-consciously, Shea realized he was half-hard and David would be able to see. He tried to grab at the sheet to cover himself, but David pulled it from his grip, tossing the covers back.

"Flip over. I need to make sure you're unhurt."

"David," Shea started, intending to argue.

"That's an order, slave."

A pleasant shiver raced through Shea's body and he bit at his lip. The word slave was starting have very distinct implications for him. It meant David wanted him, and that was only a good thing for a guy like Shea who had dreamed for so long of being the object of another's affection. He turned over, keeping his knees under him so that he wasn't lying on his rapidly swelling dick.

"Good. Hands and knees, then."

Shea groaned, turning his face away in shyness as David shifted behind him and pulled Shea's cheeks apart. Biting his lip, Shea endured some poking and prodding at both the best and worst place

David could be touching him.

"You're swollen, but that'll heal. I'm ordering you to bedrest to-day. I'll have your meals delivered and the guards will be instructed to relay any messages or requests to the rest of the staff should you need anything while I'm making arrangements."

David shifted even closer. He flattened a hand on Shea's navel, drawing him up onto his knees, guiding Shea to lean back against David's chest.

"Bring your arms up," David instructed. "Lace your fingers behind your head. Good. Just like that."

Shea was breathing harder, too aware of his erection. His head still hadn't caught up with what his instincts knew. Being ready for David didn't make the prospect of the psychological freefall any less intimidating. David slid a palm up along the underside of Shea's shaft. His cock twitched and David caressed downward to cup Shea's balls. Shea exhaled heavily, shuddering and closing his eyes.

"Why are you hard? Tell me."

"I, um," Shea floundered for words as his senses flooded his system with signals and needs that made thinking impossible. "Like the way you touch me."

"What else?"

"Your, uh... the way you..."

"Say it."

"The power in the way you talk to me, I guess," Shea answered lamely.

"You respond well to command? Is that it?"

Shea focused on breathing; every inch of bare skin that was in contact with David tingled and sparked. David tugged gently on Shea's sac and rolled his balls in a hand. Shea grunted and rocked into the touch.

"Knowing what's behind it is love instead of hate? Yes, sir," he answered breathlessly.

"Explain, please."

"Well, I've always tried to use my sense of humor to get people to like me. It's worked sometimes. Others, not so much. I like that I don't have to try to be anything other than who I am with you. I can just relax, and listen. It's nice."

"Good. Is any of this," David asked, tugging on Shea's erection, "desire for more of what we did last night?"

"Yes, Master," Shea answered, bowing his head.

"You're not too sore?"

Shea shook his head, then realized David probably wanted a verbal answer. "No, Master."

David's teeth scraped Shea's jaw. "Good. I intend to take you again tomorrow morning, slave. How do you feel about that?" David asked while he rubbed the pad of his thumb on his left hand over the pink head of Shea's cock while his right hand continued to massage Shea's sac.

Shea attempted to answer, but it was only a moaned series of sounds. He felt pre-ejaculate weep from his dick. David spread it in small circles over the tip.

"Answer me, slave."

"Good," Shea panted. "I feel good about it, sir."

"Lie down on your back in the center of the bed."

Shea whispered a curse and glanced down at David's restless rubbing of those small circles. David moved backward to give him room and Shea lay down.

Shifting off the bed, drawing the sheet farther down, David admired Shea's body and said, "Now stretch your arms and legs out widely, to the four corners of the bed."

Assuming the position, Shea lay there, spread-eagle and hard as a rock, his reddened cock jutting upward. David wandered to a cabinet and retrieved a few things. He returned to the bed with his phone and a phallic sex toy that made Shea nervous.

"I need silence during my call, slave. No moving, either. You move or make a sound and there will be punishment. Let's see how you do, hmm?"

Shea had no idea if he was capable of following those orders or not. David touched the screen of his phone a few times. Placing the phone to his ear, David moved to kneel upon the bed near Shea's middle.

"Yes, this is David Davenport calling for Mr. Goldstein. It's urgent."

Is he actually making a business call while doing this? Shea wondered, suspecting that David had more faith in Shea's abilities than he did.

That's when David pushed at a strategic spot on the toy and it started to hum. It was a soft, low sound, quiet enough to not be detectable by the phone, but Shea could feel it. The vibration moved through the air around them. Reaching out with the phallus, David touched it to the tip of Shea's cock.

Instantly, the vibrations began to shiver down Shea's shaft and he had to bite hard at the inside of his cheek to stay silent. His thighs and stomach muscles tensed and the urge to thrust upward was almost overpowering. Slowly, David rubbed the vibrating cock over his tip, down once in a while over the divot under the head. Shea stopped listening to the conversation entirely. He knew David was speaking to the person on the other end, but the words never made their way into his brain. It was all a wash of white.

He was distantly aware, not only of the talking, but of the rubbing of the toy over his cock, over his balls, and of a trembling throughout his body as he fought to stay still. He bit his lips to keep them shut and swallowed all of his groans before they could be heard.

It went on and on, but instead of torture, Shea slipped beneath the surface of awareness and floated along on pure sensations.

"Slave!" Shea heard, cutting through the flood and bringing him back to awareness.

"Yeah. Yes. Yes, Master?" Shea panted, his voice lilting.

He looked down his body and saw David was no longer on the phone.

"You did very well," David smiled.

"Thanks, sir? Fuck. *Fuck*."

"That was my lawyer," David explained while continuing to torment Shea's dick and watching his work. Shea's shaft was soaking wet, and it seemed to chase the toy, jumping at the stimulation. "He'll be coming by later."

"Awesome," Shea answered deliriously.

"If you'd like to thrust, you may," David told him with a sly expression.

"Oh thank *god*," Shea moaned.

In seconds he was coming, quaking and gasping. While he was being wiped down with a wet, warm cloth, David said deviously, "I'll allow you a pair of pants and trips to the restroom, only. Would you like your usual for breakfast? I'll let Mrs. Tinsley know before I take my shower."

"Yeah, absolutely," Shea agreed without caring. "Sounds great."

Leaning down with a chuckle, David kissed Shea's lips. "I'm not going anywhere, just down the hall to my office. I'll check back often."

Shea wove his fingers through David's soft hair and murmured, "Thank you. Maybe when you stop back, I can do something for you too."

"You already have, love. Besides, we're not done. Let me handle a few things, then we'll continue our talk, all right?" David promised earnestly.

"All right."

Chapter 29
Favor from a Master Dom

The key to everything was leverage. Though Dorian wielded significant power because of his money and connections, David was fortunate enough to have his own resources to call upon. What David
needed wasn't to cause harm or inflict pain, but to force Dorian's hand
and give him no choice but to back off. Initially, David realized his
father was suspicious of Shea because of his similarities to Trent. Perhaps Dorian had even dug up the information that Shea once had an
older sibling, though the timelines didn't match up properly, and Isaiah had died at a younger age than Trent. It was likely Dorian thought
the records had been changed or falsified to hide the identities of
Shea's family.

It was all ridiculous. Even without DNA evidence, Dorian must
have realized by now that Shea had no biological connection. That
wasn't the real issue anyway. Dorian saw Shea as a threat, intending
to go after David's money or take advantage of him in other ways, the
way he had always thought Trent had taken advantage of Donna.

Perhaps he could convince Dorian otherwise. But, whatever measures that entailed would have to be secondary to David's main strategy of psychological attack. He had to make his father believe David
was capable of defending what was his, effectively.

There were only narrow strategic avenues available to him, since
there were few things Dorian truly cared about—namely David, money, and legacy.

Seeking privacy, David retreated to his office and closed the door
behind him, leaving his guard on the other side.

He sat at his desk and pulled the phone that was connected to a secure landline closer to him.

A face floated to the forefront of his mind, sped along by another recent phone call. Severe expression, light hair, intimidating build, hypnotically seductive gaze... David remembered the first time he'd met Nicholai Zhukov in person. He'd been an invited guest at Manse. David knew of Nicholai through David's Master, Brennan. David had learned his trade of dominance from Brennan at the Master's Circle, while Nicholai, also a former Master Dom, had recently retired though he was still fairly young — not even fifty.

When Nicholai had first arrived at Manse, there had been a shift in the air. All attention drew magnetically to the former Master Dom, though Nicholai was highly selective about whom he allowed to get close to him. Only David's inner circle were permitted to share the room with him. Once Nicholai selected a submissive for the evening, the sub and David were the only ones permitted to touch Nicholai. And *oh,* David remembered the touch *very* well.

But now was not the time for that. Nicholai had other skills and connections besides those to be found in the BDSM world. Calling Nicholai was one much needed step away from asking help of Brennan himself, which, to David, was basically the nuclear option — one he'd do everything he could to avoid taking.

He took a deep, steadying breath and dialed the number.

"David?" the call was answered after two rings. The tone was questioning but warm, thank god.

"Master Nicholai," David replied with a fond hint of a grin, settling back into his chair. The connection was clear, Nicholai's rich, low voice caressing David's ear.

"Calling for pleasure, then?"

"Unfortunately not," David sighed. "I've met someone who's quickly becoming very important to me. This has seriously disturbed my father and there have been attempts made."

"Kidnapping?"

"Yes. And torture. Rape. Where this is leading, we can only guess."

Nicholai exhaled heavily into the phone. Then, after a lengthy pause, replied, "I'm sorry to hear that," with what seemed sincere emotion.

"There aren't," David began, speaking stiltedly as his own emotion crept up on him, swelling his throat and pricking at his eyes, "many I can trust, or ask for help with this. My father is used to getting what he wants, even if he has to go outside the law to make it happen."

"And now he wants your lover taken out," Nicholai guessed.

"Yes," David agreed softly. "Dorian has dangerous men on his payroll. So far we've kept my lover here at my compound, where I can keep him protected, but it's not a permanent solution. I need to bring this into the light, Nicholai. Dorian wants it to stay in the dark, but that's what will get people killed. Please, I know I have no right to ask—"

"Of course you do," Nicholai scoffed. He paused, humming thoughtfully. "You have evidence? Proof your father has attacked your man and continues to threaten him?"

"Plentiful evidence. Medical reports. Surveillance footage. Eye witness testimony from trusted sources."

"Excellent," Nicholai said with a definitive air. "We can make it all nice and official, then. How soon do you need to see action taken?"

"As quickly as possible," David admitted. "With my father, things escalate quickly the more frustrated and paranoid he gets. I've been fearing snipers, and feel like it's only a matter of time."

"Speak to your lawyers about getting a restraining order in place. I'll make some calls and get back to you quickly, my friend."

"Thank you, sir. I owe you an enormous debt for this."

"Perhaps," Nicholai replied with a little chuckle.

David ended the call but kept the phone near. He paused, taking a deep breath, and steadied himself for the next call he had to make.

As if he was moving through water, and the drag was heavy on his forward momentum, he dialed and placed the phone to his ear.

"This is David calling for Marylyn. Thank you." He waited as they put him on hold. Letting his head fall back against his chair, he exhaled a heavy breath. A moment later, his mother picked up the line.

"Darling, how are you?" she asked pleasantly.

"I need to talk to you," he said softly, with none of his usual charm or confidence, and hardly any bravery.

"David, what's wrong?" Marylyn asked with alarm. He savored the sound of it, because it felt like home and safety.

"Dorian is trying to abduct and torture my boyfriend, and believe me when I assure you that I'm not being dramatic. They broke into Shea's rooms, held him against his will, interrogated him, beat him, and violated—"

"*Who?*" Marylyn cut in, sounding much more frantic than he'd heard her in a long time. "His men?"

"Yes. He's being paranoid and cruel and I... I'm at a loss. I need this to *stop*. They're watching the property, trying to get past security undetected, get upstairs to my private quarters. We've taken measures to keep them out, keep Shea safe, but I can't hide him away forever. Mother, I'm taking action. I have to. If anything happened to him—"

"This is about Donna, isn't it? He thinks it's happening again," Marylyn guessed.

"Yes, that's been my thought," David sighed. "Look, Mother, would you like to meet Shea? I'm afraid the isolation is beginning to mentally wear him down and I want to show him I'm not the only one who will fight for him. If you would be so kind as to secure the property, we could come by. There are a few things in the works which I need to discuss with you, and it can't be over the phone."

"Of course, my love. Please. You're both welcome whenever it's convenient. Shall we plan on Saturday morning? Perhaps ten? I'll arrange a brunch and that'll give me enough time to tighten things up around here. Your father has been away at the farmhouse for weeks, and I suppose this is why. Would you like me to say something to him on your behalf? I just hate the thought of you so distressed, and of your father causing torment for such a stupid reason. He's just never been able to get past the shock of it, you know. He sees danger everywhere."

"Shea isn't a danger. He's the opposite—the gentlest soul I've ever known, which is why it's been so upsetting. Thank you, Mother. We'll plan on it. You may speak to Father if you'd like, though I doubt it would do any good. Seeing is believing with him. He sees Shea with me and that's all the proof he needs."

"Well, I look forward to meeting the wondrous Shea who has finally persuaded you to abandon bachelorhood. He must be quite a charmer."

"He is," David grinned fondly. "Saturday then. Love you."

"Love you too, dear. Be safe."

Ending the call, David immediately dialed again. Straightening in his chair, he said once the call was answered, "Yes, it's David Davenport again. I need some papers drawn up immediately, before the meeting scheduled later today at my residence. It's an emergency."

When David was finally able to rejoin Shea, he was found in the bedroom, hanging clothes in the closet. A few drawers had been pulled out as well, with some odds and ends stuffed in. Shea had dressed in a well-worn Pink Floyd t-shirt and jeans. His feet were bare. His hair was adorably tousled. An opened can of soda sat on a ceramic, hand-painted coaster on one shelf of the closet.

With one hand, Shea shoved a few shirts over on the bar they hung from, while with his other, he picked up the can and slurped down some soda.

"Hey," Shea said with a crooked, warm grin, perking up as soon as he saw David approaching. "No worries, I found some coasters with Mrs. Tinsley's help. Not gonna leave moisture rings and damage the wood when this closet is seriously nicer than closets really have any right to be. My clothes look ridiculous in here, by the way. It's like a thrift store came in and replaced the actual nice clothes that belong here as a prank."

He set down the soda again on the coaster and stood up straight, hands on his hips as he admired his work at failing to organize things in his new section of the walk-in closet.

"*You* are under orders to stay in bed," David scolded gently. He caught hold of Shea's waist with one hand and drew him in for a light kiss on the lips.

"Yeah, it's *really* boring in bed when you're not there," Shea admitted. "You should try it sometime. While you lie in bed, I'll go out on super important errands like stopping by the comic book store since I am so many issues behind by now on all of the series I'm following, and you can totally hang out in bed all day, being super bored and pining after me."

"I'm always pining after you," David said, kissing Shea again, loving the taste and softness of him. Everything about him felt so warm, and so right; even just standing in a closet together made David feel like he was exactly where he should be. "But you are disobeying direct orders from your Master."

Shea groaned and hid his face against David's neck. Catching hold of his chin, David moved Shea slightly back so that he could scrutinize him properly. With downcast eyes, Shea allowed it, holding on loosely to David's hips.

"Shirt off. Back to bed. There'll be plenty of time for closet organizing once I've made certain you've recovered."

"Keep me company?" Shea asked softly with a coaxing smile. "Just for a little while."

"Mmm," David murmured, then nipped at Shea's lower lip with his teeth. "Perhaps. Are your intentions pure?"

"Of course not," Shea chuckled.

David took a deep breath, realizing his moment was at hand, that there was too much circling around the truth, and not enough of it shared yet with Shea.

"What's wrong?" Shea frowned slightly as David grew serious.

"Come sit down. Time for the rest of our talk, I think." David took Shea's hand and led the way.

Chapter 30
Hiding Behind Walls

"I should have told you sooner, and I'm sorry for that," David began. Shea was sitting back against a pile of pillows in the bed, and David sat next to him, turned to face him on the edge of the bed.

"What's this about?" Shea asked softly.

"The past. My past. The reason for all of this," David sighed. "Hearing about your family, and how your brother has impacted your life in so many ways, it does help me to understand your perspective. I'd like to give you the same insight on how my sister has impacted my life."

"Hey, I know all about wanting to leave the past where it is. If this is upsetting for you—"

"No, you're part of my life now. You deserve to know the details. It's an... ugly story. Parts of it were discovered by the media, of course. Others were known only to myself and my parents, and we've tried to keep it that way."

His memories of that time were mostly a jumble of noise—his sister, Donna, shouting and slamming doors, police and EMTs hurrying through the house, sirens and sobbing. The quieter moments were even scarier, though, in recollection: a man David had always adored, creeping through the hall and soundlessly closing a door behind him while David held his breath out of fear of being seen, then their eyes briefly meeting anyway; thumps and clinks heard through the wall adjoining David's room with his sister's; the sound of hushed laughter, then footsteps hurrying away.

How to explain it? To convey the sense of total powerlessness and imminent catastrophe? So much noise and fret, yet none of it could have saved her. Nothing could have saved her.

When David felt Shea's hand on his arm, he looked up, realizing he'd fallen silent for too long.

"Maybe it's cruel of me to say, but I think you're lucky, Shea, to have avoided living through your brother's death. At least you don't have the memories of your family's life before, to cause you to miss what was lost. With only the aftermath to survive, you were free to disengage and leave them behind. If your father believed he was punishing you by turning you out, I think he was wrong. He was simply sparing you further harm from him and your mother. When people like that contribute so much negativity, the healthiest thing you can do is to let them go.

"You remember how I mentioned to you about Donna, my sister?" he asked. "She was ten years older than me, just like you and Isaiah, actually. She was so beautiful, and much smarter than I will ever be. She was savvy and charismatic. She was my entire world and I loved her so much. There was a lot I didn't understand then, of course. I was so young—seven verging on eight. With how much I idolized her, I didn't see what was really going on until later, running those weeks over in my head on a loop, picking the pieces apart."

David looked up at Shea and saw how he was hanging on every word, a slight frown of concern creasing his brow, and David loved him even more for it—that quiet, attentive listening.

"I imagine she felt like I did while becoming an adult, on my own terms. We grew up in our parents' shadows, and were expected to be able to do everything they could—running a billion dollar empire while always presenting a flawless image to the world, being able to carry all of this weight on our shoulders, having a narrow scope in which to express ourselves since what really mattered was the business, and appearances. Not love, or individuality, or humanity.

"She met a young man her age, Trent Cokely. Even though I was young, I remember that he always had a soft voice and good manners. And I remember he had a tender heart like you. Trent was handsome in an unconventional way instead of the traditional. Most of all, though, he was absolutely devoted to Donna. The way he looked at her made me secretly wish to someday have someone like Trent look at *me* that way, too. But his family was middle class, far below Dorian's standards for his precious little girl. My father only permitted it because he sensed Donna might act out and do something extreme in defiance if he didn't. What we didn't find out until later was that Trent's family had gone bankrupt. Their house was in foreclosure, their assets were being seized. Trent must have been panicking, just trying to help his parents and little brother, Mitchell—he was about eleven then, so slightly older than me.

"They found some of Donna's jewelry in Trent's pockets, in his car, in his room at the motel they'd started living in once the bank took possession of the house."

The sound of arguing, then a soft bang, then silence—the memory was awful. David closed his eyes tightly and rubbed a hand over them, wishing he hadn't been listening in so curiously that night. If only he'd been wearing headphones or in another part of the house, or in the shower, anything other than standing there with his ear pressed to the wall, with each noise burning itself into his mind, forever.

"I've tried," he said, "to think of Trent as the villain. It would have been so much easier if I could. I just loved Donna so much and he... he took her away from us."

Shea's fingers slid down David's arm, then folded around his hand, holding on tightly, caressing the back with the pad of his thumb. David met his gaze and said, "It was a stupid argument. She finally realized what he was doing, that he was stealing from her in order to pay off some of his parents' debts. She had so much jewelry," he explained, laughing painfully, a desperate, sorrowful sound. "It filled boxes and boxes. Diamonds, emeralds, sapphires, and rubies. She wouldn't have missed *any* of it. It was stuff—sparkly rocks and metal. She was the *only* sister I would ever have. And she was *a good person.*"

"I'm so sorry," Shea whispered, shifting closer and drawing David into a hug. He pressed a kiss to David's cheek and David tried to breathe through the trembling that shook him—filled with all of the anger and unfairness, the loss and the pain.

"He said that he pushed her off of him," David explained in a hushed, defeated voice. "When she began trying to search his pockets and screaming at him, slapping him and kicking him. She fell. Hit the edge of a marble table with the back of her head and that was it. That was enough. She was gone.

"I think he truly loved her. And she loved him. I could see it in his eyes, during the trial. I think he would have done anything to take it all back."

"What happened to him?" Shea asked, though it sounded as if he was afraid to know the answer.

"Killed himself after the first week in jail. Donna's death was ruled accidental, but because she had died during Trent's attempted robbery, he was facing an enormous amount of prison time. I don't think it was entirely the time he was facing that made him do it. I think it was the grief."

David pulled out of the hug and looked at Shea, with his fading wounds and sweet vulnerability.

"It was almost twenty years ago, but it's still not over. Dorian is still so angry and afraid, only now it's for me. He thinks you're Trent come to take me away from him, too."

The clarity of Shea's emotions astonished David, then, yet again. His remorse was right there on the surface—the sympathetic ache for what David had endured with the loss of his sister. But that wasn't all. Shea could sense it—the daunting mountain of Dorian's terror and certainty of doom; they had no choice but to scale it if they ever wanted to find peace.

"What are we going to do?" Shea asked in a small voice.

"My mother wants to meet you," Dorian confessed with a shy sort of smile, and a spark of joy. It infected Shea instantly and lifted the cloud pressing down on him. His expression lightened and David was glad to see it. "And there's something else. I have a plan and—"

The phone rang in David's pocket.

After retrieving it, David answered.

"We're on our way and should be at your residence within the hour," Nicholai said. "Try to verify your father's location. That'll be our next step after picking you up."

"No problem at all. Thank you. This means the world," he told Nicholai sincerely.

After David hung up, Shea asked with widened eyes, "Was that the plan?"

"It was indeed," David smiled, then dialed Marco's number.

"Yes, we're about to have company. Call my father's personal assistant. Pass along the message that I urgently need to see him. Make sure of his location so we can meet up. You'll come with me but we won't need any other men."

"You're going to see him?" Shea asked with disbelief once that call was over as well.

"Yes, but I'm bringing company along with me."

"Just be careful, okay?" Shea said with worry. "Everything's been getting so out of control."

"Which is why this is necessary. Would you like to meet Nicholai? He's a former Master Dom from the Master's Circle and a friend. He's on his way over now."

"Sure," Shea agreed. "Am I allowed to get dressed?"

"No need," David smirked. "He's seen it all, sweetheart. Believe me."

David stood beside Marco, watching several black Lincoln Town Cars pull up behind the building. They were near to David's private entrance with direct access to his personal quarters. Once they'd rolled to a stop, people piled out of the first car. The first person David saw was Nicholai, with his light brown hair and vibrantly blue eyes. His strong, angular jaw and broad shoulders marked him instantly as a military man. David wasn't sure just how many agencies he'd worked for or served. Nicholai had been through England, Germany, Ukraine, and now was settled firmly in the U.S.

There was something about Nicholai that appealed immensely to David. Though Nicholai rarely smiled, there was warmth and friendliness to his eyes sometimes that was more magnetic than any smile David had ever seen.

Nicholai strode over to David and shook his hand firmly, simultaneously clapping him on a shoulder. Then he gestured to the imposing man who had followed him over.

"David Davenport, this is Agent Upson," Nicholai said.

Agent Upson showed his badge, the bold letters F.B.I. unmistakable. The other agents were scanning the perimeter of the property or waiting in the vehicles.

"Good to meet you, agent," David said, nodding to the tall, fit, federal agent with fierce dark brown eyes, a dark complexion and a close-cropped haircut.

"Likewise. I'd like a word with Mr. Whittier before we see your father, if it's possible," Agent Upson told David.

"Not a problem. Come this way," David smiled. He could see Nicholai was eager to meet Shea as well.

It had occurred to David that the federal agents would want to meet and speak with Shea before tackling the confrontation with Dorian, just to get a clearer picture of David's story and what they were dealing with. Having Shea remain shirtless and barefoot was a subtle strategy to make Shea appear slightly frailer and more vulnerable, and also to showcase his recent injuries. David wanted there to be no doubt in their minds as to who was being victimized here.

When the elevator opened up on David's private quarters, David, Marco, Nicholai, Agent Upson and two other federal agents stepped out.

Shea was in the sitting area, his personal bodyguards hovering nearby, as always.

"Holy crap," Shea muttered, getting to his feet. His youthful surprise made David grin. He instantly folded his arms over his bare chest and curled in on himself slightly at suddenly being in the presence of so many intimidating people.

"This is him?" Agent Upson asked David.

"Yes, sir," David agreed, leading the way. "Shea Whittier, this is Agent Upson with the F.B.I. and my friend Nicholai Zhukov, who's been working closely with the agency. We're on our way over to see my father, but Agent Upson wanted a few words with you before we go."

"Sure, I guess," Shea shrugged. He shook hands with each of them. The other agents moved through the rooms, ensuring the space was secure. David noticed Agent Upson and Nicholai examining Shea's arm and the healed wounds along his jaw.

"Mr. Whittier, please have a seat," Agent Upson said, gesturing to the couch where Shea had been sitting. "Is it true you've been living in Mr. Davenport's home since the incident with the men in the employ of Dorian Davenport?"

"Yes, sir," Shea answered, glancing around at each of the imposing men in his company. He seemed to shrink in age and size, sitting
forward to lean his elbows on his knees, folding his hands.

"Mr. Davenport's security team provided me with a detailed account of what transpired, and I'd like to verify it with you if that's
okay."

"Okay," Shea replied, his voice faltering a little.

Reviewing a tablet in his hands, Agent Upson said, "So, the private security team hired by Dorian Davenport entered your bedroom
on the morning of March twenty-eighth, after forcibly restraining
David Davenport's security team member. They assaulted you, did
a full body cavity search on you without your consent. They forcibly
restrained you, took a blood sample without sterilizing the area beforehand and did a urethral swab. They beat you with a nightstick,
re-injuring your arm in the process. They threatened to administer an
electrical shock by holding a taser to your testicles. One of Mr. Davenport's men claims that when they entered the room and were able
to disarm the assailants, there was a nightstick being pressed to your
anus. Were you also raped by these men, Mr. Whittier?"

Shea ran his hands over his head, blowing out a breath and curling forward even more. David went to him, sitting by Shea's side,
wrapping an arm behind his back and trying to help Shea sense his
steadiness and calm.

"We're just trying to help, sweetheart," David promised. This
was the part Shea refused to talk about, about which even David still
hadn't gotten a clear answer.

"I was a, uh," Shea stammered, his voice trembling. "A virgin,
and I was so scared they were going to... you know. And I think they
could tell. They were trying to get me to talk, to confess how suppos-
edly I was planning to hurt David, and the more scared I got when
they pressed the stick against me there, the more they..." Shea exhaled
heavily and David could feel Shea's heart pounding rapidly. "They
forced it into me," Shea said quietly. "They did, uh, rape me... with
it. I tried to pretend it wasn't happening. I'm still pretending that, I
guess. I'm sorry, David."

"No apologies," David said firmly. All David had known from

the medical exam were details about Shea's physical state afterward. There had been evidence of penetration, though no severe tearing or semen was left behind. They'd also had the nightstick tested through the police by CSI technicians and had found evidence of fluids from the anal cavity upon it. Hearing Shea talk about the nightmarish experience for the first time, however, was making it quickly impossible for David to control his outrage.

"There were just so... so many of them and I'd never been scared like that. Not in my whole life. They had no problem holding me down, st-sticking things inside me, hitting me, holding that taser between my legs like they were going to..." Shea let out a shuddering exhale, his face paling. "And I didn't... I didn't want them to do that to me too. Not after everything else I'd been through. I-I panicked. They were laughing at me, calling me names, describing everything they'd do to me if I didn't talk. When they... forced the stick into me, they were all laughing. I was screaming and crying and just begging them to stop but they kept jabbing it in, yelling questions at me that I couldn't hear. Right before David's guys showed up, they'd pulled it out and were threatening to stick the knife in instead if I didn't start talking, and I really... I really think they would have done it."

Hearing those words, something inside David snapped. In a flash, he was on his feet, shouting, being held back by Nicholai. He was just trying to go for the exit, to go for Dorian. When he realized he couldn't get past Nicholai, he screamed, *"They will fucking pay for this! He did nothing! He's a teenager, for Christ's sake! After all he's been through, my psychotic fucking father does THIS?! What right does he have?!"*

"David, we'll handle it," Nicholai said calmly, his heavy hands planted on David's shoulder, anchoring him to the spot. But he was jittery with rage and needed to lash out, to hit something or tear out his hair or scream until his throat was raw. Something. *Anything.* He'd kept it all bottled up inside so long, but he couldn't do it anymore.

"I think it's best you stay here with Mr. Whittier and let us handle your father," Agent Upson was saying.

"No," David blurted. "He needs to know that he's lost me already because of what he's done. He needs to hear me say it. I'm not hiding silently behind walls anymore."

Gently, a hand touched his back. David turned to look and saw

Shea, so shaken but concerned about David. It didn't make sense, to see Shea upset for him when he'd endured so much because of knowing David. Nicholai let him go and David drew Shea into a close embrace, needing to feel him solid and secure within his arms.

"I'm okay," Shea promised softly, returning David's hug. "Because of you, I'm more okay than I've been most of my life."

"I'll never forgive him for any of this," David seethed.

"Please don't go. I need you safe, too, you know. I don't know what I'd do without you. I'd be lost," Shea whispered.

"I have to do this. I need to face him. For you. For Donna. For Trent. For everybody."

To Nicholai and Agent Upson, Shea said, "Keep him safe, okay? No matter what."

"You have our word," Nicholai replied with a solemn nod.

Chapter 31
Loyalty and Legacy

"We attempted to speak to Shea's parents," Nicholai explained in the car on the way to see Dorian. "They refused to admit he was their son, even when questioned by a federal agent with birth records at hand. He's lucky to have found you, David."

"Even though I've put him through hell?" David shot back.

"Yes. Despite what your father has done, Shea is lucky to have you. You're quite a man to have as a support system."

"Will this work?" David asked them, looking between Nicholai and Agent Upson. "Will it be enough to make Dorian back off?"

The papers were lying on David's lap, faxed over from the law firm just before they left the property. Holding them gave David hope and helped him feel armed with more than one weapon.

"It will work," Nicholai told him. There was a hard glint of determination and confidence in his eyes. David just wished he felt as sure as Nicholai.

Dorian hadn't been staying at the family's main residence and ancestral home with Marylyn, David's mother, but a smaller property they also owned, located outside of town in a much more rural setting. Living apart, though nearby, allowed each of the Davenports — David, Marylyn, and Dorian — to establish their own oases and just enough space between them to keep everybody civilized, until now. The home Dorian lived in most regularly was set up on a hill with sprawling views of the countryside in all directions. It was about an hour's drive from David's home, and two hours away from Marylyn's. As lovely as it was, with its huge wrap-around porch and careful landscaping, all David saw when he looked at it was a fortress from which Dorian could measure their approach while they were still miles away.

The whole procession parked in the driveway leading to the house and in the street out front. Before David, Marco, and Nicholai got out of their car, a team of agents, guns drawn but lowered, swept up the lawn.

A moment later, Dorian's personal assistant, an older man named Keith Poole, slowly eased open the front door and came out with his hands raised. All the guns pointed toward him and he spoke up, calling, "What's going on? Who are you people?"

From the car, David couldn't make out what the agents said, but one produced his badge and spoke to Mr. Poole. When Agent Upson got the signal, he told them they could get out of the car. Some of the agents had moved indoors, likely scouting out the house and the private security on property. One came out, nodding to Agent Upson.

"Mr. Davenport," Mr. Poole said with pleasant surprise. His gaze, though, darted around to all of the armed agents surrounding David. "Your father is in the study, waiting."

"Thank you, Mr. Poole," David acknowledged.

It all felt like a dream, really. David was soon standing across from his father, surrounded by armed federal agents.

"What's the meaning of this, David?" Dorian asked with quiet intensity. David couldn't help but wonder if Dorian suspected Shea was putting David up to all of this.

"You've been terrorizing Shea Whittier," David replied as steadily as he possibly could. "He and I are both afraid for his life as it seems there's nothing you won't do. You're having him watched, followed... you had him held against his will and physically abused, raped, tortured, and beaten simply because of your paranoia. It ends now. I know you miss Donna and regret what happened to her, as do I, but I will not let you cause harm to someone I dearly love. If it's between you or Shea, I choose Shea."

"Dorian Davenport," Agent Upson said, drawing Dorian's eyes to him. "We've been provided with plentiful evidence of your recent attacks against Mr. Whittier. We have witness testimony, documented medical evidence of the trauma he sustained, surveillance footage of men in your employ driving vehicles registered to your company, carrying automatic weapons, stalking Mr. Whittier and attempting to bypass David Davenport's home security. At this point, it is crystal clear to us that you have threatened Mr. Whittier's life. If anything were to happen to Mr. Whittier—anything at all—the federal government is prepared to hold you solely accountable."

Dorian stood there, jaw clenched, eyes wide but unfocused and David stepped forward. He set the papers in his hand on the table behind where Dorian stood, then stepped back.

"I had my lawyers draw those up today," David explained. "I'm refusing my right of inheritance. If your estate leaves any money or assets to me, they will be liquidated and given in their entirety to charities of my choosing, including international and domestic organizations that help at-risk gay youth. If you're so afraid of Shea taking your money, this should put your mind at ease. I don't want your fucking money and I don't need you as my father. We're done, you and me. From this day forward, you are childless."

"Why?" Dorian gaped, shaking his head. "Why are you doing this, David? I'm just trying to protect you!"

"From someone I love? From someone who loves me more unconditionally than you ever have? You never even bothered to try and understand who he is. You just passed judgment because of how poor he is and his lack of connections. Oh, and because he's gay. Well, surprise, Dorian. I'm gay too. Hate me if you want to, just leave us alone."

"I could never hate you, David," Dorian said, glancing with accusation at all of the eavesdroppers listening to a conversation he likely wished was private. "You're all I have left! I can't lose you!"

David heard the emotion in his father's pleading, but it didn't quite touch him. He pushed it away, refusing to let someone who betrayed him so awfully upset him. All he needed to do to refocus was remember how Shea looked—crumpled, naked and bleeding on the ground—when they'd rescued him from Dorian's thugs.

"You already have. You lost me when you lost her, because you never let it go. It's over. I'm moving on, and you should too."

"Please don't do this," Dorian asked David, giving him a hard stare that attempted to tune out the room around them, and the people in it.

"I need your word that you will keep your men away from my home and Shea, and that you will cease any attempts to kidnap or harm Shea in any way."

For a moment, there was nothing—no sound at all. Dorian only stared at David, and David stared back.

"He's taking you away from me," Dorian murmured.

"No, you're pushing me away," David snapped. "Go on, Dorian. Push. Unlike you, I'm not alone. When I go, I'll still have people who love and trust me."

"I spoke to Mr. Whittier's father," Dorian seethed. "He said disowning that piece of trash was the best thing he'd ever done, that the boy has no morals, no conscience. Just a manipulative, conniving little shit who takes everything he can and never gives anything back. His own father!"

"You know nothing about Shea or his failure of a father," David countered. "You—"

"Or his boyfriend, Ryan!" Dorian yelled, cutting David off. "The person he dated for over a year! He said *Mr. Whittier* took every cent he could and had nothing but excuses for why they couldn't be paid back. Nearly failed out of high school! Never had a job from which he wasn't fired! A prostitute in training from what Ryan told my men—willing to sell himself to make rent! This is who you've been sheltering, David. This is who you've been *fucking*."

"Enough!" David stared coldly at his father. After a deep, steadying breath, he said calmly, "I can't keep you from twisting the truth so it suits your corrupt view of the world, but I can keep you out of my life, permanently. *Your word*, Dorian, that this is over. This ends now."

Dorian scanned the room and its threatening occupants, bearing witness to the entire exchange. After a mirthless chuckle, straightening his tie, Dorian said, "You're wrong about this, and it won't be long before you pay for it, dearly."

"Is that a threat?" Agent Upson asked.

"An observation." Dorian smiled. To David, he said, "You're better than this, son."

"So are you. Or, I thought so, once. Maybe this is who you really are. I'm waiting."

For a long moment, nothing in that tense room was said. Then...

"So be it, David. You have my word," Dorian muttered quietly.

"We'll hold you to that," Agent Upson chimed in.

"Remember, Dorian, you're not the only one with powerful friends," David said to his father, his tone grim and final. As they left, he said in parting, "Donna never got to say goodbye." He held his father's gaze, and said, "Goodbye, Dorian. I hope your wealth brings you comfort, because it's all you have left."

David never forgot the look in his father's eyes in that moment— a storm of grief, regret, apology and resolve; a foreboding of consequences that would haunt David for the rest of his life.

"You're not going to miss all of that money?" Nicholai asked with a sly smirk. They were headed back to Manse and the intense dread knotting David's chest was loosening.

"Hardly," David smiled. "You need to have something first, to miss it. I never had his money, apart from my trust fund. When I was given access to it at age eighteen, I invested it entirely in my business and investments. Let's just say that business has been *very* good for me."

"Must be nice," Nicholai chuckled.

"Believe me, it's not everything," David answered wistfully.

"We'll keep an eye on your father. I don't think you'll have any more issues with him. But if you do..."

"You'll be the first person I call," David finished.

They returned David to his home, and Nicholai opted to remain behind with him, enjoying the company of the other patrons of Manse while the helpful federal agents bid their farewell and David retreated upstairs. On the way up in the elevator, David was briefed on security updates. There had been no sign of any of the vehicles which had been watching the property and Shea. It seemed Dorian had gotten the message.

That was all David needed to hear. And all he wanted was Shea.

When David got to the bedroom, he was surprised to find someone had already alerted the staff to his imminent return because there was an intimate little table set with candles near the doors leading to the terrace in his bedroom. The doors to the terrace were shut, but the curtains were pulled open wide to let in the starlight. Shea was pouring wine and still wearing his jeans – and nothing else.

Shea was beaming. He set down the wine bottle and seemed to hold himself back from running to David.

"It's so good to see you," Shea gushed. "So I heard, you know... good news. It's good news, right?"

He was biting his lip and shifting his weight from foot to foot with his hands planted on his narrow hips. The restlessness in his body spoke clearly of his youth, and it made David want to tame him, to hold him down and kiss him breathless while giving him more creative reasons to want to squirm and writhe.

Shea's recent admissions about what really happened during the attack lingered between them, though, giving David pause and making him feel quite protective of Shea.

Striding toward Shea, David tried – and failed – to hold in his grin. Grasping him by the hip, David drew him close, loving the way Shea yielded instantly to the firm press of David's body. David ran his other hand down the warm, smooth planes of Shea's chest and said, "Yes, good news. I get to keep you after all."

"Well, that was kind of a given, right?" Shea chuckled, his lips softening and eyes downcast as David touched their foreheads together. His hand came up to hook around Shea's ear, his thumb brushing the velvety hair below just Shea's ear, up on the side of his jaw where the wounds had once been.

"His men have backed off. He seems to have gotten the message. He comes near you and the entirety of the federal government will be breathing down his neck. And, I told him we were through. I had some papers drafted earlier. He can keep his damn money if he's so concerned about it."

"David," Shea sighed, his smile fading. "But you have every right to –"

"No. Not if the money means more to him than treating his son, or you, like a human being. He crossed the line. It's over."

"Okay," Shea replied with some reluctance. "This helps you, right?"

"It does. Toxic people don't get to be in our lives. That's the rule."

"That's a good rule," Shea agreed.

Glancing over at the table, David asked, "You didn't do all of this yourself, did you? You're supposed to be resting."

"Well, it turns out I have miraculous healing abilities and after getting fucked for the first time, ten short hours later, I'm still somehow able to walk," Shea said cheekily. David palmed Shea's ass through the jeans and squeezed. "But yeah, I had some help."

"Good," David hummed contentedly, kissing Shea more fully.

"So let's celebrate," Shea whispered against David's lips. "And then celebrate again. In bed."

David laughed and silenced Shea with more kisses. "It's adorable that you think you're in charge of when and how I celebrate with you *in bed*."

"I'm just, you know, *suggesting*."

"I'll take it into consideration," David replied. He could see the want in Shea's eyes, and felt the way his body moved against David's, grinding a little as if begging for more.

But the mouth-watering aroma of freshly grilled steaks and sautéed onions was in the air. It made David's stomach growl. They had all night and all of tomorrow as well. There was no rush.

"Then let's celebrate. I'm fucking starving," David admitted.

Shea chuckled, grinning from ear to ear and hurried to take his seat and uncover the platters of hot food.

Chapter 32
Creative Stress Relief

Shea woke with a groan, which was met with David's soft chuckles from just over his shoulder. David's hips were tucked up behind Shea's ass as they spooned on the large bed, wrapped in downy softness of silk and feathers. But there wasn't enough contact for Shea's liking, even though he could feel David there from the backs of his calves to the backs of his shoulders. All night long, he'd dreamt of chasing David, yet he always was just out of reach. Shea was naked, David was immaculate. Shea was desperate and horny as only a near-virginal eighteen year old could be. David was cool, composed and saw every bit of Shea's arousal. It had frustrated Shea all night, and he was still frustrated when he awoke.

David hadn't consented to sex the evening before, after they'd wined and dined in the most romantic way possible. Instead, he'd ordered Shea to bed, naked, and had him slowly masturbate while David watched avidly, but didn't touch. It drove Shea crazy. After he'd cleaned up and snuggled in for sleep, then David finally cuddled up close and let Shea feel him. But that was almost worse. It kept Shea interested but unfulfilled.

So, even before he was fully awake, he asked groggily, "Please fuck me."

David laughed with what sounded like genuine amusement and kissed the back of Shea's shoulder.

"Are you still dreaming?" David asked.

"No. Probably not."

He rolled onto his back in order to see David's face. With a subtle smile, David trailed his fingertips lightly down the length of Shea's body.

"God, *not helping*, David," Shea protested.

"What do you want?" he asked gently.

"You, in me."

"Is that all?"

Shea sighed.

"Wouldn't it be more fun if we were *creative* about it?"

Nervousness fluttered to life in Shea's belly. He began to pay more attention to the way David's fingertips were skimming over the tip of his left nipple, along the side of his abdomen and over his hipbone, then down his thigh only to come up the inside and skate just a fraction of an inch away from Shea's cock and balls as he repeated the loop.

"Nervous?" David smirked.

"Maybe. You've got a look. I'm learning, you know, about your looks."

David chuckled. He really did look like he had something particularly depraved in mind and Shea almost didn't want to know what it was ahead of time. Maybe it would be better to be held down, blindfolded, and have to go through with it without foreknowledge, just so he could take the ride and test exactly how much he trusted his new Master.

"I trust you," Shea told him, when David didn't say anything.

"How would you feel about rejoining the world a little this evening?"

"Yeah," Shea answered with some reservation, just in case it was a trap. "Of course. You know I've been stir-crazy."

"There's a BDSM play party this evening downstairs."

"Oh."

"*Oh*," David echoed, chuckling and drawing the backs of his fingers over the tip of Shea's dick. "What did you think of Nicholai? I know you didn't get any one-on-one time with him."

"He was intense."

Why was David bringing up Nicholai? He wasn't still there, was he? Was David really considering inviting a Master Dom into a scene with them, after all of the talk about no one else being allowed to touch?

"Why?"

David was watching his hand work rather than staring into Shea's eyes. He repeatedly brushed the pad of his thumb over the end of Shea's cock, stimulating nerve endings and just generally driving Shea crazy. He pushed a little into the touch, but it did nothing, gave no relief. All it did was show David how huge an effect he was having.

"I trust Nicholai as I trust few men. I meant it when I said no one touches you but me, but how would you feel about letting him watch?"

Shea gave another of those little pushes. It was just a small tilt of his hips, chasing David's light stroking. His breath caught as he imagined it. There had always been guards around when David and Shea were intimate. Even now, there was a man standing on the other side of the vast room, by the door. But, to have someone be there, *really* watching, someone who could come close, make eye contact or comment on what David was doing, or what Shea was *letting* him do...

It could be scary. It could be great, too.

"Okay," Shea answered, listening to his emotional reactions, even though he knew David could tell the idea didn't turn him off. "Just Nicholai?"

"Well," David said slowly, trailing his fingertips lower, making Shea spread for him as David stroked behind Shea's balls and down over his hole. Shea's breath caught again as David rubbed in small circles over the clenched opening. "I'd like to bring you to the party, wearing your collar. Some will be wearing masks, and if it would help you feel less *conspicuous*, we could wear masks, too. You could watch some of the others play and maybe I would touch you, just a little bit. If it got to be too much for you, you would just let me know. Then, we'll go somewhere more private."

"But Nicholai would be there? The whole time?"

Shea heard and felt the small tremors in his voice as he concentrated on David's rubbing. A dry finger entered him in a slow push and Shea let his head fall back. He angled his hips to encourage more and was breathing harder. He clenched on the finger and swallowed a moan.

"If you'd like him to be," David answered. He buried the finger completely and with his thumb, caressed the skin near the root of Shea's sac. "Look at me, sweetheart."

Shea forced himself to make eye contact, even though there was no hiding anything he was feeling or needing. Shy and unsure, he looked at David, whose gaze was so warm and steady, measuring him and every subtle cue in his body and expression.

"It's not too much, is it? Too soon? I've been impatient to show you off, but your feelings are more important. It could be some stress relief, but if you'd rather keep things private for now, that's perfectly fine."

Shea had known David was downstairs in the evenings, doing things Shea could only imagine with the gorgeous, sexy men at Manse. He'd been jealous and eager to experience more for himself. He was tired of hiding away. Sure, it scared him to show himself to people who were nearly unshockable and used to things that still massively intimidated Shea. But David would be there, and instinct told him that nothing bad would happen to him while Nicholai was near, either.

"I want to try," Shea admitted with complete honesty, some anguish showing itself in his expression as David's finger pumped shallowly.

An eager, wicked smile crossed David's face. "I'm glad," he replied. "Then I have some instructions for you, in preparation. No coming before tonight and I want you to follow the cleaning ritual I gave you and take care of any grooming. You'll wear the black shorts down to the play room, but once we're there, they'll come off. Okay?"

"Okay," Shea sighed. "I do kind of like the idea of us both wearing masks, even though with you it's probably a futile gesture. Kind of goes along with my superhero kink."

"Good," David grinned. Shea savored the feel of David fingering him, his cock swollen thick with want already, though it looked like it would be many hours before he found any relief.

David led the way into the large dungeon on the lowest level of the building. As ordered, Shea was one step behind him, with guards flanking them on all sides.

Shea would have bet all of David's money that everyone in the room knew, without a doubt and just by looking at him, that it was his first time in any situation like the one he was in. There might as well have been a big neon sign above his head that said Virginal Newbie in pink glowing letters. He liked the feel of the collar around his neck and it did give him a strange thrill to see the way literally everyone's gaze went right to it, first, when they caught sight of him. It marked him as David's, as untouchable. There was respect and something that could have been awe, fear, or jealousy in their expressions, realizing what it meant.

Half of the people in the room were wearing masks. Shea felt like he'd discovered Bruce Wayne's secret gay fetish parlor. Shea's mask covered half his face and was made of black leather. David wore a matching mask, identifying them clearly as a couple.

The farther they walked into the room, the more everyone seemed to stop and take notice. Conversations hushed and it felt like everyone was staring right at Shea, making his heart race under the sudden pressure to live up to expectations. This was David Davenport, introducing his submissive for the first time, and the importance of the moment wasn't lost on Shea just because he was new to the whole scene.

Just as Shea's worries about how he looked and if he was behaving properly made his heartbeat start to race, he heard distinct laughter, and just from one person. It wasn't the type of laughter from discreetly sharing a joke, but the kind that used to be directed at Shea in high school by the meaner guys in gym class when he would fail to catch a ball, or would trip over his own feet.

The person laughing was the slave he'd seen a while ago, and had been worrying about—Thierry. He was standing, naked, beside Elet who sat stiffly in a leather chair. Thierry, still snickering, was looking right at Shea.

Then Thierry shook his head and muttered something.

Right away, David snapped to attention. To the guard at his side, David said in command, nodding to Shea, "Stay with him."

"Yes, sir," the guard replied.

David stalked up to Thierry. Getting right into Thierry's face, causing any remaining laughter to die, fast, David demanded, "What did you just say, slave?"

"Nothing, Master David," Thierry replied. He was suddenly stone-faced and nearly swallowed the words. "My apologies."

Grabbing Thierry by the neck, David spun him around and threw him against the wall between a set of shackles.

"Get his arms," David ordered. Two other Masters hurried to secure Thierry's arms in the shackles, stretched out at his sides. Meanwhile, David went to fetch a nasty looking whip made up of braided, knotted rope. Shea realized it was a cat o'nine tails.

Shea couldn't believe what he was seeing, his momentary flush of shame at being laughed at forgotten. He would have spoken up or asked David to stop, but knew he needed to obey David's wishes, especially when he'd not even been formally introduced to the community David headed.

The Masters stepped back. David wielded the whip, cracking it more precisely than Shea would have believed possible. The tails lashed Thierry across the middle of his bare back.

Thierry screamed, his whole body tensing, recoiling in agony. Angry red lines appeared where the tails had bit.

"What did you say, slave?!"

Thierry didn't answer, only winced as the pain seemed to grow. He went up on his toes.

The lack of response earned Thierry two more lashes, right in succession. Everyone was perfectly silent, except Thierry, who screamed until his voice broke. His back was laced with red. Stunned, Shea was frozen to the spot.

"I ask for a third time and you had better fucking answer me, slave," David said coldly. "What did you say after my collared submissive and I walked into the room? After you *laughed*?"

Shea realized Elet was standing now, looking tense but with his head bowed slightly in deference to David.

"I..." Thierry gasped, crying openly now. "I said you've gotta be kidding me."

Caressing the whip's handle between both hands, David said smoothly, his emotion perfectly controlled now, funneled into action and decision. "I see. My collared submissive is a joke to you."

Somehow, that impacted Thierry even more than the whip had.

He became wild, straining against the shackles, fighting as hard as he could, shouting, "No! Master, please! I beg you! I'm an idiot! I'm jealous, all right?! I admit it! I'm so sorry! It will never happen again! I swear! Please!"

"You're officially disinvited to attend any and all functions on this property," David told him, just as calmly.

Shea wanted to say something. He needed to. But he knew he was under orders not to speak unless spoken to, and the last thing he wanted was to humiliate David by disrespecting him in front of everyone. So, all he could do was hope to catch David or Elet's eye, pleading wordlessly to speak.

Thierry was sobbing. It was hard to listen to. There was plenty of raw emotion behind it. Sniffling, he seemed to try turning the sorrow to something else, snarling and yanking at his arms, "Fine then. Hit me! Fucking hit me! Punish me! I'll do anything you want! You can't do this! I need this, Master! No one..." he panted, out of breath, running out of energy rapidly, "*No one gives a shit about me* but you and Master Elet! I can't lose you!"

The silence drew out, awkwardly.

"You want me to admit it? I will! I don't fucking care anymore. I'm not stupid. I see how the other subs all get along. They like each other and they don't have any fucking problems getting attention from the Masters. They don't even have to try. They get as much fucking respect and attention as they want. They're all friends even when they're not here. That's why I try to cut them down! They all hate me and I fucking hate all of them because they all have reasons to leave. They don't need to be here to feel normal, but I do! No one's friends with me outside of this place. As soon as I leave here and walk out that door, I'm *nothing*. Don't you think I know that? So, go on, hit me!" Thierry's fury gave way to a quieter, more broken-down type of weeping which was even harder to listen to. Shea saw some of the others in the room glancing at one another, though they didn't say a word. Sagging in the shackles, Thierry turned his face toward the wall, his pleas scraped away by his ravaged voice as he said, "I'd rather be fucking whipped to death than get kicked out for good because I'm nothing when I'm not here. Please. Please don't make me go. They can all hear me admit it. It doesn't matter anymore. I just go after the other subs to make myself feel better and it's so fucking pathetic!"

David paced behind Thierry. He glanced at Elet, then at Shea, who tried to access previously untapped powers of telepathy in order to beg David to let him say something.

"Slave?" David murmured, looking right at Shea. "You have something to say?

With huge relief, Shea said, "Yes. Thank you, Master. Please show him mercy, as a personal favor to me."

"Why?"

"Because I've felt the way he feels, to not fit in and not be able to do anything about it, and I wouldn't wish that on anyone, sir."

"I see."

David looked away, back at Thierry. He stroked the whip's handle. After pulling his arm back, he lashed Thierry again, as hard as ever.

Swallowing a shrill yell, Thierry battled through it, the violent tension in his body a visual scream, then cried, "Thank you, Master David! More please, sir!"

Five times, the whip's tails bit deeply into Thierry's back, bloody now. He grunted and gasped through it, twisting against the pain, but settling down seemingly out of sheer will.

"Unshackle him," David said softly.

It only took a moment. Thierry crumpled to the floor, moaning.

Then, he said, "Master David, may I please express my gratitude to your slave?"

"You may."

Thierry crawled to Shea, his head down, and he was still crying, his breath hitching with the force of his tears. When he got to Shea's feet, Thierry kissed them. "I'm sorry for being a dick. I owe you a lot. Thank you." He gave Shea the briefest glance, his eyes bloodshot, and Shea could tell it was sincere. His heart went out to Thierry, who kissed Shea's foot one more time, then stayed crouched there, breathing heavily.

"There will be no more chances, slave. No more punishments, if anything of this sort happens again. Is that understood?"

"Yes, Master! Thank you, Master!"

"You may stay."

Thierry laughed in relief, then started sobbing again. He folded his hands over his head and drew in on himself like he was trying to disappear.

"May I?" Elet asked David.

"Go ahead," David sighed.

"On your feet, slave," Elet said, toeing Thierry's leg with his boot.

"Yes, Master." Thierry struggled to his feet, crying out when the movement pulled at his back. Elet helped him, taking him by the arm, then led him from the room.

David walked over to Shea, whose head was bowed, his eyes downcast. Shea wasn't sure if he was allowed to do it, but he quickly lifted his mask and wiped his eyes dry before David could see the tears on his face. He wasn't sure how all of those people had just stood by while Thierry was so viciously whipped, screaming and fighting. It had echoed too much for Shea with the helplessness he'd felt when Dorian's men had attacked him. It was difficult, too, seeing David as the one actively causing Thierry's pain, and without displaying much emotional effect from it.

"I realize this is all new for you," David said quietly, "but the punishment was warranted. In time, you'll understand. That slave is much different than you. He's been cruel, and not just to you. He didn't deserve your mercy, nor mine."

"Yes, Master."

It was tempting to feel scared of David, after seeing him behave the way he just had. The other side of Shea's heart pulled at him too, though, reminding him to trust unconditionally in David, who was a good man with much more experience than Shea, especially when it came to managing unruly submissives.

David looked him over for a moment as if studying him, then cupped Shea's chin, lifting it so he could be kissed.

"I'm sorry things began this way, tonight," David said tenderly, with regret.

"It's okay, sir." It was true. With David in control, it was hard not to believe things would work out, no matter what.

"Are you all right?" David caressed Shea's cheek, waiting on him, listening to him. It helped Shea feel a little more in control and calmer.

"Yes, sir."

"I love you," David said.

"I love you too, Master."

Some people were watching them, talking quietly with each other as the party slowly came to life again.

"Should we sit?"

"Your wish is my command, sir," Shea smiling shyly.

"It is, isn't it?" David smiled fondly back.

The shorts were still covering him—barely. Shea had been told to lie on the couch with his head resting on David's lap, his legs bent and his feet resting on the couch cushion. There were maybe ten other people in the room, not counting the guards. Nicholai was there, leaning against a chair with a high back, his gaze scanning the room now and then but mostly staying focused on David and Shea, which only intensified the fluttery butterfly feeling of nervousness in Shea's gut.

Another slave was shackled to the wall and was being tickled with a large, black feather. One was bent over a bench and was being lightly flogged. In the corner, three people were having sex. The amount of activity and nakedness in the room helped to ease Shea's self-conscious feelings. For the first half hour or so, David let Shea lay there, largely undisturbed. His hand rested on Shea's bare chest, over his heart, feeling just how apprehensive Shea was. That was nice, and reassuring.

But soon Shea's arousal outpaced his reticence. He got hard and David noticed. Hell, almost everyone noticed, because David reached for the waistband of the shorts and pulled them down in front.

"Slide these off," David told him.

"Yes, sir." Shea slid them down his legs and set them on the couch at his side. Keeping his legs together at first to hide himself, Shea set his feet back down on the couch cushion.

"Let your legs fall open."

Shea hesitated, his heart pounding. Oh so slowly, he tried to comply, but he was instantly blushing and trembling a little.

"Easy," David said quietly, petting Shea's hair. "No one hurts you. No one touches you but me. You're gorgeous, slave. Don't you see how envious they all are that I get to be with you like this?"

"Yeah, right," Shea scoffed under his breath. Yet, when he was brave enough to glance around, he saw how avidly Nicholai was watching. And others, too, had paused in their own play to see what was happening over on the couch. Shea took a deep breath and let his left knee rest against the couch's back, with his right knee flat against the cushion below him. As he exhaled, David touched him, closing his hand around Shea's cock.

With a soft sound of surprise and pleasure, Shea closed his eyes. David began stroking him and Shea felt the noises of pleasure rising in his throat, needing to be voiced. It was startling to be touched by David like that while in a roomful of people who could see *everything*.

Shea could hear the noises of the others, too, as they resumed their activities. There were slaps, laughter, moans, and the wet sounds of mouths working against skin. He wanted to look, but didn't. Not yet. Minutes passed and Shea was completely hard. David's touch ventured lower, playing with his balls. It made Shea want to spread even wider and he knew he was still voicing small groans and gasps, wantonly. He chanced opening his eyes and saw Nicholai standing near the foot of the couch, facing them. He had a full view from up between Shea's legs and was nursing a drink of amber-colored liquid.

David noticed Shea had opened his eyes and it made him instantly change tactics, as though it was a cue he'd been waiting for. He rubbed behind Shea's sac and through his crack.

"Curl your legs back, all the way. That's it," David said gently. He rubbed through Shea's crease, then began to focus solely on the puckered knot of his opening, causing blood to flow there — and stares as well. "How's that feel?"

"Good," Shea confessed. His skin felt too tight, his nervousness making him a little jittery, his blood pumping hard and making him feel overheated. It was amazing, like being in a heightened state of awareness, and more alive than before. He did feel safe, and brave, and willing to do things he'd never dreamed he could. "Please more, Master," he asked.

The words seemed to flip a switch in David. Right away, in command, David said, "Come here, slave. Turn over onto your hands and knees."

Shea rolled over. David guided him up the couch so that Shea's arms were resting on the couch on the right side of David's legs and his knees were planted on the left, his ass raised right over David's lap.

"Lower your shoulders. Rest your forearms on the couch," David instructed.

Shea did as ordered and it tipped his ass up even farther in the air, his erection nudging his stomach and his balls hanging heavily between his legs. He felt David palm his ass, then, and Shea gave a startled cry as David spread Shea's cheeks. Nicholai was still back there, watching, and it only made Shea's breathing roughen, his pleasure and self-consciousness greater.

"Very nice," someone said in a deep voice.

"He's lovely, David," said another voice. "He knows we only bite if asked, right?"

"He does," David replied and Shea could hear the smile in his voice.

"It's been a while since we've had someone so shy here."

"It's fucking hot," said a softer, higher, and more breathless voice.

Shea tried to tune them out, just so he could keep control over himself. David was rubbing repeatedly over his opening and it felt so sensitive. It throbbed with his pulse and his cock was aching with stiffness, his balls heavy and full.

He heard the snap of a cap. A wet finger slid into him.

With a gasp, he bore it, hanging his head. On the other side of the room, people were moaning, clearly involved in their own pleasure and distractions.

The finger pulled out and David spread Shea's cheeks wide again, digging his fingers in near the opening to really spread it out. Shea groaned as the room's warm air caressed the moistened skin.

"What do you want, slave?" David asked him, with a dark rumble to his voice. It was brought, Shea knew, of desire.

"Anything, Master," Shea answered honestly, panting a little. He really didn't care what David did anymore, as long as he kept doing it.

The finger entered him in a swift push, making him grunt softly. At the same time, David began pumping Shea's cock, causing him to thrust and hump the hand impaling him.

"Be still," David scolded.

Shea moaned and restrained his movements, trembling, his thighs quivering. The rest of the room fell away. The voices and contented laughter, the obscene sucks, slaps, and soft squelches faded. There was only the pounding of Shea's blood in his ears, the heat in his body and the need to get off.

"Please," he begged, panting and shameless. "*Please.*"

"Are you ready?" David asked. There was a note of warning in his question, telling Shea things would not get easier once they left the party.

"*Please,*" Shea could only gasp. "Yes. I want you."

"Okay. Let's go."

Chapter 33
Displayed for Master Nicholai

As David helped him up, Shea realized how dizzy he was and how unsteady his legs were. David kept him propped upright, letting Shea lean on him if needed. Along with Nicholai, David guided Shea from the room. They followed one pair of guards and were tailed by another.

It was a short walk from the room, down one narrow hall to another, then through another doorway. Two of the guards stayed on the outside of the door, flanking it. The other two waited inside.

The suite was decadent with luxurious fabrics in royal blue and cream. There was dark, hand-crafted wood everywhere, the furniture massive and regal. David led Shea to a strangely short bed. It was only a few feet long, not nearly long enough for someone to lie on. In a moment, he realized why.

They had him lay down on his back and David brought Shea's legs back, folding him in half with his legs spread in a wide V. His ankles were slipped into leather loops to hold them in place, each strap fastened to one corner of the headboard.

"Fuck," Shea cursed. "Oh fuck."

"What do you want, slave?" David asked, caressing the undersides of Shea's thighs.

"You, sir."

"Be more specific, please. What do you want me to do to you?"

"Fuck me," Shea said in a quiet voice.

"Are you sure?"

David looked to Nicholai and said, "Hand me the smallest one and the lube."

Shea didn't look as Nicholai passed David what he'd requested. He wanted to stay focused on where David was touching him. He felt so exposed and spread open in that position. There was no hiding anything. He did catch a glimpse of David quickly spreading a handful of lubricant over a small flesh-colored phallus and Shea moaned with some dread. Touching the tip to Shea's opening, David began to feed it to him, pushing firmly as Shea's ass swallowed the toy. The pressure was intense and the sight of it sinking into him was both arousing and disturbing in its obscenity. Nicholai was watching David work the toy up Shea's ass but was also glancing back to Shea's face, reading his anxious grimace and gasping cries.

"How many times has he been fucked? He acts like a virgin," Nicholai commented.

"Once," David smiled.

"Well, no wonder, then. And he's so young, David."

Shea gasped as the toy was slowly pulled out, his cock twitching. Once the toy was out of him, David rubbed it over Shea's opening. He was so close to orgasm, his head was spinning. His whole body was strung tight, ready to shoot and release a day's worth of tension.

"You like that?" David asked with a wicked grin as the toy was thrust into Shea again in one hard push.

"Yes," Shea panted, then moaned as David kept fucking him with it.

David folded his hand around Shea's balls and tugged. Shea groaned and clenched his jaw, grinding his teeth together as David squeezed a little.

"*Ahh*," Shea gasped as the hurt grew.

"Just a little pressure." David eased up on his grip and massaged the sensitive flesh instead, rubbing the soft skin of Shea's sac. "Again."

He squeezed more the second time and Shea bore down on the toy as it thrust up his ass. David left it there and Shea couldn't shut up. The ache from David squeezing his testicles crawled up into his stomach, down his legs. The toy withdrew from his ass and Shea convulsed a little, ready to come, even with the pain.

"Nice," Nicholai commented, sipping his drink. Shea fucked air and let his head fall back. David eased his grip, rolling Shea's sac against his pelvis. His hole was rubbed with the shaft of the toy. Then it was plunged back inside and Shea made a desperate pleading sound.

"Please," he gasped. "Please."

"Please what?"

"I don't know."

David chuckled. Nicholai passed him something and Shea barely saw it.

"Oh fuck. Oh god," Shea groaned with dread, tensing up again.

The leather strap in David's hand was dragged over the curve of Shea's ass, then over his balls and shaft. David pushed the toy in until it stayed, then let go. He fit Shea's balls in the junction of his thumb and index finger, squeezing around the root of his sac and ran the strap over the soft skin. Shea growled with dread and then the slapping began. It was light, just a tease, a constant, gentle tapping against the most sensitive, fragile part of his body. Shea panted for air, shouting a little as the pain grew and grew, blooming between his legs. Soon he was grimacing fiercely, teeth bared, brow furrowed, eyes squeezed shut. David eased up, rubbing the leather over him.

The toy fucked him with deep strokes, then pulled out. He was so spread out with that position, his hole was completely exposed. As soon as David began to run the strap through his crease, Shea was begging in half-words and guttural sounds. The tapping resumed, but David was striking Shea's over-stimulated sphincter and it was a devastating sensation. The shouts erupted from him and he curled forward around the ache. David stopped slapping and rubbed again.

"Fuck me, Master, please," Shea heard himself moan.

Two fingers twisted into him and he sighed. The strap slapped hard against his left cheek and Shea flinched, his rim kissing David's fingers as he clenched momentarily.

"More," Shea cried.

"Hand me the larger one," David said to Nicholai.

His labored breaths twisted on an anxious groan, seeing the much larger phallus handed over to David.

"Control your breathing," David told Shea. "Slower, longer breaths."

Shea watched David line the toy up with his hole. Sliding his fingers back out so that only the tips were in him, David spread them out in a V to pull Shea open, then pushed the tip of the toy through the gap. The rounded end was barely in him, but David pried Shea open more with his fingers, still inside. Grimacing, his mouth working around an unvoiced cry, Shea watched David stretch him widely, giving the large toy room to burrow in.

"Push down on it," David instructed as Shea shook. He let out a pleading whimper, then worked to slow his breathing. Pushing down on the thick column, Shea felt like it was never going to fit inside.

David's fingers withdrew completely and a harder nudge at the toy saw the head tightly nestled in Shea's hole, stuffing his rim full.

Shea shuddered, trying to push down on it, but David had stopped trying to work it deeper. Instead, he left it where it was, barely inside. David held it with one hand and caressed Shea's cock lightly with the other.

"No, please," Shea begged, his voice climbing. He bit down, hard, on his lower lip, clawing at his thighs.

"It's just pressure, slave. Try to relax." He was rubbing at Shea's stretched smooth rim, hugging the circumference of the toy's end. Small tremors hit him. When David's fingering of Shea's cock triggered nerves under the head, he cried out sharply.

"Please don't."

"Relax," David said firmly. "Do you remember your safeword?"

Shea nodded.

"Do you need to use it?"

"Please take it out!"

"Take it out or put it in deeper?"

Shea's cry broke apart, his thighs quivering. Fluid dripped down his cockhead and David painted his dick with it.

"Answer please."

Shea tried to speak and couldn't manage to do it. So, David struck the side of his slave's stuffed, aching ass with the strap.

"Ahh! Fuck!"

"Answer the question, slave. In or out? Is your ass too delicate to take a cock?"

Shea glanced down between his legs at the thick, long remainder of the phallus stuck up his ass. Imagining the way it would feel to have every inch thrust into him, a pleasurable shiver raced through him from the top of his head to the bottom of his feet. His cock jumped, chasing David's talented fingers.

The strap struck again, and again, while David twisted the cock a little deeper.

With a heavy moan, watching David and Nicholai watch him struggle, Shea bore it. Every strike of the leather strap made his ass squeeze up around the toy.

A brutally hard lash across the thickest part of his ass made Shea yell.

"In! Put it in! Please, Master," he rasped.

With firm, unrelenting pressure, David forced the phallus up Shea's ass in one long push. He was suddenly being impaled on it and he yelled again, drawing back his knees ever so slightly and pushing against the inward pressure.

His cries were rough, wild, as the toy bottomed out. David squeezed once, tightly, up Shea's cock, making him purr and thrust.

"Do you like that, slave?"

"*Yes.*"

The toy withdrew in a steady, constant tugging that had Shea throwing his head back just to breathe and bear it. When the wide head caught on his rim, David worked it slightly further out to fill him there again.

"Does it hurt?"

"*Yes.*"

"Do you want to get fucked with this toy, slave?"

"*Please*, yes!"

The toy slid sharply, quickly, back in. David kept it moving, taking him with long, continuous movements, letting it ride. The more he did it, the looser Shea got and the better it felt. His cries broke apart, twisted with sweet pleading and heavy breaths.

David withdrew the phallus, lightly slapping Shea's hole with it.

"Mm," Shea frowned, biting his lip. "Please fuck me, Master."

He slipped it all the way in. With a shiver and a thrust against air, Shea grunted.

"Would you like to turn over so we may watch you fuck yourself onto this toy, slave?"

"Yes, sir."

His ass stuffed full, the toy buried, Shea lay there. He watched David unhook Shea's feet from the straps spreading his legs. David massaged the blood back into them. Then, he helped Shea turn over onto his hands and knees. There was a mirror at the head of the bed, allowing him to see the two Masters directly behind him, watching avidly.

Closing his eyes, Shea focused on the silicone cock inside him. When it began to withdraw, he pulled forward, then pushed back onto it. David held the toy mostly steady the more Shea moved, bouncing on it, the plastic balls slapping his ass on the in-stroke. He started panting, moaning.

David spanked him, kneading his ass, urging him on.

"Good, that's it. Take it harder."

Shea bounced faster, letting it nail him. He grunted softly each time David spanked him, his ass sore inside and out.

It felt like it went on forever, until David suddenly pulled the toy free, setting it aside.

"Spread your ass for us, slave. Let's see how well fucked you are."

Shea bowed his head, struggling with the idea of what he was about to do for only a moment before obeying. With his shoulders braced on the bed, he reached behind himself and pulled his cheeks apart.

Fingers rubbed his tender knot, plucking at it.

"Would you like a kiss, slave?"

Shea moaned loudly, seeing David lean down behind him.

"Yes, Master, please," he begged. "I want it."

David licked, once, directly over Shea's hole.

Panting, Shea felt goosebumps rise all over his body, his balls drawing up.

"Are you embarrassed about displaying yourself like this for Master Nicholai?"

David licked again.

"Yeah," Shea answered with a shaky laugh. "Yes. Completely."

"But you don't care about being embarrassed?"

A third lick.

"No, I really don't. Not as long as you keep doing that."

"Why?"

A fourth lick.

"I... *oh fuck*... I trust you, Master."

"What do you want, slave?"

David wriggled the point of his tongue at the gap, tickling it.

"Please more. Please give me your tongue, Master."

"Be more specific, slave."

"Please fuck me with your tongue, Master."

David pushed the tapered, wet muscle through Shea's throbbing rim, his lips gently kissed around his opening.

"Oh my god," Shea whined. David's licking was so gentle, like a caress. There was nothing better.

"You're blushing, slave."

"Yes, sir."

David pumped his tongue a few times. He pulled out and straightened up.

"What do you say?"

"Thank you, Master. Please give me your cock? I want it. Please."

His hands still spread his cheeks.

"Relax for a moment while I get ready, slave," David ordered.

He was nearly delirious. Letting go of his ass, Shea came up on his hands. Nicholai wiped a cool washcloth over Shea's sweaty brow and he was able to take a moment to catch his breath. Nicholai offered him some water from a glass with a straw as David wiped a towel over his face and got a drink of water of his own. He was already shirtless, but began opening his pants, then lubed up his dick, cradling it in a hand.

Nicholai's presence, witnessing all of this, pushed Shea hard up against his limits. Owning his homosexuality had always been his biggest struggle. Yet, David did make him feel safe. Their bond kept Shea grounded when he might otherwise have fallen apart or let the terror get the better of him.

"This isn't easy for you, is it, slave?" Master Nicholai observed.

"No, Master," Shea replied.

"But you trust Master David, yes?"

Nicholai set the water aside and hooked a bent finger under Shea's chin, keeping it tilted upward so they could clearly watch his reactions. Shea kept his eyes lowered, though. When he felt David step up behind him, his cock already nudging to get inside, Shea's breath caught, his heart hammering. Frowning, he let Nicholai tilt his chin up even higher, feeling his scrutiny.

He gave a small sob, unable to hide it or hold it in, and felt a tear slip down each of his cheeks.

"Please take me, Master," Shea asked, his voice catching.

David entered him slowly.

"Beautiful," Nicholai said when Shea keened, his anxiousness clearly showing. Shea's back was slightly arched, his ass tipped up to receive. When David filled him more completely, Shea's mental struggle with owning his submission was entirely on display.

David pulled back and started moving, setting a rhythm. Shea squeezed his eyes shut, let his lips part and whimpered as he let himself move in response, riding David's cock.

"He's trusting you a great deal right now," Nicholai told David. He let go, but Shea tried to keep his chin tilted up.

"Yes. More than you know," David agreed, grunting a little with effort and passion. Shea felt his caress up his back to his neck and writhed, sighing. "I'm so damned proud of you," David said with some emotion.

"Thank you, Master. I love you," Shea whispered, feeling so held, filled, and possessed.

David began to move faster, riding him and moaning. Leaning forward, he caught Shea's mouth from over his shoulder and they kissed. One tight squeeze from root to tip up Shea's cock had him slipping over the edge, crying David's name and reaching back to touch him, hoping he stayed close. He shuddered through his orgasm, his body locking up around David inside him, making David curse and growl, taking him harder with shallower pushes. In a moment, David was gasping, panting, and coming down.

Holding on to David, Shea knew he had the only thing that mattered. David looked at him then and said with all of the reverence of a vow, "I love you so much, Shea."

After cleaning up, David moved to lead Shea from the room. Nicholai kissed Shea's cheek and said to David, "You're a lucky man."

"Oh, I know," David grinned.

Chapter 34

The Value of Honesty

Shea took a deep breath, held it, then let it out with a heavy sigh. Stretching out his arms, he declared, "It's everything I thought it would be. It really is."

David raised an eyebrow and stayed quiet. He just kept leaning there, against the doorway leading out onto the terrace, giving Shea a mistrustful glare.

"Okay, now come back inside."

"No way!" Shea laughed, planting his feet and setting his hands on his hips. "Do you know how long I've been cooped up in there?"

The fresh air was miraculous. Unbelievably warm as it blew his hair, caressed his skin, it carried floral scents from the gardens below where a rainbow of colors were in full bloom, and woodier ones from the thick forest beyond the property. There was no one around, and not a car in sight. It was too early for even Manse's employees to be there to prep. It felt almost humid enough to be summer, no jackets or sweaters necessary; and it was just Shea and David, outside together.

But David was scanning what he could see of the road outside of the property's fences, frowning with worry.

"We should be going anyway."

"I thought we still had an hour? You said they backed off, right? Your dad's goons with the sniper rifles?"

David's expression tensed. "It's not right, dammit. Before, every-one *else* was the threat. Now it's my own goddamned father."

"David," Shea soothed. "You can't always assume the worst. You said you handled it."

"Where's the balance, between keeping you safe and becoming as possessive as he is?"

"Well, I think the balance is right here, out on this awesome ter-race," Shea grinned, pointing at his feet. "Where I'm pretty sure the only ones that can get me are the sparrows who like to sit up there on the roof and shit on everything. But you wouldn't know anything about them, since you're being a doorway lurker and all."

Stubbornness made David hold out, so Shea started to dance a little, moving his hips in small figure-eights and pulling an invisible rope to try to lure David closer. Amazingly, it got David to crack a smile.

"See, there's no resisting me and my Wonder Woman-esque in-visible lasso," Shea warned, still pulling and dancing.

David laughed, despite himself. Shaking his head, he let Shea reel him in.

Once he was in grabbing range, Shea circled a hand around Da-vid's waist. David leaned in for a kiss.

"Should I get you a bustier to go with your lasso?"

"Oh, hell no. That's never going to be a good look on me."

"Mmm," David hummed doubtfully, looking Shea over like he was imagining it.

"David, no," Shea warned. "So this was a great first step, right? I'm outside and everything. You know what would be an even *great-er* next step? Me getting a new job so I can finally fix my car. I was thinking about applying at the comic book store. When things were monumentally miserable at home when I was a kid, that's where I'd go to kind of get lost in happier places. I'm a superhero nerd. It's in my blood."

David's smirk faded, then vanished. He caressed Shea's cheek and gave him a light kiss, like he was stalling while he thought of a way to break it to Shea that it was out of the question.

"David, *please*," Shea groaned, doing a little dance of frustration in David's arms. "I appreciate the safety concerns, but I need to have a life."

"I thought you didn't like dancing," David observed, as further part of his stalling tactics.

"You're changing the subject."

"Sweetheart," he sighed, "why on Earth would you need a job? I can buy you any car you want."

"Don't you 'sweetheart' me, David," Shea said, standing his ground. He wasn't going to let David pave over this with money, bodyguards and good intentions. Reality had to start rejoining their world. Shea was on a mission to make it happen. "I can't stay in your bunker forever, and I'm not having you pay for me. You love me for me, don't you? Then let me be me. Let me get a job I love. You're already letting me live in your kick-ass sex palace where I feel safe. All of my fears of making rent are gone, along with my fears of going twenty-four hours in a row without seeing random hot guys making out with each other. Those are concerns of the past. It's a brand new world. That's a huge gift. That's plenty."

In his most suave, irresistible voice, David said, slyly, "Mr. Whittier, perhaps you're not aware of this, but you're dating a billionaire. The idea of you having a job as a comic book store clerk is—"

"Awesome? You were going to say awesome, right? I'm not taking your money, David."

"But—"

"No. And this has nothing to do with Donna. This is me. My parents didn't want to support me, and that's fine, but I need to feel like I'm supporting myself. I want to pull my own weight."

"I could train you to help with my businesses, or get you involved in running Manse, or—"

"Those are *your* things," Shea cut in. "I'm definitely interested in learning some of that stuff, eventually. For now, being able to buy my own clothes, and fix my car myself, would mean the world to me."

Hearing the sincerity in the plea, David visibly softened.

"All right," he surrendered. "But I have conditions."

Shea let his head fall back on his shoulders with both relief and the tiniest bit of dread. Then, he straightened, lost the frustrated twist of his lips and said, "Yes, Master."

"I need to make sure you'll be safe."

"I know you do," Shea allowed, surrendering in his own way, too. "Thank you."

"You're welcome. *Now* can we go?"

"You're really that eager to see your mom, huh? Weird."

The helicopter ride was one of the most thrilling, dare-devilish experiences of Shea's life, but also yet another thing in David's everyday life Shea knew he could never get used to. Shea had never even ridden in a normal airplane, let alone the cramped, confined piece of impressive technology David owned and used regularly. Zooming straight up into the air made Shea overly aware of his mostly full bladder, which suddenly wanted to void itself in terror. With his belt securely fastened, one hand gripping the hell out of his seat and one gripping David, Shea couldn't have rationalized the physics allowing them to get airborne. It was such a small space in there, and he kept expecting to fall out. The doors just didn't seem sturdy enough to hold them all in if they banked too sharply while turning. The loud whir of the blades overhead only enhanced the surreal sensation, making it hard to think past the noise and safety concerns. But, the more apprehensive Shea became, the tighter David held his hand, giving him one of those effortlessly charming smiles, too.

Marco sat across from Shea, looking wholly unfazed as only an enormous human with plenty of ass-kicking abilities could. That's the look Shea always saw on the faces of Captain America or Wonder Woman or any of his other favorites. They had their missions in mind, and didn't really care about the debris crashing down around their ears. When you were as strong as them, you got used to depending on that to get you through. As someone who had never been particularly strong, Shea couldn't relate.

The trip was a short one at barely twenty minutes. They touched down on the grounds of Marylyn Davenport's estate. While they stepped out, ducking to clear the blades and hurrying out of the swirling, kicked-up wind, a few men ran out to greet them.

Shea let David lead. David shouted hello to one of the newcomers, then let the men guide them farther out away from the copter and toward the property's main building. Shea slowly began to relax.

The first thing Shea noticed was how pristine everything was. He was sure if someone measured each blade of grass, they would be precisely the same length and all were an impossible, vibrant green. It looked more like a movie set, designed to perfection by a team of artists, rather than somewhere real people lived. There were sculpted hedges and color-blocked sections of gardens sprawling as far as the eye could see, winding around in quaint paths to small ponds or sitting areas. Massive trees which must have been hundreds of years old ringed the gardens as well as the cobblestone-paved roads leading to and from the house. The house itself was grand in a different way than Manse. It was only two stories tall but spanned outward to the left and right like a stone giant flat on its back, stretching its limbs. There were even columns of the sort Shea had only before seen on old banks and opera houses.

They were led up a winding stone staircase stretching from the lawns up to a luxurious terrace. They were met with the familiar sight of men in suits with earpieces, hands folded in front of them with wide stances as they scanned left and right from their posts spaced evenly apart.

"Who're these guys?" Shea asked David.

"My mother's security team," David told him as they kept walking and David kept a wary eye out.

"...Do your mom and dad share security?" Shea wondered nervously.

"No, not recently. They live separately, with separate accounts, separate everything really. My mother is just about as happy with my father as I am right now. She's well aware of the situation."

"And you trust her, right?"

"Absolutely. As you'll see, she does like things as she likes them but she's always had her priorities well in order. During everything with Donna and Trent, she was my anchor. The emotions of the situation at hand never trumped logic and responsibility. Just because she's legally wed to my father doesn't mean they share much beyond a name."

Leaving the terrace behind, they entered the house. The double doors were held open for them by men in grey suits who gave a little bow as they passed. A cavernous space welcomed them, with gleaming marble floors and even more columns stretching far upwards. They walked forward, then left. Eventually, they reached another doorway with more grey-suited men bowing as they ushered David, Shea and Marco inside.

It was some kind of parlor with lavish furniture, and an ornate fireplace that was as tall as Shea. Seated at a cozy table laden with food, flowers and drinks was an elegantly dressed older woman with platinum blonde hair, piercing blue eyes and an exceedingly composed appearance which exuded wealth and taste. Right away, Shea was a little intimidated by her.

When she broke out into a smile, though, which matched David's for charm and warmth, Shea began to relax.

"Sweetheart, so good of you to come!" the woman said.

So that's where David got it from.

She walked forward and kissed each of David's cheeks.

"Mother," David said with a sweetly youthful, eager sort of pride, grasping Shea's shoulder, "I'd love for you to meet Shea Whittier. Shea, this is the famous and beautiful Marylyn Davenport."

Marylyn chuckled and waved off David's flattery. "Oh dear, Shea, I hope he's not always this full of hot air. You're both likely to float up, up and away if he keeps at it."

"It's really good to meet you, Mrs. Davenport," Shea said with a smile, extending a hand.

She grasped his hand with a firm, dry grip, pulled him close and kissed his cheek as well. "Come now, you're the very first person my son has truly cared about. The occasion calls for more than a handshake, don't you think? And don't you dare call me that. I'm only Marylyn."

"Works for me," Shea replied. "Your home is insanely cool, Marylyn. It's really impressive."

"Hmm," she hummed, taking a good, close look at him and not quite letting go of his hand. Shea glanced to David to gauge his reaction to it all, but David was only smiling at them both. "So, David, if I'm to be famous and beautiful, how would you describe Shea?"

David dropped his gaze and actually looked a little bashful. "Oh, I think the same terms apply," he murmured.

Marylyn laughed brightly, released Shea's hand and lightly rested her hand on his arm instead. "Shea, what *have* you done to him? David, dear, you're gushing and glowing. I've never seen you in such a state."

"Yes, well," David said, embarrassed.

"Um, speaking of gushing... Sorry, but is there a restroom I could use?" Shea asked.

Marylyn laughed again. It was a good, light, happy sound.

"Yes, right down the hall to the left. Second door on the right-hand side," David told him. "Shall I come with you?"

"I'll be okay," Shea assured him. "If I get lost, I'll shout Marco. You shout Polo. Or Marco can just come find me. Deal?" The last thing he needed right after meeting David's mother was to be appointed a bathroom chaperone. It was time to man up and act the capable adult he kept telling David he was.

"Deal," David agreed with a nod.

"Oh, David," Marylyn admitted, sighing fondly as Shea walked away. "I do like him."

Marco shifted into the hall, watching Shea walk toward the bathroom without following. It did turn out to be a short walk, after all. Shea never left Marco's sight. Once he'd gotten to the second door across the hall, he pointed to it questioningly. Marco nodded with a grin.

Shea gave him a thumbs-up sign and went inside.

The bathroom was as huge in scale as the house. There was a sitting area and a doorway through which he could see a claw-footed tub and extravagant vanity. Through another doorway was a separate room for the toilet. Mirrors were everywhere and there were a few extra doors too. Shea never got to try them to see where they led, because he wasn't the only one in the bathroom.

Multiple reflections showed him different angles of the elderly man with the gun in his hand, pointed right at Shea's chest.

It was David's father, Dorian. He looked much more haggard than when Shea had seen him before, ages ago at the hotel restaurant. Now, he seemed wasted away, with dark circles under his eyes and the skin hanging almost limply from his bones. It was the similarities to David that got Shea, though. They had the same eyes, the same ears. When Dorian spoke, it sounded like a painful echo of the man Shea loved.

"Don't move. Don't scream, or I'll shoot," Dorian warned. The hand holding the gun shook a little. "They thought they could keep me out, but it's *my* damn house. I can get in if I really need to."

It didn't feel at all like when Ryan would threaten Shea, or when schoolyard bullies would hurl insults. All Shea felt was not his own alarm, fear, or lack of understanding, but pity. It couldn't have been plainer how scared Dorian was. To be faced with that much terror on David's behalf allowed Shea to keep going instead of freezing up. Shea had been too long in those rooms, locked away with the what-ifs. Now, finally, this was the real thing. This was as scary as it would get.

But Dorian wasn't a hired goon. He was a father, afraid for his son. Intuition told Shea that Dorian would not hurt someone as easily as his staff had. He had a different sort of conscience, borne of luxury and mistrust of the unknown.

"Okay," Shea said, slowly raising his hands. "You really do look like your son, Mr. Davenport. I'm sorry I've made you worry so much about him. He's really okay. He just worries, like you do, I guess."

"Shut up!" Dorian hissed. Shea did everything he could to maintain eye contact instead of looking down that jittering black barrel. *"Why won't you leave him alone?* What do you want from him?"

Shea sighed. "You want the truth?"

"Of course I do!" Dorian growled. A few tears slipped from his eyes. He wiped them away with the back of his free hand.

"Okay," Shea said calmly, keeping his tone as soothing and normal as he could. "Most of all, I want to make him laugh, and smile. He works too hard and worries too much for someone his age. I've never had much of anything of my own. I'm used to it, sir. I could not care less about money, or any of that. David is my *friend.* That's his value to me. I'm sorry about what happened to your daughter, and that you've lost so many years with her. You'll see her again, someday. I know she'll be so happy to see you. You want her to be proud of you, right? I know I would, if it was me. I've only ever wanted my family to be proud of me."

Shea waited for the gunshot. Maybe there would be pressure, or a burning sensation, or possibly just a big, full sort of pain, somewhere around his sternum. But it would be over fast.

At least he'd had time to love David, if only for a little while. The past few months had been the best of his life, by far. If it was to be Shea's last spring, at least it had been a warm one, full of romance, precious trust and hope of a new, happier rebirth that he might not get to enjoy, after all.

"Thank you for giving David to the world," Shea added, more quietly, dropping his gaze, when Dorian said nothing, only kept breathing hard and trying to choke back tears. "He's a hell of a guy and he does so much for so many people. It's meant so much to me to have met him and fallen in love with such a great man. He's saved me in so many ways."

More waiting. More hearing that breathing, knowing that the gun was pointed right at him, and Dorian's finger was on the trigger.

Shea's breath hitched as his fear caught up with him. How funny, to die in such a fancy, unlikely place. He imagined his awkward body lying on the gorgeous marble floor and wondered what his parents would think when they heard the news — if it would be anything more than good riddance. With all of his fading strength, Shea fought not to imagine David's screaming once he saw what was about to happen, and only prayed that David could forgive his dad, somehow. David was too good to be ruined by anger over something he couldn't have changed.

Closing his eyes, crying a little and bracing himself, Shea waited. He waited forever.

Something hit him.

It was a shove to his shoulder.

A hand gripped his chin, forcing his face upward. Light green eyes were looking at him, measuring him. He felt like he was shaking so hard, he was about to come apart in a billion little pieces.

"Damn you," Dorian hissed. "You don't love him!"

Shea opened his mouth to reply, but a desperate, terrified sound lodged in his throat at first. Clearing it, he said in an unsteady voice, "No, I really do. Even if he can't save me this time, like he promised he would. I really love him."

Where was the gun? Was it pointing at his stomach? Or upward at his chin?

He started to hyperventilate, imagining where the bullet would tear through his body. He'd seen so many drawings of violence and death. Sometimes the hero would dive in front of the bullet to save the pedestrian in danger. If it was Captain America, he'd throw his shield, deflect the bullet. There would be no last minute heroics for Shea. He was just going to die, and he'd be done. His life was over before it had really started.

Dorian pushed him again.

"Get out! Get out!" Dorian growled. Gun still in hand, he raised both fists to his head, holding it between them. He growled again with what sounded like frustration. "GET OUT!"

Finally able to make himself move, Shea burst from the bathroom, running back to David. Marco saw him first, got his weapon from its holster, coming alert fast.

"What's wrong? Mr. Whittier?" Marco asked tensely.

But Shea just kept running. His composure was about to fail him and first he needed David to understand.

He ran into the fancy parlor. Zeroing in on the only thing that mattered in all of that splendor, he sprinted to David, unable to breathe, his side cramping up and his calm fraying.

"*David!*" Shea rasped, gulping air.

"What's wrong?!" David demanded, getting to his feet, spinning around to face Shea. Shea touched David's chest, something he'd thought he'd never be able to do again.

"Gun!" Shea shouted with all of the air left in his lungs. "*My dad has a gun and—*"

In his mind, it was a year ago and Shea was running from his house, his dad behind him holding a shotgun he'd never fired.

That was why Shea startled so badly to hear the blast. A single, thunderous gunshot echoed powerfully off of the gleaming floors and pristine walls, traveling down the hallway to them.

Chapter 35

Peace of Mind

The bang faded to silence. David took two steps forward. Looking terrified, Shea grabbed onto him, grimacing, "Don't. Please. David...."

But he had to. All was frozen. There were faint sounds, but David couldn't make them out. Three symbolic things floated in the air, bigger than life, too much to fathom.

The gun.

The devastated look on Shea's face.

The gunshot.

Shea was petrified and wired — his eyes teary, his lips closed too tightly, not to mention the jittery tension in his body, crying out for help and comfort. All of David's protective instincts flared. Feeling like he was moving in slow-motion, David turned his head, glimpsing his stricken-pale mother, and looked back at Shea.

Shea was trembling, teetering on a terrible psychological edge.

God, it really was true. And there David was, once again, waiting behind walls while the unthinkable had happened.

David took Shea's shoulders in his hands.

"Don't go in there," Shea begged. "Don't."

There had been no shouting. No other remarkable sounds. Just that echoing bang.

David was walking then, and Shea couldn't pull him back.

Nearly at the doorway, David encountered Marco, who had been coming from the direction of the bathroom, where Shea had run in from.

"Stay here," Marco warned heavily.

"Like hell," David replied, pushing past his bodyguard.

"*David.*"

The pull at the center of David's chest was stronger than Marco, as it had been stronger than Shea. While David hurried forward at a steady stride, Marco rushed to get ahead of him.

The bathroom door was open.

A few more steps and David could see the back of one of his mother's guards, kneeling. Kneeling in front of —

"The police and ambulance are on their way," Marco said, with heavy implication.

"Ambulance." David echoed.

"No exit wound. I think he... missed." Marco struggled to hold David's gaze.

The bathroom.

His father was in the bathroom, where Shea had been, with a gun. A gun he'd fired and with which he'd missed.

It refused to add up to anything David wanted to accept.

There was a spreading pool of dark red creeping outward over the well-polished, off-white floors. He couldn't go closer to it. He wouldn't. Whatever had happened there was nothing he could fix.

Above all else, David needed to know exactly what had just happened, but he instantly refused the idea of questioning Shea and putting him through any more.

"There's a security camera." David looked at Marco again, jaw clenched. "*There's a security camera! Go!*"

"I'm not leaving you."

"Go!" David yelled, pointing.

All of the rooms were rigged with cameras. Especially on the main floor, even the bathrooms. After Donna, it had been one of his father's requirements, for his own peace of mind. Every Davenport residence had them, except for David's since his guests at Manse deserved their privacy.

A low groan slipped through David's defenses. The man on his knees turned and David glimpsed his father, half his head smeared in red — a soft, undistinguishable mass.

Peace of mind, David thought as he hurried back to Shea.

He was standing where David had left him, only now Shea was facing David's mother, who was grasping Shea's arm, staring at him like he had answers she needed, but didn't want. Shea's eyes were too wide, shell-shocked.

"He's still alive," David said to them. Marylyn's head turned, painted with soft wonder.

"He's still *alive*?!" Shea repeated, too loud, with a crazed sort of laugh. He ran a hand through his hair and let out a heavy breath. To Marylyn, Shea said it again, "He's still alive. Maybe it'll be okay."

Pulling Shea into his arms, and away from his mother, David wove a hand through Shea's hair to clasp his head. He pressed his lips to Shea's cheek and felt his helpless trembling. Returning the embrace, Shea clung to David with an iron grip.

"You're okay," David promised. "You're okay."

He knew he was saying it to hope it was true, not quite believing it. He said it a third time and his voice caught.

Don't think about it deeply right now. Do what needs to be done. Take control. See it through. Those had been the words Marylyn had murmured to herself immediately after Donna's death, with David a mere child at her side, holding her hand. They had stuck with him.

Now, he told himself the same things.

"Get Shea some air, David," his mother said, with all of her characteristic fortitude. "He's had a shock."

"He's had more than a shock," David countered numbly. He took Shea out of there as quickly as he could, his mother right at his side the whole time.

They sat at a small table out on the lawn. Soon the police and ambulance were pulling up to the estate's front entrance. They heard the sirens but couldn't see the lights. The house blocked the view.

David searched Shea's body for injury, despite Shea's stilted protests of, "I'm fine. David, I'm fine. I'm not hurt! He didn't... He just...."

None of them could say it, but all of them knew. Dorian had come there to kill Shea. But something had happened.

What though?

Marco appeared and gave David a tight nod.

"Stay with Shea," David commanded. "No matter what anyone else says, he doesn't move from here and he doesn't leave your sight. The police don't get to speak with him until we've figured this out."

All David could think of was how he'd lost Trent even after they'd thought it was all over and done with. Donna had died. That alone had been more than enough to handle, and yet, all of those years ago, they hadn't been finished losing people. David would be damned if fate tried to part him from Shea again, in any manner.

"Yes, sir," Marco nodded.

"What? David, what?" Marylyn demanded.

"The security video," David explained. Shea's gaze snapped up to meet his. Then he sighed, his eyes closing over with what looked like relief.

"Of course. Let's go then," Marylyn said briskly. "What are you waiting for?"

At a quick pace, she started to return to the building, with David having to hurry after her just to keep up.

"Well," Marylyn declared. "That's that, isn't it?"

They'd stopped the playback right after Dorian raised the gun to his temple with a shaking hand, before he could pull the trigger. That was something none of them wanted to see. On the screen, Marco was standing, frozen, in the bathroom doorway, trying to talk Dorian down. It was barely a second after Shea had run out at Dorian's instruction.

"He's still alive?" she asked one of the guards. They murmured a question into an earpiece. The police were there, and some of the officers had watched with them.

"Yes, he is, ma'am," the guard replied as he listened to the latest report.

"Huh. I can't decide if that's lucky or not," she said softly.

"Mother," David started, concerned for her and bracing a hand on her arm. She waved him off.

"Who does this, David?" she said angrily, pointing a finger of accusation at the screen in the small office in which they stood, with banks of monitors showing various views of the property and the emergency personnel upon it. "He would have shot that child just for being closer to you than he was!"

"But he didn't," David reminded her. "Look, I need to get back to him. The police will be intending to question him and I can't fathom what—"

"Go. Go be with him. I'll manage this mess," she said with resolve. He could tell she was using all of her strength to not fall apart, and succeeding so far. He loved and admired her for it.

"I'm so sorry to bring this down on you," he said tenderly.

She gave a pained laugh and kissed his cheek. "Oh, my love, it should be me saying that to you. Go care for Shea. That's the most important thing."

"Your father is en route to the hospital, Mr. Davenport," the guard to David's right informed him as they walked.

"Very well. Thank you," David replied, quickening his pace once he saw Shea.

Shea was on his feet, wearing an anxious expression.

"What's happening?" Shea demanded as soon as David was close enough to hear.

"What's happening? My father just tried to murder you in the damned bathroom, that's what's happening."

"But is he still alive?" There was too much worry for Dorian's sake in the question. As far as David was concerned, all that man deserved was pain. The last person who should have been worrying about Dorian was Shea.

"Unfortunately, yes." David was so angry, he wanted to scream. How had Dorian gotten past security? How had David allowed this to happen? How had he managed to put Shea in mortal danger again, despite all of their precautions? He felt like a failure, like he was doomed to lose Shea just for caring about him as David had cared for Donna and Trent.

Shea moved closer, into David's personal space, and laid his hand on David's chest. Steadily, he held David's gaze, letting him see he was okay, that he was strong. It was a different strength, though, than David or Marylyn had. Shea didn't discredit his emotions as obstacles when faced with horrifying reality. No, he processed them and found ways to carry on without closing off pieces of himself. It was the same truth and clarity which David had always adored about him.

"You shouldn't have watched that," Shea told him gently. David loved him for it, telling David what he needed to hear, if not what he wanted to hear.

"He snuck in there, for *one reason. One.*"

"But he didn't hurt me. You realize that, right? Everything he's done, all of this fuckery since I met you — that was all because he loves you. He loves you *that much*," Shea told him urgently. "Do you know how amazing that is, especially to someone like me?"

David took hold of Shea's shoulders, gripping him to see if he was really there or not. Pushing down on so much useless anger, he couldn't speak at first.

He couldn't agree with Shea. He didn't know how to.

There was no forgiveness for what Dorian had done, let alone what he might have done if different choices had been made.

"David, your dad is probably dying," Shea pleaded. "That's all that matters. You should be with him, and with your mom."

"No," David said unequivocally. "We're going home where you'll be safe. Right now."

He grasped Shea's hand and pulled him toward the helicopter.

Shea pulled him back.

"Just tell me you're not going to regret this later. I never got a choice like this when it came to my parents. *You have a choice here.*"

"I've made mine," David said, holding Shea's gaze.

Dorian didn't warrant David's concern, not when David had so much anger darkening any other emotions he might be feeling. And Marylyn would only see David's presence as a reason to distract herself from her own thoughts and feelings on the matter. She would ignore herself in favor of her son. The only thing David was willing to give Dorian in that moment was the entirety of Marylyn's attentions, focused on him and handling what she could.

The ride home was quiet, aside from the deafening whir of the blades overhead. David didn't let go of Shea once, but Shea kept looking back to where they had come from, biting his lip with worry.

"Sir, your mother is here. She's awaiting you upstairs."

"All right," David sighed. He stepped into the elevator with the guard who'd accompanied him from his office. The past few days had been spent dealing with business, flying here and there to do damage control. The guard pressed the button and up they went. He'd been hoping to use the long-awaited reprieve from work to give Shea a call, but now that would have to wait until he first dealt with whatever Marylyn had come to say. That Dorian was likely keeping David from Shea again, even in such a small way, made David irritable.

He knew he had to get used to allowing Shea freedom. The threat that had kept them in close proximity for so long was now vanquished. There was nothing keeping Shea from the life he wanted except David. No matter what his feelings were, or his tendency to want to control everything in his orbit, David refused to be Shea's jailor.

So, Shea was out, and he hadn't even needed to tell David where he was going or why.

That didn't mean David couldn't worry. He was excellent at it, after all.

The doors opened.

Inspiration struck as he stepped into his private quarters. He could call Shea with the intent of asking if he'd be available for dinner. They could make plans or just eat in, make an evening of it.

The idea brightened his mood significantly. Finally bothering to raise his gaze from the tops of his shoes, he instantly stopped short when met with the sight before him.

"Shit. I fold," his mother said, throwing down a handful of playing cards.

"Mother!" David scolded, then added with pure bewilderment, "Shea?"

"Hey, gorgeous," Shea grinned, throwing David a wink. "Sit with us. We'll deal you in!"

"What in the seven hells is—"

"He's really much more charming than you are, darling. Not

nearly such a stick in the mud," Marylyn told him gravely.

Mrs. Tinsley was screwing up her mouth with distaste as she stared at the cards in her hands, held just an inch or two in front of her nose. The three of them were seated at David's dining room table together. A pile of foil-wrapped objects sat between them. They each had their own smaller piles closer to them, and Shea's was the largest by far.

"You're playing poker?" David said with astonishment.

"For truffles," Shea said happily.

"Why... how... You aren't even supposed to *be* here!" David exclaimed.

"Well, *that* was rude," Marylyn *tsk*ed softly as she unwrapped one of the truffles from her pile and popped it in her mouth.

"It's okay. He means well," Shea explained to her. "He just works too hard. It makes him crabby."

"Yes, he gets that from his father, amongst other things," Marylyn replied.

"You've been talking about me. Fantastic," David sighed in surrender. Standing next to the table, hands on his hips, he glared at each of them, knowing he was completely outmatched.

Shea explained, "Your mother was kind enough to call my cell while I was out visiting Daisy. I was on my way back here anyway, so I just came straight up to see her and keep her company until you got back."

Mrs. Tinsley set down her cards and stood. "I'll start putting together supper then."

"Oh, but we've not finished our game," Marylyn lamented.

"How are things, Mother?" David asked.

"Fine. They're fine," she sighed. Turning to face him, she looked him over, from head to toe. "Your father had another surgery today."

"Another?"

"Yes, well, there's been a lot to reconstruct."

"What's the point if he's never likely to wake up anyway?"

She dropped her gaze, deflating a little. Shea frowned at her with worry, and David could tell he wanted to say something, but was biting his tongue.

Maybe he should have apologized for making such a cold suggestion, but David couldn't bring himself to do it. So, instead, he asked more gently, "What is it?"

Shea said, "I think if you visited him, and saw his condition, it might change your mind. I just...." He let the sentence linger, growing shy. It drew Marylyn's attention.

"Just what?" David asked.

"It was fear and stubbornness that led your dad to make the choices he did when it came to you and me. I don't want you to go down that road. You're better than that. I know you are."

He was right. David felt like a total ass.

"Well, shit," David replied quietly.

The silence drew out. Then Marylyn said to David, "I really do like him." She shared a smile with Shea, who reached out to give her hand a gentle squeeze.

Chapter 36

Control

"So, what's up with all of the late hours? You go from one job to the other and I hardly see you anymore."

"That's not entirely my fault, is it?"

Shea watched David tip his wine glass, sipping its contents while scanning the restaurant. It was the fanciest place Shea had ever been, with food presented like tiny artwork on gigantic, rectangular plates. He was even wearing a tie, and it was actually the first time he'd dressed up for David. Since it was making him uncomfortable to be gently choked throughout their date, he was trying to deflect attention away from himself. It seemed David wasn't interested in the attention either, though.

He looked tired, maybe more than Shea had ever seen. But Shea didn't have a damn clue what to do about it.

They were in a secluded alcove with a handful of guards standing here and there. Shea had become used to the constant presence of their manly babysitters, but sometimes he missed the days when he could go out and be completely unnoticed. When you brought your own entourage with you, it was hard to be inconspicuous.

"God, have we gotten to that old married couple stage already?" Shea lamented. "Avoid all touchy subjects in favor of banal small talk?"

"I'm sorry, sweetheart," David apologized, setting down his wine glass and sliding it into perfect alignment with his water glass. "Lately, things are just completely beyond my control."

"Yeah, I know you hate that."

"I do," David admitted sheepishly. "We'll talk about whatever you'd like to talk about, all right? Things have been going well for you, right? You're getting your wishes? Your freedom?"

"Yeah, I've got my freedom. I don't have you, though. And what about your wishes?"

It was June. Summer had nearly arrived. David hadn't let on about much over the past few weeks. Shea hadn't figured out how much of it was shock about the incident with Dorian, and the fact that he'd likely never have a real conversation with his father ever again. Not that he'd want to. David was still acting like Dorian was a murderer. They'd visited the hospital a few times. Dorian had been breathing on his own, but was in a coma they didn't expect him to wake from. He'd lost his right eye and the trauma to his brain indicated severe, permanent damage. During those visits, David never spoke. However, Shea had learned a thing or two about his Master in their secluded time together, and he could tell how much David was hurting. He was struggling to accept what Dorian had done and move past all of the resentment that had been conjured, because David really did hate what Dorian had done to himself, as well as everything that had been lost when that gun had been fired.

Sometimes Shea said things on behalf of both of them, just in case Dorian was listening. Even given the circumstances, Shea couldn't bring himself to write off another family member. It didn't matter that they weren't blood relatives. It seemed to help David and Marylyn with the coping process for him to be a sort of bridge from David to Dorian, and he was happy to do it.

David worked every day, seven days a week, long into the night, going from one business to the other. He woke early, stayed up late, and never stopped to rest, except to collapse in exhaustion for a few hours before doing it all again. He checked in with Shea day and night via cell phone, with energy Shea suspected David didn't have to spare, but somehow tapped into anyway. It had Shea desperately missing David.

For the most part, Shea was staying at David's home. He never visited Manse without David's permission and accompanying presence, and he didn't leave the property without an escort. Some of the old loneliness was coming back, only it had changed around on him. Now, Shea could see his friends as often as he liked, but not the man he loved.

"That's the thing about being left in control," David said sullenly. "Your wishes don't always matter. It's all for the greater good."

"What are you talking about?"

"My father's company. The board of directors have demanded I step in to fill his role as CEO."

"Holy donuts, are you serious? What about *your* company? You're already CEO of that! You're only one man, David. I mean, this is ridiculous."

"Simply put," David explained, "his is bigger than mine. There's zero chance for Dorian to make a full recovery. They want to merge the Davenport interests under me. It's good for our companies, good for profits, for shareholders, hell, it's even good for the federal government. All of the heat I brought down on Dorian goes away if I take over. Technically, once we get past the legal bullshit and changing of hats, it's no more responsibility than I already had, it's just...." David lowered his gaze, looking defeated, and wouldn't say the rest.

"You were almost free of him," Shea guessed.

David fell quiet, letting his silence answer for him.

"Fuck. I've never seen someone so melancholy over becoming suddenly even more rich and powerful." David shot him a look, which Shea bore happily, shooting one of his own right back. In a way, it was kind of wonderful, realizing how much David really did need Shea to give him a reality check. "You're *still* free of him. Don't you see that? *He let me go.* He accepted us. Accepted *you.* Now there's no more having to do as he says, or trying to please him. You won. You won *everything.*"

"Doesn't feel like that," he confessed.

Thinking of Dorian lying in that hospital bed, surrounded by medical equipment he'd likely always be attached to, now permanently missing some of the pieces of himself that made him who he was, Shea knew why David saw no victory in the outcome they'd been allotted. "No, I guess it doesn't."

David lifted his glass again and took a drink, his eyes downcast along with his mood.

"What can I do to help?" Shea offered.

"Be there when I need you," David asked.

"No problem," Shea promised.

About a half hour later, they were being whisked back into the limousine that had brought them to the restaurant. The night was clear, balmy, and the moon full. The relative coziness of the inside of the car was nice. Shea was amazed to discover he actually could think of a limo as cozy. He'd enjoyed being out in public with David, on a 'real' date. He was less sure he loved all of the curious stares or the whispering he suspected was because of them. Actually, it made him appreciate David's decision not so long ago to visit Teresa's with Elet and slum it for a few hours, trying to fit in with the average Joes.

"Where to?" Shea asked with a sideways glance David's way.

"Home." David said simply. He had a pensive sort of look, which made Shea squint suspiciously. "But first, do you remember how I said I'd like you to be there for me when I need you?"

David pressed a button to raise the privacy screen behind the driver and bodyguard in the front seat.

"I need you," David told him.

"What, now? *Here*?"

David pulled him closer so that Shea was straddling his lap, then immediately began working open Shea's pants. He slipped the belt from its buckle and tugged down the zipper, all with the diligence of someone who knew exactly how to get what he wants. There was no part of Shea that could resist David when he was this determined.

"Tired?" David asked curiously, as Shea swallowed a lump in his throat and tried not to implode with a sudden bout of shyness. He freed Shea's cock and began stroking it.

Shea laughed nervously. "Well, not anymore." He leaned forward, bracing a hand against the back of the seat behind David, bowing his head as his breathing quickened. He wanted to ride David's hand, toying with him. David played him lightly, teasing with feathering brushes of his palm and fingers around Shea's crown. It would have been so easy to push into it with small rolls of his hips, but Shea held back. David's intent was clear—to cause Shea to fall, hard, into a submissive, aroused state so David could draw it out as long as he liked. "Will you submit to me?" David whispered by Shea's ear.

"Yes," Shea moaned. Some of his control slipped. He pushed slightly into the light touches.

"Be still," David ordered. Shea forced himself to obey, humming slightly at the effort it took, and frowning against the ache. "You're good for me, you know."

"And you are the weirdest boyfriend I've ever had," Shea replied.

David chuckled, and Shea loved seeing some pleasure and happiness in him—for once, pure and undiluted by worry. That's what he wanted to be able to give David. Those were things he had such trouble finding other places, so it was a joy for Shea to brighten David's world even a little. "Partner," David corrected. "You're a hell of a lot more than a boyfriend."

The sentiment meant a lot, not that he could properly show it. Shea was fully erect and doing everything he could just to sit still and bear it.

Moving slowly but with precision, David held Shea's gaze firmly, making it clear he wasn't to look away or try to hide. He pushed Shea's opened pants lower. More of him was exposed. David slipped his free hand behind Shea and under him. Anticipating it, Shea tried not to frown or clench. He grunted and shivered as a finger entered him in a smooth, demanding thrust. A held breath broke free, parting Shea's lips, and he gasped.

"Who do you belong to?"

"You."

"Who am I?"

"Master."

"What do you want?"

"To obey."

"Why?"

"I trust you," Shea gasped, his voice lilting as the finger withdrew with torturous slowness only to push back inside. "I trust you with my life, my heart, my everything."

"Likewise, my love," David said tenderly. He chased Shea's lips and kissed away his broken cry. "So, do I take you upstairs to play, or do we stop off at Manse first? You know what night it is, don't you? Everyone will be there."

"Anything you like, Master," Shea answered, sensing all of the unfiltered reactions crossing his face, feeling self-conscious about them since David was watching so closely. He thrust inside and Shea bit his lip to hold in a groan, rearing up a little in David's lap as he fought to take it.

"Would you wear your collar for me, in front of them?"

"Of course."

"Would you wear something else as well?" David rubbed at Shea's rim. "In here?"

Shea groaned again, louder, and felt the wetness at his tip.

"Yes, Master," he managed to answer.

"I want them all to know you're mine, that I intend to take you and no one else gets to have you, or touch you, like *this*. Would you let me show them — a few of my very trusted friends — how exquisite you are when you come apart? There's such devotion in the way you submit, Shea. You hide nothing and you give everything."

Shea wanted more — more fingers, more stimulation, more of David whispering dirty, loving things.

"Would you let me come while they watch?" Shea asked, not bravely and with barely any sound.

"No, but I'll let you get close. *Very* close. They'll hear you beg me, and wonder if maybe, eventually, I'll say yes. And in the meantime..." David tapped Shea's gland and brushed the head of his cock with his palm. Shea moaned and shivered. David squeezed tightly around the sensitive, soaking tip and stars exploded behind Shea's eyes.

"*Fuck*, don't stop. *Please* don't stop," Shea pleaded. "Would you like me to fuck you?" David asked darkly, steadily holding Shea's gaze.

Shea growled and wanted to push down on the finger, to ride the hand squeezing him, but only sat there, open and willing, voicing his delicious torment.

And David, happily, only gave him more.

Chapter 37
Public Exhibition

It was an intimate gathering of about ten different couples, all gathered in one of the larger, more opulent dungeons on the basement level of Manse. There was music and masked butlers carried trays of wine, water, and lube. Shea had been by that particular dungeon before, but never inside while it was being used. The butlers were kind of hilarious, and he appreciated it as a touch of levity, courtesy of Master Davenport.

Everything from the wallpaper to the upholstery on the couches was decadently overwhelming. Of course, when Shea briefly caught the attention of a few members of the BDSM community as he and David entered, flanked by their ever-present guards, it was even more so. Dropping his gaze, feeling everyone's scrutiny, he slowed to a stop when David did. Heads were turning. Play sessions were temporarily halted. Shea felt the room going silent and his heart beat wildly under the pressure.

Ignoring his doubts in himself, trusting only in David's love, Shea persevered. There was only one thing to do, so he did it.

All eyes were on him as he knelt at David's feet, facing him. Head bowed, hands clasped behind his back, Shea leaned eagerly toward David when his hand came to rest lightly atop Shea's head. It brushed tenderly through his hair, and though Shea kept his eyes down, he sensed the don't-fuck-with-me vibes coming from David. He was probably smiling and slowly meeting the gaze of each person who dared to look, but there was no question the moment was intended to present Shea and establish his relationship to the host of the party and owner of the manor.

For a moment, as David's fingers caressed Shea's hair, it all threatened to push Shea over the edge. The terror of the past number of months, that culminating moment with Dorian in the bathroom, the silent days in which David and Shea had sat at Dorian's bedside, holding his hand, getting no response — it was all surging, right under the surface. Compared to all of that, expectations to perform socially were nothing. And, with David standing there like everything was certain and he would always be strong, Shea knew he could let it all go, and trust. It would all be okay. David would care for him, always, to the best of his ability. And, when David faltered, Shea would always be there for him, too. Facing Dorian, alone, had taught Shea the extent of his own abilities under duress.

Sometimes silence was full and it was then, almost squeezing the air from the room.

"Who am I?" David asked him. His tone was soft but his iron will lent an underlying strength to each word.

"Master of my body, and my heart," Shea answered. He knew he sounded nervous. There was no hiding it, or any need to.

David's hand carded down the back of Shea's neck. It gripped him there, tugging at the collar. Shea exhaled heavily and leaned his forehead against David's hip. The scent of him was heady and more real than anything else in that room, or his life. Kissing David's thigh through the fabric encasing it, Shea somehow felt the room get even more still. David kept the tension on the collar and it was difficult to draw down air. Surrendering to the sensation, putting himself completely in David's care, Shea let it all go. The noises he made as that circle of metal tested and choked him, were the loudest thing by far. Controlling the reflex to struggle or fight, Shea made himself trust in David, and be calm. Still, he shuddered and subtly convulsed, his hand gripping his wrist with white-knuckle tension, his opened mouth working against David's thigh.

Shea grew dizzy, his convulsions getting stronger.

David let go. Shea drank down air, nuzzling David's thigh.

"Stand," David commanded.

Shea got to his feet. David steadied him when he swayed, then led him over to a place on the wall.

"Arms above your head, held together."

A strap was looped around his wrists, holding him there without binding too tightly. David rubbed down the length of Shea's body, from wrist to chest, and chest to waist. He worked to unfasten Shea's pants.

"How do I prefer you, slave?" David asked.

Shea kept his focus only on David, not on Elet, who stood a few paces back, or on Thierry, kneeling at Elet's side, or on anyone else he recognized—and he recognized quite a few people. He'd been paying attention. He was jittery, though, and bashful. With a tremble, he answered, "Hard and wanting, Master."

David forcefully tore open Shea's fly, shoving fabric out of the way and down. Chest rising and falling heavily, writhing slightly, Shea moaned softly as he was exposed. Maybe it was his imagination, but it was as if the room drew closer once they could see the effect David was having on him. His pheromones and undeniable vulnerability were tempting the room's predators.

It didn't matter what they did. David had him now. Shea's nervousness could do nothing to dull the hard edge of his lust. David's fingertips slid over Shea's erection, now on display for the room, and David's teeth scraped over Shea's neck. Shea's head tipped to the side submissively. With panting, small moans slipping in, Shea moved in reaction to each touch, kiss and bite, writhing in pleasure, bombarded with it. His head swam.

David found Shea's mouth and used it, giving him a rough, passionate kiss. A hard groan of raw need erupted from Shea.

When the kiss was finally broken, gasping, Shea was vibrating with want. It wasn't a show David was putting on. Not anymore. It was real. It was everything. Tracking David, their eyes locked, unable to calm down or stay still, Shea knew he was being played, but David was Master and to be stimulated and shown off by him was a privilege.

David stepped back, looking around the room with a challenging stare, guarding his prize, and Shea knew no one would touch him, or get close. Heaven help them if they tried.

With a flickering tickle in his stomach, Shea noticed the hunger in the expressions of the other Masters. They tightened their leashes, metaphorical and otherwise, on their slaves, and waited. He could feel how they would all use him, fuck him, choke him, or spank him if they could. There was *a lot* they would do.

Thierry was watching Shea closely, his expression giving away nothing, but he was silent, submissive.

Shea's heart beat faster as David selected a flogger from the wall. "Turn," he ordered.

Shea spun to face the wall and stuck out his ass, widening his stance. Groaning softly with dread and anticipation that tangled with impatience for the first lash, Shea braced himself. David gently shifted Shea's pulled-down pants lower, taking them all the way to his knees. He caressed the curve of Shea's bare ass before standing back.

"Fuck. Fuck fuck fuck," Shea murmured, squeezing his eyes shut.

The leather tails of the flogger struck him full across the ass and he gasped harshly at the brutal sting. It came again, and again. He clenched after each strike, trying to control his breathing.

The flogger's target shifted. It struck lightly against the upper middle of Shea's back, then slowly, lightly trailed downward. The handle nudged between his cheeks and Shea arched his back, waiting to be entered, willing to allow it.

But Shea knew what they were all waiting for, just as he knew they didn't really expect David to go through with it. Then again, they didn't know David as well as Shea. No one did.

The flogger was handed off to one of those masked butlers.

David was suddenly at Shea's back.

Then, he felt it. Dull pressure as the blunt head of David's bare cock pressed at his opening. A hand flattened itself on Shea's pelvis, pulling him back onto the length trying to breach him. There was lube but no prep, so the stretch instantly made Shea growl and gasp in protest. Bowing his head, exhaling sharply with his discomfort, Shea made himself relax completely and bear the ache as he'd borne the flogger.

David maintained steady pressure, parting him a little at a time. Shea made a desperate, whimpered cry, and fuck, it hurt. His face grew red as he felt them all watching avidly. Surrendering to all of his faith in David, and the fathomless need in him, which Shea knew he could sate, Shea took him in. Slowly, David sheathed himself in Shea, who thrummed and panted. His entire struggle to totally submit was there for the onlookers to scrutinize.

David caressed up and down Shea's sides, then held him by the hips on the withdrawal. Growling, he gave Shea a few hard, complete thrusts, then quickly pulled out. Stepping aside, he spread Shea's ass with a hand, letting them all see. Shea bowed his head, panting. After a moment, he gave in to instinct and arched his back, pushing out his ass.

Let them see, he thought. *As long as David has me, that's all that matters.*

"Please more, Master," Shea begged, his voice breaking. "Please take me again."

With a growl, David moved back up behind him, re-entering him with a firm thrust. Shea gasped, his cry climbing and shattering as David started fucking him with complete, long thrusts. Pushing back into each inward slide of David's cock, Shea relaxed into it, hanging from his bonds and undulating on the flesh impaling him. Turning his head to the side, lips parted as he gasped, Shea sighed with sweet anguish, "Thank you, Master."

The words spurred David on. He went faster, pounding Shea's hole. Shifting his stance wider, keeping himself open, Shea bore it, his cries growing wilder and rawer by the second.

"Please, Master," Shea stuttered, half the words lost to his gasps for air.

"You want it?" David asked ferociously, scratching down over Shea's sides, kneading his ass. "You want my seed?"

"Yes," Shea sobbed, losing control, and just surrendering. No one else was there, only David. His body lax, open, given over, Shea was moved only by David's touches and thrusts. He shouted as David moved to stroke him gently, shuddering hard as he fought not to come.

David climaxed with a growl, snapping his hips, fully sheathed as he emptied his balls into Shea.

"Hand me the plug there," David said to someone nearby.

He pulled out and instantly filled Shea again with the tapered plug, forcing it through his tender rim until it was locked in place.

"Turn!"

Delirious, sweating, needing only more of David, Shea spun again.

He only had eyes for David. David was fastening his pants and wiping himself off with a towel, looking immaculate as Shea stood there, hard-fucked, hard-up, willing, sweaty and breathless. David stalked forward, hooking a hand under Shea's jaw, forcing his chin up.

He stroked lightly over Shea's cock, a deep red and dripping wet.

"Thank you, Master." Shea let David see and take as much as he wanted.

"You're welcome, slave." He squeezed then, up Shea's cock. Shouting, tensing, Shea gritted his teeth, pulling on the shackles. "Remember... control."

It was only a few strokes, but as close to the edge as Shea was, they left him screaming.

David let go, stepping back. Shea collapsed, panting, letting the shackles keep him up, his cock an angry red line, his balls drawn up tight and heavy.

"What do you want, slave?"

"You, Master," was Shea's rough plea. "Just you."

David was on him again then, kissing his breath away.

"Let them watch you a while," David decided. "Wanting to take what they can never have. Because you, slave? You are *mine*."

Shea knelt by David's feet where he sat on one of the couches, sipping water. He had no idea how long he'd hung from the shackles, hard, wet and fucked-out. When David and Elet took him down, Shea was laid out on a table, his arms massaged, then his cock. Soon, he was feeling steadier and hard as ever. The water helped refresh him. His continued erection was very much noticeable and encouraged by intermittent massages from David's talented hand, or instructions from David to masturbate for a few, precious moments. Thrumming with the stimulation, Shea reacted strongly each time David touched, letting him draw it out for the rest to witness until he decided it was time to take it back to their room for even more.

Thankfully, for the most part, everyone's attentions had returned to their previous pursuits. He'd still catch some looking, but knew that was to be expected.

Adjacent to where they sat were Elet and Thierry, as well as another blond-haired slave. When David had first taken Shea to the couch to rest, Elet and Thierry had approached. Elet and David shook hands. There had been a glimmer in Elet's eyes when he'd looked at Shea which communicated clearly that now he knew who Shea *really* was, underneath appearances, and liked him even more for it. Thierry had hesitated to look Shea in the eyes, and murmured a question to Elet and David, "May I, Masters?"

The Masters had nodded and Thierry had kissed Shea once on each cheek, then bowed his head briefly in a sign of respect. David then gave Thierry a proud grin that made the beautiful young man become quickly flustered, a fond smile of his own playing at his lips as he returned to Elet's side.

Now, Thierry was sucking Elet while the blond worked a long, sleek black dildo into Thierry's ass. It had Thierry crying out around his mouthful, his hand wrapping the shaft as he tried to steady himself. Elet wore a darkly amused smirk that made Shea wish he could stay there all night to see what Thierry's Master had in store for him. The size of Elet's cock had Shea clenching up in sympathy. It was hot as hell, though, and Shea was pretty sure David was having him watch to keep him skating the edge.

He found, after thinking it over, that he did love it—the guards, the butlers, the lush décor and the clearly defined rules in play, keeping the slaves in line and the Masters giving them everything the slaves secretly wanted but for which they might not ever ask.

There were men getting fucked, or whipped, or restrained in ways that only made Shea want more, and often. He didn't understand it all. Not yet, but he wanted to. He wanted to try everything, watch everyone, and be seen, himself, when David wanted to show him off. Seeing David's pride in him made Shea feel more valued than he'd ever dreamed he could.

Just when Shea thought the continued, strong blood flow to his swollen cock was making him truly lightheaded, David ordered him to his feet and led him from the room. Before he left, though, Shea caught Thierry's eye. Thierry winked and Shea chuckled fondly.

Shea was escorted through the labyrinth beneath Manse. A private elevator then carried them to David's suite above. After a short ride, they were on the third floor and David, stern as ever, was leading Shea at a quick pace to the bedroom.

Chapter 38
Hard and Wanting

There was a huge St. Andrews cross in the middle of the typically open floor. Lights shone down on it in a perfectly composed pool, making the padded leather and wood glow. The guards stepped inside the bedroom and closed the door behind them.

David guided Shea up to the cross with a firm hand to the middle of his back.

He positioned Shea so that he was facing the cross, and began fastening the wrist and ankle cuffs onto him to keep him there—arms wide, legs spread. David moved around the space, retreating a few steps into the previously locked section of the room, which held his fetish gear and sex toys. Shea could only stare at it all until his nervous anticipation got the better of him. Retrieving some supplies, David set them on a small table nearby.

Shea felt watched, and not just by David, but it only added spice to the heat, and another cushioned layer of security to the hard edges of the scene they were beginning. Somehow, Shea understood it wouldn't have been the same experience had it only been him and David. They both needed the guards there as witnesses as well.

After the plug was finally, slowly removed from Shea, a wet finger slid up his ass and he heard David say by his ear, "They loved to watch me fuck you." The finger rubbed and twisted around, adding vigor to his already eager hard-on. "I think you loved it, too."

"Yes, sir," Shea breathed.

"Why did you love it?" The finger slid out, replaced by the blunt pressure of a hard, cool object. David worked it past Shea's rim, making him grunt, then fed it steadily deeper.

"I, uh, *ahh*, like feeling that I'm yours, and that you take care of me, even when things are overwhelming."

"Hmm," David hummed, tugging the object out a few inches, making Shea's skin pebble. He pressed it firmly back in, provoking an aching sigh. "So, nothing to do with exhibitionism, then?"

Shea remembered feeling so watched and adored by everyone who was looking at the typically taboo sight of public sex. There had been many people there who would have loved to switch places with him — or with David.

The toy David was fucking him with dragged right over Shea's prostate, making him cry out and shudder. It happened again, setting a rhythm. His head fell forward and he rocked back, counter to the toy's movements, working himself on it.

"Okay, yeah, I liked it," he admitted, his voice roughened, "how they wanted to be the one getting fucked by you."

"Or the one *doing* the fucking," David added. "Do you realize, slave, how gorgeous you are in submission. You surrender completely, and you do so lovingly. There's no act, no performance. It's honest, sweet, and *maddeningly* sexy."

The toy began to move in long, complete strokes. It felt so good; Shea realized his climax was rushing up on him, even though David hadn't touched his cock once since they'd started.

David pinched and sharply twisted Shea's left nipple. With a pleading shout, Shea rode the wave of heady stimulation. Eyes rolling back, hairs standing on end, the over-stimulated, engorged tissues of his ass throbbing, he felt his body tense, his balls drawing up. The toy slid out, expelling with slow friction as David twisted his nipple the other way and pulled on it.

His hips stuttered forward, fucking air.

"*Please*," Shea begged, sobbing softly.

"Please, what?"

"*I'm so close.*"

David thrust the toy in, quickly, making Shea grunt. He let go, leaving it in there. Walking around to the other side of the cross, David took hold of both nipples, tugging on them and watching the effect it had on Shea's soaking wet dick, which twitched happily.

Retrieving a pair of clamps from the table, he attached both to

Shea's throbbing nipples, keeping them pinched and stretched to their limit. Shea was panting, sweating. David walked back to the table, but Shea couldn't see what he'd retrieved. Wearing one of his more worrisome, wicked grins, David wrapped a hand around the base of Shea's sac and pulled on his balls. Grimacing, Shea wanted to chase forward and relieve the pressure, but the cross made it impossible to move. David kept pulling until Shea whimpered. He squeezed, watching Shea's eyes. With an open-mouthed gasp of protest, Shea cramped up with ache.

"I know it hurts," David said. "Just a little longer."

"Please stop," Shea gasped as the pain expanded and David didn't ease up.

Finally, David let go, but there was still pressure in a ring around the base of his scrotum. That's when he realized David had bound him there with something which was still pulling on him, trying to yank his balls straight down to the floor. It was incredibly uncomfortable and he didn't like it... until David feathered his fingertips over the head of Shea's dick.

With a hard moan, Shea shivered.

"Damn it," Shea sighed, embarrassed by getting off on something he never thought he could.

He realized his climax wasn't threatening like it had been.

"Fuck, you really could do this all night, couldn't you?" Shea groaned. "Can you die from edging?"

David laughed. Shea only wished — simultaneously — that David would stop tickling the tip of his dick, and that he'd *never* stop. He pulled on the straps binding him securely to the cross, reminding himself how completely he was at David's mercy. Spread, naked, and bound, his body was David's to play with.

"Don't worry, you're in safe hands," David assured him. He trailed a fingertip over the center of Shea's cockhead, collecting the fluid there, then brought the finger up to Shea's lips. "Open."

Shea opened up and extended his tongue. David gave him a taste of himself and Shea sucked the finger clean. He'd never felt more aware of his body, how helpless it was, and how completely David might take him apart. Anything David wanted to do to him, he could. Shea was sure he'd figure out a way to make it irresistible.

David stepped up behind Shea, and suddenly Shea felt David's fingernails scratching him. They moved across the top and middle expanses of his back, crisscrossing the trails the nails left as they went back and forth. It went on and on. Soon, David scratched down lower, to Shea's ass, diligently covering it with what Shea knew must be pink trails and slightly raised welts. It woke up all of the nerve endings in his skin.

"This is to help get you ready for what's to come," David explained.

"Yes, Master."

David wandered back to the table, out of Shea's line of sight, and moved behind him again. Not knowing what would come next made Shea's pulse begin to race once more.

Something tickled in a trail over his ass, and he knew what it was.

"Damn it," he groaned.

The flogger struck with force, making him yelp, but after a few initial strikes, David set a steady rhythm right away, and the lashes continued to come with barely any pause. As soon as Shea would tense against the sting, another one would come. Too quickly, his ass was on fire. The skin throbbed with his pulse and he winced audibly against each strike. When there was a pause, he kept his butt tight, just in case, but then he felt the toy being withdrawn, and moaned heavily.

David began fucking him with it and Shea presented his ass, greedily, for more.

"Please don't stop. Oh, god, please, it feels so good. Don't... don't stop."

He was rocking counter to the movements within his ass, making the weight on his balls swing, pulling them in new directions.

"What do we say, slave?"

"Thank you, Master. Fuck, I love it. Love the way you fuck me."

The toy pulled out. Hands spread his cheeks wide, exposing his tender hole. Shea panted, waiting. A finger stroked the inside of his rim and he convulsed, trying to come, unable to but *wanting* to.

"More, please," he cried.

David let go, then something *much* thicker than the toy that had been in him was being forced inside. Shea shouted, grimacing with the burning stretch as he was stuffed full. Once it was a few inches inside, David reached around and removed the clamps on Shea's nipples.

Blood surged back to the area and Shea was breathless with the pain. As he struggled to get a handle on it, to even think past it, somehow, David kept entering him, forcing the huge phallus up his ass.

"What do we say, slave?" David said patiently.

But Shea couldn't speak. His tongue was thick and clumsy in his mouth, his head spinning, his body stormed with sensations too big to process. He was being stretched so wide with the toy; it fought viciously for his attention as his nipples throbbed with his heartbeat. David twisted the left one and Shea made a desperate, guttural sound. Pre-come wept from his slit and his eyes rolled back in his head. David twisted more sharply, slid the huge toy out, and Shea fucked air, uselessly. The head of the massive phallus caught on his rim. David rubbed an opened hand roughly over Shea's tender nipple.

"What do we say?" David demanded.

"Th-thank you, M-m—"

David's hand moved lower, wrapping Shea's shaft as soon as he began forcing the object back up his ass.

"Fuck," Shea whined. David pumped him with tight, long strokes as he was stuffed to bursting again. He pushed back onto the toy, taking it, praying for David to keep going. He hung from his shackles, wracked with gentle convulsions as David continued to jack him, quickly, and fuck him, slowly.

David sheathed the toy in him, then let go of Shea's cock.

"How do I prefer you, slave?"

Shea struggled to speak, hanging on the cross. A hand gently massaged his aching balls. He'd never felt such a high before. It was like flying. Every nerve ending in his body was awake and charged up. He would have begged, promised anything, done *anything*, to stay right there, submitting to David.

"Hard and wanting, sir," he managed in a ravaged, raspy voice.

"Would you like me to give you my cock, or shall we continue?"

It felt like David was offering the world, too many options to choose from, so he went with instinct.

"Both, please, Master."

David took off his clothes and started stroking himself, letting Shea watch. Clenching on the thick toy stuffing him full, Shea wanted it, wanted David. Shea's dick strained, dripping and throbbing for release. Picking up the flogger again, David struck Shea's sore nipples with it. The sting made Shea cry out roughly. It came a few more times, then David trailed the ends of the flogger lightly over Shea's erection and stretched balls. Staring at David's gorgeous, naked body, Shea tried to hump the flogger, trying to get off. So, David slapped him lightly with it. The tails bit the sensitive skin, briefly wrapping his flesh, and Shea shouted. Even more lightly, but faster, David did it again, drawing out the pain, keeping Shea aware of the ache in his groin.

The flogger was set aside again, giving Shea a rest. He panted for breath as David circled around behind him. The thick toy was withdrawn, then pushed steadily back in. Sighing, Shea hung from the cross, without the energy to do anything other than offer his ass for fucking.

"Oh fuck, yes," Shea purred as the toy rubbed hard over his gland on each push. He shuddered each time he was triggered. Sweating, humming, whimpering, he stayed loose and open for his Master, reacting to each thrust. He began pushing back onto the toy, wanting more of it. So, David gave it to him harder, faster. Staying perfectly still, Shea just let it take him. The sounds he made hid none of his anguish or pleasure. "Master, please," he begged.

With a growl, David slowed down, coming in to suck a kiss to Shea's neck. His teeth scraped the skin. Shea tilted his head, offering his neck, which only seemed to spur David on. He bit down, sucking as well, marking the skin. His hand moved the toy steadily and Shea shivered, gasping, keening.

"Feels so good," Shea moaned. "Please don't stop, Master."

David growled again; it was clear that something in Shea's pleading had flipped a switch in him. The more Shea let go, the more dominant David became. And the more dominant David became, the more Shea trusted and lost himself in the moment. It was a circle, turning, pushing each of them to their extreme states of being.

David yanked the toy free, stepping up behind Shea.

"Please fuck me, sir. I want it," Shea asked, with absolutely nothing clouding his lust or need. There was no fear, no uncertainty, he just wanted David.

With one, rough push, David filled him all at once.

"Thank you, sir," Shea said gruffly, his voice breaking on a harder moan. "More please."

David rode him, dragging firmly over his prostate, jacking Shea's cock. Hanging from the straps, just taking it, bearing it, Shea could only cry out. The sweeter his cries became, the more David kissed Shea's neck, giving it even harder, bombarding him with sensation.

Shea was pushed, hard, right up to the edge, needing to tip over. He convulsed and writhed, moved by the tugging and fucking. Yelling out everything he felt, he held nothing back, his whole body tingling and throbbing. There was nothing keeping them apart, then. It was only Master and slave, and Shea understood, profoundly, the gift of submission to a Master as loving as his own. He was free. There were no cares. Only love and life.

David came with a primal cry of his own, unloading deeply inside of Shea, then riding him slowly through the aftershocks. Trails of feather-light kisses dusted over the side of Shea's jaw and the junction of his neck and shoulder.

"I love you," David whispered.

Past the ability to speak, Shea could only moan in reply.

David pulled out, wiped himself off with a towel. Shea was thrumming, barely aware of anything, though tracking his Master out of raw, passionate necessity.

Circling around again, David kissed Shea's gasping lips, twisting his left nipple sharply. Then, he sank to the ground. Shea didn't and couldn't move, but through half-closed eyes he watched David lick over Shea's bound, stretched sac. It caused a shiver and a whimper. When David licked up the underside of Shea's erection, he massaged Shea's balls more than was comfortable. Shea could only choke out his reply, shivering. David licked again, then sucked on Shea's tip. The binding around the base of his balls was released. David sucked him down to the root and Shea's teeth clacked together. When he came, he blacked out.

Rising gradually back to awareness, he realized he was lying on the bed on his back. David was leaning over him, caressing Shea's forehead with a cool cloth. With a press of his fingertips, he checked Shea's pulse.

"How are you feeling, my love?"

Shea tried to speak, but his lips barely moved and only rough sounds came out. He was able to turn toward David's touch as the cloth was set aside and his fingers brushed Shea's cheek. The fingers at his pulse skated over Shea's chest, down his arm, then wove between the fingers of Shea's hand. Shea squeezed, his breath catching on a sob as the gratitude and peace overwhelmed him.

Frowning, David leaned in, kissing his lips. Then he moved to lay behind Shea, being the shield the world could crash itself against as he protected his love.

"Thank you, David," Shea cried, tears slipping down his cheeks. He pulled David's arm across his chest and began to doze, knowing while he was in David's embrace, he had everything he could ever need.

Chapter 39

Happily Ever After

"Guess where I am right now!"

"Um, in your ivory tower?"

"I'm in my car! Driving to work!"

"Wow, you're super excited about that, huh?"

"I totally am!"

"You're fucking chipper and everything."

"Damn right I am."

Shea glanced in his rearview, from which hung a string of green, plastic beads a cute guy had thrown at him on Mardi Gras last year. The black Lincoln was right there, tinted windows and everything. It was easy to ignore. He just pretended it was a random car in the traffic flow.

"Look, I'll call you later, okay? If my bodyguards see I'm on the phone while driving, they'll totally tattle on me."

"Seriously, how is this your life? Do you even hear yourself?"

"Nah, I don't ever really listen to what I say."

"Love you, babe," Daisy chuckled. "Have fun peddling superheroes to the masses."

"Love you too, but don't tell David!"

"Got it. Over-protective is his middle name. Later, Whitt."

"Later 'gator."

He ended the call and discreetly set down the phone, glancing constantly in his mirrors. Soon, he was pulling up into the small lot next to Comics and More. The leaves of the trees along the road had changed color, brightening the view with splashes of red, orange and gold. He swung into his favorite spot, where there was just enough shade to keep the car cool but not enough tree cover to encourage the birds to shit all over his baby.

The black Lincoln parked nearby.

Two guys — Bruce and Jason — got out. They adjusted their well-pressed dark grey suits and started their visual scan of the area. Bruce had his hand to his ear, relaying information to the dudes at headquarters.

"'Sup, Jason! I've got a buddy stopping by in an hour with some donuts. No shame in enjoying some freshly-baked pastries, you know."

"Of course, Mr. Whittier," Jason replied, all business as usual. Shea actually found it kind of hilarious how these guys were always on, kind of like the guards outside the palace in England. You couldn't resist trying to get them to crack a grin now and then.

Mrs. Phan across the street in the nail salon stood at the window, scowling in their direction as Shea got out his keys to open up the store. He gave her his most charming smile and a wave. She pretended to smile back and then started relaying the gossip to her co-workers, though he couldn't hear what she said. Probably something about that weird teenager who was obviously using the comics shop as a front for the Irish mafia, given the types of guys that followed him to work every day and stood at each entrance from morning to night. Maybe he'd order the nail salon employees some donuts, too, as a peace offering.

"Do a sweep of the first floor and secure the rear," Bruce told Jason.

"Yes, sir," Jason replied. Shea tried to ignore it. Bruce accompanied Shea into the store, not budging from his side. They hung back while Jason did his sweep of the shop, moving from front to back, his weapon drawn but lowered. From experience, Shea knew not to go too far into the store, yet. Better to play along than freak them out any more than necessary.

Soon Jason was back. "All clear," he told Bruce. Shea would have felt like he was stuck in some exaggerated TV cop drama if this hadn't become the weirdness of his actual life every single day. Shea, and his shadow, finally walked to the office to turn on some lights and boot up the computer. Sunlight shone prettily through the bullet-proof glass windows, illuminating cardboard promotional cut-outs and a few life-size replicas of Batman, Superman, Captain America and Wonder Woman. In the corners of every room were small cameras, their unblinking red eyes peering down at him constantly. He repressed an urge to give a wave to them, too, mainly because then he'd have to start apologizing for being weird again.

He reached for the Captain America shield charm hanging from a chain around his neck, feeling the slightly raised rings and star under the pad of his finger. Wearing the necklace was more habit than something he needed anymore. Once, that charm had been the symbol of all of his hopes and dreams. Its reality had helped him believe that miracles could happen and heroes did exist. Now he knew that was true. David had saved Shea, but it wasn't as cut and dried as that. Lines had blurred and Shea felt more powerful and heroic than he'd dreamed in his wildest, geekiest fantasies.

Now, instead of giving him a reason to go on, the charm helped remind him to look for ways of his own to give back, even if it just meant giving neighborhood kids a cool, safe place to come and set their imaginations free.

The rest of the staff who'd been scheduled to work that Friday were due to arrive soon. Shea glanced at the chart on the wall and saw it was Eric and Margo. Eric was also a submissive from Manse. Being personally vetted by David had gotten him through the brutal interview process and security clearances that much faster than some of the other hires. One of the benefits to working at Comics and More was being safeguarded by the best security money could buy, but it came at a hefty price for those just looking for some entry-level work.

After fetching the cash drawer from the safe, Shea brought it out to the register. His shadow tailed him, taking his post behind and to the left of where Shea would hang out behind the check-out desk, drinking his coffee and eating his donut. Mahendran was bringing the breakfast fare by after his night shift security detail. Shea looked forward to seeing him. It'd be good to catch up with his former roomie.

Perching his ass on the stool by the register, Shea looked around his little realm of fantasy, adventure, and art, and smiled. It was going to be a good day.

Later that day, when four p.m. rolled around and he still hadn't heard from David, Shea decided to head upstairs for a nap or some lounging on his raggedy thrift-store couch while he paged through a few issues of their newest stock.

"Hey," he called to Eric. "I'll stop down around nine to help close up. You know where I am if you need anything."

"No problem, Shea," Eric smiled back, playing it totally normal, as per usual, even though they frequently saw each other naked and getting fucked in various ways. Eric was cool like that.

He walked out of the shop's front entrance and straight over to the door beside it. Bruce was already there and held the door open for Shea to walk through.

"How was your day, man? Get to frisk any customers or anything?"

"Not today, Mr. Whittier," Bruce replied seriously.

"There isn't anything you're not telling me, is there?" If there was ever a real threat, Shea wasn't sure he'd know about it. His team would likely just take care of it and report back to the boss. Keeping Shea from having to worry was part of their job, too. David liked Shea calm and comfortable, at all costs. Luckily, Shea's absolute faith in David helped quell any unease about things being kept from him.

"Of course not, sir."

"Hmm. Okay."

At the top of the stairs was a landing. A huge wall of a man stood there, dressed in the same grey suit as the rest of the team. He was behind a wall made up of the same bulletproof glass as the windows. As soon as he saw it was Shea, he remotely disengaged the lock to let him through.

"Looking good, Tony," Shea smiled, walking past. Behind Tony was the guard station that was manned twenty-four hours a day, seven days a week, whether Shea was there or not. He never asked what it cost in order to make that happen, but he imagined it wasn't cheap. In front of Tony was a bank of monitors, displaying views of the area all around the building, as well as within it.

"You too, sir," Tony replied.

"Ooh, was that subtext?" Shea smirked.

"Just being polite, sir," Tony said with a small grin.

"Sure, we'll go with that," Shea replied with a wink.

Beyond the guard station was the actual entrance to his apartment, which he never locked, because... why bother? If Tony didn't keep the burglars out, nothing would.

Because security took up so much of the second floor, that level of the apartment mainly consisted of Shea's kitchen and entryway. He dropped his keys and wallet on the counter, then ascended the spiral staircase to the third floor which contained his living room, bathroom and bedroom.

As soon as he rounded the last bend, he saw another grey suit and chuckled with a sigh.

"How did you get in here without me seeing you?" he called out loudly. The third floor had an open plan layout, so he knew David would hear him no matter where he was. The bathroom didn't even have a door.

"I have my ways," David answered with a grin from where he lay reclined on the bed, propped up on pillows with a hand behind his head. "You really mustn't flirt with the staff, sweetheart. You make them nervous."

"*I* make them nervous?" he laughed. "Ironic."

David looked so perfectly arranged there, in the wonderfully cobbled-together, less-than-pristine setting of Shea's new home away from home. Somehow, David's home had also become Shea's, in actuality as well as name. He spent most nights there, if there was any chance David would be coming to bed at some point during the evening. Otherwise, he hung out in his apartment above the store.

Everything beyond the fortified exterior was homey and eclectic. On his days off, when David was busy with work, Shea scouted out local flea markets with Daisy and his ever-present shadows. That's where most of his furniture, kitchen gear, and decorations had come from. Finding and buying everything himself with the money he earned at the shop was more empowering than he could have dreamed. It made it a real home, and his, instead of something he hadn't earned.

Crossing to the bed, and the dreamy vision David created there—a masterpiece nestled in the mundane—Shea began to say, "So, did they *tell you* I was flirting or are you just—"

At that point, Shea tripped over a design in the hand-woven, well-worn but colorful throw rug beside the bed and almost went sprawling on his face. Catching himself — barely — he laughed it off.

"Please be careful, love," David asked with a wince.

"I'm fine," Shea chuckled, recovering and climbing onto the bed, and David. "People trip. It happens. Doesn't mean you need to coat the floor in bubble wrap or have Bruce carry me everywhere. Besides, that would be *really* emasculating." He slid his hand up David's chest, over the crisp ivory of his button-down shirt which probably cost more than the contents of the entire room. Beneath was nothing but firm, warm, familiar contours of muscle. "I thought you had to work tonight. That's the only reason I'm here instead of at home, you know."

"Change of plans. More important things to do, like planning that party we were talking about earlier," David smirked. He twisted a fist in Shea's shirt and dragged him down for a slow, lingering kiss.

Shea loved lying on top of David, feeling the whole length of him, in every sense of the word. Straddling David's thighs, Shea rocked in a slow grind against him, inspiring David to palm Shea's ass and squeeze.

"Oh *hell* no," Shea whispered seductively. "That party's supposed to be for your birthday, and planning it is my job. Don't you dare get any ideas."

"Too late. Maybe we should make it a trip instead of a party. I've shown you off at Manse so often; I want to take you somewhere entirely new. How about Paris, or Naples if Paris is too ordinary?" David tempted, his eyes lighting up with excitement. There was no telling what he was imagining, and which Doms he knew in Naples.

"Oh, *far* too ordinary," Shea agreed, almost but not quite managing to keep a straight face and not laugh. "You're crazy. And what the fuck am I supposed to get you for your birthday anyway? You got me a damn building for mine!"

"Does that mean you don't like it?" David asked. "Should I get you a larger one?"

Biting his lip, Shea reached between their bodies and squeezed David's cock.

"Is that supposed to be some sort of payback?" David laughed, thrusting into Shea's squeeze.

The day of Shea's nineteenth birthday, David had presented him with a set of keys and a deed to the building containing what would become the Comics and More store and his apartment above, complete with his own security detail. It was the strangest and most magnificent thing anyone had ever given him. Nothing would ever top it.

"Or maybe I'll just hire uglier guards?" David said thoughtfully.

"Mmm, jealousy. I detect it," Shea grinned triumphantly.

David easily dislodged Shea's grip on his genitals and brought the arm up instead to rest beside his head, then looped both arms behind Shea's back.

"This is cozy," David murmured, kissing Shea again.

"Slumming it still does it for you, huh? Who'd have thunk?"

"All I want for my birthday is somewhere to be with you without any sort of work to distract me for a full week with no interruptions."

"But plenty of sexual supervision, I'm guessing."

"Of course," David smirked. "You know I love to show off how thoroughly I'm able to fuck you senseless."

With a groan and an interested twitch of his cock, Shea sank more deeply into David's arms.

"So, you're off for the *whole* night?"

"I am." He guided Shea back far enough to get a good look at his face, and said tenderly, "I've missed you."

"I missed you too," Shea agreed, feeling so full of love, he would have happily drowned in it.

"Father asked for you," David said quietly. Something sentimental and fragile moved like a shadow behind his eyes. "Again. Mother told me earlier."

"He's just a fan of my famous slapstick routine. You know I stepped on a ballpoint pen the last time I was there and rolled a few inches, arms flailing, the whole nine, while he laughed?"

David chuckled, smiling widely, eyes crinkling at the edges.

"I really don't think he knows who I am," Shea admitted reluctantly after a pause. "I'm just the smiley guy who watches cartoons with him every few days."

"I want to believe he does. I *do* believe he does." David closed his eyes. The smile fled, replaced with a furrow of his brow and tension in his mouth as the worries hit him again. Shea had seen it happen too many times to count.

"Hey," Shea sighed, rubbing David's chest.

His voice thick with emotion, David said, "It means *so much to me* that you visit him and that you treat him *so kindly* after everything that—"

Shea kissed him quiet. It went on and on, until David was once more composed, yet still reluctant to let Shea pull away very far.

"He loves the hell out of you," he told David. "He always has. That means a lot to *me*."

"And I love the hell out of *you*," David replied, nearly getting teary again.

"I have a brilliant idea," Shea began, raising one eyebrow and feeling deviously inspired. "Let's walk down to Gino's and get chees-esteaks, then rent a cheesy movie and lay here for hours until Tony gets bored watching us."

"That *is* a brilliant idea," David agreed, taking Shea's hand and weaving their fingers together. "Am I allowed to attempt to distract you from the movie and the sandwiches?"

"Oh, you can *try*. I love me a lazy night in with the love of my life, though, so you'll have to be creative."

"Challenge accepted."

Author's Notes

This story is a prequel of a prequel, with ties to two other series (*Deliver Us* by myself and *Don't* by Jack L. Pyke) in a shared universe called The Society of Masters, including works by myself and Ms. Pyke. All of that sounds incredibly complicated, but at its heart, Loving the Master is purely a romance. I wrote it to simply experience these two wildly different men falling madly in love, and to have fun along the way.

David and Shea's relationship had already been established in both *Bound by Lies* and *Learning from the Master*. The history was already there. They had made it through many years together, and happily so. With that mental cushion in place, I peeled back many layers to get to the core of who they are and why they work as a couple. We have a billionaire CEO and Dominant trained in the Master's Circle committing himself to a relatively average guy stuck in the middle of a run of bad luck. Why? The puzzle of that is what drove me along.

I will admit to loving Shea first, before David. Even back in *Bound by Lies*, when we didn't even meet Shea, I was curious about who he was, and why David protected him so fiercely. As Jenner finds out in *Learning from the Master*, the reason behind this is because Shea is David's heart. That's why David safeguards him. Shea is out there, walking around, making his own choices, and the danger of it scares David to death, even as David knows he owes Shea the ability to shape his own life.

Because of who David is, and how his internal coping mechanisms had been firmly established before we meet him in this story, I knew David would need to fall into the pattern of being Shea's protector right from the start. It's a role that suits him, and in which he thrives. He's comfortable there. He can, however, get carried away, and so it becomes Shea's job to help David relax, to let go, enjoy the simple things, and to really live. While David is using all of his strength to ensure everything is running smoothly and according to plan, Shea is there tempting David to come dance badly with him and laugh at themselves. There is no doubt that world needs those like David, but it even more desperately needs people like Shea, cherishing each moment with an honest smile and the kindest of intentions.

There is a lot of David in me, which I didn't see at first. I grew to appreciate him just as much as Shea for the quality of David's steadfast efforts to do the right thing and his passionate need to not let anyone down. He's every bit the hero Shea sees him as, but even the strongest need a loving presence at their side to keep the motivation flowing and to provide reminders of what's really important, underneath it all.

My wish is for my readers to take away from this story the sense that none of us are perfect, and those flaws are nothing if not possibilities to grow and enrich our lives, if only we would look a little more closely and compassionately at those who are wildly different than ourselves.

Thanks must go to the brilliant and generous Jack L. Pyke for lending me Master Brennan. I'm shipping him back over the pond to the Master's Circle headquarters, where you can read more about him in her *Don't* series.

Special thanks must go to my wonderful editor, Rylan Hunter, for pushing me to do justice to David and Shea and for being so understanding of my chaotic emotional state these past few months, during which my life was turned as completely upside down as Shea's at the beginning of this story. Equally heartfelt thanks must go to Dany (D.M. Atkins) for her wisdom, kindness and encouragement. I don't know what I'd do without either one of you.

Finally, thank you to my readers, without whom I wouldn't have this wonderful world of writing in my life. I am truly grateful for you each and every day.

— Lynn Kelling

About the Author

Website: www.lynnkelling.com

Lynn Kelling began writing in order to tell stories that aren't afraid of the dark, don't hold anything back and always strive to be memorable, forging lasting attachments between character and reader. Her inspiration comes from taking a closer look at behaviors and ideas lurking at the fringes of life — basically anything that people may hesitate to speak of in mixed company, but everyone wonders about anyway. Her work is driven by the taboo in order to expose the humanity within it. Lynn is an artist, designer and lover of any form of creative self-expression that comes from a place of honesty and emotion, whether it's body art or opera. She has had multiple novels published, has written over seventy works of erotic fiction of varying lengths, and always has several novels in progress.

Works by Lynn Kelling:

Deliver Us Series:
Deliver Us
From Temptation
Forgive Us

Twin Ties Series:
My Brother's Lover
Dual Affairs
Double Heat

Manse Series:
Loving the Master
Learning from the Master
Bound by Lies

Other Works:
Whatever the Cost
Arctic Absolution
Song of the Lonesome Cowboy
Threshold (Anthology)
Cursed Blessings (short story)

The Society of Masters

In the shadows, behind the scenes of the world you know, exists a secret world of professional domination and submission. All over the world, there are men who love men, who also love pain and discipline. Some are masters; some are willing slaves. Others... not so willing. One thing they all have in common is a desire to seek others with their inclinations, to seek respite and satisfaction among the society of masters. The Society of Masters is an overlapping, multi-author universe exploring the men of this world.

In the world of The Society of Masters, major "players" include:

- The Masters' Circle is an exceptionally discreet English society club, with members placed in the highest positions in British government and society.
- The Company is an American criminal cartel, supplying prostitutes to rich men and women with exotic tastes and hardcore fantasies.
- Diadem is a fetish club and pornography studio.
- The Manse is an exclusive gay nightclub where the Doms and subs come out on Saturday nights.

You can find out more at the Society of Masters page
at http://forbiddenfiction.com/collection/som/.

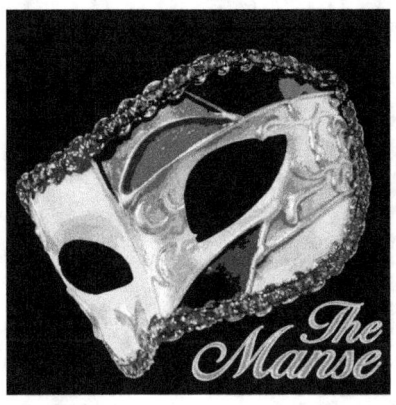

The Manse is a private club in rural Pennsylvania, catering to gay men. David Davenport runs the club as he sees fit, and he's used to getting his way. So when he decides he wants to fill the place with gorgeous men in masks for a night, that's exactly what happens. The Manse series focuses on the lives of men who play at the Manse.

About the Publisher

ForbiddenFiction.com is a publisher devoted to writing that breaks the boundaries of original erotic fiction. Our stories combine intense sexuality with quality writing. Stories at Forbidden Fiction.com not only arouse readers through sensations, but also engage them emotionally and mentally through storytelling as well-crafted as the sex is hot.

ForbiddenFiction.com is also designed to be a social reading environment. You'll have fun even if just reading the latest post each day, yet you will have the chance for so much more. Readers and authors can be part of ongoing discussions of specific works and individual authors as well as more general topics.

Sign up for a FREE Membership today at ForbiddenFiction.com